Totally Bound Publishing books by Sandra Carmel

The Cure
Capture
Discover

I0646179

The Cure

CAPTURE

SANDRA CARMEL

Capture
ISBN # 978-1-83943-810-3
©Copyright Sandra Carmel 2019
Cover Art by Erin Dameron-Hill ©Copyright August 2019
Interior text design by Claire Siemaszkiewicz
Totally Bound Publishing

Published in 2019 by Totally Bound Publishing, United Kingdom.

CAPTURE

Dedication

For Simon, whose inspiring idea helped complete
the vampire physiology puzzle.

Acknowledgements

Writing a novel is not simple. If it weren't for the high-quality input from those listed below, this book, as you see it, would not exist. A massive and heartfelt thank you to the following:

Famous Five Write Now for the brilliant writerly chats and your continued encouragement and support,

Melbourne Romance Writers Guild (MRWG) for your assistance particularly regarding development of my writing skills and knowledge around marketing and promotion,

Romance Writers of Australia (RWA) for providing up-to-date industry and writing craft information,

SavvyAuthors for providing me with the opportunity to connect with my publisher through participating in pitchfests,

The Totally Entwined Group and especially my editor Jamie Rose for believing in my work,

Jane Routley, my mentor during the early incarnation of my book, for suggesting my idea be made into a series, and recommending I join RWA,

Margie Lawson for significantly enhancing and revolutionizing my writing and editing skills,

Lily Malone, my generous author friend, for your inspirational ideas and practical, honest feedback,

David Speyer and Elisa Garzarella for providing general guidance and connecting me with great legal support,

Andrew Logie-Smith, from Logie-Smith Lanyon Lawyers, for your clear legal advice and recommendations,

Damira Rogoznica, Margaret Midwood, Marie Riley and Raewyn Bright, my beta reader friends, for your constructive and valuable feedback,

Jim Kane, my musician mate and work colleague, for the incredibly useful and enjoyable brainstorming sessions and creative industry discussions over the years,

Karen Ingram, my author friend and work colleague, for your encouragement and faith in me as a writer,

Christine Smith, Jim and Helen Kirko, and Johnny and Meri Tsiglev, my good friends, for your ongoing support of me and my writing,

Simon Damevski, my husband, for your thought-provoking conversations which have given me the confidence to take on new challenges and helped me evolve and grow into the person I am today, and

Mum and Dad, and my sister Jai Simeone, for your love, generosity and longstanding support.

Chapter One

Lady Luck?

Hobart, May 1965

"I need to know her."

Richard Hall edged nearer to the beautiful woman waiting at the Sub Rosa Corporation lifts. There was something about her blue-violet eyes — Elizabeth Taylor-like, but bluer. They drew him to her, teased and tugged, until his whole mind, body and spirit tangled together with an insatiable craving.

And it knocked him. Hard.

She turned toward the tinted window, the soft, autumn morning light catching the violet in her spellbinding irises. A magical aura seemed to surround her, like she was a muse and he a nomad, being summoned to her calling.

A Sub Rosa name tag was clipped onto her sexy C-cup chest but her handbag strap obscured her name. He needed to get closer and talk to her. She stood listening to her female friend, her silent yet captivating presence rendering him a wordsmith with no words...except 'hello'.

Hello. Such a simple, yet powerful foot in the door to start the flow of conversation. He psyched himself up to make a move but the doors opened and the stunning woman and her chatty friend drifted into the male-dominated lift that was too crowded to admit him.

The mesmerizing dark-haired rose disappeared among a pack of very lucky thorns. As the doors closed, he couldn't miss the check-out-the-foxy-babe-onboard look on his workmates' faces, the nudging body language between them, alerting each other to the presence of pure beauty.

He had to meet this girl. And he'd find a way. Richard had never had it easy, had never had things given to him, though he usually got them in the end.

It should help shorten his search, seeing as she worked at Sub Rosa too. But in what department? Not research. It brimmed with blokes, the boys' club beaming a *Back Off, Keep Out* forcefield.

Women. Exactly what their department needed. It wouldn't happen, though—not in Australia in 1965, definitely not in Hobart, Tasmania and especially not while he was the outvoted newcomer.

How to find one gorgeous girl in a thirty-story skyscraper of sweaty blokes. *Hmmm...* She had to work as a Girl Friday or a secretary of some sort. That narrowed down the options, but he'd still be forced to make inquiries. He could just imagine how that conversation would go.

"Can I help you?" the receptionist would ask.

"I'm just trying to find a girl I saw in the lift. She has blue-violet eyes and long, dark brown hair, and I've got the hots for her."

The receptionist would give him a professional, sure-thing smile then press the intercom. "Security…"

Okay, so he couldn't really chase her around the building…unless he wanted to risk his dream job and get a reputation as a stalker. Luckily, his chances of running into her were good – great even. The situation just called for patience.

Richard yanked the stifling scarf from his neck and stuffed it in his black bag. *Me, patient? Ha!* When he wanted something, or someone, he couldn't relax until he had it.

More staff arrived and waited for the elevator. Men, men, men and more men oozed a cloying mix of colognes and spoke in confident, testosterone-laced tones. The tall, short, thin, fat-suited male landscape stretched out around him, with a sprinkling of bob-haircut, mini-skirt-wearing, Mod-style women. But his mind was snagged on his singular, elegant beauty.

Mine.

Richard shook his head, trying to shake some sense back into his two-track mind – them, together as a couple. *What has gotten into me?* Obsessing over a woman was totally not his thing, especially a woman he hadn't met.

Lust at first sight was the only explanation – heart-hammering, mind-bending, limb-trembling lust. His cock needed a companion…but so did his heart.

Fire simmered in his stomach. She hadn't just gotten under his skin. She'd burrowed into his heart, head, soul. How would it be when he actually spoke to her, touched her? *Am I twenty-five or fourteen?*

He closed his eyes and took a deep, get-some-fucking-control-over-yourself breath.

The lift doors opened, and he glanced at the gold cogs in his skeleton watch—eight-thirty-one. Time to get to work...and do some research.

* * * *

Eva walked into the regular clash of perfumes in the noise-polluted, open-plan office and dropped her handbag beside her electric typewriter. Her eyes snagged on the letter, the one that had stomped on her heart—the letter she should have scrunched up and tossed away, like all the others.

"Hey, Eva, did you see the hunk staring at you this morning?" Greer Circe's voice cut through the hum of chronic chatter, ringing phones and incessant taps and dings of surrounding typewriters. Her best friend never missed an attractive man. If only she had a speck of Greer's hunk-hunting talent.

"Where?"

Greer rolled her office chair closer. "Waiting for the lift. In the hip threads. Golden brown hair. Dreamy green eyes."

Eva selected and replayed the morning's, busy, men-filled-foyer memory. "No."

Greer shook her head, not a hair moving in her perfect, chocolate-brown beehive. "I can't believe you didn't notice him—black leather jacket, red and green tartan scarf, tight black pants, nice buns..."

"How did I miss him? He sounds divine." Eva went through the conversational motions, her mind on *that* letter. The latest private investigator's report drew her gaze like a solar eclipse. None of the PIs had found the father she'd never met, not even a lead.

It was as if someone had taken an eraser to her past and scrubbed him out, like he'd never existed. And she'd have believed it, except for the note he'd sent her all those years ago, now yellow and frail and preserved like a precious piece in a museum.

"Are you okay?"

Shit. Eva couldn't confide in her friend about the search for her father. Not yet. Greer wouldn't get it, not with her *Leave It to Beaver* childhood. She wouldn't understand her need to track down a stranger – an absent, disinterested, gene-sharing stranger.

"Yes. Just a bit tired. Still settling into the new place." Her own place. A rental, but the first place that felt like home.

"Good. Because you need to start dating. That guy from this morning? He noticed you. More than noticed." Greer's gaze went all melted-marshmallow gooey. "I wish he'd noticed me."

"You've got a boyfriend." Eva slipped the report beneath a stack of files. No more PIs. Not for now, anyway. She needed the money for rent and to focus on important things she had more control over, like finding a husband and starting a family of her own.

Greer reorganized Eva's pens and pencils into an off-kilter heart shape. "We've been out a few times but it's not official. And anyway, there's nothing wrong with window shopping."

"It's more than window shopping. You like to try, try, try before you buy." Unlike her friend, Eva didn't want a string of Friday night dates. She'd rather hold out for Mr. Forever.

"You make me sound like a floozy."

Eva smiled. "If the stiletto fits..." Teasing her coworker added a bit of lighthearted fun to their chat, though in truth she needed an outgoing, risk-taking friend like Greer to spur her on or she'd turn into a pitiful, loveless loner.

"Very funny. Stop trying to change the subject. We need to find a cool cat for you. We need to find Mr. Gorgeous Green Eyes."

"I didn't even see the guy! What if I don't like him?" It looked like the universe and Greer had ganged up on her. Eva turned and started filing.

Greer joined her at the tall, gray filing cabinet. "Come on, Eva. Give him a go. You've locked lips with a couple of deadbeats and it hasn't worked out. Big deal. Move on. The past is the past. You're almost twenty-one. If you don't find someone soon, you'll be left on the spinster shelf."

Eva put the last file away and pushed the drawer shut. Her left ring finger stood out, bare, pale and ringless. She shoved her hands on her hips. "Says who?"

"Society."

Her gaze locked on Greer's. "Since when do you care what society thinks?"

"I don't. But you do." A smug smile curved Greer's glossy-pink lips.

Eva dropped her hands and her shoulders sagged. Her colleague had nailed it. Eva did care—about her reputation, about finding her soulmate, about being too old to start a family.

Greer's big eyes glimmered with an I've-got-a-brilliant-idea-you're-not-going-to-like look. "I know. You're coming with me to the dance on Friday night. And don't try to squirm out of it."

Eva's eyes stretched so wide that cold air rushed in and nearly freeze-dried her eyeballs. She blinked then blinked again. "No. No. You know how I feel about *those* dances."

"You're coming. You owe me. I spent my whole weekend helping you move. Remember?"

A tumble of excuses rolled around in her mind. Unpacking and tiredness wouldn't save her from Greer's husband-searching mission this time. *Shit.* She'd been backed into a corner not even Houdini could escape.

Chapter Two

The Break

Salvator Aalem held the vial of bright blue liquid up to the blinding light in the lab. *Will the memory drugs work as expected?*

"How is everything coming along?" Harry 'Nosy' Kennedy blocked the lab doorway. The Sub Rosa Senior Manager's signature catchphrase and beach-ball body were impossible not to recognize. He spent his day swanning around between his palatial office and the research department, looking important, delegating and sticky-beaking.

Salvator rarely had many visitors. He worked in a state-of-the-art special projects' lab, alone. *Solitary confinement*, as he called it, could be lonely but it had its benefits.

He put a stopper in the vial and slotted it into a wooden holder. "The good news is, the memory eraser and filler drugs are finally ready for testing. The not-so-good news? I've been trying to come up with possible animal trials, except none look like they'd yield useful results."

"Why not?" Harry asked.

"I can test for memory changes in mice, rats and even chimpanzees, but the testing isn't sensitive enough to determine whether their memories have been completely erased. And forget about the memory filler. I can't do anything more until human testing has been ratified." Salvator snapped off his rubber gloves and threw them in the metal bin under the bench.

"Unfortunately, there's no budget for that, and even if there was, where are you going to find human volunteers?"

Salvator took off his safety spectacles and rubbed his eyes. The Sub Rosa protocol required animal testing before even considering experimentation on humans. Usually, he'd agree but it wasn't possible in this case. He had to provide strong clinical reasoning to go straight to human trials, and he'd identified just the population group that could benefit.

"Returned and Services League of Australia. Returning servicemen or others experiencing post-traumatic stress or lingering trauma might want to forget." Salvator had experienced the devastating after-effects of war firsthand.

His father had committed suicide the year Salvator turned seventeen and his mother had died of a broken heart soon after. And all because a frontline soldier couldn't un-see the horrors he'd seen, the memories persisting, making him relive the events moment to moment to moment and spreading grief through the family like cancer.

No one deserved such suffering. The memory drugs Salvator was developing were a way to stop the pain, to give people back some quality of life.

"Good idea, though we still need to get ethics approval," Harry said.

He'd seen that look on Harry's face before. Stalling. Most likely to fall in line with another proposal dictated by the agency.

"That could take months!" And now, with the Vietnam War, it had become even more pressing to have a safe, clinically proven pharmaceutical 'forget' option for return soldiers.

"And it will. So, to expedite the process, get the documents to me as soon as possible and I'll send them to the ethics committee, then to the board and senior management for approval."

"And in the meantime?"

A smile broke onto his manager's sweaty, triple-chinned face. "You can start working on a cryogenics project." Harry lumbered over, his rubber-soled shoes squeaking against the linoleum, and handed him a wad of typed pages.

"Cryogenics?" The big, bold title just about jumped off the page, the agency's agenda spelled out in hard-line black and dirty white. Salvator skimmed through the pile. Fairytale stuff, even more risky than the memory drugs. "I've read about it in scientific journals. They're touting it as the new frontier. I'm still not convinced."

"Think of this as your chance to test your hypothesis. We've received some recurrent funding to look into cryogenics and its uses. At this stage, we want to focus on its potential for storage of samples, and whether once unfrozen, they can be brought back to life."

"So, you have the budget for cryogenics and not for the memory drugs trial?" Salvator didn't want to rock his research boat, but come on.

Harry turned and stepped toward the door. "Don't worry. I'm still lobbying the government. It'll help once we have ethics approval."

Salvator slapped the enormous document down on the work bench and stared at Harry's dismissive back. "But they're happy to pour money into something like cryogenics without it?" He kept his tone pleasant, as usual, though anger pumped through him like an over-inflated tire.

Harry stopped and faced him. "So it seems."

It didn't make sense. However, that's what happened when the people at the top, far removed from the experts, made decisions about what was important. They had no idea and put research dollars into projects based on personal interests, personal motives and the economic outcome on their personal bank accounts.

Fury caused a chemical reaction in Salvator's blood, turning it to cold, viscous sludge. Somehow, he swallowed back his frustration. He didn't have any power. He was just the expert. "Fine. I'll complete the ethics approval request forms for the memory drugs trial and, once they're done, I'll start on the cryogenics bri—"

"Excellent. I'll leave the rest of the cryogenics documents in your pigeon hole."

The rest? Harry had already handed him almost half a ream. "And I assume I'll continue to consult on the Norway Experiment."

"That's right."

Plus, Salvator had his secret pet project, the one he'd been working late for. One of the advantages of being a researcher in a high-end facility was he could access the available resources and stay after hours without being questioned, with management assuming he had passion and dedication to his work.

And he did. Mostly. He had to if he stood any chance of saving lives and achieving his Nobel-Prize-winning-scientist goal. His private project had kept him motivated and re-energized, especially when dealing with the day-to-day management politics and general ignorance-inspired rubbish.

Salvator forced his most convincing grateful smile. He had to shut this conversation down before he said something he shouldn't. "Thanks for the update."

Harry left the lab, the floor practically quaking under his knee-buckling weight.

Salvator's jaw ached from clamping his teeth together, and he picked up the memory-eraser-filled vial, careful not to crush it in his tight-fisted hand. He entered the dark, windowless sample storage area and slid the vial into a small rack, with five other memory-eraser-drug ampoules, in the fridge.

"At this rate, I may expire before you ever get tested." A row of pink memory-filler vials sat on the shelf below. "And that goes for you as well."

He shut the fridge, the room returning to film-developing darkness, and kept hold of the handle. Maybe he could sneak in some time on his special project after he submitted the memory drugs ethics approval request.

He could say he'd been following up Norway Experiment research, which wasn't exactly a lie. Salvator had been exploring gene-eradication options to apply to the captured vampire subjects, when he'd found the ancient, alchemic formula.

A Norwegian missionary from the Middle Ages living among the warring Jade and Violet vampire clans had developed it. The missionary's translated notes on the impact of precious metals, as well as various herbs and flowers, such as rose, lavender, thyme, basil, clove and calendula, on emotions and body chemistry were fascinating. Inspiring. So Salvator had combined the information with his knowledge of pheromones from perfume companies and had developed his own special formula.

He opened the fridge door again, a slice of yellow light penetrating the dim room, then reached to the back and pulled out a little white box. Inside sat four ampoules filled with his deep red rose-colored Soulmate Serum. Once he added a minim of patchouli, they should be right for trial...and he'd be the first human test subject.

A rush of adrenaline spiked his nervous system. Tonight would be the night...for the rat trial, for starters. Then, if all went to plan, he'd be next.

Salvator returned his prized package to its spot in the back of the fridge, headed to his desk and got to work on the ethics approval request, including a project update summary for management.

Memory eraser — *An injectable blue drug that infiltrates the bloodstream and targets the brain. It invades the memory centers and erases stored images, thoughts and emotions, leaving a blank canvas, a receptacle ready for reinvention.*

Proposed target group — *Those suffering with persisting mental and emotional anguish and trauma, particularly those experiencing post-traumatic stress.*

Memory filler — *An injectable pink drug that suffuses the bloodstream and targets the brain. It fills the void in the memory centers left by the memory eraser. The principle is to render recipients open to suggestion and allow the laying down of new, fed memories. It works similarly to hypnosis but bonds the new information seamlessly into the spaces, so the subject really believes he or she has experienced the events.*

Proposed target group – As per memory eraser.

He put the information, along with a note about trial options and formal request for ethics approval, in a secure yellow envelope and delivered it to Harry's locked, mailbox-style pigeon hole in a tucked-away alcove near the lifts.

A couple of researchers hurried past him, juggling piles of paperwork, and re-entered the sterile-white hallway leading back to the labyrinth of labs.

Salvator twisted the dial on his combination-lock pigeon hole and opened the small door. A chunky, sealed A4 envelope with his name on it and a red 'Classified' stamp almost filled the inside. He detoured past the lunch room, grabbed a strong, black coffee, sat at the long, empty table and started reading the cryogenics brief.

The paperwork called for the basement level of Sub Rosa to be converted into a lab with a designated section for cryogenics. A large cylindrical tank able to house four specimens would be installed, along with all the other associated cryogenics equipment, in a restricted access area. A slow smile leached onto his lips. It would make the perfect place for him to conduct his little extracurricular projects as well.

Salvator poured himself another coffee and continued wading through the information package. Once Sub Rosa had installed the tank and he'd familiarized himself with how cryogenics worked, his role entailed exploring the best options for its use and putting forward a business case outlining up to four different research trials.

Footsteps.

He shot his gaze toward the door and a new guy, around his age, strolled into the room. The man had to be a fellow scientist—however, with his hip, golden brown hair, fashionable clothes and model good looks, he appeared more like a movie star.

Salvator rammed the confidential brief back into its envelope, knocking his cup and spilling hot, brown liquid across his lap.

"Ouuw!" He jumped up and yanked the wet patch away from his scalded skin. *Disfigured genitals. Just what I need.* Definitely not the kind of lasting impression he wanted to make on his fiancée. And on top of that, he'd have to sit around in wet jocks and stinky woolen slacks for the rest of the workday. Thankfully, he looked young-ish, too young for his colleagues to think he had an incontinence problem.

"Are you all right?" the model researcher asked. His deep, raspy voice had pitch-perfect tenor notes, giving a graceful edge to his strong masculinity.

Salvator glanced up into the man's concerned, light green eyes and smiled through the searing pain of embarrassment. "Should be." *Hopefully.* "We haven't met. I'm Salvator. I would shake your hand but..." They both glanced at his coffee-drenched pants and wet hands.

The guy laughed like they were old buddies. "I'm Richard," he said and handed him some paper towels.

Salvator mopped up the excess moisture on his thighs and private parts. "Which area do you work in?"

"Genetics. I'm the new-ish go-to genetics guy. You?" The absent lab coat signified Richard hadn't yet progressed past desk jockey. If Salvator's first few months were any indication, management had the poor man buried in paperwork, the standard Sub Rosa initiation to prove his dedication and worth.

"I'm across a few different research projects at the moment. I go where I'm needed." *Where management can rape and pillage my scientific expertise for their own gain.* Salvator stopped himself before he purged his frustrations about the organization out loud.

Richard epitomized new and enthusiastic. Salvator shouldn't bombard him with his bitterness. "If you ever need a second opinion, general advice or even just a debrief, my lab door's always open."

"Thanks. Ah…" Richard scrunched up a paper towel and rolled it between his hands. Back forth, back forth, back forth. "I could do with some general advice, if you've got a minute."

Salvator stopped patting his pants and gave Richard his full attention. "Of course. How can I help?"

Richard's light jade eyes seemed to pierce Salvator's soul. "I'm trying to track down a beautiful woman…"

Salvator smiled. "Aren't we all." He couldn't complain. Not really. He was engaged to a wonderful woman—or so he kept telling himself. If all went to plan, he'd know for sure soon.

Richard laughed and dropped the ball. It rolled to a stop by his foot and he bent to pick it up. "She works at Sub Rosa. But on what floor, I have no idea."

"Unfortunately, you won't find her here. No females are employed on this level. I'd try one of the admin floors."

"I thought so, but just wanted another opinion. Make sure I hadn't missed something."

Salvator collected the soggy paper towels and threw them in the bin by the kitchen sink. "Good luck with your search." He returned to Richard, the breeze cooling his crotch. "When you find her—or another woman you're keen on—if you want to check if she's your soulmate, let me know."

Salvator looked around the room, leaned in and whispered, "I'm looking for volunteers to trial a serum I've developed that should confirm either way."

"Impressive. I'll keep it in mind." And Richard looked like he meant it, too. He seemed the open type, willing to take research risks. Excitement at the possibilities replaced the residual burning on Salvator's skin.

"Oh, and if you ever need help with applying a genetics lens to any of your work, I'm happy to assist." Richard looked at his skeleton-style watch, the gold hands glinting under the bright fluorescent lights. "I better get back."

Not only was Richard a superb male specimen but he was also kind and conscientious—and obviously smart. Sub Rosa had a reputation for only hiring the best. There had to be something wrong with him. No one could be that perfect. Could they?

Salvator returned to the lab, read the rest of the massive document and squeezed in a bit more work, which took him up to six p.m. He still stung a little down below, though he'd managed to avert a major disaster.

He got up from his desk and snuck in and out of each office, lab and toilet on his floor. *Deserted.* The time had come. Nervous energy swirled like a cyclone in his stomach. The moment had finally arrived to trial his Soulmate Serum.

In the lab, Salvator set up four cages with a horny male and female rat in each. They scurried, climbed, played and sniffed each other's behinds, as though feeding off Salvator's anticipation and excitement.

Eyedropper in hand, he administered three drops of the red rose serum into the throat of each rat. Within seconds of returning to their cages, three out of the four pairs kept apart, their white fur pressing through the metal bars on the opposite side of their enclosure, as though the middle had a thick, invisible barrier — like they could no longer stand being close, let alone touch.

In contrast, couple number four were going at it, rat porn style. Salvator stared, his gaze glued to them, observing their every move. Fortunately, one pair of the four rat samples were soulmates, otherwise the serum could have appeared to have the opposite outcome — to turn off people's attraction to one another.

Would the one-in-four ratio of finding a soulmate carry over to humans? The vacuum cleaner blasted nearby, jolting him back to the present. The cleaners had arrived. It had to be after midnight.

He packed the rats away, one at a time, leaving the amorous couple until last. By the hypnotic drive in their aroused pink eyes, they weren't letting him separate them, not without a bite. Best he saved his prying hand and left them together for the night.

Curiosity gnawed at his mind, leaving Swiss-cheese holes of unanswered questions. How long would the serum work? Could the body break it down? Would the effects wear off or tattoo permanent changes into the subject's DNA? They were all things he needed to test before he plunged himself into a possible pool of regret.

Or did he?

Inside the fridge, he reached for the small white box at the back, selected a fresh vial of blood-red serum and clutched it in his sweaty hand. Either his fiancée proved to be his soulmate or not. There was only one way to find out.

Chapter Three

Dancing with Fate

It seemed the universe took requests. Only a few days after Richard had spotted the blue-violet-eyed fox at work, there she stood, on the packed dance floor at Hobart's hippest Friday night dance.

She waltz-hopped across the floor with a toe-stomping partner, her hair whipping and swishing with her violet swing dress. A polite smile remained on her lush, pink lips, never giving away her pain. *So sweet.* He liked her even more.

She finished the dance, exchanged a few words, still exuding kindness, and returned to her busty friend, who flirted with some slick-suited, Beatle-esque Mods.

With a broad smile, her friend made introductions, but after some brief chit-chat, the blue-violet-eyed babe stepped back into the shadows — a heavenly, intoxicating wallflower. He couldn't steal his eyes away from her, willing the blooming beauty to return his stare. And, in seconds, she did. He tried to hold her gaze but she averted her eyes to her fidgety feet.

Richard had to take a chance now or risk missing out again. He drew in a few deep breaths, shook out his steel-tight shoulders and approached her. His heart pounded so hard he thought his ribcage would splinter.

She was still staring at her shoes, her chest rising and falling in sync with his, like she knew he'd come over. The thin, black belt strained against her narrow waist, accentuating her hourglass shape. His cock stirred with appreciation.

Richard loosened his cravat. "Hello, um..." Since when had he been so nervous, fumbling for words around a woman? Not for years. Not since he'd turned sixteen and fondled his first naked breast.

The air crackled between them, heightening the intensity a hundredfold, like she was a live wire and he a conduit, awaiting the shock of arousal from her touch.

Her brilliant blue-violet gaze lifted up and met his eyes.

He swiped his clammy hand against his black pants and extended it to her. "Would you like to dance?"

A shy smile toyed with her luscious lips. "Um..."

"I promise I won't bite...unless you'd like me to." His attempt at humor created a coating, a translucent veneer covering a core of mischief, a hint of the real him.

Every muscle in his body tensed in anticipation of her answer. There were only two possible paths she could choose. Slap and walk off or stay and connect.

Her eyes widened.

Did I blow it?

Then she laughed and grasped his hand. A potent zing shot up his arm, way more powerful than he'd prepared for, nearly blasting him off his feet. An intoxicating mixture of joy, lust and relief poured into his soul. Hers wasn't a simple stay and connect. It suggested something much, much more special. *Does she feel it too?*

With his blood rushing in his veins, Richard led her onto the dance floor and held her close, their bodies swaying in time to *Hold Me, Thrill Me, Kiss Me* by Mel Carter.

"I love this song," she said, her voice a come-hither call to his cock.

His pulse picked up to stair-climb pace. *I love your sexy body.* Had his mind been hijacked by a caveman in heat? It was so unlike his usual, controlled response to lust and focus on deep, cognitive connection.

Sure, he drooled over attractive women, though this felt different, like her pheromones had synced with his and created an overpowering chemical combo, altering his mind and body. "Me too."

Other couples crowded onto the dance floor, which he normally hated, but not tonight. Not when it forced her breasts to rub against him, driving him almost insane with lust. He gagged a groan and held her tighter. She didn't resist.

Her rose and cinnamon scent further stoked his desire, daring him to run his hands through her lustrous, long hair and kiss her soft, pink lips. A burgeoning hard-on pressed against his pants and he pulled his pelvis back. He'd hate for her to think he was a sleaze.

"I'm Richard, by the way," he said, weaving them a little woodenly across the glossy, timber floor.

She glanced up at him, all long lashes and parted lips. "I'm Eva. Eva Fjelstad. Nice to meet you."

"You work at Sub Rosa, right?"

She stiffened, her don't-tell-me-you're-some-crazy-stalker stare searching his eyes. "Yes, but how...?"

"I saw you waiting for the lift a few days ago. I work there too...in the research department."

"Oh..." The rigidity in her muscles melted away and she relaxed into him. "I'm secretary to the Personnel Senior Manager."

I knew it!

The song finished. *No!* He couldn't let her go. He kept hold of her hand and steered her through the cigarette-smoke haze to an empty table in a quieter area in the back.

"I thought we could talk for a bit...if that's okay."

She smiled and cast her eyes down in a cute, shy way. "Yes."

"Um...can I buy you a drink?"

"A glass of red wine would be lovely, thanks."

At the bar, he bought a couple of glasses of merlot and picked up some paper coasters. They could come in handy for exchanging phone numbers, if he was lucky. He stuffed a few in his back pocket and returned to the table.

Eva sat on a chair against the back wall, facing the dance floor, legs crossed and her dainty foot swinging to the music. Or did it shake with anticipation? Maybe both. *Don't get ahead of yourself.* Difficult not to, though. With her skin so pure and smooth, he longed to explore every inch of it.

Richard swallowed his lecherous thoughts and sat opposite her. "Your drink, milady. I hope you like merlot."

Eva took the wine glass, her fine-boned hand brushing his. "I love merlot."

He raised his glass to hers, his skin still tingling from her touch. "Me too. Cheers."

They each had a sip without breaking eye contact. "How long have you worked at Sub Rosa?" Richard reached into his back pocket, pulled out a couple of coasters and laid them on the table.

"About two years now. I started as a bit of a Girl Friday and moved into my current position about six months ago. How about you?" She put her glass down, a blood-red drop of wine seeping into the pristine white paper and spreading into an abstract heart shape. Or was it a woman's... *Whoa.* His own personal ink blot test proved revealing — so revealing that it didn't take a psychologist to work out what dominated his mind.

Richard stopped staring at his X-rated interpretation of her spilled wine and cleared the residual lust from his throat. "I only started six weeks ago, so you could say I'm still in the honeymoon period." He wouldn't mind being in the honeymoon period with her right now too. The image of him and a naked Eva tangled together embedded into his brain and he tugged at his cravat to release the building heat.

Eva smiled, seemingly oblivious to his obscene thoughts. "Your line of work sounds pretty interesting. I can't imagine it becoming boring."

The silky sheen of her lip gloss lubricating her lips was the perfect enticement, inviting him to lick and taste... *Think non-sexual.* Or she would catch on. And run off. *Puppies and kittens, puppies and kittens, puppies and kittens.* "You're right. The great thing with Sub Rosa is they offer a lot of research options and possibilities, so losing interest is pretty unlikely."

He took a large mouthful of wine, and his gaze returned to her, like his eyes were a compass and she due north. "You're really beautiful, you know that?" The words slipped out before he could vet his wayward thoughts. And he couldn't blame the wine. He hadn't even had half of it yet.

Eva grabbed her glass and gulped down the rest of the red.

Her beauty, combined with her close physical presence, worked like a battering ram, breaking the door down on his inhibitions. "I'm sorry. Was I a bit forward?"

"No. Yes. But thank you." Her flushed cheeks looked wine-stained. And deliciously hot.

Barbara Lewis' *Baby I'm Yours* started, as though responding on his behalf. An unrelenting craving to hold her again made him restless, and he stood and held out his hand. "May I have this dance?"

She slid her palm against his and they both shivered. Did she feel the potency of their connection too? Richard led her back onto the dance floor. The smile on his face had to look like he'd taken a special trip down sexy lane.

"I love this song too," she said, her lips within kissing range.

"Not just a great song, also a great sentiment, as long as it's demonstrated by actions and not just words." He pulled her close, even closer than before, and they fit together like two perfect pieces in a 3D puzzle.

"Yes..." She looked at him like he'd said the most groundbreaking, poetic thing in the world.

Had the music gotten louder or had his awareness around her heightened? The physics of the situation suggested both. He leaned in close to her ear to be heard over the blaring band. "How are you getting home?"

With a shaky hand, she pointed to her friend, swarmed by a mob of Mods. "With Greer. She gave me a lift."

Damn. Although, her friend hadn't stopped flirting, like she wouldn't mind going parking by the end of the night. Maybe he could offer to drive Eva home, test the romantic waters. Now that they'd spoken, he'd become thoroughly besotted.

"Um..." He hesitated, the words hanging on the edge of his tongue.

Her big, bright eyes encouraged him to continue.

"I could drive you home. If you'd like."

She dropped her gaze, though didn't pull away. "Oh...um..."

"If you don't want me to, I understand. It's just...it wouldn't be a problem. In fact, it would be a pleasure."

They kept dancing but she didn't answer him. Was she still thinking about it or did her non-answer mean *no*? If only he could mind-read.

The song finished and she looked into his eyes. "Okay."

She agreed? "Okay?" he asked, just to double-check.

"Yes, I'd like that...for you to drive me home. Thanks." She gulped. "Wait here. I'll just tell Greer."

Richard stood off to the side of the dance floor and savored the swing of her hips as she hurried over to her friend. Eva tapped her, then they exchanged a few words and looked over at him.

Greer squealed, whispered something in Eva's ear — most likely warning her against the dangers of wandering hands and lips in the confined space of a car — making her blush, and, in moments, Eva slid back in by his side.

His hormones continued to wreak havoc with his usually rational brain, but no matter what, he needed to show some control. He needed to show her his respectable nature, that he epitomized the sort of man she'd want to be with, the sort of man he usually was, the sort of man he was proud to be. Even his past girlfriends would agree.

"Ready to go?" he asked.

"Yes." Her voice sounded all want-wrapped-up-in-a-parcel-of-nerves breathy.

Exactly how he felt.

He brushed his fingers against hers and lingered, hinting he wanted to hold her hand, silently asking for consent. And she silently gave it, opening her hand and sweeping her palm across his in the gentlest, most erotic way he'd ever experienced. Eva had no idea of her seductive power.

Richard interlaced his fingers with hers, rejoicing at the renewed skin-on-skin contact, and led her out into the busy street. People dotted the pavement—sober, drunk, flirty, shy, dorky, cool—smoking cigarettes and making out. Fog gathered around the antique iron lampposts, sending out a scattered halo of glowing, golden light.

They stepped around the mini congregations of dance-goers and turned the corner to revving motors. A gang of Bodgies and Widgies propped against their motorbikes, drinking, smoking and leering. Richard slipped his arm around Eva's waist, pulling her against him like a protective boyfriend.

Not only did she go along with it, but she also nestled tighter into his side. He stifled a sigh. The smell of exotic spices in her hair stimulated his appetite for a non-food feast. *Mmmm…*

Restraint would be hard, harder than he'd ever known. Did their closeness spark the same desire in her too or had she snuggled in for safety? *No. Not only for safety.* Nothing about her touch felt safe.

Richard paused by the passenger side of his red MG, reluctant to let her go. He hesitated then shuffled around in his pocket for the key and opened the door.

She sat and ran her hand over the dashboard. "Cool car."

If only he could trade places with the dashboard. *Get a grip.* His body, now absent of her, went cold, yet throbbed with the hot thrill of more to come. "Thanks."

He got behind the wheel and started the engine. "Where to?"

"Seven Swan Street, Sandy Bay. I'll direct you."

"No need. I know exactly where it is. It's not far from work. Lovely spot."

In five minutes, he'd parked in front of her whitewashed, single-story house—green lawn, picket fence and all. He accompanied her to the imposing white wood door and they stopped in the shadows, couched in the dim, misty shimmer of a distant street lamp.

"I just wondered… Could I get your number? I'll call you tomorrow."

She shifted her weight from one delicate foot to the other. "Oh, um…yes, it's—"

"Hang on." He pulled out a blank coaster, and a pen from the inside pocket of his jacket, then pressed the round white card against his thigh, pen poised. "Okay, go ahead."

"Two, two, three, nineteen forty-four."

Richard jotted it down and slipped the precious piece of paper back into his pocket. "Thanks." Then on another blank coaster he wrote, *Eva, you're intoxicating,* and underneath it scrawled, *Richard Hall, 223 1939.*

"And here's my number," he said, and handed it to her.

Eva read his note, kept her head bowed and smiled, her hand shaking as she filed it away in her bag. Her shyness around him was the sweetest thing. Combine that with the sexual tension surging between them and Richard careened toward combusting.

He had never wanted to kiss a woman so much in his life. Would she consider it too bold? They weren't even on an official first date. They'd hardly spent a couple of hours together.

"Um…I suppose it's goodnight then." Good to know his do-the-right-thing conscience always won out, even though it could be frustrating. Like now, when he wanted to taste her tempting lips.

"Yes…" she said, without looking up, but she didn't move.

Hope sprang into his heart, speeding up the sporadic beats. *Is she wishing for more too?* "Eva…"

Her bewitching gaze reconnected with his then dropped to his mouth, and before he could stop himself, he kissed her. Instead of pushing him away, she molded her mouth to his, warm, supple and welcoming. Eva sighed, the remnants of red wine on her breath sending him straight from tipsy to drunk…on her.

Richard clutched her face and deepened the kiss, engaging their tongues like lustful lovers. She pressed her palms against his chest and leaned into him, sending his pleasure receptors into overdrive. He trailed his hands down her arched back to her sumptuous behind.

What am I doing?

Rational thoughts shackled his desire and he pulled back. "I shouldn't have… I'm sorry," he said, his persistent hard-on betraying his words. He had it so bad.

Eva grabbed her house keys out of her bag, opened the front door and turned to him with a coy smile. "Don't be," she said, and disappeared inside.

A broad grin burst onto his lips. She'd liked it as much as he did. *Yes!* Now for their upcoming date. He had to work out where to take her, what to do and when — with the aim to keep his and her pants on like a chastity belt.

Chapter Four

A Date with Destiny

It backfired. Salvator's love potion panacea backfired. He pulled away seconds into his fiancée's doomed kiss.

"I can't do this," he said and began to leave her home, still recovering from the change in her touch.

The result was absolutely fascinating, from a scientific perspective. His skin had gone from tingling with the anticipation of pleasure to heaving with revulsion. 'Revulsion' might be a little extreme but it felt like kissing his sister instead of a lover.

Wrong, wrong, wrong.

No longer could he enjoy her lips on his, her breasts pressing against his chest and her hips rubbing against his pelvis, making him hard. Every ounce of lust and what his heart had assessed as love had been stripped away, snuffed out, leaving a romantic void. It felt as though she'd sucked every bit of it from him, like an emotional vampire.

She grabbed his arm, biting heat puncturing his flesh. He tried not to flinch as he turned to face her.

"What do you mean?" she asked, her words trying to pick the lock to his closed heart.

Salvator stumbled away from her and attempted to swallow what remained of her unwelcome spit without gagging. He forced a smile but the drop in her face told him she could see beneath his façade, his mask.

Things were different. Things had changed to chasm-like between them and she couldn't understand why. Even though his feelings had done a one-hundred-and-eighty-degree flip, she seemed as into him as ever. More so, if that were possible.

From the bottom of the front steps, he stared up at her, still standing in the doorway. "I'm sorry. I have to call off the wedding. It's nothing to do with you. It's me...all me."

She averted her gaze, her mouth opening and closing with absent words, silent tears streaming down her face. Part of him celebrated. By doing this, he'd allowed each of them to go forth and meet the right person.

I've done the right thing.

Haven't I?

The devastation on her face screamed that he hadn't, but maybe he'd confused her response with shock and grief. She'd come around. She'd have to. He could never, ever be with her. How could he marry a woman whose romantic touch repulsed him? He couldn't even hold her hand now, forget about sharing her bed.

Salvator got in his car, his head a jumbled mix of conflicted feelings, her distraught face branding a permanent spot in his brain. Had taking the serum really been worth it?

* * * *

Eva placed her hand on top of the telephone receiver, as though to send a telepathic request for Richard to call. *Richard.* Her stomach fluttered, setting off a thudding in her heart and she flattened her palm over her chest. Hard and fast beats rattled her ribs. *GagungGa-gungGa-gung.*

So, he was *the guy* — the one Greer had said couldn't keep his eyes off Eva while they'd waited for the work lift a few mornings ago. And her observation couldn't have been more right. Richard personified 'dreamboat'. And he liked her. Had kissed her even.

She closed her eyes and touched her lips, every detail returning her senses to that magical moment. His ragged breathing, his deep caressing voice, the intensity in his gorgeous green eyes and those incredible lips and hands taking her to sensual places she'd never been before, detonating an internal grenade of desire even now.

Their kiss had been on repeat in her mind, following her into sleep, her dreams and still there when she woke. Her body craved the dysfunctional 'stop' button but her hand protested, her wrist sore from several bouts of self-pleasure. And still, the yearning lingered. So unlike her Miss Prim, always-the-good-girl persona. The heat of embarrassment scorched her cheeks. If he knew…

The phone rang.

Eva jumped and her heart almost shot through her head. Was it Richard? Had he tuned into her salacious thoughts?

It rang again and she lifted the receiver to her ear, her arm shaking like she'd overdosed on espresso. "Hello?"

"Hi, Eva? It's Richard. We" — he cleared his throat — "we met last night."

As if she could forget his handsome face, his panty-stripping voice, the way he flicked her pleasure switch... "Hi, Richard."

"Sorry to call so late in the day. I had to attend an extraordinary work seminar and — "

"Don't worry about it." Did she sound too breathy? Desperate?

"I hoped you'd have dinner with me tonight."

"Tonight?" She leaned back against the wall for support.

"If you don't have any plans...and you want to."

Of course I want to! "Um...yes. Thank you. What time?"

"I'll pick you up at six-thirty and maybe afterward we can see a movie."

"A movie? At the drive-in?"

"Yeah. How does that sound?"

Perfect. Fab. Fantastic. Except, what would people say, seeing her alone at the drive-in with a guy she'd just met? Not that she should care — she didn't have a certain reputation to uphold to her family. She didn't have one — no mother, siblings, uncles, aunties, cousins. Only the hint of a father, as far as she knew.

But her reticence wasn't just about her social standing. What if she didn't have much of a connection with Richard beyond the physical? How could she cut the night short and have him take her home without hurting his feelings? They hadn't spoken much, so she had no idea if they were compatible on a deeper level. Yet every cell in her body gravitated toward him like it had accurate, unexplainable knowledge they were attuned.

Should she trust her intuition? No matter what she felt, reality held the truth, and Richard may be all wrong. A Saturday night drive-in session tended to be pretty busy, though, so if he tried something untoward, she'd be able to get someone's attention, wouldn't she?

"Eva?" Something in the timbre of his voice said *trust me.*

"Yes...um...good. That sounds good."

A short while later, Eva stood in front of her large bathroom mirror and applied thick black eyeliner then a couple of coats of mascara and brushed lip gloss onto her lips, surprised at the steadiness of her hand, given she'd be seeing Richard any second.

The doorbell rang and a tidal wave of suspense rolled through her stomach.

"Coming!" She ran into the bedroom, grabbed her black coat from the wardrobe and glanced at her alarm clock — six-twenty-five. "Reliable *and* punctual," she murmured, and hurried down the hallway.

She opened the front door and Richard stood on the porch, wearing a black leather jacket, red shirt, black jeans and a panty-soaking smile.

"Are you ready?"

For their date or for him? She dragged her yearning eyes from his best-candy-in-the-box body and met his potent gaze. "Yes." To both.

They reached his car and he opened the passenger door for her, like a true gentleman.

"Thank you." She sat on the cool vinyl and buckled up her seatbelt. Would the true gentleman theme carry through the night or had Richard planned on getting to second base? She still couldn't believe they'd already made it to first!

The memory of his hungry lips on hers, his tantalizing tongue and his hot hands brushing over her bottom invaded her mind, for the thousandth time. Heat pooled between her legs and rose right up into her cheeks.

She shifted in her seat, searching for a cold swatch of vinyl to control the fire burning in her core. Eva hadn't wanted him to stop the kiss the previous night and her body had ached with disappointment when he had. So maybe she'd allow him to get lucky. But not too lucky…yet.

Richard turned to her from the driver's side, his green eyes glowing in the dusk light. "I put the top up. I hope you don't mind. It's a bit too chilly to have it down."

His close proximity shot her internal thermostat up to sweltering, making it easy to forget the coldness outside. In fact, she could do with a cool breeze to fan her stirred-up body right about now.

"Not to mention the mess the wind would make of my hair," she joked, trying to distract him and herself from her hypersexual response.

He chuckled. "Exactly. So, I made a reservation at Café Destino for dinner. They're the only place in town that cooks steak the way I like it. Any objections?"

"None whatsoever. I love a good steak." Something red, rare and bloody.

When they got to the restaurant, a waiter directed them to an intimate nook, next to a window overlooking the deep, sapphire sea

Eva studied the menu, and when she looked up, Richard's gaze zeroed in on her eyes. "I'm sorry if I keep staring but your eyes are amazing. The blue-violet color is so striking, so unusual, so beautiful."

"Oh, um…thanks." Eva glanced down, her cheeks going from simmering to roasting. Again.

"So, ah…what would you like?" he asked, as though sensing her need for deflection.

You. Eva stared so hard at the menu she swore she could almost see smoke rising off it. Yet the words were a blur, her mind flooded with R-rated images of Richard and her, naked, in all sorts of erotic positions.

What the hell? Her mind must have taken a wrong turn down a debauched detour. She'd fantasized about men, but never to the I-need-an-ice-bath-to-cool-my-scorching-thoughts level.

"Eva?"

She fought the urge to mop her brow with the white cloth napkin. "Oh, sorry. I got a bit lost in thought there for a minute." *Obscene thoughts, in fact.*

"Anything you'd like to share?"

Her cheeks flared like a furnace on full blast. "No, not at the moment."

Richard grinned and she could have sworn he could read her mind.

"What's so special about the steak here?" she asked, desperate to change the subject.

"Well, I like it rare, whereas most people seem to prefer charcoal. The chefs here cater to my request. I've found most places won't."

"I can't believe it! You're the first person I've met who likes their steak done the way I do. I normally cook it at home because most people think it's strange, eating it bloody."

"I know exactly what you mean." His gaze lingered on hers and he licked his lips. "Anyway, let's order. All this rare meat talk is making me hungry."

Hungry in more ways than one, by the looks of it. And me too.

Richard grabbed the waiter's attention and ordered a rare steak with baked vegetables and an accompanying glass of merlot for each of them.

His probing gaze fixed on hers. "Tell me more about yourself. Do you have any family?"

"Unfortunately, there's not much to tell." A sharp sting stabbed at the back of her eyes and she looked at the shiny tabletop. "On my seventh birthday, I received a trunk with some belongings and a letter from my dad but that's it. I don't know where he is or even if he's still alive. I've used up all my savings hiring nearly every private investigator in town to track him down...and nothing."

She slammed her hand to her mouth. *Shit.* She'd never told anyone about her quest and yet with Richard, an almost total stranger, the words bled out like a burst artery.

"Are you okay?" He reached out, curled his fingers around her hand, and gently tugged it away from her lips.

She nodded, unable to speak, the opening of her mouth a tripwire, ready to set off a bomb of tears.

With his thumb, he stroked her skin in soothing little circles. "I don't know my dad either. Never met him but I'd like to, if he's still alive. So I understand," he said, his tone a pressure bandage, stemming the flow of her internal grief.

She shifted closer, curiosity overriding her sorrow. "And how about your mum? I have no idea about mine. My dad left me at an orphanage as a baby and I got brought up in boarding school."

"I grew up in boarding school too." A devilish smile leached onto his lips. "And let me guess... You hate garlic, prefer the cold and dusk is your favorite time of day."

Eva stared at him, her jaw slack with surprise. *Is he some sort of psychic?* "Yes."

Richard leaned in, the golden flecks in his brown hair flickering like embers under the dim romantic lighting. "You know, if anyone heard our conversation they'd think we were vampires."

She laughed. With just a few simple words, he'd lifted her right out of her sadness. "We really do have a lot of weird things in common."

"No wonder I like you so much."

What? Her heart skipped a beat, then another, and another, and kicked back into a rocketing rhythm.

The waiter placed their wineglasses on the table and headed toward the kitchen.

Richard raised his glass with his free hand and looked her in the eye. "To many more enjoyable nights together."

A bolt of desire struck her nerves, making her hand tremble as she lifted her glass to his. "Cheers." She had a large, steadying sip of wine. "Enough about me. Tell me about you."

Richard put his glass on the table, out of accidental-knocking distance. "The highlights-package version... I went to boarding school in Launceston and worked hard to win a scholarship to Melbourne Uni to complete a Master of Science degree with a specialty in genetics."

He picked up his wine, swirled it around and had another swig. "Not long after I finished the course, I received a letter from my dad's brother, Bram, asking to meet up in Hobart. Up until then, I 'hadn't even known I had an uncle. I didn't think I had any family. So, of course, I agreed. We hit it off so well he invited me to stay with him at his place in Fern Tree. I refused at first but he convinced me it was the perfect solution, for both of us."

A spike of envy speared her heart. "You're so lucky to have found each other. Though it's a shame he didn't make contact earlier."

"I guess he didn't want to get my hopes up. He didn't know if he'd stay in Tasmania — something about a past romantic relationship that had gone wrong. I'm just glad to have him in my life now. Better late than never, as they say."

Eva stared at their still-joined hands, the dark wood table contrasting with their pearl-white skin. "I wish I had someone close. I mean, Greer's great but…" What made her confide so much in Richard? It felt like he'd dosed her up with truth serum, freeing the feelings imprisoned in her fortressed heart.

She gulped down another massive mouthful of wine.

He caressed her cheek and her gaze reconnected with his. Green unwavering intensity. "You have me."

What? Sizzling electricity shot through her flesh and her breathing stalled. He looked totally serious. How could he be so certain this early on in their relationship? How could he make such an intimate promise? "That's very kind of you, though don't you think it's a bit premature? I mean, we've only just met."

Richard moved closer and cocooned her hand between his. "Look, Eva. I'll be honest. I'm twenty-five and I've had a few girlfriends. But I've never felt like this about any of them. Ever. And I can't imagine feeling any better than when I'm with you."

Could this be a strategy he used to get to second base — third even — by reading women's vulnerabilities and targeting them? Saying what they needed to hear? Emotionally entrapping them? Or was he genuine, speaking from the raw depths of his heart?

"Sometimes things can feel amazing at the start then fizzle out."

"Of course. But something in here," he said, holding her palm to his heart, "tells me that's not the case for us."

His heart beat strong and steady against her hand. *Us?*

Everything he'd said had sounded sincere and he'd backed it up with persuasive, unblinking eye contact. However, he might be a world-class con artist, a heartbreaking gigolo.

No matter how much she wanted to believe him, how much his words resonated with her emotions, how attracted she was to him, she needed to keep a clear head. She needed to slow things down, to make sure they got to know each other before she did something she might regret.

The waiter brought their meals and Richard let go of her hand, breaking the addictive flow of energy between them.

Shock.

Withdrawal.

The classic signs were there. Frustration, obsessive thoughts, physical craving… And all because he sat opposite her like a dangling piece of rare meat, just out of reach. Slowing things down would be a struggle.

As the waiter retreated to another table, Richard said, "You're going to love this," jolting her out of her rambling reflections.

Eva cut into her steak and it bled onto the plate. Perfect. Tender, red, juicy, just as he'd promised. She savored the raw, metallic taste in her mouth. "Mmm...you're right. This is exquisite."

Richard polished off his wine and stared into her eyes. "You're exquisite."

Her cheeks went from smoldering to aflame. "Thank you. You're very kind." Mixed signals? There were none. He hadn't even tried to hide his attraction to her. A good start, a very good start, but he needed to find her mind and character desirable too—baggage, faults and insecurities included.

"I'm just telling you the truth."

She peered into his eyes, trying to get a glimpse through the windows of his soul into his essence. "Are you? How do I know for sure?"

"You don't. You just have to trust me. For a relationship to work, there has to be trust, don't you think?"

Definitely. She should trust him until he proved otherwise. "Yes."

He smiled and rubbed his hands together. "Okay, now that that's cleared up, let's finish our steaks so we can indulge in some dessert."

They ate the rest of their meal in flirt-tinged silence, with the occasional heated glimpse at each other in between mouthfuls. Their searing kiss from the other night popped into her mind and hijacked her senses.

Soon they'd be alone in his car at the drive-in, away from prying moral-police eyes, and just the thought of what other intimate activities could happen made her pulse pound.

Once the waiter had removed their plates, Richard stared into her eyes. "Now, about that dessert..."

Eva patted her stomach. "I've had more than enough. Maybe just a coffee."

"Come on. Let's at least share something. Don't quit on me now."

Quit? Who said I quit? The hackles stampeded up the back of her neck. He really did have a knack for identifying and exploiting a weak spot.

She glanced at the cake display cabinet over his shoulder. "The lemon meringue looks pretty good."

"Done. I love lemon meringue."

"Really?"

He did the sign of the cross over his sturdy chest. "Cross my heart."

"What else do you love?" Eva asked.

The look he gave her didn't just spark with heat. Something deeper glowed in his eyes, a sort of adoration, and for a wishful second, she thought he'd say, *you.* "Hmmm…outside of excellent company and good food, observing and interpreting people's behavior and what causes it…"

No surprises there.

"Genetics, deciphering puzzles, poetry, reading novels and going to the opera," he continued.

"Wow. We really do have a lot in common. Though I'm not too *au fait* with genetics or solving cryptic puzzles."

"I bet you're better than you think," he said.

She raised her eyebrows in a 'think again' expression.

He chuckled, the sexy sound traveling like celebratory bubbles of champagne through her bloodstream. "All right, I won't test you…yet. I'll stick with something safe, something in your comfort zone."

She rolled her eyes, a response not even years of the strap at boarding school could beat out of her. "You're so considerate."

"I am, aren't I?" He grinned. "Tell me, what's your favorite book?"

"Of all time? That's a hard one." She ran through the catalogue of book titles stored in her brain. "I'm going through a bit of a classics phase at the moment... If I had to choose one of those, I'd say *North and South* by Elizabeth Gaskell."

"Ooh, great choice."

"You've read it?" Could this man surprise her any more tonight?

His lips curved into a so-proud-of-myself smile. "I sure have. I don't mind a bit of the classics. Great for my poetry."

Smart, handsome, kind, creative. Richard represented her own earth-dwelling Eros. "You write poetry? I'd love to read some of your work."

A sexual undercurrent flowed in his eyes. "I might even let you inspire some of it."

Chapter Five

Mixed Messages

After Richard settled their dinner bill, he held Eva's hand, sending a shiver of delight straight to her sex. They walked back to his car, and he drove them to the nearby Elwick Drive-in to see the late showing of *The Sound of Music*.

Richard parked at the rear and turned to her. "Would you like something else? A drink, popcorn, ice cream? I'm going to have a Gaytime. I can't resist those bloody things!"

Eva laughed. She could always squeeze one of those in. "All right, I'll have one too. Thanks."

A roaming mobile cart vendor passed by, and Richard bought their Gaytimes and slipped back into the seat beside her. He handed her one then installed the metal drive-in speaker onto his window and wound it up, shutting out the frosty night air.

Eva peeled back the golden paper packet and bit through the biscuity, chocolate-covered shell and into the creamy, golden-vanilla ice cream. "Mmm... I haven't had one of these in ages."

"Then we must do this more often," he said, with a do-I-have-plans-for-you twinkle in his eye.

A yes-please shudder spiraled up her spine.

"Ice cream. Probably not the best choice on a cold night, huh?"

He'd mistook her body's response to him for the ice cream. And she wouldn't correct him or they'd be on each other like randy rabbits.

"Yes, something hot would have made more sense."

"I could get you something hot if you want." His smile said he meant every bit of insinuation in that sentence.

"No, I'm fine." If fine meant totally turned on. Her panties dampened more with each moment in his car's close quarters.

Eva focused on her Gaytime, sucking the mini balls of biscuit and licking the remaining ice cream off the wooden stick. She could feel his eyes all over her and glanced up, tongue poised mid-lick. Richard was watching her, all right, with an I-want-to-do-that-to-you glint in his eyes.

"You look like you *really* enjoyed that," he said with a wicked smile that could just about melt off her clothes.

A heatwave soared under her skin and she licked her lips. "I did." Two could play his titillating game.

He shifted in his seat, giving away exactly where his mind went — the dirtiest end of the gutter. She couldn't help but smile. Now he knew how she felt being around him with his sexy masculine scent, irresistible green eyes and alluring, muscular body. A small moan escaped her lips and she covered it up with a cough.

Richard shifted closer. Would he make a move? Would he kiss her again? Between her hammering heart and labored breathing, she was seconds away from having a full-blown desire attack.

His personal space began to intersect with hers, and he stopped and chuckled.

"What?" Her voice sounded breathy, her body still recovering from his silent, unfulfilled promise of a kiss.

Richard reached up and caressed the corner of her mouth, sweeping away a ball of biscuit.

How embarrassing!

He cupped her face. "Saving it for later on?"

Her heart thumped so loud that he could probably hear it over the chattering speaker in his window. He tilted her chin up, his gaze switching between her eyes and her lips and he dipped his mouth to hers. His gentle kiss brushed her lips, tentative this time, as though checking to make sure she wanted it as much as he did. And she did, maybe more.

Eva parted her lips, welcoming his tongue, and she wound her arms around his neck. A groan sounded in his throat and she pressed into him, desperate to hear him do it again. And he did — deeper, longer.

Richard sank his hand into her hair and tugged just enough to set off a wave of warm tingles rolling across her scalp. He delved his tongue farther into her mouth, stroking and sucking on hers until he teased out a moan. His other hand traveled an achingly slow path along her curves and came to rest on her bare leg.

Each of her nerve endings pinged, like scoring in a game of pinball, and he was the expert player. She wanted to shed her clothes and be naked with him. Suddenly she didn't care what society thought. Being present in the sensual moment with Richard mattered most.

Where had this extra-sexualized Eva sprung from? Obviously, she'd been stuck somewhere deep in her psyche, so deep she hadn't even realized her alter ego existed. It was like she represented Excalibur and Richard, King Arthur, the only man who could free her sexy side from stone.

She slipped off her shoes and he swept her legs along the length of the front seats so he lay on top of her, her dress bunched up around her thighs. The coarse denim of Richard's jeans scratched a ripening need into her skin and she trailed her hands down his back, his muscles rippling beneath his shirt.

Richard explored her ear with his lips, the length of her neck and continued down the plunging neckline of her dress.

"Ooooo," she moaned, hooking a leg around his waist and pressing her pelvis into his. She'd never felt a man so…hard. His breath hitched and he rubbed his bulging cock against her panties, taking them from damp to wet to drenched.

Their breathing accelerated, matching his thrusts, like a steam train speeding toward the ultimate destination. The delicious throb in her sex intensified until she teetered on the brink of screaming. They were going to do it…on their first date…and she didn't care. Right now, she wanted him more than she'd ever wanted anything or anyone.

Richard slid his long fingers under the fabric of her dress and stroked her bare breast, her nipple erect under his expert attention. Then he pushed the material aside and took the aching point in his mouth.

She dropped her head back and clamped her teeth together, extending every last second of elation. He sucked and licked and kissed, a low rumble of approval humming in his throat.

Buds of ecstasy sprouted in her clitoris and bloomed in her core. "Richard!" she cried and bucked beneath him as she came.

"Eva!" he grunted, and stilled, following her into climax.

Then, all of a sudden, he sat up, disentangling himself from her, and threw his door open, a rush of chilly air invading their intimate space. "Excuse me," he said without making eye contact and stepped outside.

The experience they'd shared rated as one of the most incredible moments of her life and *that* was his reaction? Fault lines of confusion spread across her forehead. *Does he regret what happened?*

Richard exited the drive-in toilets a few minutes later with his head hanging forward, and trudged back to the car. He dropped into the driver's seat and covered his face with his hands. "Sorry. I'm *so* sorry. I don't know what came over me." Richard paused and lowered his hands, his eyes filled with remorse. "Actually, yes I do. I can't resist you."

"I know the feeling," she said.

He smiled, but it didn't erase the harsh lines of shame etched into his face. "It's not a good enough excuse. Caveman behavior is never acceptable. I should have had better control."

Eva smoothed out her dress and tamed her sexed-up hair. "It's okay. Don't blame yourself. I could have stopped things too, but I didn't." *I didn't want to. Greer will be super proud.*

She glanced at the movie, and the family was taking a huge risk, leaving the comfort of their home and trekking across the mountains into the unknown. Eva had taken the risky, unknown path herself tonight.

It had been the first time a man had seen and touched her bare breast, the first time she'd allowed herself to let go and the first time she'd come in a male's company, yet she didn't feel self-conscious or even awkward.

Being with Richard felt so right. He seemed to be the unique key to open her locked heart...and free her libido. Though, after his deflated response, her emotions were an oil-and-water mix of elation and guilt. *I can't believe we nearly went all the way!* They'd just about had sex with their clothes on...to *The Sound of Music* soundtrack, of all things.

Bright lights beamed back on as the credits rolled. "I should drive you home." He stared straight ahead, with not even a glimpse her way.

"Yes..."

Within twenty minutes they parked outside her place. "Would you like to come in for a drink?" she asked. *What am I doing? He'll think I'm that sort of girl.* Too late to take the words back now, though. And her actions? Her response to him in the car had been pure textbook bad-girl behavior.

Richard's clearly conflicted gaze met hers. "I'd love to, but I don't think it's a good idea." He held her face between his hands. "How about I take you out for lunch on Monday?"

Eva exhaled, her lungs letting go of her hijacked breath. He already wanted to see her again. An excellent sign. Obviously, her forwardness hadn't put him off. "That sounds really nice." Then she leaned in and kissed his delectable mouth.

* * * *

On Monday morning, a solitary note sat in Eva's pigeon hole. She unfolded it and scanned the elegant, backward-slanted writing.

Hi Eva,
Unfortunately, I have to cancel lunch today.
Sorry about the short notice.
I'll be in touch soon.
Richard

Her heart caved in like a spoiled soufflé. Canceled? Head lowered, she dragged her feet back to her desk, the weight of his rejection heavy in her hand. Surely he needed a lunch break.

His antics were classic brush-off behavior, done on paper instead of in person. She'd obviously let things go too far on Saturday night. Maybe he'd pegged her as the free-love type and it had turned him off.

She closed her eyes, trying to quash the rising wave of worry. Maybe he'd just been inundated with work. Eva flopped into her office chair and fumbled with the dictation pad on her desk. She really should give him the benefit of the doubt and not jump to conclusions.

Greer wheeled in beside her. "Hey, what's with the sad face?"

"Richard had to cancel lunch."

Greer grabbed Eva's arm, forcing her to look up. "His loss. Think of the positives— You get to hang out with me instead."

Her friend's attempt to cheer her up almost worked. "Yes..."

"Don't sweat it. It sounded like everything went great on Saturday night."

"I thought it did." Eva pushed her notepad aside.

Greer's eyes took on her signature no-nonsense stare. "It did."

Eva lifted her shoulders into a halfhearted shrug.

"Come on. Smile. It won't hurt."

The edges of Eva's lips twitched and broke into a resigned smile. When Greer went on a mood-lifting mission, she stuck it out until she got results. And with Eva, she always did. Eventually.

The rest of Monday and all of Tuesday dragged, with no further word from Richard. By Wednesday night, she'd started to give up hope that he'd contact her.

Eva was standing over the stovetop in the kitchen, cooking, when the phone rang. Hope rose in her thundering heart. *Richard?* Rational thoughts flooded her brain and drowned her joy. She doubted it, given he'd avoided her ever since their date on Saturday night.

Self-doubt plagued her, picking at the emotional scab she'd thought had healed. First her father left, now Richard.

She took the frying pan off the heat and strode down the hallway to stop the persistent ring. "Hello?"

"Eva, are you okay? You sound a little flat."

Richard. Excitement effervesced in her stomach. His deep, sexy voice reminded her of a favorite song, triggering nostalgic memories. *Hang on. He can pick up on my low mood from just one word?* "I'm fine, thanks." *Sort of.* "How are you? What have you been up to?"

"Work, work and more work, unfortunately."

"I see." *Now comes the I'm-really-sorry-but-I-just-don't-think-our-relationship's-going-to-work speech or maybe the it's-not-you-it's-me breakup bullcrap.*

"I'm so sorry about canceling on Monday. What are you doing Saturday night?"

"Nothing, why?"

"I'd like to take you out."

Really? "Where?"

"It's a surprise. Make sure you dress up and be ready by five-thirty."

Oh. Could he still be interested? Or maybe he planned to do the gentlemanly thing, treat her to one last fancy, thanks-but-no-thanks date and break up with her in person. The only way she'd know was if she agreed to go.

Eva struggled to sleep that night, nervous and excited about their upcoming date. When she got home from work the next day, a brown paper package with a card and a single red rose greeted her from the front doorstep.

Richard. Has to be. She didn't have any other potential suitors. With a smile so large that she imagined it could be seen from the moon, she picked up the parcel, plucked out the rose and sniffed its glorious perfume.

She went straight into the lounge room, sat on her comfy couch and lifted the card out of the mini red envelope. Richard's backward-slanted handwriting flowed in neat lines across the small space.

Dear Eva,
I've really missed you this week.
Looking forward to seeing you again Saturday night.
Richard
P.S. I couldn't resist getting this for you. Hope you like it.

Two rips later, a collector's edition of *North and South* peeked out from the torn paper. She freed the precious hardback, ran her hand over the black and gold cover and flipped through the gold-edged pages. It had that heady, old-book smell. Such a thoughtful gift, not to mention the sweet message attached. It had to mean romantic interest, right?

His words were one thing, but to prove he'd meant what he wrote, he had to follow through with consistent boyfriend action, including physical intimacy — assuming he considered himself her boyfriend.

Chapter Six

The Code Breaker

Trondheim, Norway 1937

Abe's roommate pushed his textbook off the desk and it slammed onto the floor. "Come on! You know you're a genius with code. It's just one night out. It won't hurt you. You can finish revising tomorrow."

The guy had a point. Abe had always been a math whiz and loved creating and solving puzzles. If 'cryptographer' had a picture next to it in the dictionary, it would be his. One night off from studying might even do him good. It might help settle his nerves, which were the real problem.

They got ready and walked to an underground club close by, a popular place, apparently frequented by beautiful women — or so his roommate assured him. *That* had been the clincher.

Swing music pounded against the closed, double doors, guarded by two burly, blond security guards. His friend shook their hands, exchanged a few words and led him inside, into a wall of smoke.

Abe's eyes adjusted to the dark room. Clusters of spiffy-suited men and slinky-dressed women filled the vast area. A band played on stage to a crammed dance floor, with swirls of smoke wafting into the upbeat air. A small cloak room stood to the left and a bright, shiny bar ran along the rest of the left wall.

"Let's get a beer," his friend said and drew him along a convoluted path to the closest bartender.

"My shout." Abe pulled some kroner from his wallet and ordered and paid for their drinks.

Then he saw her. The most beautiful creature he'd ever beheld. Her jade-green gaze cut through the haze and met his across the bar, and it was as though little invisible hands shot out and nudged him forward.

"Sorry, got to go." Abe handed the beers to his mate without taking his eyes off the woman, and started walking toward her.

"Abe?" His roommate's voice sliced through the noise.

But Abe kept going, like a train on a track to an exciting new station.

"I'll see you back at the dorm, then." Or, at least, that's how he interpreted his friend's drowned-out words.

The closer he got to the intriguing lady, the more his body hummed with single-minded harmony, as though her aura had wrapped him in a welcoming blanket and blocked out the rest of the world.

Glorious golden hair framed the beauty's face and fell in waves over her svelte shoulders. "I have not seen you here before." Her accented English cemented her as a native Norwegian, a tall, slim, sexy local. Movie star material.

His heart thumped to the rhythm of the big band beats. "N-No," he stammered. "No. I'm staying at the university. The University of Science and Technology, Gløshaugen campus." He hadn't even answered her question. She must think him a Class-A moron.

"Um...I haven't ventured out much. I'm on a scholarship. I've been focused on study. I can't afford to lose it." Oh yeah, that sounded a lot better. Full marks for making a great first impression. Now she probably thought him an unadventurous nerd, too.

She smiled as if to say, 'makes perfect sense' or maybe 'I don't know why but I'll give you a chance', and extended her fair-skinned hand. "I see. I am Rhoda, also a student, and I just live down the street."

Is that an invitation? He shook her hand, shivers of delight jumping from synapse to synapse. "Abe. Nice to meet you." *Really* nice. His loins agreed.

Couples congregated onto the dance floor. He should ask her to dance then buy her a drink. That's what typically started the courting ritual in Australia. In Norway, still so foreign to him in many ways, he had no clue. The etiquette couldn't be too different, though, could it?

He cleared his throat. "So..."

"Would you like to escort me home?" Hope shone from her eyes like focused beams of torchlight.

What? "But I just got here. We just met."

"It is only a short walk. We can get to know each other better on the way. It is hard to talk here."

Either she was extremely forward or he'd totally misread her. Normally, he excelled at reading people, situations, codes. But so far nothing had been normal about their interaction. "Um..."

"Come on. Live a little." She grabbed his hand and steered him to the front door.

The icy air outside grated, like scraping flesh with a frozen peeler. Abe shivered and pulled the collar up on his coat, whereas Rhoda seemed unaffected, not even a goosebump on her exposed skin, like she had immunity to the cold.

They turned left and strolled along the promenade. "Are all Norwegian girls this…bold?"

She laughed, a rich, harmonic siren song. "You have an accent. Where are you from?"

"Tasmania, Australia. You didn't answer my question."

"Depends on the girl. Are all Australian men so…presumptive?"

"Presumptive? I'm not presuming anything."

She stopped, her enticing jade-green eyes staring into his. "A girl invites you to walk her home and you do not have any assumptions, any expectations?"

He chuckled and they kept walking. "You got me. I'm curious more than anything."

"As to what might happen."

"Yes. I'm trying to have an open mind about it."

"That is the best way."

He glanced at her balanced profile. "Do you often ask men to walk you home?"

"Would it matter if I did?"

"No. What you do is your business."

"No."

"No?"

"I do not normally ask men to walk me home. This is the first time."

"Really?" This woman was a riddle not even he could crack. Sanguine, attractive, flirtatious, yet innocent?

"Why is it so easy for you to believe I have done this before but not that it is the first time?"

He rubbed his clean-shaven chin with his icy-cold hand. "You just seem so confident."

"I am...about you. You seem upstanding and trustworthy."

"Now who's assuming?"

She laughed her soft, beguiling birdsong again.

They arrived at a large, gothic, sandstone mansion, with a Psyche and Eros fountain babbling away at the front. "Wow. You live here?"

"Yes. The house has been in my family for generations."

They walked up the well-worn steps to a large oak door with curvaceous black hinges and ring knocker. She let go of his hand, fished in her pocket and pulled out an antique brass key, like something from a museum.

Rhoda stepped inside and continued down the dark hallway. "Are you coming in?"

Even with the distance between them, he remained within her bewitching bubble. Abe followed her, like an adoring pup on an invisible lead. A staircase led up on the left and she turned into a dim room on the right, with low yellow flames and orange embers flickering in the fireplace.

Rhoda grabbed a poker, adjusted the wood and added a couple more logs, reinvigorating the fire. She sat on a carved, decorative loveseat, licks of gold and amber splashing across her face and body like she was an abstract art canvas. She gestured for him to join her.

Heat radiated from her closeness and the flames, further stoking his desire. Abe fought the urge to slide his hands over her skin and under her flowing white skirt. And those eyes weren't making it any easier. The predatory look in them said she wanted to devour him in a good way—a very good way. "Isn't there anyone home?"

"Probably not. Supper is not usually until after nine p.m. and it is not even eight yet."

A nervous smile sandbagged the corners of his lips. "Right...um...so tell me more about you and your family."

"Are you sure you want to know?" A sense of warning tinged her tone.

"Of course. Isn't that the point of this?" Then it struck him. Maybe she'd picked him up purely for sex. He hadn't ever done it on the first date, though her beauty made her almost irresistible. Abe snatched his gaze away from her and sat on his hands.

"You look—what is the English word? Anxious?" she said.

"Probably because I am."

She laughed. "I will not bite, unless that is your...predilection." Rhoda stared right into his eyes. "Would you like something to drink?"

His aroused, suspense-filled brain did not need plying with any more disinhibition. He needed to try to think straight, which was becoming more and more difficult the longer he sat with her. "No, I'm fine at the moment. Thank you."

"All right, then tell me about Abe. A summary of the man you are." Her husky voice and hypnotic eyes were captivating.

Abe dropped his gaze to his lap. If he kept looking at her, he couldn't trust himself to remain a gentleman. "Aren't you supposed to be telling me about you first?"

"Does order really matter?"

"Sometimes. If I wrote you a letter and you read it right to left, it would make no sense whatsoever."

She curled her legs onto the couch, leaned her elbow on the top of the backrest and propped her head on her hand. "What are you studying at the university?"

"Cryptography. It's the science of—"

"I know what it is, Mr. Code Maker—or is it Code Breaker?"

"Both."

"Figures."

Her lips twitched as though struggling to contain a smile. *Is she laughing at me?* "Excuse me?" he said, sitting up straighter.

"Did you not get my little joke? Code...figures?"

Clever. The built-up defensiveness drained from his body.

"You are so cute when your pride overcomes you," she said.

He grinned. "Only then?"

"No. You have a very—what is the word in English—sexy? You have a very sexy smile, too."

Look who's talking. "Thank you."

She knocked his thigh with her slender knee. "I am still waiting for your summary."

Abe scrambled to recover from her heart-hammering touch. "As I mentioned earlier, I'm on a scholarship, studying over here."

"So you are intelligent...at academic work, anyway." A cheeky grin curved up the corners of her mouth.

Abe plowed on, struggling to stop himself from planting a kiss on her tempting lips. "I'm loving the change of culture..."

"So you enjoy traveling."

"The countryside is breathtaking..."

"So you are a nature-lover, a man who enjoys simple, untouched beauty."

Untouched beauty. Had she referred to herself or the landscape? He stared into her jade eyes, so close to the edge of seduction that the smallest step and he'd fall into their depths. "Yes."

Without warning, she closed her soft, sultry lips over his, stealing his breath, and moved nearer, slipping her slender arms around his neck. He wound his hands around her tiny waist, delved his tongue into her mouth and explored its hidden delights. He hardly knew a thing about this woman, but the one thing he did know? She could kiss…well, *extremely* well.

He broke away to suck down some air. "You did that to distract me, didn't you?" His voice sounded hoarse with lust.

"The question is, did you enjoy the distraction?"

If she had been sitting on his lap, she'd know the answer without him saying a word. "Very much. You?"

"A lady does not kiss and tell," she said with a mischievous smile.

He chuckled. "Fair enough. But you at least owe me the Rhoda highlights."

She relinquished her hold on his neck and glanced down, her leg shaking.

Now it was her turn to be nervous. "I'm waiting," he said.

Her gaze returned to his. She opened her mouth and only a sigh escaped.

She responded like she had something to hide, like she lived the life of a secret agent or femme fatale.

"I…" She inhaled another diaphragm-deep breath as though to give her extra time to compose her thoughts. "I am a music major. Piano is my instrument of choice.

I am hoping to make it to the symphony orchestra but I am doing my teacher's degree as a fallback."

"So you're artistic and creative."

"I have lived in Norway all my life and have never traveled abroad…"

"So you like the comforts of home and are close to your family."

"And…" She hesitated. "How am I going to say this?" She tapped her trembling fingers on her delicate chin. "My…" Clam-up clashed with come-clean in her worried eyes. "My heritage is…complicated. I am a half-caste…"

"So? If you're a half-caste that makes me a mongrel, a convict."

She averted her eyes and shook her head. "You do not understand. I am half Jade."

Jade? What the hell does that mean? "I'm sorry. I'm not familiar with the different Scandinavian familial groups."

"Not many people are. I just thought there might be rumors at the university. Some students are very…smart."

Abe held her hand. "Rumors about what? What's so special about this Jade heritage of yours?"

Her gaze pleaded with him. "As long as you promise me that after I tell you, you will not run away."

He balked. "Run away? Of course not. How bad can it be? Are they a Scandinavian crime family full of mass murderers?"

Her dead-serious facial expression shut down his attempt at humor. "You promise."

"Yes, I promise." He stroked the smooth pale skin on the back of her hand.

Rhoda took a deep breath and stared at their interwoven fingers. "There are two clans — the Jades and the Violets. And they do not get along, not since the Middle Ages."

"Let me guess... The prejudice still exists."

"Yes. Personally, I do not have a problem with the Violets, but that is not the issue."

Abe squeezed her hand. "Then, what is?"

Her gaze reconnected with his. "The Violets and the Jades are" — she hesitated — "creatures of the night."

"Creatures of the night? You mean like to" — he fashioned quotation marks with his fingers — "have a good time?" So they weren't conservative, no-sex-before-marriage types. Big deal. It didn't bother him. Times were changing anyway.

She shook her head, her beautiful blonde hair swishing across her shoulders. "No. I mean...vampires."

He laughed. "You really do enjoy a joke, huh? It's a very attractive quality."

Her somber expression didn't budge. "I am not joking this time."

"Are you trying to tell me I'm sitting here within the clutches of a vampire? Did you lure me here for supper? With me as the main course," he said, trying to tame the laughter cramming his throat.

She huffed and let go of his hand. "This is not going quite how I expected."

It hadn't gone anywhere near what he'd expected either.

"How can I convince you?" she asked.

"Hopefully not by making a meal of me."

She closed her eyes for a long second, as though stringing together thoughts to make him see sense.

"The Jade clan is identified by their jade-colored eyes and fair hair. The more vampire genes they have, the deeper the eye color and the fairer the hair. Whereas the Violets have dark hair and violet eyes.

"You need to understand that the majority of us do not drink human blood. Half-castes like me eat a diet similar to what humans have, except I need to add some animal blood once a week or else I get fatigued, irritable."

Fear spread like an aggressive cancer from his brain right through to the rest of his body. Could it really be true? Surely no such thing existed, not in reality. But she seemed so genuine. "And I'm supposed to believe this?"

"Why would I make it up?"

He shrugged. "I don't know, psychosis? Maybe you've decided you don't really like me and want to scare me away? Maybe you had a bet with a friend?"

She stared at him, her tenacious expression unwavering. "I promise that I am telling you the truth."

"You said not many people know about Jades and Violets. So, if it's meant to be a secret, why are you telling me?"

"Because I like you and it is important you know the facts, what is involved if…you like me. And I think you do."

She did look and sound serious. Did that mean vampires weren't just some myth? That they were real? *And even though she said she doesn't snack on humans, should I be scared?* Probability suggested she'd be physically stronger and more invincible. *What if she gets hungry?*

He sprang up and stepped away from her, his head spinning. He'd just kissed a *vampire*. Well, part vampire, but vampire all the same.

Her eyes filled with sadness. "You promised you would not run."

Abe gulped, his body's fright-and-flight alarm activated. "I'm not. It's a lot to take in. I need to think about things." He edged backward toward the door. "I've got final exams to study for. I really need to concentrate on those at the moment. Sorry. I'll contact you as soon as I can."

Her eyes glazed with unshed tears, like she didn't believe he'd follow through. "Promise?"

I'll try. He fidgeted, not convinced he would, once out of her reach, once safe. "Yes. Um…goodnight."

The journey back to his university dorm room could only be described as a drunken blur. But he wasn't drunk, not from alcohol, anyway. His mind darted all over the place, tumbling from thought to thought, feeling to feeling like dirty clothes being tossed around in a washing machine. *What the hell kind of country do I live in?*

Meeting Rhoda had turned his whole belief system upside down. It had opened his eyes. Wide. A whole world existed out there that he knew nothing about. He'd been living in his own little sheltered reality, shaped by his middle-class upbringing and associations.

Rhoda had made him think beyond his safe, self-constructed borders. She'd challenged and unsettled him and he enjoyed a challenge, thrived on it. By nature, he took risks, but did she pose too much of a challenge, too much of a risk?

Abe fell onto his bed and stared up at the shadowed ceiling. His lips still tingled from her kiss. Whether part vampire or not, sharing that intimate moment with her had been incredible. And not just his lips felt the force of it, the sensual aftermath continuing to sweep through his keyed-up body.

He needed to sleep. His subconscious needed some time to piece everything together before he could respond to her.

And his body needed to recalibrate too. It still craved Rhoda after her confession. *Absolutely ridiculous.* The sexual attraction component shouldn't *ever* hold as much weight as rational, practical thinking. He'd been caught out before, so he should know better. This felt different, though. More intense, more consuming.

Enough!

His mind stepped in, trying to repel her, out of self-preservation or panic? He didn't want to be the sort of person who reacted out of fear and ignorance. If she'd wanted to suck his blood, she'd had plenty of opportunities. But she hadn't taken advantage of any. Maybe she really was harmless.

Going by her response to his kiss, she did like him, though was it in a romantic or food-type way? *How can I find out?* He didn't have any vampire mates to run it by. Or maybe he did and just didn't know.

Abe pressed the heels of his hands into his closed eyes. What to do… Forget about her or give her a chance? Had she woven a spell over him, making him crazy? *No.* If he took the emotion out of it, she'd taken a big risk too, confiding in him so early on with such an enormous secret. It must mean she trusted him, yet he'd far from afforded her the same respect.

Abe sat up and looked out of the window into the dark night, across to the lights lining the street to her house. He should give her the benefit of the doubt, shouldn't he? He'd expect that from her. But was trust worth risking his life?

Chapter Seven

Assuming the Worst

Hobart, May 1965

"Wow!" Richard's gaze wandered over Eva, the second she opened the door. "You look" — he sighed — "ravishing, with a capital 'R'."

Her heart didn't just flutter, it flapped as though a pair of doves had been released from its depths. "Thanks." He looked pretty hot himself, dressed in a suave black suit, white shirt and paisley cravat. Very cool, very James Bond.

He smiled his sexy, core-caressing smile and gestured toward his car. "Let's go."

"Where are you taking me?" She studied his outfit some more, hoping it would give her a hint. Somewhere dressy, obviously, but other than that, she had no clue. Though, she did notice a fun little coincidence. The electric blue in his cravat matched the shade of her body-hugging velvet dress, like they'd rung before their date to color coordinate.

He opened the passenger-side door, his light green eyes gleaming. "I told you. It's a surprise."

Hmmm... No kiss hello or hand holding, though he did seem happy to see her. And he had sent her that thoughtful and, by the looks of it, expensive gift. She couldn't work him out. He was like one of those cryptic crosswords she always struggled with.

They soon reached the city and Richard parked in the Theatre Royal carpark. It was still a bit early to see a show. His crafty cloak-and-hidden-dagger demeanor suggested he'd planned for more than just a simple lead-in dinner.

Instead of entering the theater, they continued past it, crossed the street and stopped in front of a solitary, carved wooden door.

"Here we are," Richard said with a sly smile and pulled the door open.

The welcoming aroma of marinated meat wafted into her nostrils and sparked her salivary glands. She gulped down the gush of saliva and her stomach growled.

"After you," he said, being too damn gentleman-like. Then again, he could be using the opportunity to check out her behind. By the roguish flash in his hooded eyes, she'd go with the 'behind' option.

At the top of the stairs, she entered a posh dining area, decked out in gold, cream and red, with a large, glowing chandelier hanging in the center of the room. A grand piano sat in the corner and an odd cross-section of people from Bodgies and Widgies to Mods to Hippies and Upper Class milled around, holding drinks and talking within their select groups.

Richard's hot palm against Eva's lower back startled her like she'd been struck by a bolt of lust. He steered her toward the bar, ordered them both a glass of wine and a waiter showed them to their table. Richard pulled out an ornate gold chair with red velvet seat for her and sat opposite.

Floor-to-ceiling windows lined the perimeter of the room, offering a spectacular, three-hundred-and-sixty-degree view across the dusky mauve, pink and gold-dappled city.

He looked into her eyes and raised his glass. "To another wonderful evening."

Just like last time. Eva squeezed her legs together in an attempt to stem the longing ache building between them and chinked her glass against his. *I hope.* "Cheers."

They both took a sip and put their glasses down on the red and gold tablecloth.

"I'm assuming we're having dinner then seeing a show?"

A grin spread across his lickable lips. "I thought you said you weren't good at puzzles."

"Cryptic puzzles," she said, correcting his broad-brush statement. "How did you find this place?"

"I saw an ad in the newspaper for a special meal deal that looked perfect for us. They hold it once a month in different venues and I noticed this one seemed close to the theater so teed up tickets for the same night."

"You thought right. I love the theater and this place is…" She sighed. "It's really lovely."

Lust-fueled fire flared in his eyes. "Like you."

Her gaze hit the table, heat throbbing in her cheeks. What he said shouted *I'm totally into you*, then he'd negate it by his reluctance to touch her. Richard really was an enigma wrapped in a paradox.

He had another drink of wine. "The venue's great but…I think you're going to appreciate the whole experience."

"I don't doubt it. Thank you. Though you have to stop spending so much money on me. The gorgeous gift you sent me yesterday plus tonight must have cost you a fortune!"

"I wanted to do it. I wanted to treat you."

Touch me then! That's all she wanted, along with his undying love and devotion. Not much at all really. She laughed to herself. "Just spending time with you is enough. Honestly. Quality time means much more to me than material things."

He smiled like he'd just won *Pick a Box* and she was the grand prize. "Me too."

Then show it! "Though this place is pretty amazing."

He laughed. "And unique. Wait until you see what's on the menu."

Meat, meat and more meat. She'd heard of indulgent degustation meals in fancy French restaurants but never anything raw-to-rare-meat-themed. The selection was a true meat fetishist's paradise. And going by the fifty or so diners in attendance, there were a lot more people with their sort of taste than she'd thought. A percentage of those would only be there for the novelty, but she didn't care. It was just good to know events like this existed.

Appetizers consisted of a range of colorful raw meat canapés, followed by Steak Carpaccio, then Steak Tartare for first course, rare-eye fillet and roasted vegetables for main course and fruit mince pies done the old-fashioned way, with actual meat, for dessert.

Richard couldn't have made a better dining choice. Everything was perfect, filling and scrumptious. And they said the way to a man's heart was through his stomach. The meal tasted like pure seduction. If Richard wanted to kiss her at the table right then as a post-meal digestif, she'd be reluctant to stop him.

But no. He stuck with his almost-no-touching stance, paid the bill, and they made their way to the theater. She'd just have to angle for a kiss on the lips later. Going by his recent behavior, it would be the closest she'd get to finishing the night with a bang.

The winter-cotton-sheet crisp air amplified to freezer frosty without Richard's body heat. Eva shivered, focusing on the illuminated square and the cream building with forest green trim, only a few more footsteps away. Columns adorned the archway leading into the packed front foyer, where ushers stood on a couple of raised platforms selling programs to the opera, *La Sonnambula* by Bellini.

"We're upstairs," Richard said, grabbing her hand and weaving through the crowd.

His skin on hers electrified yet soothed her nerve endings. "Have you seen it before?"

"No. You?" They reached the top of the stairs, and he let go of her hand and pulled out their tickets from his inside jacket pocket.

"No. But I love Bel Canto, and Bellini was the master," she said.

"I agree."

From their front-row dress circle seats, she surveyed the surroundings. The gold-cream, red and green themed décor continued into the theater's interior with a large, red velvet curtain draping across the stage. They were in the perfect position to watch the action play out, without patrons' heads bobbing into their view.

During the first act, Eva got absorbed by the elaborate sets, singing and storyline, but not so much that she didn't notice Richard's frequent glances her way, yet continued avoidance of physical contact.

He leaned on the armrest between them, brushing his arm against hers, then retracted it, giving her only a moment's pleasure. Maybe she should reach for his hand and see what happened. No. Not yet. She could be patient. She'd save her little strategy for Act Two, the climax.

They had a drink and bathroom break during the interval and spent the rest of the time talking about the impressiveness of the production. Then the bell rang, notifying them to return to their seats, and round two of Eva's physical touching campaign. The jostling crowd had its benefits. Eva counted five times Richard's body pressed against hers, pushing her arousal meter from seven to nine out of ten.

Sneaking in a handhold formed step one in her seduction plan. She glimpsed sideways at him, searching for a chance to make her move. However, he sat up straight, hands in his lap, staring at the show, and stayed in that position for the entire second half. So much for a climax. He'd seemed to anticipate her intention and ensured she had no opportunity.

Plan A may not have worked but she still had Plans B and C. Push to have a post-show coffee in a small booth where she could slide in beside him or break into his personal space when he drove her home.

With her coffee suggestion shut down, she prepared to put Plan C into action. They pulled up in front of her house and she took a deep, steadying breath. *Here goes...* "Would you like to come in for a coffee?"

His attempt at a smile stalled on his lips, turmoil raging in his eyes. "I'd love to, but I can't."

She shuffled closer, swallowed, swallowed and palmed his knee. "Yes, you can. It's still early."

Richard's gaze shot to his knee then back to her eyes and he went to speak but stopped, as though his heart and head were at war with one another and he couldn't decide which side to take. "Eva, thank you, but I can't."

Frown lines ran across her forehead like cracks in a wall, and she grasped his cold hand. "Please."

He slid his hand out from under hers, leaned across and gave her a swift peck on the lips. "I'll call you tomorrow."

Except he didn't. Disappointed and confused, Eva pulled her doona over her head and curled into a butchy-boy ball, as though to protect herself from the outside world. *Is Richard playing games with me?* He didn't seem that type, but she had very little experience with men. She had to talk to him about it on their next date, so she knew where she stood, once and for all.

* * * *

They were meant to catch up Friday night. *Tonight.* When Eva got into the office, a folded note sat in her pigeon hole. From Richard. *Canceling. Again.* She called his work number but he didn't answer. Several more unsuccessful attempts later, a tension headache morphed into a full-blown migraine and her manager sent her home.

Eva went straight to bed and woke up to blackness. She fumbled for her bedside lamp and switched it on, a shard of artificial light stabbing her sensitive brain. Through squinted eyes she glanced at her gold marcasite watch—nine-fifteen. Was it too late to call Richard? *No.* She had to try to speak to him, while she had the courage.

She dialed his home number and waited, her nerves in strangle knots, listening to the phone ring and ring and ring.

"Hello, Hall residence." A woman's voice. A young, cheerful woman.

"Who is it?" Richard called out in the background.

Eva slammed the phone down and stumbled away from it, her emotions flinging her around like a rowboat on a raging river. What had Richard been doing at home with a woman?

Scrap that. She knew exactly what he'd been doing, ditching her for another date. Her worst fear had been founded. Richard had abandoned her like everyone else who'd claimed to care for her.

Silent tears welled in her stinging eyes and slid down her cheeks. Better she knew sooner rather than later. Though rationalizing the situation did nothing to settle her distress. She stumbled back to bed, her feet lead-lined heavy. She should have known Richard was too good to be true. A passion like theirs could only peter out, and in their case, as quickly as it had started.

Disappointment and sadness clung to her like a cold, heavy fog throughout the weekend and by Monday morning, she had hardly slept. The whole drive into work, the impending confrontation with Richard played on loop in her mind and made her gut contort.

The lift doors opened on her office level, but she couldn't see him. Her heart sank to the bottom of her stomach. She'd been nervous as hell, assuming he'd be waiting. Now disillusionment stagnated in her veins like slow-moving sludge. Instead of choosing to meet her in person, he'd dumped another note in her pigeon hole.

Dear Eva,

I'm so sorry about Friday. Something came up that I couldn't get out of. I tried to call you all weekend but you didn't answer. You're not upset with me, are you? I really missed seeing you and hearing your voice.

I'll call you later.

Love,

Richard

Her heart fluttered, and a surge of joy pumped through her system. *Love.* A first. He'd never signed off with 'love'.

Stop it!

Love was just a word — the right one, granted, but not enough. The best way to test the strength of his sentiment would be to speak to him in the flesh. The most reliable lie detector would be whether his body language matched his words. However, he'd said he'd call. And she had to decide whether she'd pick up.

Chapter Eight

Cracking the Love Code

Trondheim, Norway 1937

The door flung open and Abe's roommate strode in. "Looks like you're staying."

"Pardon?"

"The results are up. You blitzed! Top of the class." The guy's ecstatic eyes gleamed, as though they were his results. "You can drop the shocked face, Abe. I'd understand shocked if you'd averaged B's."

"Thank you. That's great news," Abe said with zero enthusiasm.

"Then why do you look like someone just died"?"

Abe massaged the back of his tight neck. "I've had a lot on my mind."

"Such as?" He sat down opposite Abe on the blue, single-seater couch.

"I've been thinking about transferring back to Tasmania to finish my degree."

"I thought you loved it here? And wouldn't leaving negate your scholarship?"

"Yes…and yes."

His friend leaned forward, his eyes pleading. "Then you have to stay, not just for you, but for me, too. Without your help, I don't know how I'll pass the compulsory code components."

That's it. How had it not occurred to him before? Abe could write Rhoda something in code and if she figured it out, it was his sign to give her a chance.

His roommate snapped his fingers. "Hello? I'm talking to you."

"Yes, sorry. Don't worry. I'm staying…for the moment. You just helped me solve a problem that's been plaguing me for the past couple of weeks."

As soon as his mate went out, Abe sat at his desk piled with neatly-stacked textbooks and lecture notes and pulled out a blank piece of paper. He picked up a fountain pen and tapped it against his lips. Delicate rays of sunlight spilled in through the window, casting soft shadows across the room.

What to write? His mind got stuck in a censoring rut. Maybe physical, pen-to-paper contact would free the flow of thoughts. He dabbed the gold nib in the half-full inkwell and pressed it to the page.

Dear Rhoda,

Please forgive me for the delay in getting back to you. I've been thinking a lot about the night we met, what you said, that incredible kiss, and I'm ready and willing to give things a try. I'd really like to see you again, to give us a chance to get to know each other and make a more accurate decision about whether our relationship has a romantic future.

If you still want to give me a chance, let's meet in front of the Nidaros Cathedral at midday on Friday. I'll wait for an hour. If you don't come, I'll assume that's a 'no' and I promise not to contact you again.

I very much hope to see you then.

Abe

Done. First go. He read and reread the letter, just to make sure he hadn't missed anything. Nope. Now he just had to decide on a code. Something hard but not so hard Rhoda had no chance of deciphering it. Why even bother if he wouldn't be fair? His heart rooted for her to get it, though the jury was still out in his brain.

Abe picked up his lecture notes and reviewed the coding examples they'd covered in the course. A numerical code. Something where 1 equaled A, 2 was B, 3 equaled C and so forth. It seemed the best mid-range option. So his letter became...

45118 1881541,

161251195 6151879225 135 61518 2085 4512125 914 7520209147 21311 2021 251521. 9'225 25514 208914119147 1 121520 12152120 2085 1497820 235 13520, 238120 251521 19194, 218120 9143185492125 1191919, 1144 9'13 1851425 1144 23912129147 2015 79225 208914719 1 201825. 9'4 1851121225 129115 2015 1955 251521 171914, 2015 79225 2119 1 3811435 2015 7520 2015 11141523 5138 15208518 1144 131115 1 1315185 13321181205 45391991514 12152120 2385208518 152118 1851212091514198916 8119 1 1815131142093 6212021185.

96 251521 192091212 2311420 2015 79225 135 1 3811435, 12520'19 135520 914 618151420 156 2085 14941181519 312085418112 120 13944125 1514 61894125. 9'1212 231920 61518 114 8152118. 96 251521 41514'20 315135, 9'1212 1191921135 208120'19 1 '1415' 1144 9 161815139195 141520 2015 31514201320 251521 171914.

9 2251825 132138 815165 2015 1955 251521 208514.
125

When the ink dried, he folded the note, wrote her name in clear block letters on the front and hand-posted it, to make sure Rhoda received it in plenty of time.

Two days later, Abe stood in front of the Nidaros Cathedral, struck by the beauty of the stained-glass, Gothic rose window. No matter how many times he'd seen it, it always offered something fresh, a new detail woven into the intricate design.

As a mathematician, he didn't believe in religion or faith, and yet, the place radiated calming energy, though not enough to appease his teeth-gnashing anxiety.

Today he tottered on edge, which didn't make sense. If Rhoda didn't show, they weren't meant to be together. And if she did, then he had to uphold his promise and give her a proper go.

Unease weighed him down, like he'd swallowed a medicine ball. But was he more worried about her making an appearance or not showing up at all? He glanced at his watch…twelve-o-five. She still had fifty-five minutes. If the first five minutes were anything to go by, it would be the longest, most dragged-out hour of his life.

He patted the front pocket of his pants, hiding the gold and black cross pendant and matching ring his parents had given him.

"It's to protect you while you're away," his father had said. And hopefully it would today, if Abe needed it.

"And to make sure you don't get mixed up with any non-Christian girls," his mother had warned.

If his mum were alive, he could picture her aghast face at him contemplating not only a non-Christian but also a half-caste vampire. Bless her. No one could ever have been good enough for her only son.

In the distance, a fair-haired woman approached. Not *her*. He shook out his cold, stiff arms and legs and glanced at his watch again…twelve-o-nine. Would she make him wait? Give him a double dose of his own medicine? He probably deserved it.

Abe went over the coded message in his head. Had he made it too tricky? His stomach lurched. Maybe she didn't have a puzzle-solving brain. Maybe he should have kept it simpler. But how much simpler could he have made it?

Forget the cryptic clue path — that style of code was even more difficult to decipher. Maybe he should have tested the coded letter on some non-cryptography students just to check. Too late now. He'd made his decision and he had to live with the consequences.

A few people trickled out of the cathedral and walked to the park across the road. The path and rooftops were dusted with snow that sparkled in the struggling sunshine, and without a breeze, the air temperature felt around five degrees. By Trondheim standards, it was a lovely winter's day.

He rubbed and blew on his black-gloved hands and zipped his jacket right up under his freshly-shaved chin. Some stubble would have helped insulate his face against the chilly air, but he'd chosen the respectable track at the expense of warmth.

A breeze started and carried molecules of skin-biting ice, as though straight from the Arctic. The cold almost burned, chiseling a deep aching hole into the core of each and every bone.

"Think warm thoughts," he mumbled to himself, and an image of Rhoda invaded his mind. Next thing, she stood just meters from him, seemingly materializing out of nowhere, like some illusionist trick. Relief, joy and terror ripped through him and he stumbled toward her, hand braced over the pocket containing the cross amulets.

Rhoda smiled, a broad, teeth-gleaming smile with no sign of fangs. But he'd double-check when he got closer, just to make sure. Her golden hair splayed out from under a black knitted hat and fell over her fur-trimmed jacket. The pants she wore, paired with long black boots, made her legs look like they reached to the sky. And those eyes, those unmistakable, jade green eyes... Gorgeous. Irresistible.

"Impressive. Was that a test?" she asked.

Guilt welled up inside him and his gaze plummeted to his frozen feet. "Of sorts..."

"And if I failed?"

"We weren't meant to be," he said in a hoarse, humbled whisper.

"And now I have passed?"

He glanced up into her eyes and smiled. "I'm happy to report you've successfully reached round two."

She frowned. "Does that mean I need to do this again—or something like it?"

He chuckled. "No. My exam ended up assessing me more than you. I had to pass my own test."

"And have you?"

Hope shone from her impatient eyes, making it clear she'd give him another chance. "I think I have. Actually, I know I have." He clasped her gloved hand and interwove their fingers, disappointed that the double-knit barrier prevented skin-on-skin contact. "Shall we go for a walk while the sun's still out?"

"I thought you would never ask." No one could say sarcasm wasn't her strong suit and he liked it. Spirited women stimulated his mind, body and soul, but none he'd met ever had as much as this feisty female.

They meandered past the cathedral, crossed the road to the park and strolled along the winding river. "There are so many things I wanted to ask you but do you think I can think of them now?" he said.

She laughed and wiggled her fingers between his so they wove tighter together.

The increased contact made Abe just about hum all over. He glanced at her. "Maybe you could just tell me about being a Jade. What are the differences? Is there anything in particular I should know, other than keeping my vampire knowledge quiet?"

"Differences..." She thought for a moment. "I have less tolerance to sunlight than you, but more than my full or three-quarter Jade relatives. It is to do with an elevated white blood cell count. The more vampire genetics, the higher concentration of white blood cells, causing fairer skin and decreased tolerance to the sun. That is why we live in colder climates with less intense sunlight."

"How about crosses?"

"No effect. Pure fiction, like most of the *Dracula* story."

Abe's hand clamped over the jewelry in his pocket. Thank God things had gone to plan...so far.

"And neither does garlic. It is a deterrent, but it does not kill us. Again, because I am a half-caste, it affects me less than those with more Jade genes."

Her flawless, pearl-white skin scintillated in the sunlight and he couldn't stop staring. "And what about a stake through the heart?"

"It does nothing to three-quarter or full vampires, but it will kill or badly injure half and quarter castes just like it would a full human, due to the increased human genetics and weaker body."

"Makes sense. And how about your teeth?"

Her rose-pink lips curved into a smile. "Ah, yes, you did not notice any fangs. Again, only full Jades have full fangs and even then, they only come out when the Jade is angry or about to...feed."

Now for the clincher. How she answered this one decided their relationship's destiny. "And what about humans being bitten and changed into vampires? Could that happen if you accidentally bit me, for example?"

She laughed and when it wouldn't stop, she doubled over, grabbing her belly and trying to suck in air between chuckles. Instead of being offended, he soaked up the sweet sound, its harmonious tendrils spreading straight to his heart.

After a good minute, her laughter subsided and she stood, mirth still dancing in her eyes. "Sorry. I should not laugh, though some of the things you humans say are so funny and ridiculous. Fear and, the English word...ah...ignorance. Fear and ignorance do this. Let me set you straight."

Rhoda grabbed both his hands, her glowing green gaze fixed on him. "Do not worry, I cannot change you. Only three-quarter to full castes can do that by creating a blood bond. It happens when the vampire sucks out blood in a continuous stream while injecting venom. If

93

I nipped you or even bit you hard, the area would swell and redden for a few days but nothing more."

"Like a love bite."

"Yes, similar." She kept hold of one of his hands and they resumed walking. "Anything else you want to know?"

"What causes death?"

"It depends on how strong the vampire gene is. For full vampires, the main causes of death are starvation due to lack of red blood or over-exposure to sunlight. Otherwise, they will live forever and never age from the moment they were changed. For those of us who are less than full-blood vampires, we age but at a slower rate and can die from human ailments, if we do not look after ourselves."

A frosty breeze blasted his face, shooting icy shrapnel into his eyes. "Let me get this right. You can only become a full vampire if changed by a three-quarter to full vampire," he said, mopping the stinging tears off his cheeks.

"Yes. All part-castes are born that way."

Her eyes hadn't been affected at all by the bitterly cold wind. Did her vampire genetics protect her or was her immunity due to her native Norwegian human genes adapting to the freezing conditions?

"What happens if two half-castes conceive a full vampire?"

"It dies. It cannot survive because it will be frozen at the embryo stage and is miscarried."

"Of course. Anything else I should know?"

"Nothing I can think of."

"Except you'll age slower and I'll eventually look like I've gotten myself a trophy wife."

She laughed, a husky, sexy little tune that played right into his pants. "One minute you were not sure you wanted to see me again and the next, you are talking lifelong commitment. You are making me dizzy."

"We should stop a minute then, so you can get your bearings," he said, and kissed her.

It felt so good, amazing, better than the first time, having her whole body pressed against him. Their thick clothes created an almost insulated quilt between them, and even though it provided extra heat to contend with the cold, he grew desperate for bare skin contact. Just her physical presence put him under her sensual spell.

He forced his lips away from hers and whispered, "Let's go somewhere warm."

They found a cozy café and chose a table near the fireplace with a window overlooking the shimmery, sunlit river. They took off their gloves and coats and Abe went to order them a couple of glasses of mulled wine.

When he returned, he sat opposite her and said, "I have something to confess." He gulped down a couple of mouthfuls of the warm, spicy wine and placed his glass on the dark wood table. "You're going to laugh..." *Hopefully.*

Abe reached into the front pocket of his jeans. "Um, you see, I didn't know how today would go so I..." He plonked the cross jewelry onto the table next to his glass. "I brought what I thought offered me a bit of a safeguard, if things didn't go well." He poked the cross pendant with his finger. "When I packed them, I had no idea they'd be useless."

Her wineglass hovered mid-air and she stared at the necklace and ring. He couldn't read her face. *Is she angry? Disappointed? Insulted?* Hopefully he hadn't ruined everything.

She had another sip of wine, put her glass down and grinned. "Lucky I ate breakfast then."

Spirited, stunning and a sense of humor. The perfect package. He chuckled. "Consider them a gift. I want you to have them."

Her eyes widened with surprise. "No, I cannot—"

"Yes, you can."

"What if things do not work out between us?"

He put on his best serious face. "You can give the jewelry back."

Tiny lines of disappointment scored her forehead.

"I'm kidding. Honestly, I want you to have them. Maybe they'll provide protection for you some day."

"You are sure." Her eyes scrutinized his.

He'd never been surer in his life. The pieces of jewelry seemed to vibrate at the same energy as Rhoda. They belonged to her. "Very." He picked up the necklace and undid the clasp. "Let me put this on you."

She took off her woolen scarf and leaned forward, offering him a breath-hitching view of her breasts. "Where did you get them?"

Abe averted his gaze and gulped down the swell of desire rising inside him. "My parents gave them to me...to ward off danger." *And unsuitable women.*

He did up the clasp and hid his smile as she sat back. The dark pendant contrasted with, yet complemented, her radiant, alabaster skin. "It looks lovely on you."

"Really?" She pulled out a gold, engraved compact from her handbag and reviewed her reflection.

"So...mirrors aren't a problem either?"

Rhoda laughed hard, tears welling in her eyes and making them an even deeper jade. When she settled enough to speak, she said, "No. All Jades and Violets can see their reflections."

She laughed some more. "Sorry, though I am sure you understand. It is like me asking if Australians live in the desert with kangaroos and crocodiles as pets. I am sure you would laugh too."

She had a point. He smiled. "Yes…" Abe picked up the ring and slid it onto her right, middle finger. "Hmmm… It's a bit big but we can have it resized."

Rhoda stared into his eyes and fingered the cross pendant, her ringed hand over her heart. "No, it is perfect."

Chapter Nine

Things Aren't Always as They Seem

Hobart, June 1965

After letting Richard stew, Eva arrived at work to another neatly folded note in her pigeon hole.

You didn't answer your phone. You're upset with me. Let's talk about this so we can sort it out.
I'm coming to your place tonight at seven.
Hope to see you then.
Love,
Richard

Persistent. She had to give him that. Eva tucked the note into her handbag and returned to her desk in a distracted daze. Richard wouldn't try so hard to resolve things if someone else had captured his interest...unless the other woman hadn't worked out.

Stop. No more focusing on the negative, on assuming the worst. He'd come over, she'd let him in and they'd discuss everything—in depth, like mature adults.

Stiffness seized her body, like she'd been coated head to toe with tension spray. Confrontation was far from her forte. But if their relationship stood a chance, they had to be open and honest with each other.

At seven p.m. the doorbell rang. *Punctual as always.* Eva took a deep breath in and a long, slow breath out, in an attempt to steady her sprinting heartbeat. *Calm and confident. Calm and confident. Calm and confident.*

She opened the front door and Richard stood on the porch in all his package-hugging, blue-jeaned glory, looking as devastatingly handsome as ever. He searched her eyes, as though trying to assess her mood...and his best course of action. Worry and confusion lined his tight face...or was it sadness?

"Come in," she said and led him into the lounge room. "Would you like a drink?" Her voice sounded formal, businesslike, not how she wanted to be with him at all. However, it helped control her emotions and keep her heart intact, at least until she heard what he had to say.

"No. No thanks." He raked his fingers through his golden-brown hair, making it messy — a reflection of their relationship at the moment.

Eva sat on her two-seater leather lounge. "Please, have a seat."

He hesitated, taking off his black leather jacket and checking out the lay of the lounge-room land, whether he should risk sitting beside her.

He did. And they were so close, she could feel waves of heat and tension rolling off him.

Richard looked into her eyes. "Eva, I know I've had to cancel a few of our dates recently and I'm really sorry. I can't tell you how sorry. I've wanted to see you more than anything. It's just… I'm the new guy at work and I need to make a good impression."

"So, it's purely work getting in the way?"

A deep V formed between his brows. "What else would it be?"

She shrugged. "I don't know – lack of interest, another woman…" Her voice cut the air, sharp as broken glass.

Richard reached out and hesitated, hovering his hand over her arm. "I know I've not been perfect boyfriend material but I'm going to try harder. I don't want you to feel like this. I want you to trust me."

"*Trust* you? Kind of hard when you're home with another woman on a night we were supposed to go out." The acerbic edge to her tone sliced the air.

Richard dropped his hand, his face wrinkling with confusion. "What other woman? What are you talking about?"

Her accusing stare shackled his eyes. "I rang you last Friday night to speak about things. A woman answered, and I heard you call out to her in the background."

He buried his face in his hands and shook his head. "That was you."

"Yes." She strained to hold back the building bank of tears.

"She's my uncle's housekeeper. She comes in twice a week and one of those days happens to be Friday."

Eva sniffed back a sob. "Really? At nine o'clock at night?"

"Yes. She starts at eight and finishes at ten." He slipped his hand around hers and gently squeezed, drawing her attention back to his green-eyed gaze. "I'd just walked in the door when she answered the phone."

Eva dropped her head and tears trickled onto her cheeks. "And I'm supposed to believe you."

"Yes. Speak to her or my uncle, if you want. I wish you'd take my word for it, though. Honestly, I only have feelings for you."

His plea definitely sounded heartfelt and it seemed a reasonable explanation. But it didn't explain the sudden lack of physical affection. "Then why won't you touch me anymore"?"

"I touch you."

"Here and there but—" A sob cut her sentence short.

He tilted her head up, anguish filling his eyes, and hugged her to him. "Eva…" His soft voice slid over her, tender as a lover's caress. "It's not that I don't want to. The problem is I want to too much. Way too much."

"How's that a problem?" Her words muffled against his muscly shoulder.

"I worried things would get too out of hand. I mean, we nearly had sex on our first date. And it would only escalate from there. The more I touch you, the harder it is for me to control myself. Normally, I have great willpower, but with you… You're too much temptation."

His heart beat a strong, steady rhythm against her ear. "When I got home, after I pawed you at the drive-in, I thought about what you'd said at dinner—lustful attraction can die out—and it got me thinking. I wanted to make sure that what we have together has substance and can last the distance. If I kept touching you, I worried it would affect my judgment. I didn't want to make a decision or ignore things based on my physical attraction to you."

Richard stroked her hair, sending tranquilizing tingles down her spine. "I probably should have spoken to you about it. I didn't realize it'd end up causing so many problems. I thought you'd be relieved to have a boyfriend who wanted to get to know you and not just your body."

A deep pang of guilt slashed through her heart. "I should have been more upfront with you instead of jumping to conclusions." She pulled back and looked into his eyes. "I should have trusted you. I'm sorry."

Richard smiled and swept strands of stuck hair off her wet face. "No worries. We just need to learn from this. We need to have open, honest communication for us to work."

"I agree." She had to look a weepy-eyed, red-nosed sight, and yet he stared at her as though she'd just stepped on stage for the bathing suit round of Miss Universe. Did she look at him in that special I-want-you way too? "So, what are we going to do about the touching situation?"

He sighed. "It's a hard one, excuse the pun."

She laughed and sniffled. "How about we discuss it over dinner?"

"Great idea. Where shall we go?"

"How about here? I picked up a few things on the way home."

His eyes searched hers. "You were optimistic."

"Let's just say I hoped it would work out." She got up and reached for his hand. "Don't think you're getting out of helping," she said with a cheeky smile.

Eva put the vegetables on to steam while Richard poured them a glass of wine. "I'll look after everything from here."

She squinted her eyes at him. "I know what you're doing, Mr. Control Freak. You want to make sure your steak isn't overdone."

"Was I that obvious?"

"You and your bloody steak," she murmured. "Pun intended."

He laughed, washed his hands and placed the lamb in the pan.

Watching him, combined with the scrumptious scent of cooking meat, made her mouth water...and not just her mouth.

They ate dinner, devoured a Gaytime each for dessert then returned to the lounge room with black espresso. Richard placed their cups on the coffee table and they sat beside each other again, the air no longer thick with stress. Now, instead, not even a chainsaw could sever the sexual tension.

Eva rubbed his denim-covered knee. "We didn't decide on the touching rules."

"Are you a little tipsy?"

"Maybe, but it doesn't mean I'll let you deflect. The touching subject is important...at least it is to me."

His sincere, steadfast gaze held hers. "Me too."

"What do you—?"

His lips connected with hers, cutting her off, and the gentle tease developed into a slow, sensual tongue kiss.

"You're tipsy as well." Her breathy voice brushed against his lips.

He kissed her again.

"Excellent distraction technique. You'll do anything to avoid—"

He smothered her lips with his and lifted her onto his lap.

She gasped. "The rules aren't quite as strict as I thought they'd be."

He chuckled, then a serious, I-want-to-make-love-to-you-this-instant look shone in his eyes. Did she stare back at him with a resounding *yes please*? Because she wanted him to, and her body agreed, going by the throbbing ache between her legs.

Richard kissed her again, then his mouth traveled down her neck and he nibbled on her earlobe. "How about," he whispered, his voice as sexy as a striptease, "we agree to kiss and caress as much as we like, but with our clothes on. That's the boundary, the one limiter."

She moaned and angled her neck, allowing his magic lips greater access. "Can we let things go as far as our drive-in date?"

"Yes, except my hand won't be slipping under your clothes."

"Not even under my skirt?"

Richard tore his mouth from her skin and stared at her, flames of lust flickering in his eyes. "Okay, maybe under your skirt, but not beneath your underwear."

"What if I don't wear any underwear?"

"Eva." His tone rumbled with a mix of desire and warning. *So hot.* Hotter than a firestorm in hell.

"Well, you don't want there to be any gray areas, do you?" A saucy smile played on her lips.

He laid her down on the couch and pressed his body against hers. "The same rules apply to you too. No sneaking your hand beneath my clothes either."

She ran her palms along his back. "Not even under your T-shirt or shirt?"

"You're making this difficult."

"Look who's talking!"

A swift kiss later he sat up and had her straddling him, face to face, pelvis to pelvis, need to need.

"Okay, these are the exceptions. We can touch each other's bare skin as long as it's not in an erogenous zone."

She massaged his chest and his nipples puckered. "Does your stipulation include these? Some men would argue their nipples are just as sensitive as a woman's."

His head fell back and he sighed. "I suppose technically you're right, but in this instance, we'll deem my chest a safe zone. Okay?"

"I hoped you'd say that."

His head jolted up and he stared into her eyes. "You set me up."

And I did a bloody good job too. She grinned. "Maybe…"

"What am I going to do with you?"

"I can think of a few things."

"And unfortunately, a lot of those things will have to wait…for the time being."

She pouted. "I know."

Richard ran his tongue along her bottom lip and gave it a little nip.

"Do you want to stay over?" she asked.

"Eva…"

She tugged the hair at the nape of his neck and he groaned. "I just want to make sure you're safe to drive. You have had a bit to drink. Plus, it's Saturday tomorrow and now, with these new rules in place…"

Richard raised his eyebrows. "What am I going to sleep in?"

"Your underwear…assuming you're wearing some," she said with a mischievous smile.

"Is this the wine talking or are you always this… suggestive?"

"A bit of both."

A bolt of desire flashed in his eyes. "I like it."

"I'm not surprised."

He laughed, deep and husky. "Maybe I better sleep on the couch."

"Of course. What were you thinking?" she said, acting all innocent.

A you-got-me smile spread onto his suckable lips.

"I'm kidding. You're more than welcome to sleep with me...literally, of course." Blistering heat burned her cheeks. She couldn't read his thoughts, but going by the lustful glint in his gaze and the poke-your-eye-out bulge in his pants, it was pretty clear where their minds had gone. The gutter. Maybe their minds could make a home there, together.

Using the pad of his thumb, he stroked soft circles on her cheek. "Are you sure it's okay for me to stay? I mean, neighbors might talk if they see my car parked out front all night."

"It's fine. The only opinions I care about are yours and Greer's. Hey, did you tell your uncle where you were going? Maybe you should let him know not to expect you home. You don't want him to worry."

Richard gave her a lingering kiss. "You're so sweet, in every sense of the word. I'll give him a call."

Eva climbed off his lap and he walked out of the lounge room, leaving her drooling over his flawless physique. His tight, white T-shirt emphasized his V-shaped body and his denim jeans clung to corded muscles in his butt and legs. He symbolized the perfect Levi's advertisement.

Her pulse raced to 'ready-to-faint' and she reflexively fanned her face. How she would love to get him out of those clothes and study his assets up close. *Mmm...*

Richard re-entered the room. "All done."

"What did he say?"

"Be careful and be a gentleman."

"He doesn't know you too well then, does he?"

"Very funny." He strode over to her but instead of sitting down, he scooped her up into his strong, sinewy arms.

She gasped. "What are you doing?"

"Taking you to bed." His words spoke straight to her libido, shooting it right up to eleven out of ten on the I-want-you-so-bad-it-hurts scale.

He headed down the hallway and she pointed to her bedroom ahead on the left.

"What happened to being a gentleman?"

Richard grinned, his gorgeous green eyes crinkling at the corners. "No point trying to be something I'm not."

They entered the dark room and he lowered her gently onto her bed, pinning her against the doona with the weight of his body. Lovemaking flooded her thoughts and stimulated her body, and his too, going by the steel-hard swell in his jeans. But they'd agreed to the clothes-on rule, so she just had to make the most of it.

"If we're going to do this, I'm going to throw on something more comfortable."

Panic gripped his eyes.

She brushed her lips against his. "Don't freak out. I'll go into the bathroom and you can get changed here."

Eva slid out from under him, rummaged through her nightwear drawer and selected a short, white satin and lace slip and panties ensemble she'd been saving for her wedding night.

In the bathroom, she had a quick shower, shaved her legs and bikini line, threw on her outfit and inspected herself from all angles in the mirror. Eva turned scarlet.

Her nipples were like soft pink stars and her panties a white flag of surrender beneath the thin gauzy fabric.

Either Richard would scold her for pushing the boundaries—though technically she was well within the clothes-wearing rule—or thank her for just staying in them.

"Here goes." Each beat of her heart reverberated through her jelly-like limbs.

The bedside lamp spotlighted Richard in his magnificent manliness, eyes closed, lying flat in only blue paisley boxer shorts, his hands behind his head. Saliva surged into her mouth and her core clenched.

The bathroom door clicked shut behind her and she made her way toward the bed.

"What took you so—" He opened his eyes and they nearly bulged out of their sockets. "Whoa!" He breathed out hard and sat up, staring at her like a starved man and she represented a buffet spread.

She tugged at the lace hem on her slip. "Do you like it?"

"Like it? *No.*"

Oh. She shrank into herself, feeling exposed and embarrassed. *How could I have gotten it so wrong?*

"I love it." His deep, jagged voice scraped, as rough and sexy as second-day stubble.

Her gaze shot up to meet his. Pure, raw desire shone in his eyes. The exact response she'd aimed for.

He patted the bed. "Come here."

Eva rejoined him and he grasped her face between his hands, kissing her with heart-thumping urgency, as though she were his sexual lifeline. She wound her arms around his neck, the exhilaration so intense she could hardly breathe.

He kept his lips locked to hers and ran his hands down her body, pausing over her breasts. The heat from his warm palms seeped through the fabric to her sensitized skin, and he rolled her nipples between his thumb and index finger.

"Uuh," she moaned, already close to climax.

He laid her back against the bed and moved to nibble on her ear, then he kissed her neck and her breasts, stopping over each nipple and giving it a good lick and suck through the sheer negligee.

Eva threw her head back. "Richard!" She panted, rejoicing in his sensual worship.

He continued down her stomach, along her inner thighs, then he dipped his head between her legs and, *oh my*, kissed her right *there*. He planted a row of kisses across her mound and she bucked against his mouth and moaned.

"Mmmm...you smell incredible," he whispered, his hot breath stroking her skin. He trailed his tongue along the same sizzling path as his lips, licking her moist panties, and she weaved her fingers through his hair, anchoring him to her.

"You taste delicious too. Mmm..." He hummed through the satin and lace, cranking up the arousal dial on her clitoris. Then he took the small nub into his mouth and taunted and teased, prolonging her journey up the pleasure path.

Crazy with building desire, only garbled sounds came from her lips. Her body cried out *now please*, and miraculously he understood, switching to harder and faster licks until she came, screaming his name.

He peppered her wet panties with light kisses. "Serves you right for dressing like this."

Eva laughed. If a mind-blowing orgasm was her penance, she'd do it again and again and again. Richard's special attention down below was the best punishment ever.

He rolled them onto their sides, positioned her top leg over his waist and rubbed her panty-covered clitoris with his massive hard-on.

Eva gasped. Even with her limited experience, she could tell he was big. Would his size be 'ouch' or 'wow'? He sank his hands in her hair, thrust his tongue between her lips and picked up the pace with his pelvis. She massaged his bare back, working her way down to his firm butt.

"Oh, Eva," he groaned, his climax shuddering through his body.

Her name, a passionate plea on his lips, pushed her over the edge again. "Richard!"

They kissed and held each other close while their breathing returned to normal.

"Just going to the bathroom." Richard kissed her forehead and looked into her eyes. "Be right back."

He returned a few minutes later and snuggled with her under the doona. No sign of self-consciousness or awkwardness stirred within her, even after Richard had nuzzled his face between her legs. Instead, being so intimate with him felt natural, made her feel…whole.

Eva played with the sprinkling of golden-brown hair on his chest. "It's not true what they say. You can have a lot of fun with your clothes on."

He tilted her head up and looked into her eyes. "You certainly can." A *knowing* rang in his tone and showed in his stare.

An injection of jealousy shot through her veins like a slow-acting poison. "You sound like you've done this before." *With someone else.*

"Does it matter if I have?" His eyes searched hers, a hint of worry creasing his brow.

Yes! Though, should it? The idea of being each other's first was romantic but more and more unrealistic. In the swinging sixties culture, it no longer seemed a necessity, especially for a man. "No. Whatever experience you've had has made you who you are today." The man she loved. *Loved? So soon?*

"I'm glad you feel that way because, as I mentioned, I've had a few girlfriends." His gaze softened into a reassuring stare. "But we didn't have sex."

Relief rolled through her. Rationally, what he'd done with other women didn't matter to her, but emotionally it did. "Were any of them serious?"

"I thought one could have been. Physically, we were really compatible. I think we both thought upping the sexual intimacy would bond us more and it did initially. Then the attraction started to fizzle out, with no friendship or romantic love to fall back on."

Eva propped up on one elbow and stared down at him. "That's why you backed off. You were worried our relationship might go down the same path."

He tucked a lock of hair behind her ear. "Yes. But my plan doesn't seem to be working too well."

She laughed. "Sexual chemistry aside, we do get on great, don't you think?"

"I do. It's definitely different with you. With us." Richard leaned on his elbow, his enticing lips within licking distance. "How about you? Any boyfriends?"

"Not really. I've only kissed a couple of guys...so I need all the practice I can get." *Hint, hint.*

Richard nestled into her neck and trailed a string of hot kisses along her skin, stopping at her ear. "I'll see what I can do," he whispered, his sultry breath re-igniting the fire inside her sex.

After another round of...fun, she fell asleep in his arms.

* * * *

Eva woke up to a stream of sunlight shining through a gap in the curtain. What an incredible Richard dream. "Richard," she murmured, his name clutching onto her breath and cramming her body with longing.

"Mmm?"

Air caught in her windpipe. She turned over and the man himself lay beside her in the flesh, wearing the sexiest of sexy smiles.

"Good morning."

"You're here." She reached out and grasped his face, just to check.

He put his arms around her and pulled her flush against him, as though to prove his physical presence.

She smiled at her dream-come-true morning. "How did you sleep?"

"Not too well. It's hard to sleep with such a beautiful, half-naked woman lying beside me."

She sighed and kissed his succulent lips, the lips that had tasted her most intimate parts.

"What would you like to do today, assuming you don't already have plans?"

"Stay in bed."

His hard-on pressing against her inner thigh told her exactly what he thought of her idea. He stroked her hair, the added hit of pleasure, sending her into a heightened arousal stupor. A couple more caresses and she'd purr. Literally.

"Great suggestion, but it looks nice outside. We should get out and do something, make the most of it."

What? His words were in total contrast to his body language.

He smiled, big and broad. "Plus, I want to show off my stunning girlfriend."

Oh… Girlfriend. There, he'd said it. They were officially a couple. Euphoria swept through her, like a post-child's-party sugar high. "How about we spend until mid-morning in bed, then go out for brunch?"

"Mmm…I like the way you think. Best of both worlds." He brushed his lips against hers. "Then after we eat, I'll take you for a drive, drop you home after dinner and—"

"When will I see you again?"

He brushed the soft, plump pad of his thumb across her lips. "Soon. Very soon, I promise. I've got to finish a few work assignments…"

She frowned. Him and his work. She admired his dedication, but were all those extra hours really necessary?

"I'll call you tomorrow night and we'll arrange a catch-up this week."

"Just one?" After what had happened, didn't he want more? She already ached for him. And he hadn't even left yet.

"Believe me. I wish I could see you every day, every night but—"

"I understand." *Kind of.*

Richard pressed his lips to her forehead, tip of her nose, mouth, collarbone, earlobe. "What do you suggest we do for the next couple of hours?"

Hmmm...her chance to remind him what he'd be missing. Eva pushed him onto his back and straddled him. "A few ideas come to mind."

Chapter Ten

Life-Changing Proposal

Trondheim, Norway 1938

Tap, tap, tippity-tap

A lovesick grin spread onto Abe's face. *Rhoda.* He could tell by her distinctive knock. "Coming!" He did one last check in the mirror, smoothing his thick, ash-brown hair, adjusting his black tie and straightening up the collar of his long, black coat. His gray eyes were bright with anticipation. Tonight was *the* night.

When he opened the door, Rhoda wore a breathtaking smile and an open, black coat with the hint of a clinging, gold dress underneath…that he was dying to peel off.

Either the room had shot up ten degrees or he had an off-the-charts temperature. The needle on his hot-o-meter hovered near sex o'clock. The not-until-we're-married territory, except for the occasional stolen taste and touch.

Abe almost had to roll up his tongue and pick up his jaw from the floor. Rhoda looked like a real bombshell—not a gussied up, over-indulged actress, but a true, natural beauty. She'd give Marlene Dietrich a flat-out run for her money.

"I'll be the luckiest man there. You look ravishing," he said and kissed her porcelain cheek.

"Thank you. You look pretty dapper yourself."

Abe smiled. "Thanks." He checked his watch. "We'd better go or we'll miss the start."

"The start of what?"

His smile deepened, seeping into his cheeks. "You'll see."

Hand in hand they walked twenty-five minutes to reach the Frimurerlogen Concert Hall on the other side of the river. An antique, cream, box-design building, it glowed with golden light shining through the tall, arched windows. Groups of people gathered around the front, chatting, laughing and some lined up to head inside.

Rhoda's wide, jade eyes soaked up the lively scene then refocused on him. "We are seeing the symphony orchestra."

"See? I told you. You're a natural at solving puzzles."

She laughed and tugged on his hand. "Can we go in?"

A glacial gust of wind clawed his face as they joined the crowd of people filing through the entrance. The warm, cream coloring continued inside, with trimmings of glittering gold. Very classy, just like Rhoda.

Before the performance, during the interval and after the show, Abe had a champagne more as a medicinal nerve tonic than for the taste. The time had nearly come and he needed to prepare himself. He needed to get his thoughts in order.

On the walk to her home, Rhoda threaded her arm through his, raving about every detail of the performance. Close contact with her normally shifted his heart from idling to top gear but not tonight. Tonight, his erratic mind and heart ticked away like an anxiety bomb ready to explode.

Abe struggled to string a sentence together, and when he did, the words tripped on his tongue. He stared into the clear, star-filled sky for some inspiration, some focus.

Rhoda rubbed his arm. "Are you all right? You seem a bit...agitated."

"Maybe I shouldn't have had that last coffee." Abe chuckled nervously and tried to change the subject. "Why is there bad blood between the two clans?"

Her forehead creased. "Where did that come from?"

Nerves. Anything to distract him from the looming, life-changing task. "You mentioned there are differences between the clans and they don't get on, but you never told me why. And I'm interested. Anything to do with you interests me."

She smiled and snuggled into him. "It is hard to know the exact reason. My family says the story has apparently been handed down by word of mouth since the civil war began in the Middle Ages. Though it is difficult to know how much of it is truth and how much is fiction. It is a bit like a story from the Old Testament—a verbal account without evidence to confirm what is real."

"What does the story say?" He struggled to get the words out, his mouth as dry as the Sahara Desert.

"Depends whether you ask a Violet or a Jade. But being the integral person I am, I promise to give you the least-biased answer," she said with a sassy smile.

"Basically, a Violet boy met a Jade girl and they fell in love. Jade and Violet relationships were not and never have been allowed, so they ran away and married. Not long after, they were captured by Jades. They released the Jade girl but imprisoned the Violet boy and sentenced him to death for kidnapping and rape."

They crossed the bridge, the arctic night air stinging his hard-working lungs. "So, they were star-crossed, forbidden lovers. Like *Romeo and Juliet.*"

"Yes, though the ending of their story is open to interpretation. Some say they were killed in a fire that broke out in the Jade jail cell, and others say they made it out together and went somewhere far away where no one could ever find and separate them again."

They approached the main street. Clamminess coated Abe's hands. *Not long now.* "Once they disappeared, why did the war continue?"

"Fear, greed, politics. Up until both communities got involved, they had lived a blissfully ignorant life. However, once they intersected, it created competition. They argued over land, food, women, men—anything and everything.

"As the years passed, the violence reduced because Violets and Jades went back to living in their own segregated communities again. Most have moved on, but some will not let go, out of principle."

They entered the bottom of her street, and his pulse pounded like a snare-drum solo. "What about religion? Often it plays a part, too."

"Not here. Neither clan is religious in the traditional sense. Most vampires do not even believe in God, given most will never die. Retaining culture and lifestyle is their religion." She stopped in front of the Eros and

Psyche statue, the gushing of the free-flowing water, echoing the anxiety percolating in Abe's stomach.

"Would you like to come in for a drink or some late supper?" Her eyes held encouragement for a *yes* — or was it the reflection of himself, staring back at him?

He swallowed the block of fear barricading his throat. "Um…there's something I need to speak to you about first."

She took a step toward the door, her gaze unwavering. "We can talk inside."

"No. I need to do it here, where we're alone." Abe released her hand and smoothed out his wrinkle-free jacket. "Um…" He hesitated, and inhaled a lungful of crisp, fresh air.

A crinkle of confusion divided her forehead.

"We've been courting for five months now, and I feel it's time to move on to the next step."

"The next step," she repeated.

"Yes." With a quivering hand, he pulled out a gold ring with a brilliant cut, solitaire diamond from the pocket on the inside of his jacket.

"I really should've done this in code. So much easier," he mumbled, and cleared his throat. "Rhoda, I love you. It's as simple as that. I love you and I want to spend the rest of my life with you. Will you agree to be my wife?"

A film of moisture brought out the jade in her brilliant green eyes. She threw her arms around his neck and hugged him so tight he almost couldn't breathe.

A shooting star sparkled on its path across the clear night sky, and he smiled. "I'll take that as a 'yes'."

The clock clicked over to four a.m. by the time Abe crept into his pitch-black dorm. He tiptoed past his roommate's bedroom and continued on to his, closing the door behind him and leaning against it.

Rhoda had said 'yes'. His body felt like an outgrown receptacle, straining at the seams with joy. And to think, not long ago, he had considered never seeing her again. That would have been an enormous mistake.

They had their differences, though a lot in common too—their love of Norway, music, fine arts, academia, culture, nature, kissing... *Kissing. Mmm...* Neither of them could get enough.

Dreams of marriage, having a family, traveling and excelling at his cryptography work were things he still wanted to do but with her by his side. The sexual chemistry between them sizzled hot too. He couldn't wait for them to be married so he could enjoy the full naked benefits.

They'd agreed on an end-of-June wedding date, only five weeks away, with lots of organizing to do. He'd start tackling those tasks tomorrow. Too wired to sleep, he had to expel some creative energy, and what better way than through poetic code.

Abe got changed into a T-shirt and pajama pants and slipped into bed. He grabbed the small notepad and pen he kept on his bedside table, and began to compose.

Rhoda
A jade gem
Jewel of my eye
Key to my heart
Arousing my mind
Stirring my soul.

This time he used a different cipher. He'd done numbers to death throughout their courtship, and he now needed a code to reflect that they'd taken the next step in their relationship.

Abe scrutinized his poem for a few moments then it came to him. He could capture the theme by taking the next step with each letter so that a equaled b, b was c, c equaled d and so on.

Sipeb
B kbef hfn
Kfxfm pg nz fzf
Lfz up nz ifbsu
Bspvtjoh nz njoe
Tujssjoh nz tpvm

Once done, he slipped the coded poem into an envelope, wrote her name and address on the front and posted it the next day.

* * * *

Tap, tap, tippity-tap

"Rhoda..." he murmured and rushed to the door.

She waved his coded poem in his face, strode past him and dropped onto the living room couch. "I cannot solve it." She slammed the poem onto the coffee table and huffed.

"You need to be patient. It'll come to you."

She crossed her arms and stared at his undeciphered poem. "I doubt it."

"I have faith in you. You've gotten every other one so far."

"This is different."

"You've got that right."

"Not good enough. *Argh!*"

She looked so damn cute, even frustrated. He stifled a laugh and sat down next to her. "Just relax, think about something else and let your subconscious do the work behind the scenes."

"I cannot see how letting my mind wander will help."

He locked his eyes on hers. "Trust me, it works. I'm a code specialist, remember?'

"I cannot think of anythi—"

He covered her lips with his and traced his tongue along the inside edge of her mouth. She stiffened but soon relaxed, giving in to his persuasive lips. Abe slid his hands into her golden hair, teasing her tongue with his and she pressed her yielding body against him.

She tightened her arms around his waist, and passion thrashed through his veins, heightening the intensity of the kiss.

Without warning, she pulled way. "I have it!" Her face lit up. "Get me a pen? Please."

Now? Really? Terrible timing. His nether regions agreed. However, he sprang up as best he could with a mountainous erection and handed Rhoda a pen and paper. She scrawled out the answer so quickly he hardly had a chance to blink.

"See? I told you that you could do it." *Though not quite so fast!* "You just have to give it some time to let your brain piece it together."

Rhoda read over the deciphered poem, smiled and leaned against the backrest. Something in the lightness of her expression told him she was proud of her efforts. "Very lovely. Thank you. But promise me—no code on the wedding invitations, okay?"

* * * *

In May 1939, at age twenty-four, Abe had taken on three new-ish roles—as a husband, an ecstatic father and a qualified cryptographer. Things got better and better by the day until the announcement of the Second World War in September of that year. But he and his family were lucky. So far it hadn't impacted on them.

Abe packed a picnic basket of goodies and waited in the front foyer. The gorgeous, sunny, eighteen-degree day seemed like the perfect conditions for a first outing with his wife and baby.

Rhoda came down the stairs, cradling their rugged-up, sleepy son in her arms, and placed him in the pram. A tuft of his golden-brown hair stuck up and a dash of pink tinged his pudgy cheeks. With his head poking through the top of the swaddled blue blanket, he looked like a caterpillar in a cocoon.

They strolled to the park by the river and looked for a suitable dry spot. A jogger sped toward them, his deep jade eyes wide and erratic. He kept turning his head, scanning the grassy knolls and forest to their left, his blond hair whipping across his frightened face. Not a leisurely run, more like running for his life.

"Are you all right?" Rhoda asked, as he barreled down the path, nearly bowling them down like skittles in a strike.

He stopped just past them, hiding behind Abe, and bent forward, his palms on his thighs, catching his breath. He peered at Rhoda and said, "You need to get out of here."

She surveyed the area. "Are we in danger?"

His gaze darted between Abe, their son, then returned to Rhoda. "You and me, yes—and maybe your baby."

"From what? The Nazis?" Abe asked.

"No. Yes. But the real threat is Sub Rosa. They're collecting Jades and Violets and experimenting on them." The man's eyes yo-yoed between them and the serene-looking surroundings

Their son whimpered and Rhoda rocked the pram. "The research organization that opened up just outside the city center?"

"Yes."

"How do you know?"

"I just escaped." His impatient voice became restless, and he almost jogged on the spot, as though desperate to keep moving.

Lines of worry creased Rhoda's forehead. "But Sub Rosa is staffed by humans, yes? They do not have the strength or the speed—"

The guy fidgeted, stepping from one foot to the other, his gaze shooting past them, between them, back to them. Repeat. "Taser guns. They blast out some sort of sunlight. It's paralyzing…"

What he said sounded pretty far-fetched. However, so was the whole notion of vampires, until he'd met Rhoda. Either the man had descended into the middle of a psychotic break or his words actually held some truth, in which case, they should be worried. Very worried. Abe caught the guy's gaze and held it. "How did you get out?"

He edged away from them. "It wore off and I broke out of my cell. But I have to go. They're after me and they'll be after you, too." The man turned and bolted toward the cathedral.

Abe's gaze reconnected with Rhoda's. "Could his accusations be legitimate?"

"I am not sure." Her stare followed the fleeing man's back.

"It's either that or he escaped from the sanitarium."

They resumed walking. "He did seem genuine. Very scared."

His gut agreed, but where was the evidence? So far there'd been no sign of anyone giving chase. "I know. Though so can someone who's in the throes of a psychotic episode."

Within the month, the answer bordered on blatant. Some of Rhoda's family and vampire friends started disappearing and Sub Rosa became the main suspect. Now Rhoda and their baby were in double danger — from the Nazis *and* Sub Rosa. So, Abe made a pre-emptive strike and applied for a transfer to the University of Tasmania, Hobart, his hometown, and he and his family set sail to Australia.

They arrived in mid-November and he knew exactly where he wanted them to live — Fern Tree, located not too far out of the Hobart township and still fairly quiet. He drove Rhoda past the area, dotted with signs promoting plots for sale.

His wife stared out of the window. "This is lovely."

Abe pulled over in front of a large block of land on a hill with rolls of lush green grass and an abundance of trees and bushes. He glanced at her. "What do you think about living around here? It's not too far from town or the university but far enough away to feel like we're in the country, to have some privacy. To be safe."

"How about cost?"

"Very reasonable. We'd still need to take out a loan, of course, though we shouldn't have any problems paying it back."

"It sounds too good to be true."

A little cry pierced the car cabin. "Feeding time," she said, and moved to the backseat to start breastfeeding their baby. "Oh, definitely hungry!"

The way his son's small mouth latched onto Rhoda's beautiful breast looked like he couldn't get enough milk. He sucked and sucked like an industrial vacuum cleaner without an off switch. And yet he looked so angelic swaddled in a light, white knitted blanket.

"What do you think? Should I put an offer in for the property?"

Rhoda winced, her free hand moving to caress their son's head, a body language sign to slow down. "Yes. But I have one request—to have some input into the house design."

Either their son didn't get the message or he ignored it because he kept on feeding like preparing for an impending milk shortage, like it was a matter of survival.

"Of course. Do you have something in mind?"

Rhoda persevered with trying to soothe their insatiable son. "You will probably think this sounds silly but I would love to recreate my family home here. It would look perfect on this block. Our own version of our beloved Norway."

"Though not as cold."

Her smile cut through the bitten-back pain on her face. "Definitely not as cold."

They rented near the university while finalizing the plans for their proposed home, and after dinner one night, Rhoda put their son to bed and Abe rolled out the architectural drawings on their small kitchen table. "I wanted to show you one more addition to the design."

She came and stood beside him and he put his arm around her. With his free hand, he pointed to a spot a distance away from the back of the house. "I thought we could do with a bomb shelter."

"A bomb shelter? Tasmania is safe, though?" Her worried voice wavered.

Abe didn't want to scare her but he needed to be upfront. He didn't want to create any false expectations or for either of them to be too blasé, too complacent. In reality, nowhere could ever be a hundred percent safe. "The government wants us to believe that and maybe it is, but you never know. We're at war and we also have the Sub Rosa complication."

She stiffened. "Yes…"

He stroked her hip and her muscles relaxed beneath his hand. "I thought of building the shelter underground, about a kilometer away from the house, with a secret door leading to it from under the stairwell, as well as through the Eros and Psyche statue. It's important to be prepared. I'd rather us have it and not use it than not have it and wish we did."

They got into a routine and the months passed. One evening, Abe finished work early and found Rhoda on the couch, head in hand, charcoal smudges beneath her heavy-lidded eyes. She glanced up at him, a weary smile tugging at the corners of her lips.

He leaned down and pressed a gentle, loving kiss to her forehead then her mouth. "You look exhausted." His son slept in the bassinet bedside her. "How about I take him out and give you some respite?"

Relief whooshed from her like air from a freed balloon. "Yes, please. You are wonderful."

Abe lay their baby in the pram and stepped into the glorious sunshine, the long, golden rays streaming into the stroller. His son squinted and started crying. Abe grabbed the pram top and pulled it over his baby's head to shield him from the bright sunlight.

He settled straight away. Sensitivity to the sun was a Jade sign, one of many his son now displayed.

In the grocery store, customers fawned over his child like he had some sort of power, like the spellbinding attraction that had first drawn Abe to his wife. Their response solidified his presumption. His baby had to have the Jade gene, but at what percentage? Quarter or half-caste? It was still too early to tell.

Loaded up with bread, bloodied meat and a fresh supply of sterile white nappies, he and his son strolled home, the brittle autumn breeze sending a chill winding up Abe's spine.

When he reached the house, the front door gaped open.

"Rhoda?"

Nothing.

Unease churned in his gut and he rushed inside with the baby.

"Rhoda?" he called out, parked the pram in the front foyer and searched, searched, searched every room. No sign of her. His heart and mind were speed racing, jumping to a blitz of crazy conclusions.

Gone. She was gone. He shot back to their bedroom. Her clothes and jewelry were still there…except the black and gold cross ring and pendant. The ones she always wore. Her black leather handbag still sat in its usual spot, slumped on the vanity. A bad sign. Very bad.

Not a robbery.

Taken. She had to have been taken.

Sub Rosa.

"No, no, no!" He slammed his fist against the wall, sending jagged cracks across the plaster.

Their baby started crying.

Abe hurried to his son, picked him up and tried to soothe him, to soothe both of them.

He had to find her. Save her. He could be a victim or a hero but being a victim wouldn't get Rhoda back.

Chapter Eleven

All in the Family

Tasmania, June 1965

After Richard and Eva's incredible reconciliation session, he called her most days after work, and the days he didn't call, he left 'I miss you' notes in her pigeon hole. Then, two Fridays in a row, he came over to her place for dinner and stayed the night, and they spent all of Saturday together, mostly in the car, exploring different parts of Tasmania — and each other.

On the way back from their wonderful Saturday trip to Freycinet National Park, Richard said, "How about dinner at my place tonight? I want you to meet my uncle. He's really keen to meet you, too."

Meet his uncle. So early on. Did that mean he considered their relationship serious? Her heart fluttered as if it held a swarm of butterflies about to break free. No way would she introduce a guy to her family unless he was something special.

In less than two and a half hours, they arrived at a large wrought-iron gate in the outer suburbs of Hobart.

Richard reached out his window, pressed a small black button and two, large, wrought-iron gates swung open.

Lush Australian native trees wove in with English cottage-garden-style plants in a beautiful blending of cultures, and lined the driveway leading up to a grand, sandstone house, perched on top of the hill.

Her mouth dropped open. "This is *your* place?"

"Well, it's my uncle's but yeah, it's my home."

"Wow. Just wow."

He chuckled.

At the top of the driveway, a marble Eros and Psyche fountain bubbled away in the last of the dusk light. *Eros–Richard.* The connection had come up twice now, as though it was a sign pointing her heart in the right direction.

Richard rolled the car to a stop between the fountain and a green and white Holden parked in front of a large bay window and came around and opened her door.

He took her hand and they walked up a few steps, lit by a couple of black wrought-iron lanterns, and stopped on the patio outside a wooden door with black curved hinges and ringed door knocker. Richard pulled an ornate, old-fashioned key from his jacket pocket, slotted it into the lock and swung the door open.

"Welcome," he said, and guided her inside, her hand still in his.

The hallway glowed with soft, amber light, and opened up to a lofty stairway on the left. He continued along the corridor, and a fluffy, charcoal-gray cat appeared at the foot of the steps.

Richard shook his head. "I can't believe it! Normally Smokey hides when we have visitors."

Eva released Richard's hand and approached the stairs. "Oh, he's gorgeous." She bent down to pat the cat and he circled around her legs, purring like a little motor.

Richard crouched beside her and Smokey shunted between them for pats then trotted past them down the passageway. They both stood, and Richard embraced Eva, his hard body flush against hers. She gasped, and he dove in, planting a long, passionate kiss on her lips.

"A-hem."

They startled and split apart like sprung, sex-crazed teenagers. Eva's gaze connected with a handsome man in his forties, with ash-brown hair and kind gray eyes. He and Richard had such a strong family resemblance—the same broad shoulders, the same square jaw, the same roguish smile—that Bram could almost be his father.

"Uncle Bram, um…this is Eva."

Great first impression…if she were a courtesan. "Hi, Mr. Hall," she said, her cheeks throbbing with the heat of embarrassment.

He stepped forward and shook her hand. "Bram, please. It's a pleasure to finally meet you, Eva. Richard hasn't stopped speaking about you."

A flush of redness crept up Richard's face. "Let's show Eva into the lounge room, shall we?"

"Follow me," Bram said with a knowing smile and led them into a large, Regency-style lounge-dining room with a roaring fireplace. It looked exactly how she imagined Mr. Darcy's Pemberley.

"Please make yourself at home," Bram and Richard said in stereo.

Eva took off her black coat, hung it over the back of the black double-ended chaise lounge and sat in front of the fire.

Bram handed each of them a red wine. "To the lovely couple."

"Cheers," Richard said and they chinked glasses and had a sip.

"So, Eva, Richard tells me you're the secretary to one of Sub Rosa's senior managers."

A fleeting glint of hardness flashed in his graphite-colored eyes, as though just saying the name Sub Rosa brought back unpleasant memories. Richard hadn't mentioned his uncle had any connection with them, though. "Yes, the Personnel Senior Manager."

"How do you find him?"

"Okay. He keeps me pretty busy, but I can't complain. My work finishes when I leave the office." She tilted her head toward Richard. "Unlike some people."

Bram laughed. "I keep telling him if he doesn't ease up, they'll put his picture next to 'Workaholic' in the dictionary."

Ah…maybe Bram doesn't like how Sub Rosa takes advantage of his nephew.

Richard's gaze shot across to his uncle. "Look who's talking. I think your workaholic ways have rubbed off on me."

Oh. So, the over-committed apple didn't fall far from the Hall family tree. And Bram probably didn't want Richard to take the same path. Workaholism seemed to be a genetic trait in their family. From what she'd seen so far, once Richard set his mind on something he became almost tunnel-visioned.

"I hope not. It's a way of existing for people who don't have a life or are trying to distract themselves from something. And you don't fit either of those two categories."

That definitely sounded like experience talking. "What do you do, Bram?

"Outside of role-modeling poor work-life balance?" He grinned. "I'm an academic, a professor in the Science, Engineering and Technology Faculty at the University of Tasmania."

She crossed her leg toward him. "How do you find working at the university?"

"Interesting, challenging, even fascinating at times. And that's just the students."

Eva laughed. This guy was a real character, really likeable. His students must love him.

Bram glanced at the mantle clock. "I'd better go and check on dinner. I wouldn't want to overcook it. I hear you like your meat done the same way as my nephew."

Looked like they needn't worry about him being the third wheel. She smiled. "I certainly do."

He winked at Richard. "I'll be back in a few minutes." Then he disappeared into what must be the kitchen.

"Have you two got some sign language letting each other know when to go?" Eva asked.

Richard chuckled. "Not exactly. He's very good at reading people, picking up on the vibe." His glowing green eyes flicked between her eyes and lips and he leaned in for a kiss. "You're going to stay tonight, aren't you?"

Stay? With Bram just meters away. "I can't."

"Yes, you can. He knows we've been sleeping together."

What? "Did you tell him?"

"No. But he can put two and two together."

Just because his uncle accepted the idea didn't mean they should flaunt it. "I should go home. I've got nothing to sleep in."

"How about your underwear...assuming you're wearing some," he said with a wicked grin.

She smiled and shook her head.

"Seriously, don't worry about my uncle. He's great. He won't judge."

Bram called them to the table to eat dinner, and after a plate of yummy rare roast lamb with baked vegetables and brandy-snap baskets with mixed berries and cream for dessert, they returned to the fireplace to drink their coffee.

"What about the dishes?" Eva asked. "I'm happy to help."

Bram waved away her offer. "No, no, just relax. My housekeeper will sort them out."

So, a real housekeeper did exist. She didn't doubt Richard, but it reassured her getting confirmation from someone else.

"Richard tells me you had a similar upbringing." Bram held his coffee cup suspended above his lap, his gray gaze studying her response through the curling ribbons of steam.

"Yes. I don't remember my parents and I grew up in boarding school." Richard massaged her hand, his strokes, soft, soothing, reassuring. "Though, I did get a letter from my dad once, when I was little. He apologized for not being able to care for me. I've tried to find him but...it's no use. No one has found anything, not even a trace of him. Nothing. I just wish I knew why he had to give me up and what happened to my mum."

"I'm sure your parents struggled to let you go. They'd have wanted you to be safe. They'd have wanted the best for you, which sometimes means making big sacrifices." Bram's eyes filled with a mix of hurt, sadness and remorse, like he could relate. Maybe he'd turned to workaholism to try to cope with a terrible event in his past. Richard had mentioned some sort of romantic disaster.

"You're right. Of course, you're right." Eva stared into the delicate black and gold coffee cup, like it could tell her fortune. "I hope this won't keep me up all night."

"I hope it does," Richard murmured. "Biscuit?" he asked, all innocent, and offered her the plate.

She glared at him and took a Tim Tam. They were impossible to resist—a bit like Richard, really.

"What have you two got planned for tomorrow?" Bram shot his steaming espresso like liquor, as if his tongue was coated in Teflon.

"I'll drop Eva home. Then, unfortunately, I've got work to do," Richard replied.

An I'm-not-impressed facial expression sent Bram's smile into flatline. "Sub Rosa is really piling it on."

"They sure are," Eva said, happy to have Bram on her side. Maybe between them, they could make Richard see some sense.

"I suppose they're making the most of their employee investment. But in the end, it's just work." He stared at Richard, a steely edge to his eyes. "Make sure you factor in plenty of time for each other." Then he glanced at Eva. "Try not to put too many things off. Things don't always turn out the way you expect."

She shivered. *A warning.* He'd given her a warning, one that resonated with her whole body and soul.

"But I want to set up a stable financial base"—Richard squeezed Eva's hand—"for the future."

Her heart swelled like a frozen bottle of fizzy drink. *He sees me in his life long term.*

Bram patted Richard's upper arm. "Just try to get some balance. That's all I ask. It's easy to get sucked into the hamster-wheel-of-wages and building-for-the-future thinking, though once you're in there, it's hard to get out. You can always have more, be better off, but at what expense? You need to think about what's most important to you."

Silence hung in the air, allowing Richard time to digest Bram's words.

"I'm just going to the bathroom," Eva said, jolting him out of his thoughts and leaving him alone with his uncle.

Bram scrutinized him, like Richard was a foreign language text he aimed to decipher. He went to speak and stopped. Went to speak and stopped. He rubbed his chin as though it were a magic bottle able to summon the stuck words. "You two are being careful, aren't you?"

Richard gulped. Somehow, he didn't think he meant wearing seatbelts in the car. "Careful?"

"Using contraception."

Who'd have thought he'd have his first birds and bees conversation at twenty-five with his uncle…while on a date? "No…" *Slightly awkward.*

"No? You really should. You're both young. You don't want to get in trouble."

"Thanks. I appreciate your concern, though there's nothing to worry about."

He stared at Richard like his nephew was a captured fly and Bram held a magnifying glass to him in the hot summer sun. "Isn't there? You've been spending *a lot* of time together."

"Let's just say we're enjoying each other, but we've got an agreement."

"What sort of agreement?"

Every muscle in Richard's body went rigid at the prospect of explaining. If he'd known his uncle longer or if it had been his dad, it might be different, easier. However, they were relative strangers. Then again, that could be a bonus.

His brain stumbled over words, trying to come up with the best combination under pressure, but he couldn't think of the perfect phrasing. Plain and honest and straight to the point would have to do. "A no-penetrative-sex agreement, for the moment."

A relieved breath gushed out of Bram's lips. "Okay, good. Well, not good...smart. It's better to be sensible about these things. You both need to be ready."

"You sound like you're talking from experience." His chance had arrived to find out more about his uncle's locked-away personal life.

Soft footsteps echoed on the hallway floor, and he followed his uncle's gaze to the door.

"Ah...Eva, you found your way back," Bram said, and met her halfway across the room. "And just in time for me to say goodnight."

Damn. Would he ever find out the deal with his uncle? Bram continued to remain cagey, guarded, closed off about his past. Something terrible must have happened. And it seemed like he'd try his best to prevent Richard and Eva from the same fate.

Eva entwined her fingers with Richard's outstretched hand and he welcomed her back to the couch with a kiss.

He raked shaky fingers through his hair and swallowed hard. "There's something I've been meaning to ask you."

Special dinner, meeting his uncle, planning for their future. Could he be preparing to propose? A rush of euphoria saturated every cell in her body.

"Um, Eva, as you know, I have really strong feelings for you. I realize we haven't been going out long but…"

She stared at him, heart hammering, pulse pounding. He really was going to ask her to marry him.

He edged closer and held both her hands. "There's a researcher called Salvator who I met at work and he's after volunteers to trial his Soulmate Serum."

What? Excitement expired from her like a leaking balloon, deflating fast. "A Soulmate Serum?"

"Yeah. Apparently, it identifies a person's soulmate through touch."

"And what? You want us to volunteer?"

"Yeah, what do you think?"

"What do I think?" She snatched her hands out of his. "Are you kidding? You want us to be guinea pigs? What if it doesn't work? What if it has side effects?"

He attempted to clasp her hand. "Eva…"

She retracted it, like he'd poked her with a branding iron. "You're willing to not only risk our relationship but also our lives just to see if some potion identifies us as soulmates?"

"You're angry." His tone sounded calm, yet surprised.

No joke! "No, I'm not angry. I'm furious, disappointed, confused," she said, squeezing out her reply through tight lips.

"Eva, listen to me."

She shook her head and turned away. *Can he really be serious? I thought he cared about me, about us…*

"Please."

She didn't respond.

"It was just an idea. I thought, if it worked out…"

Eva gnashed her teeth together. "And if it didn't?"

"We wouldn't waste any more time and could move on."

She spun around and glared at him. "You're calling these past six weeks wasted time?"

"No, of course not. They've been great, better than great. But don't you want to be sure you're with the right person? It'd save a lot of time in the long run."

Although she didn't want to admit it, what he said made sense on a practical level, not so much on the emotional. How could he be so…so…so sensible about feelings? She shook her head. Always boiling things down to their base. Always searching for the factual truth. Always the scientist.

And she loved him for it. Richard, forever the rational Yang to her emotional Yin. Together they were balance.

Richard got off the couch and crouched in front of her. "How about we both meet with him and get a bit more information. Then, if we agree it sounds reasonable and safe, we can decide to go ahead…or not."

In some ways, the concept of the serum sounded romantic. It surprised her a male researcher showed enough interest to investigate the idea.

Part of her liked the prospect of knowing for sure whether Richard was the one, but the rest of her had become so invested in him that she didn't want to lose the best man she'd ever known. And the Soulmate Serum made it a real risk that she might.

Whether he was her soulmate or not didn't mean she and Richard couldn't have a fantastic life together. Then again, her life might be even more amazing if she found her kindred spirit.

"Please don't be angry with me." His pleading tone almost made her look up. "I just want what's best for us, both of us, even if it means we're better off as friends instead of lovers."

Her emotions were so scattered she didn't know what to think, let alone say. Tears rose in her eyes and rolled onto her cheeks.

Richard reached up and wiped them away with his thumb. "Oh, Eva, please don't cry. I didn't want to upset you. I didn't want tonight to work out like this. I thought the serum would interest you. Forget I ever brought it up."

Her gaze reconnected with his. "Richard..." She sniffled. She had to be honest with him. They'd promised that to each other after their previous miscommunication. "The truth is, I like the idea of it, but I'm scared — scared of side effects, scared of losing what we have, scared of losing you. You're right, though. Living in fear isn't the answer. Sometimes you do have to take risks to find something better."

His eyes filled with hope and relief. "Does that mean...?"

"I'm willing to speak with Salvator and find out more. Then we'll take it from there. I'm not promising anything," she said in her best no-nonsense tone.

Richard clutched her face and kissed her. "Thank you."

* * * *

Eva woke up wrapped in Richard's arms and encased in a gold and black doona, surprised she didn't have to send out a search and rescue party to find him in his massive four-poster bed.

After a good-morning kiss, cuddle and cavort, they dressed, and Richard led her out of his penthouse-sized bedroom, with en suite and study-come-private library, and directed her into the conservatory for breakfast.

A white linen tablecloth and three place settings covered the round timber table. Bram knew she'd stayed...in Richard's room. A rush of heat swarmed beneath her skin.

After their disagreement, Richard had spent several hours making it up to her, treating her to orgasm, after orgasm, after orgasm. Hopefully his uncle hadn't heard her moans of pleasure.

Bram entered through the kitchen doorway with a white apron over his clothes. "I hope you don't mind, but I've taken the liberty of cooking breakfast. I thought you both might be hungry."

"Thank you," Eva said, embarrassment threatening to turn her cheeks neon red. *No. Not this time.* She would try another tack to see if she could fend off the looming awkwardness and play along with his uncle's innuendo. "I'm ravenous. I don't know about Richard."

"Yeah, I've definitely worked up an appetite." Richard grinned, joining in on the little game.

"Then I've got just what you need to re-energize." Bram re-entered the kitchen and a few clangs later returned, juggling three dinner plates stacked with bacon, eggs, toast, avocado, mushrooms, tomato and homemade hash browns and set them down in front of them. He'd gone all out.

A positive sign, a sign that he approved of her. She and Richard. Together.

"How long have you been in this house, Bram? And how did you find Richard?" Eva asked.

He finished his mouthful of bacon and loaded up his fork with tomato and avocado. "Richard's parents moved here from Norway when Richard was a baby and they bought the block. They were hoping to create a sense of Scandinavia but in kinder conditions.

"Then just before they were to start building, Richard's mum went missing. All her belongings were left behind. She disappeared with no trace, not even a note." Bram looked into Richard's eyes. "She never would've chosen to take off and leave you. You meant everything to her."

Richard set down his cutlery. "Did my father suspect foul play?"

"Yes. He reported it to the police but they hit a dead end. He was so distraught that he couldn't be a father to you—not a decent one—and he worried about whoever took your mum coming back. So, he made the hardest decision of his life and put you into care, so you'd be safe. Then he traveled the globe, staying out of sight, searching for her."

Eva propped her elbows on the table and leaned forward. "What happened?"

Bram stabbed an egg and the yolk bled out onto his plate, soaking the remaining slice of toast. "While working at the university, my brother contacted me and asked if I'd oversee the building of their home. He hoped he'd have found his wife and they could return to the finished house, collect Richard and live as a family again.

"Once completed, I moved into their home and waited for further word but I didn't receive any." His flint-colored eyes sparked and he stared at Richard. "When both of them had disappeared, I worried about your safety, so I kept an eye on you from a distance. I planned to make contact when things seemed more settled, less of a threat. And here we are."

Richard's knife and fork sat on the edge of his plate, his meal growing cold...like the trail of his parents. "Could I still be in danger?"

"I don't think so. Your parents' disappearance happened a long time ago now, so I'd say if you were a target, the person or people behind the kidnappings would've already sought you out."

Richard rammed his hand through his bed-tousled hair. "Why have you never told me this before?"

Bram mopped his mouth with a napkin and dropped it onto his sticky, yellow-stained plate. "I tried to, but I couldn't. The time just never seemed right. Though now that you appear to be carving a life out for yourself with Eva, I thought you both had a right to know."

"Yes..." Richard seemed to focus internally. No doubt bombarded with thoughts about what had happened to his parents. If they had been kidnapped, Bram would have received a ransom request. Common sense said they were dead. However, their bodies had never been found, meaning they could still be alive somewhere.

They hadn't tried to make contact, but it could be because they were still being held captive, or had somehow lost their memories or been brainwashed, like she'd heard about in POW camps during the war.

Maybe her parents had met a similar fate.

Sadness tore at the seams of Eva's heart. "This whole thing must have been so hard for you."

Bram stared at his messed-up plate. "It's been incredibly difficult, especially living in their house, living what should have been their life."

"Did you ever find someone special?" she asked.

A melancholy smile pressed at the corners of his mouth. "Once. Things didn't work out and I've never gotten over her."

Richard touched his uncle's arm. "The right woman for you is out there. Don't give up. You're such a good man, and you deserve to be happy. I'm so lucky to have you."

And he was. Extremely lucky. A pang of envy poked at Eva's heart. She'd be ecstatic if she found a relative even half as great as Bram. She'd be rapt just to find a living family member.

Bram smiled and patted Richard on the back. "And I you. Your parents would be so proud of you, you know." He stood and started clearing their plates. When he got to Eva, he stopped and said, "I'm sure you weren't anticipating such an intense initiation into the family. I hope I haven't scared you away. It definitely wasn't my intention."

Quite the contrary. The similarities between their lives drew her to Richard even more, like a thread of destiny sewing them together. "Not at all. Every family has skeletons stashed in the closet." And, in their case, the cupboards and drawers as well.

Chapter Twelve

Mum is the Word

Tasmania, 1940

Only minutes after Abe and her son had gone for a stroll to the local shops, Rhoda had come out of the bathroom and *zap*. She dropped to the floor, convulsing, paralyzed, her insides frizzled. Two human Sub Rosa men holstered strange guns and reached down to cuff her.

They dragged her into a waiting car and carted her off, mute, immobile, leaving her no time to scream let alone leave a note. Tears of agony squeezed from her eyes. *Will I ever see Abe or my son again?*

Each time the tingle of sensation returned, they blasted her with more potent shots, keeping her still and quiet until they got her back to Norway, courtesy of what appeared to be the company jet. The men made it a memorable first time on a plane for her, but not in a good way.

They threw her in a dungeon-like cell in a derelict compound, her still chained up. The facility now spanned over a huge section of land including her family's property and that of surrounding families. Trondheim would never feel the same. It had gone from a place of fun, opportunities and freedom to one of terror and torture.

"What is in the guns?" she asked, breathless, shivering — not from the cold but from the unknown.

The burly guard smirked. "Sunlight."

So that runaway Jade had told the truth. "How does a gun manufacture sunlight?"

"I don't know. Ask one of the scientists. All I know is the thing works." He walked out of her cell and locked it behind him.

Helpful.

The shorter, stockier gunman returned a couple of hours later with a cup of overcooked stew, placed it down about three feet in front of her and quickly stepped back toward the cell door. Given her worn-out state, she really needed blood, but some food was better than nothing.

"Before you go, can I ask you a question?" She did not wait for his reply. "How do the guns work?"

"I don't know if I'm supposed to tell you." His voice shook with nerves.

"If you tell me, you have nothing to lose. You are still the one holding the gun."

He thought for a moment, looked around and whispered, "There's a pool of guns. The ones used today, we hand in to the research department and they give us a fresh gun to use the next day, while the other charges."

Drips splashed around her at irregular intervals, adding to the dank, musty smell. "How does it charge?"

"With sunlight. It captures it somehow. I don't know the specifics."

She shifted forward on her bottom and reached for the cup with both hands. "Can you remove the handcuffs while I eat?"

"Nope."

He waited as she held the cup in her restrained hands, brought it to her mouth and wolfed down the tasteless, watery stew. Then he took her cup and left.

The damp ground numbed her bottom and a cold ache seeped through her skin and settled in her bones. She tugged at her handcuffs, and they gave a little. *Maybe I can split them?* She had never tried breaking metal, though her Jade genetics made it within the realm of possibility. Rhoda tugged and tugged, the links weakening.

Without the shots from the stun guns, combined with the energy boost from the meal, she cracked them open in less than ten minutes. If a half-caste like her could do that, it would be impossible to contain full vampires, unless staff starved them of blood and tasered them every thirty minutes.

Can I escape? It was one thing breaking metal cuffs but quite another to muster enough energy to bust out of her cell. She had to try, though.

Rhoda pulled on the metal bars and bent them enough to squeeze through. Warping them was much easier than she had thought. She ran into town and hid down an alley. Without quick access to money, where could she go? To really escape, she had to focus, think things through, make a solid plan. She had to find a way to get back to Abe and her son before Sub Rosa caught up with her.

"Out of my spot!"

Rhoda peeked from behind the alley wall.

A Jade crossed her arms. "It's not yours. It doesn't have your name on it."

A Violet stepped closer, standing over the unmoving Jade. "I said get out."

The Jade did not budge. She just sat, cross-legged, like a retaliating yogi.

The Violet yanked on the Jade's long, blonde hair. The obstinate Jade gritted her teeth and tried to hold her grip on the wet, stone ground. The Violet dragged her a few meters, threw her against the high brick wall and took her secret hiding spot amid rubbish bags and bins.

The evicted Jade jumped up, her hands wound into tight fists, her face twisted with anger, and strode back to the offending Violet. She tapped the Violet's shoulder. When she turned, the Jade threw a punch, striking her right in the stomach.

The Violet dropped to the ground, winded, and the Jade continued her assault, kicking and stomping on the Violet until she rolled into a round, blubbering ball.

"Fuck you, you fucking Violet!" the Jade muttered and repossessed her perfect hiding place.

Rhoda glanced from her to where the Jade had left the Violet, but she had gone, like she had dived under an invisibility cloak. Maybe the Violet was one of the select group of vampires she had heard about who had special powers.

Sudden scuffling echoed down the alleyway and a squad of Sub Rosa guards appeared. And with them, the jaded Violet.

"She's over there," the Violet said, grinning, and pointed to the no-longer-secret spot.

The guards marched forward and Rhoda pulled her head back from the corner, her heart hammering. If they continued down the alley, they would find her, trapped in a dead-end dog leg.

"Let go of m—!"

Z-Zap!

Rhoda flinched, the sound setting off a trauma switch in her head.

"What the fuck are you doing?" The Violet's voice. "But I led you to h—"

Z-Z-Z-Zap!

Rhoda's already-tattered nerves frayed further.

They obviously did not care. Sub Rosa wanted to get as many vampires as they could and, by the looks of it, there were no exceptions.

The footsteps trailed away, departing the way they had come. Rhoda slid down the cold brick wall and dropped to the icy ground, her body awash with relief. Though she would have to come out to find food…and soon, leaving her vulnerable to re-capture.

By day twelve her stomach had gone beyond growling to gnawing. She needed sustenance but not just any fuel, something bloody. Rhoda dragged her feet and her shoulders hunched forward. Her internal warning light flashed, indicating her battery had hit a disturbing low.

Sniff sniff. Blood? She drifted toward the scent with renewed energy, desperate not to lose the trail. The strong lure made her forget about everything else.

She hardly noticed the Violets skulking across the street, the family of Jades darting in and out of the shadows ahead of them or the horde of humans, pointing and whispering at her disheveled dress as they passed. She hardly noticed the birds singing or the frosty wind taunting the leaves. She hardly noticed anything.

Except a dead rat, down a secluded street—away from the main township, lying in the gutter in front of a bunch of bins. Rhoda reached the dying rodent, bent down and inhaled the blood dribbling out of its wounded neck.

She ran her tongue along the lesion, her mouth filling with saliva. Never before had she killed to satiate her cravings, her needs. Instead, she had bought freshly slaughtered animals from the local butcher and drained the blood off to drink.

Survival.

It had a way of pushing her past her limits. With bared teeth, she went for the weak pulsing artery in the animal's neck and got flung backward, whacking her head against the road. Passing out was not possible with her body jolting, buzzing, shuddering.

Shock, confusion and paralysis replaced pain, until two Sub Rosa guards stood over her, smirking like a couple of wily mice that had caught the careless cat.

For over forty years Rhoda continued to frequently break out of Sub Rosa, but each time her captors caught her only a short time later. Much to her frustration, her freedom never lasted long enough to make it out of Norway.

The revolving-door escapes had taken their toll on her but she refused to give up, not while a chance remained to be reunited with her husband and son. She lost count of how many times she had broken out.

Then Sub Rosa threw in a little sweetener. They revamped the cells to make them more comfortable, more homely. But in 1986, they followed the refurbishment with a pill so bitter it burned, like swallowing poison. *Every. Waking. Second.*

The sunlight barricade system.

It stopped all the captives.

The options were simple. Stay in your cell or die.

The night of the system installation, a flare went up —
or so it seemed, until a loud thud dropped a flaming,
twitching Jade in front of Rhoda's cell. When the fire
went out, a black person-shaped sculpture collapsed on
itself, the embers flaking into dust particles that puffed
into the air.

The resulting dark shape formed a Jade-black hole, a
literal outline of where a murder had taken place.
Though, of course, Sub Rosa management deemed it a
suicide. They claimed the Jade ran at the bars, knowing
the consequences. They could skew anything. Fear
propaganda had a way of keeping the rest of the
prisoners in place.

Once secured in her updated, sunlight-protected
accommodation, Rhoda received a sack of mail...from
Abe. Sub Rosa had obviously intercepted his letters,
thinking she would lose hope and stop trying to break
out. Why they had held on to them and given them to
her now, she did not understand.

Maybe to increase her anger, her grief? Reinforce all
she had missed? Snuff out any last remnants of hope?
Sub Rosa always had their strategic reasons. Ultimately,
with the sunlight locking her in, whether she had hope
or not did not matter. She could no longer flee.

With great care, she tipped out the fragile contents
and stared at the white envelopes and yellow packages
covering the floor. Her jumbled emotions could not
decide whether to grieve or rejoice. She sat among the
sea of correspondence and began picking through it,
creating date-ordered piles.

With her super vampire speed, she had the task done
in a couple of hours then started reading through his

carefully coded messages. Finally hearing from her husband felt good, yet she missed him so much it ached, deep in her chest, as though part of her heart had been torn from her body and had never healed.

But having his words gave her a sense of home, curled up in a comforting blanket. It helped her deal with the constant prods and pokes and fluid sample extractions taken by the research staff.

Exhausted from her draining day, she selected the next unread Abe letter and sank into bed.

Po uijt svcz dfmfcsbujpo
J bn dpmtvnfe xjui Kbef.
Bmuipvhi bqbsu,
J uijol pg zpv fwfsz ebz.
Uiptf gjstu gfx zfbst
lfqu uif gjsf cvsojoh
Lfqu nz ifbsu bgmbnf
Gps zpv boe
Pomz zpv
Gpsfwfs.

Using a step forward code, she transcribed it as —

On this ruby celebration
I am consumed with Jade.
Although apart,
I think of you every day.
Those first few years
kept the fire burning
Kept my heart aflame
For you and
Only you
Forever.

A love poem written to commemorate their fortieth wedding anniversary. Tears prickled her eyes. He still had faith, too, even though he would be in his early seventies now. Her heart swelled, ripe with love and longing. She ran her hand over his words as though the simple act could conjure him up.

Rhoda pulled open her bedside drawer and filed the note in her 'favorites' pile for easy re-reading. Then she got out of bed, and grabbed the next note and the next and the next. Her voracious appetite for his updates, for a connection to him — any connection — kept her up late, reading, imagining, remembering.

She had to stop. She had to stop and get some sleep. But the next envelope on top of the stack came with a package and she could not rest without knowing its contents.

On her return to bed, she crept across the vinyl floor, trying to keep the noise down, but when she jiggled open the flap on the back of the yellow parcel, the paper crackled, breaking the two-a.m. quiet. She froze, waited, but no-one complained and no staff came. A relieved sigh escaped her lips.

Propped up by pillows with her legs tucked under the warm quilt, she tipped the package contents onto her lap. No note fell out this time, just a picture frame with three photos — a portrait of her and Abe on their wedding day, a candid shot of their adult son and his wife coming out of a small bluestone church on the day of their marriage in 1965 and a picture of Abe and their son, leaning against a Psyche and Eros fountain, with the inscription, *Deep inside the chambers of my cavernous heart lay secrets, truth and eternal love* running between them.

Her gaze moved from picture to picture to picture but kept straying to her son — her handsome, married son. She stroked his face. *My beautiful boy.* His wedding photo had been taken over twenty years before, so she assumed he had stayed married. He probably had children. She still had several letters to read through. Maybe Abe would mention them.

Odd he had not given her an update on her son and his wife since the mid-1960s. Had they lost touch? She sat forward, her heart squeezing in her chest. Had something happened to him? As long as her son remained safe and happy. She kissed his image and flipped the frame over, searching for an inscription from Abe.

A sequence of strange letters ran underneath a red rose motif. She scrutinized the squiggles for a long time, turning the frame and viewing it from different angles, but the answer eluded her.

When she and Abe were courting, she had always been able to solve his codes. This one had her stumped. She needed his distracting kiss to give her subconscious a springboard.

The writing almost looked hieroglyphic, like she needed a specific key, a sort of Rosetta Stone to unlock its meaning. Maybe she just needed to be patient and let her subconscious do the work, like he had always encouraged. She had the time. She would not be going anywhere in a hurry.

Several more years passed and she still had no luck deciphering the message. Abe's letters continued but none made any reference to the obscure inscription, their son or grandchildren. He provided her with no more clues, no more hints.

In 2007, Abe's letters stopped.

Chapter Thirteen

The Soulmate Trial

Hobart, July 1965

Eva paced her kitchen floor – up down, up down, up down. If she kept it up much longer, she'd wear right through the black and white linoleum tiles. It had only been a few days since Prime Minister Menzies had declared that Australia was in a state of war in Vietnam. She fisted her hands so hard that her nails dug into her flesh and drew blood.

The next national conscription lottery loomed, along with the Soulmate Serum trial date, both threatening to take Richard away from her. Things were already uncertain enough yet he had her agree to experimentation on their relationship. How had he swayed her to go ahead with something so risky?

A magical knack, that's what he had – a special, almost supernatural ability to push her out of her comfort zone. And so far, the risks had been worth it. Would it be worth it this time? If it backfired, then what?

Eva had spoken to Salvator, the Soulmate Serum inventor, on the phone, earlier in the week, to tell him she intended to volunteer, and she'd used the opportunity to ask him some questions. But his answers still hadn't allayed her concerns.

She strode down the hallway and lifted the phone receiver. She needed another opinion, someone to either back up or shut down her second thoughts. Eva started to dial Greer's number and stopped. On the notepad by the phone, Richard had written a message in his distinct, backward-slanted handwriting.

No matter what, I will always love you.

Her heart melted into a puddle of how-can-I-say-no-to-him-now. Ever. Even at a distance, he wove his trialing-the-Soulmate-Serum-is-the-right-thing-to-do spell on her. She ripped the note off the pad and pressed it to her chest. Then she pulled it away and read his words again and again and again. But could he really still love her if they weren't soulmates, knowing they weren't destined to be together?

The busy signal beeped in her ear and she put the receiver back in the phone cradle. It didn't matter. In all Greer's men-and-relationship experience, not even she could answer her questions.

So it looked like Eva would go through with the trial. Hopefully the Soulmate Serum backed what her gut had already confirmed, what she'd felt the moment she met Richard.

He was the one.

* * * *

Richard and Eva pulled up in the Sub Rosa car park. Outside of a blue Chevrolet, the dark, deserted place only had street lamps offering a splash of light. The quiet, Thursday-night creepiness slithered up her spine.

Richard held Eva's hands and stared into her eyes. "Are you ready?"

"I don't think I'll ever be ready for this."

He kissed her, the taste of challenge and excitement on his lips. In the short time they'd gone out, Richard had made it pretty clear that he thrived on testing boundaries, on taking risks, which she admired but didn't embody. She had more of a cautious, ruminating let's-plan-everything-out-in-detail style. Maybe they would balance each other out.

Keeping hold of one hand, he walked with her to the main door, opened it with his office key and pressed the 'up' button for the regular lift and the 'down' button for the restricted access service elevator the researcher had told them to take.

Richard turned to her. "It's already after seven-thirty and I just need to quickly pick up some paperwork from my office. How about you meet Salvator in the lab and I'll join you there shortly?"

"Okay. Don't be too long."

He clutched her face and gave her a swift kiss. "I promise I won't be."

* * * *

Salvator grabbed two vials of the red serum from the fridge and returned to the work bench. He slotted them into a small stand and checked the wall clock. Richard and the other volunteer, Eva, should arrive any minute...assuming they hadn't reconsidered.

She arrived first. His back was to the door, but the distinct click of stiletto heels struck the tiled floor.

"I'll be with you in a minute." Salvator finished recording a research note, shoved his pen behind his ear and swung around to face her. "Thanks for com—" He stopped mid-sentence and swallowed hard. He couldn't believe his luck—early twenties, long, dark, lustrous hair, blue-violet eyes, an hourglass figure. She was the most beautiful woman he'd ever seen.

"Hello, Salvator? I'm Eva. I'm here for the trial." A smile hesitated halfway on her lips and she joined him in the middle of the room, her black and white polka-dot dress flouncing about her shapely legs.

Salvator only just managed a strangled, "Um...can I get you a drink?"

"No, thank you."

Salvator moved in closer, eager to make physical contact. "Ah...if you don't have anything else planned after this, maybe we—"

"Hi, Salvator," Richard said and joined them, offering his outstretched hand.

Damn. "Good to see you again, Richard." Salvator shook his hand with as much masculine force as he could muster then gestured to the enthralling woman at his side. "And this is Eva."

Richard and Eva shared a look, a special sparkle, the chemistry between them clear. Like divine intervention, destiny had stepped in and selected them to do the trial. "Thank you both for coming and volunteering to be my guinea pigs."

A worried look flashed across her face.

"Sorry. It's a research joke." He fiddled with the buttons on his white lab coat. "As I mentioned on the phone, I haven't conducted any human trials, though I have done a succession of rat trials with no alarming side effects." If he didn't count the serum's influence on the breakup with his fiancée of two years and being unable to find a woman whose romantic touch he could tolerate ever since.

"In theory, and from what I've observed with the rat trials, there's one consistent outcome. Once the drug is ingested, only soulmates will connect. So, forget wanting to have a fling with someone. You won't feel pleasure with anyone but your soulmate."

Worry invaded Eva's enchanting face. "What if I never find him?"

"Then I'm afraid you'll be on your own. You'll have your friends and family, of course, just not a romantic partner. You see, there's no antidote...yet. I'm still working on it."

Turmoil tossed around in her eyes like a raft in stormy seas. "Oh."

Salvator could almost see her mind's gears cranking over, weighing up all the pros and cons. Should I? Shouldn't I?

Richard's light jade eyes searched hers. "Don't you believe in *us*?"

They knew each other. They'd come in separately, but they were together. *Is she the woman Richard was searching for the first time we met?* If so, no wonder he'd scoured the hallways, desperate to find her. A beyond-beautiful woman like that...

"Of course I do."

"Well then, there's nothing to worry about, is there?" Richard said.

Her resigned blue-violet eyes stared into his. "No, I suppose not."

Richard held her trembling hand. "Look, we don't have to do this, if you really don't want to."

"I know. Though it'd be a shame to miss such a great opportunity." Eva's tone sounded full of faith rather than belief.

"Exactly."

She took a deep, shaky breath and swallowed. "Okay."

"Just over here," Salvator said, directing them to the nearby benchtop to sign consent forms.

He handed them each a vial containing one fluid ounce of the red oral serum. "Just so you know what to expect, the drug is rose-flavored and takes effect immediately. However, you won't feel any different until you make physical contact with someone. You'll still feel attracted upon sight. Everything will be the same, except when you touch. Then you'll know straight away if the person is romantically right for you or not."

Richard and Eva looked at each other, excitement beaming from his eyes, while hers streamed with fear.

"No guts, no glory," Richard said, and gulped his down like a shot of whiskey.

Eva inched the vial to her lips and tipped it so a single drop dripped onto her tongue. She shivered and screwed up her nose like it tasted toxic. Then she stared at the remaining serum, one, two, three seconds, and chugged it back.

"Thanks, Salvator." Richard shook his hand. "We'll let you know how we go."

"Great. Just remember, from this moment on, you'll have a result as soon as you touch."

Eva stood just far enough away from Richard to avoid physical contact...for the moment. She seemed to be concentrating on her breathing, her eyes closed, as though to psychologically prepare herself for the outcome.

The forever-altered Richard and Eva left the lab, his cool, rock-bohemian style perfectly complementing her outfit. They continued along the lonely corridor, drawing nearer and nearer and nearer.

Then it happened.

Their hands brushed, and they stopped and turned toward one another, an intense, almost visible forcefield connecting their eyes. They leaned in, mirroring each other, as though two halves of a whole, and they kissed.

Salvator wanted to give them some privacy but he couldn't look away. As a scientist, it thrilled him to observe such immediate, compelling results. As a man with hormones and emotions, he wished it were different. He wished Eva felt that way about him. However, after taking the serum, she had no choice — or him either — when it came to romantic connection.

* * * *

Richard embraced Eva so tightly she worried her ribs would snap. "I told you it would work out. I knew our connection was way too strong not to mean something special." He caressed her hair and kissed her lips again and again, like a beloved treasure he couldn't stop stroking.

His enthusiasm radiated out of every pore and entwined with her own elation. The outcome had turned out perfectly. They'd never have to question their interest in each other ever again.

Richard's reasoning now made sense. Knowing they were soulmates eliminated a lot of unfounded worries and doubts. "Sorry I lost my temper when you brought it up last weekend. I should have trusted you, I should have trusted us," Eva said.

He caressed her cheek with the pad of his thumb. "By giving this a shot, you proved you trusted me and us. That means more to me than the results of the serum."

She stared at him with a you've-got-to-be-kidding look.

"Okay, maybe not more than the results."

They returned to his MG and climbed in. "Let's go back to my place and celebrate!" he said.

"What did you have in mind?" Hmmm…maybe he'd drop the *clothes-on* rule tonight. Butterflies morphed into flapping doves in her stomach.

"Champagne and a home-cooked dinner take your fancy?"

"It's a good start."

They reached his house by nine p.m. and were three-quarters through a bottle of champagne by the time they ate dinner, with no Bram in sight.

Eva swallowed a forkful of rare beef salad. "Maybe he's on a date?"

"I hope so. But somehow I doubt it." Richard had a sip of sparkling wine. "He's probably working on something in the shed or has gone to bed."

She had another mouthful of her meal. "You know, I'm so glad we decided to take tomorrow off. I think we would've needed it either way."

"If we keep drinking at this rate, we'll really need the extra day off. We'll both be nursing hangovers."

"Right, no more celebratory champagne tonight. I want us to enjoy the extra time together." And hopefully bask in the afterglow of a passionate night of lovemaking.

Richard's eyes sparkled with promise. "Oh, we will. I'll make sure of that."

They finished their dinner, piled their dirty dishes in the sink and retired to the lounge room. Richard stoked up the fire, sat beside Eva on the couch, and they made out like it was the first time.

Every single sensation amplified like a finely-tuned musical instrument—and she'd thought their interactions beforehand had been amazing. She hadn't noticed the increased intensity when they'd touched post-serum at Sub Rosa. Maybe the drug took a while to have its full effect. Given they were the first human subjects, Salvator wouldn't have known about the added benefit. She'd have to make a mental note to tell him.

Richard ran his palm over her breasts and her nipples stood to attention as though he'd reached beneath the barrier of her dress and stroked her bare skin. A flame of desire shot up each nerve ending, sending the telegraph-like signal through her body until she blazed with a raw, animalistic heat. Eva reached down his jeans and rubbed his engorged cock through his boxer shorts.

He groaned and pulled away, breathless. "I think we'd better stop."

She kept her hand in the same position, her fingers teasing and caressing. "Shouldn't that be *my* line?"

He grabbed her hand and held it. "Believe me, I don't want to, but—"

She pouted. "But what? We know we're perfectly suited."

"I know it sounds old-fashioned, but I want to do things properly. I feel like I owe it to my parents—our parents—and my uncle, too."

What a major disappointment. But she respected his reasoning. She had always wanted a gentleman and he kept proving he met the criteria. "Fair enough."

Richard kissed her palm and the underside of her wrist then released her tingling hand into her lap. "I'm going to make us some coffee. I'll be back in a minute."

He stood and headed toward the kitchen. Eva's skin and lips still throbbed from the aftermath of his kisses and she wanted more—much, much more.

She clamped her gaze on his broad shoulders and taut butt for one last hit of pleasure before he disappeared behind the door. The ache between her legs flared, gaining momentum and bombarding her brain with X-rated thoughts. She needed an orgasm. Badly. But from him, not her hand.

Naked preferably.

There had to be a way to persuade him. She sighed and rested her head against the back of the couch, picturing them in their own private adult film.

Smokey slinked over and curled up beside her. She gave him a pat and he purred in appreciation—a bit like how she felt when Richard touched her. And she was ready, more than ready, to succumb to his every sensual stroke. Tonight.

Mmm... She closed her eyes, then they rolled open like a loose awning and finally drifted closed and anchored shut.

Asleep? He hadn't been gone that long. Richard placed their coffees on the lamp-side table and sat next to Eva. The rise and fall of her sumptuous breasts hypnotized, aroused, tempted.

How he'd love to get her out of her dress and explore every bit of her body with his eyes, hands, mouth. He'd had the chance, too, and had blown it. Both of them were keen to take things further. However, they should be mature, do the right thing and hold off...or so he kept trying to convince himself.

"Eva," he whispered, and she stirred but didn't wake. He pressed a soft kiss to her lips and she shifted and snuggled into his chest. "I think it's bedtime," he said, and carried her upstairs.

Richard removed her clothes as though unwrapping a fragile gift, leaving her in her underwear, and tucked her under his doona. Eva was out as cold as their abandoned coffees. All the anxiety leading up to the trial must have exhausted her.

Still on edge from their make-out session, Richard showered, hard-on in hand, and imagined Eva kneeling before him, her hot mouth on his erect cock. Seconds... Within seconds he came, bracing himself against the wall, a guttural groan echoing through the en suite. With the fog of pent-up passion partially lifted, he finished his shower, threw on his paisley pajamas and went into his study.

Richard sat at his desk and pushed aside the documents he'd brought home from work, outlining his new research project. He had hoped to get a head start on it, but it would just have to wait.

The almost-full moon shone through the window, and that, combined with his Eva-inspired release, lit up his brain with creativity. Richard grabbed a piece of paper out of the top drawer, and with fountain pen in hand, started scribbling out a poem.

Eva opened her eyes, disorientated until Richard's arms tightened around her bare waist. In his bed again, her soulmate's bed. Every bit of her exposed skin erupted in goosebumps. Not from cold, from desire.

A shiver licked up her spine. *How did I get to his room?* In her last waking memory, they were making out, then Richard went to make coffee and she drifted off into an erotic daydream. Had they enacted any of it? She'd had a few drinks, though she'd gotten nowhere near drunk. She would have remembered if they'd gone all the way. Wouldn't she?

"Are you awake?" Richard whispered into her hair.

Eva patted her hand over the front of her body. Her underwear remained in place, suggesting she hadn't missed one of the most anticipated events of her life. Thank goodness. "Yes. Sorry to conk out on you last night."

"Don't worry about it. You can make it up to me this morning." His voice fanned the rising flames of her libido.

"I'm at your service. What would you like?" Her tone dripped with seduction.

He kissed her shoulder. "For you to sit on the edge of the bed."

"The edge of the bed?" And leave the comfortable spooning cocoon? She didn't want to move. They were in the perfect position to take things further.

"Yep." He jumped up, a blast of cool air hitting her back.

Curiosity, and the absence of his warm, aroused body, convinced her to do as he asked. *What is he up to?*

He snatched a folded-up piece of paper off his bedside table and stood in front of her. "I couldn't sleep last night. I kept thinking about things – about you – and inspiration struck. "I remember you asking me a while back to hear some of my poetry and I never followed through. I don't like breaking promises. So, here's a short one I wrote last night, in honor of you. It's called *That Special Fire.*" He cleared his throat.

You set
a raging fire inside my heart,
spreading, consuming, transforming
Everything in its path
Until we are wholly connected,
Joined
Forever in love.

Eva stared at him, his heartfelt words warming her insides into love mush and sending her mute with emotion. So much had happened in six short weeks. For the first time, her life had clear direction and purpose, outside of endless searching for a familial connection.

For the first time, she'd found a place she belonged – beside Richard, the missing piece in her romantic puzzle, completing the picture.

Her gaze met his and he fidgeted, restless, waiting for her response. "Beautiful. So beautiful. Thank you."

A large, relieved smile replaced his obvious stress. "I'm so glad you like it."

Then he strode over to his bedside cabinet, took something out of the top drawer and returned with his hands behind his back.

"I didn't envisage doing things this way, but it just feels right. Um...where do I start?" He paused and looked into her eyes. "Eva, I'm sure you know by now you mean not just the world, but the universe to me. Our incredible whirlwind romance has exceeded all my expectations. And last night was the juicy rare steak on top—the solidifier.

"I know it might seem premature, though I figure why wait, when we know we're perfect for each other." He dropped to one knee. "I love you, Eva. I'm in love with you and I want to be with you every day, every night. I want you to be my wife. Will you marry me?"

"Yes!" She threw her arms around his neck and kissed him, deep and long.

They came up for air, and, keeping one hand on her thigh, Richard opened his other hand and a gold and ruby heart ring sat in the middle of his palm. "This betrothal ring has been in my family for centuries. I hope you like it."

"I love it. It's beautiful. I feel like a princess," she said, in between post-kiss gasps.

"I must be Prince Charming then."

"Obviously." A joyous droplet descended her cheek.

Richard wiped it away with his thumb, pressed her back against the bed and kissed her like his survival depended on it. She rolled them onto the side and curled her leg around his waist so they were intimately intertwined. He cupped her behind, then loosened his grip and drew large, lazy lines along the length of her thigh. "There's no need to rush, is there?"

Sure there is. She'd been starved of affection for years and he could offer her true intimacy and more. Right now. 'Waiting' had to be one of the worst, most frustrating words in the world. Eva rubbed her damp panties against his arousal, trying to further stimulate his sexual appetite to match her growing hunger. "I thought we might make love to celebrate."

He shook his head, but his eyes and cock said *yes, yes, yes*. "Uh-uh. Not yet, not until we're married."

She huffed. *Mr. Do-The-Right-Thing strikes again.* "And when will that be?"

"Next Friday."

Her eyes widened. She thought knowing when would take the spice out of it, but counting down the days added a surprising level of suspense and anticipation. "A week from today?"

"Yep. What do you think? We can hold off longer if you'd like."

"No, Friday's perfect. Though, don't we need a priest? And how about arranging invitations and time off work?"

He caressed her cheek and she imagined how his hand would feel gliding inch by exploratory inch across her bare body. "Leave it to me. I'll sort it out. All you need to do is decide on an outfit and turn up at the church."

She kissed his temple and nuzzled her nose into his skin, his man-scent like sexy smelling salts. "We should find your uncle and tell him the good news." Before she lost all control and slid her hand down his pajama pants — the out-of-bounds area…until Friday.

* * * *

Later that day, Richard took Eva home and she called Greer.

"Where have you been? I rang several times yesterday and today and nothing. I started to worry."

Eva sat at the hallway table, twirling the telephone cord in her hand. "Relax. Everything's fine. More than fine."

"You've been with Richard, haven't you?"

"Yes."

"And you've gone all the way."

Eva crossed her legs. "No. He's a gentleman."

"What a shame," Greer said, her voice drenched with disappointment.

"Though, we have been...intimate."

"You'd have wanted to by now...and?"

"He proposed and we're getting married next Friday and I'd love for you to be my maid of honor."

"You're getting married? Next Friday? And you've only known each other less than two months. Don't you think it's a bit soon? I mean, you haven't even gotten it on yet," she said, concern coating her words.

"We don't need to. We know it's right. I don't expect you to understand, but you're like family, so I'd love you to be there and support me." *Seeing my dad can't.*

"You're not just doing this so you can have sex with him?"

"No!"

"Good. Okay."

"So, does that mean you'll do it?"

"Yes, I'll do it."

Relief melted away all the tension in Eva's muscles. "Thanks, Greer. Richard's organizing a dinner at his place on Wednesday night to go over the finer details. I know it's short notice—"

"I'll be there. I need to reschedule one of my dates, but you know what they say. *'Treat them mean, keep them keen'*." Her husky laugh echoed down the phone line.

"Hey, Eva..." Richard called out from her bedroom.

"Who was that?" her friend asked.

"No one. The radio." No point explaining, not to Greer. She would never understand the sleeping arrangements. For her, sleeping together meant sex, or else, why bother?

"Oh right," she said, her tone laced with suspicion.

"Anyway, I'd better go. See you at work on Monday."

"Sweet dreams." Greer's voice spiked with innuendo.

* * * *

Monday morning, Salvator sat at his desk wishing he could feel sad about splitting up with his fiancée. But instead, he mourned his inability to connect with his own soulmate and the death of his hope for her to be Eva.

Envy at Richard and Eva finding each other so quickly, that their intuition had been so spot on, was spliced with admiration. No matter what Salvator's situation, his new friends made a lovely couple and no one could deny it or take their incredible connection away from them.

In the afternoon, while plowing through the mail in his pigeon hole, he came across a thick, off-white envelope. The paper quality and embossed design confirmed it definitely wasn't work stationery. And with his name written in black cursive font on the front, it looked like the invitations his fiancée had planned to send for their wedding.

Salvator slipped his finger under a break in the seal on the back flap and lifted it open without any damage. Inside, a gold family crest sat atop more elegant black calligraphy.

A wedding invitation.

For Richard and Eva.

They were getting married on Friday.

This week.

He stumbled back, still in shock when he reached his desk. It shouldn't be a surprise. They were soulmates. Why wait any longer?

His phone rang and he picked up the receiver.

"Salvator, it's Richard."

"Yes, um, I believe congratulations are in order."

"Thank you." Richard cleared his throat. "Ah...this might seem a little unexpected, but how would you feel about being an official witness?"

"As in groomsman?" *He has to be joking. I hardly know him.*

"Yeah. What better person for the job than the man who helped Eva and I realize we're soulmates?"

"I'm flattered but—"

"No buts. We'd love for you to do it. Consider it your gift to us."

"If you're sure." Because Salvator wasn't. A shy, single-minded science nerd with a crush on the bride-to-be didn't quite meet groomsman standards.

"Very sure. Come around for dinner at my place on Wednesday night and we'll fine-tune the plans."

Chapter Fourteen

Violet Preconception

Norway Compound, 2005

Ethan had just finished dinner — the same time every night, after night, after night. He left his bowl by the blasted beams of light and went into his bedroom. Although still too early to sleep, he needed a rest — from the memories, from the guilt. His mind filled to the brim with reminiscence that started to spill over.

He slumped onto his military-style, neat bed, reached under it and pulled out a bottle of purple home brew. His stash had been confiscated after a drunken altercation with a couple of guards, but he had Beauregarde — a full Violet who couldn't be contained — who could squeeze in just about anywhere with his bottle of salvation.

Popping the cork sparked his saliva flow, in anticipation of not only the taste but also the medicinal mind-numbing. He brought the bottle to his lips, chugged back half the contents, re-corked it and shoved it back under the bed. Then he lay down and waited.

His brain bled with regurgitated images, thoughts and feelings, recapping his life to date, like a preparatory autobiography for if he ever met his daughter. His sweet, sweet little rose…

* * * *

Hobart, 1942

Ethan's dad took him aside into the vast drawing room of their Tasmanian home. "You cannot be serious. A human girl? You proposed to a full human?" The refined, constructed veneer on his voice reverted to his native Norwegian accent. Ethan hadn't heard his dad slip since he'd rescued Ethan from a Jade camp, near death. His father had to be on the far outer limit of flustered.

"Yes. I'm more serious than I've ever been in my entire life."

"How long have you known her?" His dad recovered quickly, his well-spoken façade faultless in his harsh whisper.

Great. Instead of celebrating, instead of congratulating him on the wonderful news, he'd gotten the inquisition. He shouldn't be surprised. Surprised would have been if his vain, self-absorbed father showed interest, some happiness for him. "Long enough."

His dad stared at him as if to say, 'don't be smart with me'.

Ethan huffed and adjusted his amethyst cufflinks. "Eighteen months. I met her almost as soon as we migrated in 1941." He looked his dad in the eye. "I'm twenty-three, old enough to know what I want and who I want to be with. And I want to be with her."

"Why is this the first time you brought her home?"

"Because I knew I'd get this response and I didn't want the negativity."

"Have you told her parents?"

"Yes."

"And they are happy, are they? Do they even know about you? About your heritage?"

Ethan's gaze fell to the floor and he shoved his balled-up hands in his pockets. "Not exactly. They know I'm Norwegian."

"But not part Violet." His father ran his palm over his smoothed black hair.

"Well, it's none of their business. They don't have to live with me."

"Have you told her?" His dad's probing violet eyes searched his.

"Of course!"

"And do you plan to have children?"

"Dad!" The sex topic was a no-go zone. They'd never even had 'the talk'. Then again, most topics were a no-go zone with his judgmental, know-it-all father.

"It is important. If you do, it is a huge risk to her."

"I'm a half-caste, not a full Violet."

"It doesn't matter. There can be complications at the best of times, but especially when mixing in a part vampire."

Ethan's accusatory eyes glared at his fop of a father. "You'd do anything to break us up, wouldn't you?"

His dad stood firm, preening himself in the elaborate, gold-framed mirror above the soot-filled fireplace. "No. I am just making sure you know the ramifications—and her too."

Ethan crowded into his narcissistic father's personal space. "Don't you dare say anything to her!"

His dad didn't even flinch, seemingly unable to tear his eyes away from his own reflection. "If you do not tell her, I will. So you'd better get to it...tonight, before you continue with the wedding plans."

Ethan shook his head. He'd expected the announcement to be difficult, to get some resistance from his parents, but not this much. They were more prejudiced than he'd realized. And they thought humans were bad.

"Fine. Will you at least give us your blessing?"

His father turned back to him and laid a well-manicured hand on his shoulder. "I am sorry, son. We cannot do that, not when you're making the biggest mistake of your life. Whether you like it or not, tragedy is inevitable."

He shrugged out of his dad's grip, stormed from the room and left with his confused fiancée.

Ethan strode to his car, his jaw teeth-crushingly tight. "They're unbelievable!"

"Don't they like me?" she asked, almost running to keep up with him.

"It's not that, exactly. They think we're making a mistake."

"Because I'm full human."

They stopped in front of the passenger-side door and he tipped her chin up, tears teetering on the brims of her blue eyes. "Yes."

She smiled, but a tinge of sadness seeped through. "We'll just have to prove them wrong."

They got into the car and he drove her home. "There is one other thing I should tell you." Damn his dad for bringing up something that would probably not affect them. He had to let her know the risks, though, no matter how remote. And hope it didn't scare her into someone else's arms. "If we decide to have children, we're going to need to be really careful."

"Careful? In what way?"

He stared at the road, his hands strangling the steering wheel. "Even though I'm only a half-caste, if any vampire genes are transferred to our baby, it will increase the complications for you. The baby will grow quicker, bigger, be a lot stronger."

"I don't mind," she said, her voice soft, gentle, accepting.

Ethan parked the car in front of her house and looked at her. "You're sure? It might cause you more pain. The baby might be born premature without giving your body time to adjust. It might be more demanding physically and emotionally."

She smiled and stroked his cheek. "There are a lot of 'mights' in there and not many 'definites'. It doesn't sound like too much of a risk to me."

He covered her hand with his. "It is a risk. Being with me is always going to be a risk."

"And it's one I'm willing to take, Ethan. I love you. I can't imagine feeling like this about anyone else."

Ethan exhaled a long, relieved breath. "I love you too."

* * * *

They married in March 1943, with Ethan's parents not present at the wedding. And by September, his overjoyed wife announced her pregnancy and rendered him speechless, his whole body shaking with shock and stress. They'd been careful — very careful — but not careful enough.

Bloating, chronic nausea and two lumbar spine fractures, and his wife still smiled, even as she went into labor seven months later and had their baby daughter.

A young nurse in a white dress, starched hat and short, hematic cape approached Ethan in the waiting room. "You can come and see your wife now."

He followed her into the bleached, sterile room and jolted to a stop. His wife lay flat with her eyes closed, her skin whiter than the white sheets and she was hooked up to a drip and monitors.

Ethan rubbed his eyes to erase the false picture from his mind and reset. However, the scene stayed the same. She looked exsanguinated, drained of all nutrients, a torture victim in a concentration camp.

He turned to the nurse. "What happened to her?"

"I should probably get the doctor to explain." She adjusted his wife's drip and left the room.

Ten minutes later, a middle-aged man in a white coat and stethoscope dangling from his neck arrived and shook Ethan's hand. "Congratulations on your daughter. Have you seen her yet?"

Ethan tensed, so desperate for answers he nearly crushed the man's knuckles. "No. I need to know what's wrong with my wife."

The doctor winced, rubbed his released hand and gestured to the closest spare chair. "Please, sit down."

Ethan sat and the doctor pulled up a seat next to him, stale cigarette smoke clinging like a dark aura around the man. "She's sedated at the moment. She lost a lot of blood —"

"Is it serious?"

"During the course of the pregnancy, the baby caused a lot of internal damage and depleted your wife of many essential vitamins and minerals, significantly lowering her immunity. I've never seen anything like it."

Ethan shot to the edge of his seat. "Will she be all right?" He studied the doctor's face as though the answer would appear on his skin.

"I wish I could guarantee she'll be fine, but... Her condition is still very unstable. It doesn't help that she insists on breastfeeding." The doctor stared at him, his eyes grave and unblinking. "If you really want to help her, talk her out of it. She needs to conserve the little nutrients her body has left. The only way she can do that and start building up her strength is to bottle-feed your daughter. I know it's not ideal, but neither are the circumstances."

Ethan scoured his face with frantic hands. How could something so perfect turn so precarious? He glanced at the statue-still doctor, whose coffee-tainted tobacco breath lay like a stagnant cloud between them. "Thank you for being so candid with me. I'll convince her to stop."

The doctor smiled, cracking the somber mask, but it hardly curved the edges of his down-turned mouth. "Now, why don't you come and see your daughter?"

In a daze, Ethan shadowed the doctor to the nursery. Babies upon babies—big, tiny, bald, hairy, cute, crying, sleeping—lay in cribs, swaddled in blue or pink blankets. It bordered on overwhelming...until he spotted *her*.

The doctor pointed through the glass. "Your daughter is—"

"I know," Ethan said, mesmerized by her tiny, pink-wrapped body. A hint of rose colored her little round cheeks and a splash of raven hair covered her head. She slept peacefully, oblivious to the carnage she'd caused. And it was all his fault. Ethan hadn't wanted to lose the love of his life by pushing her away, never realizing that holding on to her could end in the same devastating result. *Worse.*

Given the circumstances, he decided not to tell his parents about the birth. His father wouldn't be able to pass up the opportunity to spout his favorite fucked-up words—*'I told you so.'* Ethan gritted his teeth, bristling with anger. He had to get a grip. He had to focus on saving his wife, on being a good dad to his baby girl.

All the way home and into the night he tried to think of ways to make sure that happened. With hardly any sleep, he arose early the next day and returned to the hospital, eager to speak to his beloved wife and discuss feasible, practical options.

He walked in on her sitting up, supported by pillows, breastfeeding their daughter, and strode over. "What are you doing?"

A feeble smile hesitated on her lips, like her facial muscles no longer had the energy to move the edges of her mouth. "Feeding our baby."

Frustrated, fearful thoughts and feelings swelled his brain, like an over-filled pressure cooker, ready to explode. "The doctor said to bottle-feed. Remember?"

His wife's gaze fell adoringly on their child, who lay in her frail arms, sucking the life out of her. "I need to give her the best start."

Ethan tilted her chin up so she looked him in the eye. "And you have. You nurtured her in your womb and gave birth to a very healthy baby, considering her prematurity."

"I won't feel like a mother if I don't breastfeed her."

"If you don't stop breastfeeding her, you may not even have a chance to be her mother."

Her drawn, wrung-out face dropped.

"I'm sorry. But we spoke about this and you agreed…" He swallowed back the rising hurt and anger. "I don't want to lose you."

"You won't." Not even her voice had any power.

He sat on the bed next to her skeletal body and looked into her weary, dark-rimmed eyes. "I don't think you understand how serious this is."

"I understand. I just think they're being over-cautious."

Her mothering role was smothering her ability to gain perspective, to think straight, totally blinded by the bond with their baby. And that, along with the malnutrition, created a lethal combination. "They're not. Believe me. You're very unwell."

"Okay. I promise I'll stop breastfeeding…after this. Just let her finish now, then she can be bottle-fed until I'm well enough."

Thank goodness, she seemed to get it. Finally. "You promise?"

"Yes. I love you, Ethan. I'd do anything for you."

A relieved smile eased the tension in his tight jaw. Now she just had to stick with what she'd said. "I love you too. Make sure you get some rest."

The day after, on the way to his wife's room, her doctor intercepted him, a grim edge to his chain-smoker-lined face. "I tried to call you earlier… Can I speak to you for a moment?"

"Is everything all right?"

The doctor ushered him into a nearby consulting room and closed the door. "Please sit down."

Insidious unease spread like a malignant tumor through his system. "What's going on?"

The doctor hesitated.

Ethan grabbed a handful of the guy's white coat and twisted it into a fist. "What. Is. Going. On?"

Short puffs of stale tobacco breath blew onto his face. "Your wife... She didn't make it."

"What?"

"She passed away."

His heart stopped and plunged like a lift with a severed cable, crashing into the pit of his stomach. *No!* He shook his head, and lost his grip on the doctor, his arm falling by his side. "When?" The word croaked out of his strangled vocal cords.

"Her rostered nurse went to take her observations this morning and found her."

Ethan stumbled backward, gasping for air. "No, it can't be. She promised... She promised she wouldn't breastfeed. She promised she'd get some rest." His lungs constricted with grief, disbelief.

"And she did both those things." His compassionate tone sounded like the type he used for dealing with distraught relatives. "But too late. Her heart gave out. Too much damage had already been done."

Ethan's jaw twitched, anger warring with anguish, and he glared at the doctor. "Did you even try to revive her?"

"Yes. We tried everything. We worked on her for over half an hour without even a trace of a pulse. I'm so sorry."

He buried his face in his hands, barricaded, unshed tears pounding at the back of his eyes for release. "And our baby? How is she?"

"Fine. She's doing wonderfully."

Ethan ran his shaking hands through his hair, still struggling to breathe. "Can I see my wife?"

"Of course. Come with me."

Laid out on the hospital bed, shrouded by golden daylight, she looked so peaceful, rested, like she'd just fallen asleep. Her sallow color looked almost better than when he'd last seen her. He bent down and kissed her icy skin. Guilt tore through him. With everything going on, he hadn't even told her parents about the birth.

He'd convinced himself his wife would improve, then he'd let them know when things were more stable. Now, instead, he'd robbed them of the chance to see their daughter alive one last time, to hug her warm body, to say any last, loving words. They were going to hate him. They were never keen on him in the first place, being a foreigner, but after this...

Ethan drove to his wife's parents' home, tension and sorrow tearing at his insides. He swiped at his stinging, waterlogged eyes, with the back of his hand.

His eight-year-old brother-in-law, William, opened the door, his eyes wide with excitement. "Has my sister had the baby?"

Ethan tried to smile. "Yes. Can I speak to your parents please?"

"Come in," he said and stepped aside. "Is it a boy or a girl?"

"Girl."

He frowned. "Oh. Better luck next time."

If only fate had given them a next time.

The boy ran ahead to the back sunroom. "She's had the baby! It's a girl!"

Ethan's mother-in-law put her crossword puzzle on her lap and glanced up. Her enthusiastic smile faded when she saw his face.

"What's happened?"

He didn't answer. He couldn't. Not yet. Not without turning into a hysterical mess.

His father-in-law put down his pipe and pushed his recliner chair into an upright position. "Go to your room, William," he said, his dark blue eyes locked on Ethan's.

"But, Dad…"

"Just go, please."

William sulked off, dragging his feet and slamming his bedroom door shut.

"The baby's very early. How is she doing?" his mother-in-law asked.

"The baby's fine. She's doing very well, actually." Ethan started to pace, his heart rate racing like a ticking time bomb. "It's your daughter. She lost a lot of blood…"

His mother-in-law jumped up and turned to her husband. "We have to go and see her."

"Wait, please." Ethan sighed, his accelerated pulse thrashing in his throat. "I haven't finished.

Their combined stare beamed like an interrogative spotlight.

A fresh onslaught of tears flooded his eyes. "She passed away this morning."

"Passed away? How?" His mother-in-law collapsed onto the nearest seat and started crying.

"Her heart stopped. Gave out. While pregnant, the baby caused some internal damage and stripped her of vitamins and minerals, which compromised her immune system. So that, with the blood loss…"

His father-in-law put a consoling arm around his wife. "When did she have the baby?"

Ethan closed his eyes and braced himself on the back of the couch in front of him. "Three days ago."

"Three days ago? And you only told us *now*?" his father-in-law yelled.

"We could have seen her. Why did you stop us from seeing her?" his mother-in-law said in between sobs.

Ethan's watery eyes focused on hers. "I waited for her to be more stable, to get better. I thought she would. I'm so very sorry."

His father-in-law pointed to the door. "Leave."

"I understand you're upset but—"

"Leave. *Now*."

"She's at Royal Hobart Hospital and so is the baby…if you want to see them," Ethan said, and left the blur of his in-laws behind.

Chapter Fifteen

Gifted

Hobart, July 1965

The wedding gown selection was a cinch. In addition to the letter Eva had received from her dad on her seventh birthday were some sepia photos and a mass of off-white silk — her grandmother's wedding dress, also worn by her mother — contained in a wooden trunk with brass fastenings. The moment she saw the delicate lace and silk adorning the hanger, she'd fallen in love with it and sworn she would wear the dress for her own wedding.

The real challenge became what outfit to choose for the engagement dinner. Eva needed a new dress to commemorate the beginning of a new life. And who better to have helped her pick something than her new beau, Richard?

Standing in front of the full-length, wrought-iron mirror, she slipped into a slinky, black, strapless dress with a pink rose and green chiffon overlay covering her arms and up to the base of her neck. She scooped her hair over one shoulder and could only do the zip three-quarters of the way up her back.

"Richard, could you give me a hand, please"?" she asked, and slid her feet into black court shoes.

He walked out of his en suite, looking sharp and sexy in a black suit, white shirt and a tie matching the print of her dress.

Richard adjusted his gold and jade cufflinks and glanced up. Her gaze met his. "Do me up?"

"With pleasure," he said, with a devilish grin.

He grabbed the zip, his hot, capable fingers gliding along her skin as he eased it up. Heat shot to her core, and she imagined all the fun they could have if he eased it down instead. Then he wound his arms around her waist and kissed the back of her neck. "You look beautiful, stunning. I'm a very lucky man."

If she didn't move away from him right now, they would never make it downstairs. "You certainly are." She turned and planted a cheeky kiss on his lips.

He held her hand. "We should go down…"

On each other. If her thoughts continued along that theme, she'd need a few moments alone with her hand — or Richard's — to clear the sexual fog from her brain or she'd struggle to hold a decent conversation.

"Salvator and Greer will be arriving soon."

Always Mr. Practical and Responsible, while she deviated into sexual-fantasy land, contemplating how to get her urges met. Not going all the way had kept her core shifting between simmering and boiling over. And right now, she bubbled close to boiling. Lucky their honeymoon was only two days away.

They walked into the lounge room, the aroma of raw meat tantalizing her taste buds, a welcome distraction from her salacious thoughts. "Let's check on the cook," she said, hoping to sneak in a sample of the dinner offerings.

Richard led her into the kitchen, where an apron-clad Bram had laid out peeled potatoes, onions and carrots in an oiled baking tray and stirred chopped, continental parsley into a meatloaf mixture.

Eva tried to keep the pooled saliva from spilling out of her mouth. "You really didn't have to do this."

A kind smile curled onto Bram's lips. "It's the least I could do. Consider it part of your engagement present."

"Thank you," Eva and Richard said in stereo.

Bram went to place the meatloaf into the tray. She had to stop him. She had to have some. Raw. "Um...could I please try a bit...just to check on the seasoning."

The look he gave her had a spark of recognition, as though something had clicked into place. "You two really are alike, aren't you?" He picked up a fork, scooped some uncooked meatloaf onto it and passed it to Eva. Then he glanced at Richard. "Would you like some too?"

"Do I really need to answer that?"

Bram loaded up another fork and handed it to him.

Eva wanted to take her time and savor the taste but she couldn't. A primal, animal craving overtook her and she gobbled it down. "Delicious!"

She sucked on the fork tines and licked her lips, indulging in every last morsel of raw meat. It was far from ladylike but better than snatching the bowl, tearing off chunks of the mixture and shoving it in her mouth, which was what she really wanted to do.

Richard hoed into his sample. "I agree. Pity we have to cook it," he said with an impish grin. But the ravenous look in his eyes showed some truth to his words, and she concurred wholeheartedly.

Bram placed the tray with the remaining meatloaf and vegetables in the oven. "Why don't you two make yourselves comfortable in the lounge room and I'll bring you some wine while you wait for your friends."

Within ten minutes, Bram joined them with a glass of red in front of the fire. "To Richard and Eva, may you have a long, happy, healthy, prosperous life together."

"Thanks, Uncle Bram." Richard lifted his glass.

Eva raised her glass to Richard's and Bram's. "Cheers."

"Before the guests arrive, I want to give you your engagement gift." Bram reached into his pocket, pulled out a hematite, diamond and ruby ring and looked at Richard. "It's a bonding ring, given to your dad to help reunite him with your mum. It's meant to keep soulmates together. Though, in saying that, it's nomadic in nature and is apparently designed to move on to those who need it most."

"How did you end up with it?" Richard asked.

"Your dad sent it to me with his last letter. He'd given up on it reconnecting him and your mum. It needed your mum's energy to solidify the bond. Anyway, I'm sure he'd be really happy to pass it on to you and Eva, as a gesture, a symbol of you making a positive start together."

Bram dropped the ring into Richard's palm. "Now hold it in your hand so it absorbs your energy."

Richard's awestruck eyes met Eva's gaze. "It's got a real warmth to it, almost an energy of its own."

"When it feels right, put it on Eva's right ring finger," Bram instructed.

Richard lifted her right hand, brushed her knuckles with a slow, reverent kiss that shot desire straight to her sex and slid the ring onto her finger. It fit perfectly, like a jeweler had made it for her. Throbbing heat spread through her flesh and a flush of love and adoration for Richard radiated from her skin, like the ring recognized him as the one, too, like it had soulmate selection powers.

Eva kissed Bram on the cheek and gave him a hug. "Thank you so much. You've been so supportive of us, so caring. You've made me feel part of the family. You've made me feel at home. I can't tell you how much it means to me."

Bram smiled, his eyes glassy with an emotion she couldn't quite read. Possibly happiness intermingled with a tinge of sadness, maybe even regret. "You're very welcome. You're like the daughter I never had."

The doorbell rang and just in time, before happy tears streaked her face and ruined her makeup. Excitement swelled in her stomach. She and Richard were not just an official couple. They were soon to be husband and wife.

Together, they opened the front door and Greer and Salvator stood on the doorstep. Greer wore a sly smile and held a fancy gift in her hands, and Salvator clutched a bottle of wine.

Richard shook Salvator's hand and ushered him into the lounge room, while Eva and Greer hugged then hung back in the front foyer and continued chatting.

"Okay, now the men have gone, I want you to open my gift," Greer said with a glint in her eye.

Eva accepted the shiny white box and went to read the card. Greer snatched it out of her hand. "You know it's from me. Just open the box before they come back."

"I thought this was supposed to be an engagement gift for me and Richard?"

Greer grinned. "Believe me it is—or should I say, will be."

Creases of confusion crinkled Eva's forehead and she tugged on the big gold bow on top of the box. The ribbon dropped open, and she lifted the virginal white lid. Gold tissue paper puffed up, and underneath lay a white translucent fabric.

She pulled it out and a pair of tiny, see-through panties fell on the floor. Eva picked them up and held them next to a white chiffon, baby-doll negligee with shoestring straps. Her gaze shot to Greer's eyes and she could see her red-faced reflection.

"Don't you love it?" Greer gushed.

"It's see-through."

"You don't miss a thing, do you?" she said with a satirical smile.

"I'll feel like a lady of the night!"

"No, you won't. You'll feel super sexy."

Eva's face burned as though there were hotplates stuck on high, beneath her skin. "What's the point of wearing something see-through? I may as well wear nothing at all."

"You can do that, too, but I suggest teasing your man a little first. Believe me, he's going to love it! He won't be able to keep his hands off you—and not just his hands." Greer's smile exuded pure sin.

"Eva, darling..." Richard called.

She threw the scanty items back in the box and tried to tame her erratic heart. "Be there in a minute."

Eva directed Greer into the lounge room then ran upstairs and hid the pornographic gift in her overnight bag. Could she really pull off wearing something so…skimpy? Her friend seemed to think so. Now she just had to believe it herself.

When she returned downstairs, Greer was full-on flirting with Salvator and Bram, flaunting her buxom cleavage. Both of them were polite and played along, but neither looked like they'd bite. Bram was old enough to be her father and Salvator? It surprised her he didn't show any interest. Her pretty, sociable, sexy friend rarely got turned down.

Richard met Eva halfway across the room and slid his arm around her waist. "What kept you?"

"Greer gave us a gift."

"You should have brought it to show me."

She gulped. "It's a surprise." *For later.* She called Salvator over, saving him from Greer's seductive onslaught. "Thanks so much for the wine. Merlot's our favorite."

He fidgeted with the collar of his crumpled brown suit. "It's just something small. The main part of the gift will be delivered tomorrow."

"You don't need to get us anything else. Your presence is present enough," Richard replied in a brook-no-argument tone.

"I want to do it. Please just accept it. I'll be offended if you don't." Something about the intensity of Salvator's hazel eyes suggested that he needed rather than wanted to pass on the wedding present.

Greer sashayed over in her siren-red dress and clung to Salvator's arm. "I'll be offended if they don't make good use of my gift, too."

He froze as though turned to stone by Medusa.

"Everyone, please take a seat at the dining table. Dinner is served," Bram announced.

Salvator squeezed between Bram and Richard, further distancing himself from Greer. *Fascinating*. Like Salvator was Superman and Greer his kryptonite.

Over the meal, they finalized the wedding plans, then afterward, Eva commandeered Greer's attention to give Bram and Salvator some respite. Plus, she needed answers to a few questions that had been plaguing her since Richard had proposed.

They sat on the couch in front of the fire while the men remained at the dining table, talking all things research.

Eva had a large swill of her third glass of wine, the liquid courage wearing down her wall of inhibitions. "I just wondered, you know, when you're with a man—"

"Sexually?"

"Yes, um—"

"How do you please him?" *Scary*. Greer answered like she'd read her mind.

Eva nodded.

Her friend smiled and held her hands up to the flames. "There are three things men love—having their cock sucked, having sex and having their cock sucked."

"You said that twice."

"Because that's how much they love it."

Heat seeped into and sizzled across every inch of Eva's skin. "Oh."

Greer crossed her leg toward her, a wicked gleam in her clear, brown eyes. "Don't look so worried. It's easy. When you take him into your mouth, just keep your teeth out of the way and use your tongue and lots of saliva to lick and suck—but not too hard."

Greer glanced over at the men, then her gaze reconnected with Eva's. "Guys especially like the underside of the head licked, it's real sensitive. And make sure you let him come in your mouth at least some of the time. And swallow. They *really* love it when you swallow."

She slapped her hand down on Eva's knee, as though to hold her in place, as though to physically infuse her pointers. "Oh, and don't forget to give his balls some attention as well."

And there it was…a recipe for successful cock-sucking by the connoisseur herself.

Eva's face throbbed with self-consciousness. "What does *it* taste like?"

Greer moved closer, her eyes flaring with excitement. The sex act, as well as sex talk were two of her friend's favorite pastimes. And going by what Eva had heard, Greer excelled at both. "His cum? Depends on the guy. If he eats well and looks after himself it'll be a bit salty and sometimes even a little sweet."

Eva gulped. Would Richard be salty or sweet? Entrée or dessert? She'd soon know. "And the sex part? How does it feel…the first time?"

"Again, depends on the guy. My first time bit the big one. The guy totally focused on himself and shoved his cock in me when I wasn't ready, so it hurt. A lot. But if Richard takes things slow and makes sure you're really wet, you should be fine. It'll sting a little at the start, then settle. With Richard, I don't think you've got anything to worry about."

The rest of the night flew by, with Eva and Richard not making it to bed until one a.m.

Richard lay on his back and held her against him. "I think our little get-together went really well."

In lots of ways. "Yes. Everything seems to be falling into place for Friday."

"Which is only two — actually, officially only one day away now. I'm so excited!"

"Me too!"

"Did I tell you my uncle is loaning us his car for our honeymoon?"

She rubbed his bare chest, playing with the smattering of golden-brown hair. "No. That's very generous."

"He thought it would handle the Cradle Mountain conditions better."

"Yes, I don't imagine a soft-top could keep out the cold too well." She snuggled into him. "Is there anything we've forgotten?"

"There is one other thing." Richard took a deep breath and his heart rate quickened. Whatever he planned to say made him nervous and sent a whirlwind of assumptions storming through her mind.

He cleared his throat. "Do you need me to get some...protection or are you already taking something?"

Heat blasted into her cheeks. The practicalities of sex. Her excitement about their impending intimacy made her forget about the baby side of things. "Um...I'm not taking anything, but I'm due a few days after the wedding, so we won't need protection."

He tilted her chin up and looked into her eyes. "Are you sure?"

"Yes. We should be fine."

Joy spread across his slightly-stubbled face. "I had really hoped we could make love without any barriers, just skin on skin, especially the first time."

"Me too." Eva rested her head back on his bare chest.

Richard brushed her hair from her face and kissed her temple. "We should get to sleep, since we have to get up in just a few hours."

She kissed his sternum. "And we want to make sure we're refreshed for Friday. It'll be a big day."

"And night," he said, his raspy tone tinged with pleasure-filled promise.

* * * *

Richard dropped Eva home after work on Thursday, and they had dinner together in the comfort of her small kitchen.

He helped her collect the dirty dishes and pile them in the soapy sink, ready for washing. "I'm going to miss you sleeping beside me tonight."

"Even my small bed is going to feel empty." She looked into his eyes. "I wish you could stay."

"I can. It's just…"

"I know. It's bad luck for the groom to see the bride before the wedding." She scrubbed the cups, plates and cutlery, rinsed them in the second sink and loaded them onto the dish rack.

Richard grabbed a tea towel off the oven-door rail and started wiping. "I'll stay as late as possible." *As long as I'm in the car by eleven fifty-five p.m.*

She pulled the plug out, let the dirty water drain and washed her hands. "Good."

When they'd finished putting everything away, he scooped her into his arms.

"What are you doing?"

He carried her down the corridor. "Celebrating our last night of being single."

"And what did you have in mind?"

He lowered Eva onto her bed, enjoying her body's telltale signs of arousal — flushed skin, dilated pupils, erect nipples. "How about some nearly naked sex? It seems to be our specialty."

Eva laughed, bubbly, light and husky. She was cute and sexy rolled into one adorable package.

He lifted her block primary color dress over her head and peeled off her long black boots and stockings. One more night and he wouldn't have to stop there. His cock grew so hard it hurt.

Richard kicked off his shoes and unbuttoned his shirt while she undid the buttons on his fly and pulled down his jeans. He stepped out of them, threw off his shirt and socks then lay beside her.

She pushed Richard onto his back and straddled him, her long hair draping over her barely-there bra, and her panty-sheathed pelvis pressed against his, sending him into a dopamine daze. He wanted to grab her hips and spread her legs over his face, pull her panties aside and lick and probe her sweet pussy until she came, screaming his name. But eating her out was reserved for tomorrow night.

Eva leaned down and kissed him, delving her tongue into his mouth with slow, deep strokes, extinguishing all the thoughts in his head. She moved her lips along his neck, to his ear. "I love you," she whispered, and trailed kisses down to his chest, where she created a large love bite on his pec. The mixture of pleasure and pain nearly sent him spiraling into orgasm.

"Eva…" He groaned, weaving his fingers through her hair.

She targeted his navel next, then his inner thighs and rubbed his throbbing erection through his boxer shorts until he charged toward release. She seemed to sense it and slowed down, planting a line of soft kisses along his length.

Eva alternated between rubbing and kissing until, hardly able to breathe, he begged her to make him come. She kissed his shaft one more time then climbed back on top of him and ground hard and fast, the friction driving him to climax in seconds. Bright, white stars of ecstasy still exploded behind his eyes when, moments later, she joined him in beyond-this-world bliss.

She fell against him, and they panted in rhythm.

"How was that?" she asked in between ragged breaths.

"Amazing. You're amazing." Now he really couldn't wait until tomorrow.

After cleaning himself up in the bathroom, Richard gave Eva a parting kiss that left his head spinning and his cock ready for round two. He arrived home after midnight and found his uncle still up, reading in front of the fireplace, the embers glowing red as the flames died out.

Strange. Bram usually went to bed by ten p.m. "Making sure I made it home?"

Bram glanced at him above his reading glasses and grinned, unable to hide the nervous twitch on the corner of his lips. "I wanted to ask you how your evening went, but the huge smile on your face says it all."

"Be prepared for a face-splitting smile after tomorrow night."

"I should hope so." Bram put his book face down on the couch. "I'm assuming that means you're pretty confident with everything? If you need to ask me anything, I'm here for you."

The conversation scarily dipped back into birds-and-bees territory — and on the eve of his wedding. Was this his uncle's way of broaching the sex-tips subject without being emasculating? "Are you referring to the wedding or the wedding night?"

"Either, both."

Just how he imagined he would talk with his father. Were his dad and Bram similar? Close? Richard had never even seen a photo of him. Okay, not exactly true. He'd seen pictures of his dad as a baby, right up until he'd reached puberty. Then...nothing.

The family resemblance was undeniable. But what about personality? Could his father be as approachable and down-to-earth as Bram?. What were the odds of having two impeccable, almost identical characters in the one family? "I think I'm on top of everything with the wedding. The wedding night? Not so sure."

"I see."

Richard averted his eyes and shifted his weight from one foot to the other. He should probably tell him. "Eva's actually my first."

"And are you hers?"

"Yes." Richard glanced up to gauge his uncle's reaction.

This time, Bram's smile reached his kind gray eyes. "Right. Well then, my advice to you is this." He patted the seat beside him and Richard sat down. "You need to make sure you look after her needs before your own. So, lots of kissing, caressing, compliments..."

No judgment, no making Richard feel inadequate or unmanly. Bram seemed genuinely interested in helping.

"With plenty of attention between her legs, from your hands and mouth."

Whoa! And being extremely open. *Slightly awkward.* Richard squirmed in his seat.

Bram continued, unfazed. "You need to give her at least a couple of orgasms this way first. Sex is still probably going to be a bit painful for her, though, so be gentle, and make sure you keep asking her how things feel and adjust accordingly. Open communication is essential for great sex and a great relationship."

Heat blistered Richard's cheeks. "Thanks." Bram had stepped into the father role so easily, naturally, and Richard really appreciated it, even though it felt a little uncomfortable speaking about the ins and outs of successful lovemaking. In the end it had helped and that's what mattered. It had definitely been worth the weirdness.

"Any time. You'll be fine." Bram gave him a man hug, slapping him firmly on the back. "You're a very caring, thoughtful young man." His uncle pulled back, the sheen of unshed tears in his eyes. "Oh, but the main reason I waited up was to let you know you had a rather large delivery. I didn't know where you wanted it."

Such a kind, loving man. Although not his dad, Bram behaved just like the kind of father he'd always craved. Richard had really won out in the relative department.

They walked into the conservatory and found a large crate taking up space in the center of the room, with a note from Salvator.

Dear Richard and Eva,
Congratulations on your engagement and impending wedding. Please find my present to you enclosed in the accompanying crate.

Let me start by letting you know the history of the gift. Up until a few months ago, I, too, was engaged to be married, but unfortunately, I had to break it off. What I'm sending you is the treasured gift my sister arranged for me and my fiancée. Instead of returning it, I gave her the money, but I just don't feel right using it. The gift had been meant to celebrate a union… that never happened, and it's a constant, painful reminder.

As soon as I received your wedding invitation, I thought it would be perfect for you, to commemorate a positive match, as a gift is supposed to. Then, when I visited your home last night, it further reinforced my decision.

I thought if you knew the truth, you'd be more willing to accept it. I hope you won't disappoint me.

Looking forward to seeing you both tomorrow.

Best wishes,

Salvator

"Are you going to open it?" Bram asked.

Richard put the note down on the table and stared at the enormous wooden container. "Yeah. I wonder what it could be?"

Smokey sauntered over to the giant box and rubbed himself against it. "Whatever it is, it's big and Smokey seems to like it," Bram said, and handed a drill to Richard. "I thought you might need this."

"Thanks." At the loud, buzzing sound of the drill, the cat disappeared out of the door. Richard removed the screws on the top panel, lifted off the lid and peered inside. Layers of bubble-wrap covered the object, distorting its appearance. "It looks like furniture of some sort."

The front panel came off next, so he and his uncle could get a closer look. Bram passed him a pair of scissors, like a surgical nurse involved in a delicate operation, to cut open the plastic packing. They pulled off the bubbled layer, revealing an ornately carved, black Gothic desk with a small black jewelry box sitting on top.

Richard opened the box and a gold chain with a rose-topped, gold-key pendant and a small note lay on the black velvet base. The message explained that the key opened a lockable drawer, hidden behind a front panel of the desk, adorned with a carved, red-painted rose.

"What a great idea," Bram said over Richard's shoulder.

"What a generous gift. I mean, we only recently became friends."

"It looks like you've both made quite a strong impression on each other."

Oddly enough, Richard had felt a rightness about Salvator from the moment they'd met, similar to when he'd first met Eva, except on a purely platonic level. Richard slid his hand over the desk's shiny black surface. "Yeah...where are we going to put it?"

"I think it would fit well in your study."

"Upstairs? Ugh." Richard groaned.

"Don't worry. I'll arrange removal of your old desk and replace it with this one while you're on your honeymoon. Speaking of which, it's getting late, and tomorrow you've got a long day, a long drive and a long night. You'd better get to bed."

Richard hugged him. "Thanks, Uncle Bram. You've been such a big help. I really appreciate all you've done for me, for us." He stood back and looked him in the eye. "I feel so grateful to have you in my life. Even though we've only gotten to know each other in the last twelve months, it's like I've known you forever. You're like a father to me."

A moistness coated Bram's warm gray eyes. "You'll always be a son to me."

Chapter Sixteen

The Endless War

Hobart, 1944

The funeral happened a week after Ethan's wife's death. And if looks could kill, his mother-in-law's gaze would have sent him hurtling into the hole in the ground to join his wife. His parents-in-law, their son and the rest of his wife's extended family stood as far away from him as possible, all decked out in black, in sympathy with the occasion and the gloomy, overcast day.

Straight after the burial, Ethan went to the hospital and held his daughter — the little piece of his wife he had left. He loved their child, even though she'd killed his wife and torn his life apart. But she'd had no control over the damage she'd caused. He was to blame, not an innocent baby.

He should have known it would end in disaster when his wife had become unwell straight after conception. Though, given her strong Catholic background, she never would have considered an abortion. And he never would have pushed for one, never could condone murder. And yet, his decision had led to death, the death of the love of his life.

His daughter stirred in his arms and squawked like a hungry baby bird. One of the nurses approached him with a bottle. "She's due for this. Would you like to feed her?"

"Ah…"

"Go on. Give it a try. You'll need to get used to it. You'll be doing it on your own when she's discharged, which should only be about a week away."

On my own. The words were a reality-jolting reminder of his harsh new world. He accepted the bottle and guided the teat into the baby's mouth. She clamped onto it and sucked like she hadn't been fed for days. Her insatiable appetite suggested she'd put on size and weight at a good rate.

When she'd finished, he gave the empty bottle to the nurse on duty, and she provided instructions and a demonstration on how to burp and change his daughter, then placed her back in her crib.

He stared at the ID card with his surname and no first name. With so much going on, he hadn't been up to naming her. In the end, he decided on her mother's name. It suited her sweet little face and voracious appetite. It created a living memory.

* * * *

Nappy change after nappy change, bottle-feed after bottle-feed, sleepless night after sleepless night… The regimented routine and reduced rest felt like being back in the Violet army instead of home.

On top of that, Ethan had to resume work and provide for them but he couldn't look after his baby and hold down a job at the same time. And he couldn't afford to employ someone.

Ethan stared at the silent phone, sitting alone on the hallway table. Seeing his wife's family wanted nothing to do with him, he pushed past his reluctance and dialed his parents' number.

No answer.

After his daughter woke from her nap, he tried again. Still no response. *Odd.* They rarely went out in the afternoon sun. So he packed his daughter into the car, and drove past their mansion. Mail spewed from their letterbox and the grass had grown to jungle proportions.

Ethan put his daughter in a hand-carry bassinet, walked up to the front door and knocked. Nothing. He tried the handle and it opened. The stench of stale food struck him in the nose like a nauseating punch.

In the kitchen, food decayed in a saucepan on the stove, and on the bench, two plates sat covered in dust. They'd left in a hurry. He hadn't seen his parents since his engagement, a couple of years before, and, by the look of the place, they'd gone soon after.

Had the extremist Jade faction found them and taken them prisoner? Or maybe the Sub Rosa Corporation? He'd heard on the Violet grapevine that they were collecting vampire specimens.

Ethan glanced at his sleeping daughter. No matter which explanation, he and his baby were at risk. He needed to get her somewhere safe, somewhere away from him.

Possibly his parents-in-law. If he promised to stay away and fully gave her over into their care, surely they would look after her. Their granddaughter remained the closest connection to their deceased daughter.

Ethan drove to his in-laws' home and stood on the doorstep, rocking the bassinet and preparing himself. The outcome could go either way. He pressed the doorbell, his heart pound-pound-pounding in his chest.

William opened the door, jumped back, held up two fingers in the shape of a cross and slammed the door shut.

Confusion slapped him hard across the face. Did they know about him? He rang the bell again and this time, his father-in-law answered.

"Leave us alone, you freak!" he said, his voice a venomous bite.

Freak? They must have found out about his background. Somehow. "Please, hear me ou—"

"No!"

"Think of your granddaughter," he pleaded.

"Listen here and listen good. We don't want anything to do with you or your spawn. Go and take her away from here. We never want to see either of you again. Do you understand?" The man's anger stabbed at him like knife slashes to his heart.

Spawn? They had to know about his Norwegian-Violet heritage. But how? "Don't you understand? She's half your daughter."

"She's half you, too," he said, and slammed the door in his face.

Ethan drove home, trying to keep his mind on task, trying not to be persuaded by emotion. Being in the army had taught him to switch off, to focus on the bigger picture, the greater good. And if he had any chance of making the best decision now, he had to employ the same tactics.

Yes, he wanted to keep his daughter with him. Yes, he wanted to look after her and teach her right from wrong. Yes, he wanted to be able to tell her all about her wonderful mother. But he couldn't.

No matter how devastating, no matter what he wanted, he had to face facts. He had to do the right thing for her, and that meant arranging a life away from him, at least for the moment.

When he got back to the house, he fed, burped and changed his sweet little rosebud and packed her things while she slept. He'd found an orphanage for girls in Hobart—St Joseph's—a large, sterile-white building run by Catholic nuns. He preferred an environment without a religious agenda but he didn't have much of a choice.

Ethan wanted to leave it until tomorrow but he knew, if he did, he might change his mind. He couldn't allow himself to falter, to reconsider keeping her with him, no matter how much it hurt.

Once he'd packed all her belongings, he drove her to the orphanage. Ethan held her in his arms one last time. "Hopefully you'll see it in your heart to forgive me." He kissed her forehead, sleepy eyes and rose-tinted chubby cheeks.

She opened her blue, violet-tinged eyes and stared into his, as though comprehending the need for a new beginning. He cuddled her. "I love you, and I always will."

* * * *

Not even six months later, Ethan trudged deep down in the trenches in Papua New Guinea with a rifle in his hand, waiting. His troop had been trekking through rugged tropical terrain for days in rainy, humid, muddy, miserable weather.

Men had died all around him, not from shotgun wounds or bomb blasts but from mites and mosquitoes and the poor sanitary conditions. Living in such close quarters, with restricted access to nutritious food, created the perfect breeding ground to develop and spread disease.

However, his half-Violet status gave him an edge. His additional white blood cells made him stronger, fitter, more resistant to disease, quicker to heal when wounded and a lot harder to kill. Plus, he could top himself up on animal blood. And given the revolting conditions, there were plenty of rodents around.

Sweat dripped off his face and ran down his back. An almost-permanent film of moisture coated his sore, fatigued body, reappearing within seconds of drying off after a wash.

It was disgusting. The one thing he didn't have over the humans was tolerance to sunlight. He stayed covered in his army gear, including a broad-brimmed hat, most of the time, which didn't help with the heat but had become essential to prevent him petering out.

Ethan stopped under the shade of a tree, lifted off his hat and poured some tepid water over his sweat-soaked hair and face. Then he guzzled down half the contents of his canteen and sank to the ground.

"Are you okay?" one of his crew members asked.

Ethan glanced up. He desperately needed time out from the sun, a decent shade break. However, his troop commander wouldn't let him fall too far behind. So, no, he wasn't okay—far from it. "I just need to rest for a minute. I'll catch up with you."

The soldier squatted down, looked around him then fixed his gaze on Ethan. "What would you say if I told you I could get you out of here?"

"I'd say you're suffering from heat-stroke-inflicted delusions."

"Seriously, mate. I know a way."

Ethan laughed. "Sure you do. Death."

The guy chuckled. "Mark my words... By the end of the week, you'll have more shade than you know what to do with."

More shade. How did the guy know cover held so much importance to him? Was he one of the few humans who knew of his kind? And if so, why did he want to assist him? Suspicion spread like tentacles and twisted around his gut.

"I'll believe it when I see it." He stared into the soldier's clay-colored eyes. "Why do you want to help me, anyway? We've hardly spoken two words to each other."

"I can see you're struggling, particularly during the day. Some of the guys are concerned you're a liability, putting the troop in unnecessary danger with all your frequent shade stops."

That might be part of the agenda, though the guy hid the rest. Ethan could see it in the soldier's insincere smile and the over-excited flicker in his chameleon eyes.

"I definitely don't want to put any of you in danger. So, I'm assuming you've arranged night detail for me in a more static location?"

"You could say that. I can't give you any further information at the moment, but as soon as everything is organized, you'll be contacted and shipped off."

* * * *

Zap!

Ethan awoke to a buzz of pain, shuddering and jolting. Two soldiers stood over him — the clay-eyed chameleon and one he didn't recognize — holding some sort of stun guns. He tried to move and couldn't. His sensation had shut off, leaving him totally at their mercy.

They cuffed him, loaded him onto a plane, and while the unknown man played pilot to an unknown destination, his army colleague stood watch, dosing him up with shock after shock to force his surrender. *Where are they taking me? And for what purpose?*

They landed, dragged him off the plane, and it all made sense. He was back in Norway, a prisoner of war of a different kind, captured not by the World War II enemies — the Germans or Japanese — but by full humans. By Sub Rosa.

The soldier had been right. He did have access to increased shade, inside a dingy cell in the frosty Trondheim climate. Although he preferred it to the humidity, he was trapped. He languished in his confined quarters for days, teetering on the edge of unrelenting tiredness

Blood. He needed it, relied on it to rejuvenate him. Would they provide some? So far, they'd only offered sloppy, overcooked meat or fish and vegetable stew. It stopped his hunger pangs, temporarily, but he needed to quench a deeper thirst, a deeper hunger.

Sniff. Sniff, sniff, sniff.

Ethan struggled to his feet, his nose drawing him to his cell door. The distinctive earthy aroma of rat. He didn't care, as long as he got a red blood boost. Now. Without it, he could function, barely, but ended up with accelerated depletion of white blood cells, which led to chronic fatigue. Heavy, slow and lethargic, it felt like running on fifty percent less fuel.

Regular ingestion of red blood was a required staple to provide the white blood cells with enough nutrients. Ethan cringed at the thought of how the three-quarter and full-caste Violets were coping. Their red blood requirements were exhaustive, impossible for staff to meet, which could only lead to one outcome — mass starvation and multiple deaths.

He stopped, clanging his cuffed hands against the metal. The strong scent dissipated. He must have sunk so far into delirium that his mind had started playing tricks. He couldn't see a rat, not in reality. It had to have been a malnutrition-inspired mirage.

A guard peered through the eye-hole of the thick, metal door. "Move back."

Ethan did, and, using an adrenaline-fueled emergency store of energy, sped past the dumbfounded man, setting up a merry-go-round of escape and recapture, escape and recapture. Until the sunlight bars happened in the mid-1980s.

They stopped breakouts.

Dead.

According to Beauregarde — the Violet escapologist and spy — Sub Rosa used a combination of natural sunlight together with solar power, to stream through the concentrated beams of light twenty-four hours a day to keep the rest of the vampires captive.

Considering how his life had turned out, Ethan almost rejoiced at his decision to give his daughter away. He'd hate for her to be a prisoner, to live a life of restriction and heartache. He reached into his top bedside drawer and pulled out a picture frame with a photo of her as a baby. She would be a grown woman of sixty-one now.

He kissed the photo and held it to his chest. Having inherited his Violet genetics, she'd have some of his coloring and look half her age, assuming she'd stayed alive. His gut insisted she had. Hopefully, she had found a good man, one she loved who could love and support her…as he never could.

During one of his short escapes in 1951 he had sent her a keepsake and brief note, but he hadn't mentioned anything about her lineage, mostly to protect her, in case packages were intercepted and checked. Whether she'd received it and ever thought of him, he had no clue.

Ethan sat up, had another swig of special purple wine and put his daughter's photo beside him on the pillow. That familiar floaty, alcoholic buzz really started to hit him. The beautiful mind-escape, tipsy state felt so good…at the start.

But the more he drank, the more buried memories floated to the surface, until he almost drowned in a montage of horrific images from his days in the Violet army, before he and his parents had emigrated to Australia in 1941, before he had gotten captured by Sub Rosa. When he'd only had to worry about the civil war between the Violets and the Jades.

Even though over sixty years had passed, he relived the same incident over and over like a recurring nightmare.

* * * *

Jade POW camp, northern Norway, 1941

Deep jade eyes bored into Ethan's. "Tell me what you know."

Sunlight-infused chains bit into Ethan's body and burned his ankles, wrists and torso. He was too weak to break away, but he remained strong enough not to give in. He closed his eyes and refused to respond.

"Tell me what you know or you'll regret it."

Regret it in what way? Any decent soldier would fight to the death for his cause. He stared back, his defiant silence further riling up his Jade captors.

"Okay, if that's the way you want to play it," the leader said and pushed Ethan's chair into the bright sunlight. Normally, he wouldn't care too much. Most places on earth had respite from the sun for at least a few hours, but not the northern tip of Norway in the peak of summer.

Ethan sat out in the unrelenting sunshine, the chains scorching and blistering his skin. The longer they left him out there, the more it felt like sitting in the middle of a bonfire with flames frying his body and burning right to the bone marrow. He could almost hear the sizzling and popping of each cell, like popcorn thrown in a scalding saucepan on the stove.

The barren landscape looked desert-like, but instead of sand, boulders dotted the bald patches of grass. The sea stretched out ahead and he licked his parched lips as though to lap up any lingering moisture from the misty air.

Water. It was the only word his brain could conjure. His gritty eyes stung and he closed them to conserve what little liquid he had left. Blurry images of polar bears and woolly mammoths pouring water down his throat played in his mind and he dropped his head forward, giving in to delirium. He started mumbling, a nonsensical blathering of incoherent words.

Shade. The Jades pulled him into the shade. He opened his eyes — back in the hut. Welcome respite. The leader shoved his face right in Ethan's. He had combustible green eyes, pasty white skin and a snide smile. Ethan was barely conscious and his head lolled. He was too out of it to be scared.

"Tell me what you know."

You mean about Violets moving in to overtake Jade-occupied areas?

The Jade's blunt finger poked at the weeping welts on Ethan's chest. "Tell me what you know."

Ethan groaned and clamped his teeth together to close off any pain-induced outbursts.

"Tell me what you know."

About the bomb scare we're planning on the Jade quarters. "Never." He collected the little strength he had in reserve and sat up straight, his eyes fierce with loyal determination.

"Who else is involved?"

Ethan dropped back into the 'no reply' strategy, his lips sealed tight.

The leader grabbed him by the throat. "Who. Else. Is. Involved?"

Ethan stared at the splintered timber walls, enemy sunlight slipping through the cracks, his short, sharp, suffocated breaths, eating up the silence.

The Jade released his death grip and Ethan gasped in lungfuls of life-sustaining air. "If you don't tell me, your family will pay." The corner of the man's mouth flickered with his signature snide smile again.

Fucking bastard.

Ethan's stomach tensed, though experience had made him an expert at masking his fear. *Do they know about my parents?* Of course they did, just like the Violets knew all the ins and outs of the Jade faction members. But would they really hurt them?

So far, both sides had only targeted group members. They'd threatened harm to their families, but none had actually gone through with it.

However, he wasn't a Jade. Ethan wouldn't put it past their current, emotionally unstable-looking leader. The rest of the Jade pack had to okay it, though, and Ethan couldn't see that happening. They'd do their best to avoid bad Jade press.

If they attacked one of Ethan's family members, they'd sink below the Violets, in the Jade community's estimation, and the Jade army couldn't stand that. Some Jades might even abandon the cause if they thought the group unreasonable, a rogue mob refusing to represent their community's best interests.

Ethan stayed silent, but his glare said, *Go ahead and try it. You'll have hell to pay.*

The Jade gritted his teeth and stormed off. The rest of the crew dragged Ethan from the decaying timber hut and threw him, still bound, back in the sun, where he withered into unconsciousness.

He woke up at home, in his own bed, with no knowledge of how he'd gotten there. Covered in bruises, burns and scaly, red blotches, his skin stung like he'd suffered severe sunburn. His whole body slumped with heavy-limbed weakness, and he felt hot and tight all over.

After a few days, his body near healed, his Violet compatriots visited, told him about the raid and praised him for not cracking under the pressure. A week later, under protest, his parents lugged him onto a boat to the other side of the world, to Tasmania, Australia.

The steady glare and hum of the sunlight bars returned Ethan to the grim reality. Out of his half-dozing half-inebriated post-traumatic stress state. Still living, if it could be called that, in a cell inside Sub Rosa in 2005.

One of the by-products of Sub Rosa's vampire collection had been the disintegration of the Violet and Jade factions.

Capture.

Imprisonment.

Segregation.

When the Violet and Jade faction members weren't being experimented on, most of them sat, wasting away in their Norway compound cages, like him. But the unresolved civil war continued to simmer below the surface.

Ethan's mind still swam from the alcohol-fueled trip down every dark corner of memory lane and he turned to his daughter's picture, lying on the pillow, and touched her sweet, innocent face. Now he'd do anything to get back to Tasmania — to get back to her.

Chapter Seventeen

The Tie that Binds

The wedding day, July 1965

The doorbell rang. Eva's eyes snapped open and she reached for her watch on the bedside table — nine-o-three. She had a quick stretch, threw on her dressing gown and opened the front door. On the patio lay a bunch of velvety red roses with yellow centers — classic Eva roses, going by the accompanying information card.

Her palm pressed against her pounding heart. *Richard.*

She carried the lightly perfumed bunch of flowers into the kitchen and put them in a crystal vase. Then she ripped open the small red envelope, attached to the red and gold wrapping paper. On a white card, Richard had scrawled a poem in his elegant, backward-slanted handwriting.

Ode to Eva

Bewitching blue-violet eyes

Rich cocoa-brown hair
Cascading
Over porcelain perfection.
Alluring angel
Possessing my mind
I crave your holy touch,
You've carved a place in my heart
A supernatural living space
Of synchronistic bliss.
My true soulmate, destined for
Dual paradise
Together, eternally.

She squealed and held the card to her chest. Then she read it again and again and again. Excitement exploded inside her like crackling, popping candy.

Still buzzing, she had a shower and returned to her room to pack her overnight bag. Greer's gift lay in a messy *maybe* pile on the bed. Should she take it? Eva held up the sheer white fabric to the light. Seriously, what was the point? Richard would see everything through it.

Greer had given the gift to both of them, though. Eva owed Richard the pleasure of a close-up view, so he could make up his own mind. She shoved the negligee set into her overnight bag and struggled to close the zip. She should take some clothes out. Honeymoons weren't known for wearing many outfits, outside of a birthday suit.

Eva peeled the plastic off her grandmother's wedding dress, removed the hanger and carefully stepped into the delicate folds of material. She did up the tiny buttons at the back and inspected herself in her bedroom mirror.

Exquisite lace covered the upper bodice of the off-white dress, right up to her neck, and the sleeves flared out from her elbow to her wrist in a bellbottom design. The smooth silk continued in a figure-hugging style past her hips, highlighting her petite, shapely body, then fell into a soft, A-line cut with a small train.

She left her hair out and still had to secure the waist-length, chiffon veil. In her overnight bag, she included a fur wrap for later. Although it was a sunny, cold winter's day, her nerves acted like a faulty thermostat, cranking up the heat.

Eva had just finished her eye makeup when the photographer arrived. He took a series of shots, with and without her veil, in and around the house, then he drove to Richard's place before heading to the church.

An elegant, black 1920s car arrived to pick her up at two-forty-five p.m., and she made it to the church in ten minutes. Greer met her outside, wearing a body-hugging, cleavage-boosting, hot-pink dress and holding a colorful bouquet of wildflowers.

"You look killer!" Greer said, grabbing her hand.

"Thanks. So do you."

They walked up the steps leading into the cute, bluestone church and Greer reached into a cardboard box inside the entrance. "Oh, and here's your bouquet. Can't forget your flowers."

She handed Eva a bunch of hot-pink roses with greenery woven through them. "They're beautiful. And they smell divine."

"Thanks, I thought you'd approve."

The priest joined them. "Are you ready?"

"Yes." A rush of nerves scrambled through Eva's system.

The wedding march started and Greer walked her down the aisle. Eva wobbled on weak legs, like a leaking air mattress ready to deflate.

Richard and Salvator stood at the front, with leadlight windows casting a rainbow of scattered light across them and the guests seated in the two columns of pews. Suave and sexy were the only words to describe Richard in his black suit, hot-pink paisley tie and matching rose buttonhole corsage. Salvator scrubbed up a treat, too, in a similar, though slightly creased suit.

When Eva reached Richard, he smiled the happiest, most seductive smile she had ever seen. He found her hand and love and warmth emanated from his touch.

After the ceremony, she and Richard were attacked with colorful confetti and swarmed by the small group of guests offering their congratulations. Bram squeezed his way in first, gave them both a huge hug and kissed Eva on the cheek.

Greer followed with a squishy hug and kiss, then Salvator shook Richard's hand, moved to her and hesitated, like he wasn't quite sure what to do. Eva smiled, and he finally leaned in and gave her a chaste kiss on the cheek.

The cozy little party walked to a nearby sandstone pub to start the reception. After dinner, Eva and Richard had their first dance to *Hold Me, Thrill Me, Kiss Me* by Mel Carter.

Eva threaded her arms around his neck and rested her head against his chest. "I love this song."

"It's special to me, too. It's the first song we ever danced to."

Her gaze met his and she fought back the advancing army of emotion. "Thank you for this, and for all the lovely, thoughtful poems and gifts. You're a true romantic, you know that? I'm so lucky."

"I'm the lucky one. Look at you. You're beautiful...in every way."

She blushed and nestled into him. Not only was her husband considerate but also a great mover, on and off the dance floor. Her stomach twisted with anxiety and tangled with elation and anticipation. In only a few hours, they would physically connect for the first time as husband and wife.

Baby I'm Yours by Barbara Lewis came on next, and the rest of the guests joined them on the polished timber floor.

She stared into his eyes. He'd also remembered the second song they'd danced to, the song that seemed to strengthen their bond.

Richard smiled at her in an it-would-be-impossible-to-love-you-more way.

At five-thirty p.m. they cut the wedding cake — non-traditional lemon meringue — thanked the guests for coming and had a final, farewell dance.

While the party continued in the pub, Bram ushered Richard and Eva to his green and cream Holden. "Before you go, I just want to wish you a safe and enjoyable journey and let you know I'll be away when you return. I've been planning to travel for a while and I think this is the perfect time."

Eva clutched his arm. "Please don't go because you think we need time alone."

Bram patted her hand. "You're a very sweet young lady. Just think of it as part of my wedding gift to you...along with the house."

Richard's eyes nearly shot right out of their sockets. "No. We can't accept the house."

Eva shifted away from Bram and stood by her husband, her hand slipping around his. "That's way too generous."

"No, it's not. It's rightfully yours, anyway, Richard. I'm just handing it over a bit earlier."

"You're coming back, aren't you?" Richard asked.

"Yes, but I've built myself a place a kilometer or so away."

Eva couldn't stop the frown from showing her displeasure. "You don't have to move out."

"I know, but I want to. No matter what you say, it's good for you to have some time together, just the two of you as a couple. Don't worry. I'll be coming over for dinner every night." The cheeky twinkle in his eye reminded her so much of her husband.

Richard hugged his uncle. "I don't know what to say except thank you and have a safe trip."

Eva embraced Bram next. "And don't be away too long." For some reason, it felt more like 'goodbye' than 'see you soon'.

"You two had better get going or else you'll be too exhausted to enjoy the best part of your special day." Bram's giant grin sent a rush of heat to Eva's cheeks.

* * * *

"Eva."

She jolted awake and opened her eyes. A light shone through the window of a quaint log cabin, breaking through the darkness.

Richard had the car door open and held her hand, his green eyes sparkling with seduction. "We're here."

Frosty wind sliced into her skin like razor blades, and she shivered. Richard assisted her still-sleepy body out of the car and put his arm around her. He led her up the steps to the cabin, the snow fresh and powdery beneath her shoes. Pristine white snow also coated the roof, icicles hung from the eaves like stalactites and the crisp air smelled of smoked pine and eucalyptus.

They stopped on the landing while he opened the front door then he whisked her into his arms and carried her over the threshold. She clung to him and he lowered her onto a love seat in front of a crackling fire. "Our humble abode, or should I say 'love shack', for the next couple of nights, Mrs. Hall."

Mrs. Hall. Excitement bubbled up inside her like a surging hot spring. *I have a husband.* And, tonight, they were going to explore every part of their newlywed status. Passion pumped through her veins at the prospect.

The cabin felt snug and much warmer than she'd expected. The large window at the far end of the room had to be double-glazed. With below-zero temperatures outside, indoors remained comfortable without a coat. Most likely the owners had fitted the cabin with heating and the fireplace was more a decorative feature, to create a romantic atmosphere for couples. It worked.

Richard grabbed a bottle of champagne from the bar fridge, filled a couple of tall glasses and joined her on the couch.

"What about our bags?"

He handed her a glass. "I already brought them in."

She stared at the champagne, fizzing and popping — totally opposite to her fizzed-out response to Richard on the drive over. "I'm so sorry. I must have slept most of the way."

"Don't worry about it. You can make it up to me tonight, seeing you're nice and refreshed," he said, his tone imbibed with mischief.

Scorching heat scalded her skin.

He raised his glass to hers. "How about a toast — to my wonderful wife."

"To my handsome husband."

"Cheers!" they said in unison and had a drink.

Eva put her glass down on the coffee table and Richard lifted her onto his lap. His cock nudged her hip, hard and ready and raring to go right now. Her heart rate doubled in a single second.

He covered her lips with his and she wound her arms around his neck, her nipples straining against the corseting bodice of her dress. They made out like reunited lovers, and he began unbuttoning her wedding gown, his cool fingers brushing her flushed skin.

She pulled away, breathless, and had a sip of champagne. Why was she suddenly so anxious? For weeks she'd been dying for this moment and now, she felt nail-biting, core-clenching nerves. It had to be the high expectation of the occasion. *What if I don't satisfy him? What if the sex doesn't meet our expectations? What if it really hurts? No.* They were confirmed soulmates, so the sex should be sensational.

Richard tilted her chin up and looked into her eyes. "Is everything okay?"

"Yes." *Sort of.* A smile stalled on her lips. *Is he nervous too?* If so, he hid it pretty well. "Um…I'll be back in a minute. Stay here, okay?"

He brushed his lips against hers. "Don't be too long or I'll come in after you."

With a stammered laugh, she hopped off his lap and hurried into the bedroom. She needed to transform from virginal bride to sexy wife. Maybe the skimpy outfit would boost her confidence and give her the edge she needed for a successful seduction.

Eva turned on the lamp and stared at her bloated overnight bag, sitting rigid in the corner. She unzipped it and pulled out the gift Greer had bought them.

You can do this.

She ducked across the narrow passageway to the compact bathroom, had a quick shower and threw on the translucent chiffon negligee. From her waist down, no hair remained, thanks to Greer. During the week, she'd persuaded Eva to shave her legs, bikini line and deep into the depths of her pubic area as well.

Her friend's parting words were branded in her brain. *'Richard will love your soft, smooth skin, and you will too when you feel his tongue –* '

She blushed and her core clenched.

"Eva, are you okay?" Richard called out.

"Yes! I'll be there in a minute."

Her reflection looked startled – scared, not sexy. "Think hot, think foxy and he will, too." She sighed. "I need to do better than that!" She thought for a moment. Whether he liked her outfit or not, the outcome would be the same. She'd be out of it in seconds." She laughed to herself. "Okay, here goes…"

Eva stepped out of the bathroom and tiptoed down the hallway to rejoin Richard. However, he wasn't where she'd left him. Her gaze darted across the room to where he was topping up their glasses with more champagne. His unbuttoned shirt hung loose over his pants, and he'd rolled up his sleeves, sending her heart racing at a thousand beats per minute.

She took another step and a floorboard creaked beneath her feet. He turned to her, nearly dropping the bottle in his hand.

"What do you think?" she asked.

"What do I think?" Richard put the bottle on the small dining table and focused all his attention on her. "You're like my own, beautifully wrapped, perfect present, in every sense of the word. You look" — he sighed — "mouth-watering."

Eva's heart danced with delight at his enthusiastic response.

His gaze roamed over her barely-clad body and he licked his lips. "Let me guess...our present from Greer."

"Pretty obvious, huh?"

"Remind me to thank her when we get back." He met her in the center of the room, his green eyes dark with lust.

Richard reached up, undid the flimsy tie between her breasts, and the negligee fell open, revealing her bare chest and tummy. He breathed out hard and ran his hands over her hypersensitive skin. Then he stepped aside and slowly circled her, checking her out from every angle and murmuring in appreciation.

When he faced her again, he slipped the shoestring straps down her arms and her negligee dropped to the floor. With shaking hands, she pushed his shirt off his broad shoulders and moved to undo his belt and pants, brushing his hardness with her fingers. Richard groaned and kicked his trousers off onto their small pile of discarded clothing.

He knelt before her, hooked his fingers into the corners of her see-through panties and slid them down. She tried to tame her loud, labored breathing, her body pulsing with budding physical need. Richard tossed the scrap of material aside and kissed her navel, sending shivers of desire deep between her legs.

"You're so beautiful." He covered her skin with light, teasing kisses where her pubic hair used to be, then he paused and took a long, deep breath. "You smell incredible."

Her knees nearly buckled with the weight of his wonderful words.

Richard returned his mouth to her skin, his tongue warm and moist, his breath hot. Pure, wicked pleasure pulsed through her, just as Greer had said. Eva closed her eyes, ran her fingers through his thick hair and held him close, savoring every scintillating sensation. She had never felt so wanted, so adored, so special.

He trailed his lips back up her body and stood, holding her face between his hands. He leaned in and kissed her parted lips with such tenderness and longing that any lingering trace of worry disappeared. Being with him felt like home—welcoming, comfortable and exciting.

She tugged on his boxer shorts and his cock sprang free. *Oh my!* So big—pushing eight inches big, she'd guess. Richard stepped out of his boxers and pulled her in, skin against skin. She gasped, electricity soaring through her body like a lightning storm of lust.

Eva slid her arms around his neck and he picked her up and carried her to the king-size, canopy bed. He lowered her onto it, his lips still locked on hers, his hot body contrasting with the cool, white sheet against her back.

The silver-pink moonlight streamed through the window, highlighting Richard's rippling muscles as he explored her. He paused over her breasts and licked each nipple with the tip of his tongue, then used the flat of it on the hard buds, one at a time, until she whimpered and writhed.

He sucked on one nipple and rolled the other between the pad of his thumb and finger, the ache between her legs growing stronger, deeper, so close to coming. And he hadn't even reached her throbbing pleasure point yet. He continued the journey down her body, seeming to be everywhere at once with his hands and mouth, instigating a rapturous sort of torture.

Eva desperately wanted to climax but didn't want the foreplay to end. And he kept her right on that delicious edge.

Then he claimed her sex with his mouth. She jolted, a surge of pleasure spreading from her core to the tips of her toes. Eva bent her knees and spread her legs wide for him, allowing Richard full access to her inner depths, and he licked, sucked and tantalized her flesh, groaning in approval. She hovered on the edge of climax, and he pulled back.

Nooooo! She stared up at him and mewled with frustration at her unmet need.

A roguish grin coated his wet lips.

"Please—" Before she could finish her plea, he returned right to where she needed him most. But instead of giving her aching, swollen bud the attention it required, he licked her entrance and thrust his tongue inside.

She gasped. Fingers or his cock, she'd expected, but his tongue…?

He slipped it straight out and his gaze found hers. "Is that okay?"

She dragged herself away from the haze of new feelings. Not exactly okay, though not bad, more...weird, invasive, intimate.

Eva nodded, too overwhelmed to form words, and he slid his tongue along her seam and right back inside her, where he began a steady, rhythmic plunging pace. In .and out. In and out. In and — his fingers joined the mix, rubbing her highly aroused mound — *Oh. My. God* — out.

The sensations had shifted to good-weird. *Really* good-weird. Glorious weird. Greer had gone on and on and on about how amazing internal stimulation felt but Eva had never been game to try it, not with her own fingers and definitely not with a man. Until now. Until —

"Richard!" she screamed, ecstasy culminating into an earth-shattering orgasm. However, he didn't stop. He continued his sensual assault, his tongue feather light at first, delving into every little crease, peak and crevice, drawing out the immense pleasure.

"Mmm...you're so sweet and wet," he said, his voice husky with want. He focused on her clitoris, picking up the licking speed and pressure, and this time he gently inserted two fingers inside her. She pushed into him and a building ache exploded into another body-shuddering orgasm.

"Oh yes!" she cried, hardly recognizing her shameless voice.

He kissed her sensitive sex as though he worshiped it — worshiped her — and she grabbed his head and tilted it up so she could kiss his moist lips. Tasting herself on him was an unexpected surprise, a gift of bliss that kept on giving. His green gaze was wild with longing and he shifted above her.

"I need you. *Now*," she whispered against his lips.

With a tender thrust, he entered her with his large cock. Eva flinched, the sting from his size slicing through the euphoria.

He locked his gaze on hers. "You okay?"

She tried to relax the pain-induced tension in her face. "Yes."

He eased out and in again, bit by painful bit, and she kissed him to disguise the discomfort.

His eyes searched hers. "Are you sure?"

She nodded. Although it hurt, she didn't want him to stop. She'd adjust to it. She just needed some time to stretch—or so Greer had said. And Richard had given her so much pleasure already that she wanted him to enjoy his own release.

Richard persisted with slow, cautious thrusts, keeping his eyes focused on hers the whole time, the experience intense and profound and other-worldly. As renewed pleasure overtook the pain, she began to move with him, encouraging him to thrust deeper, faster.

He hit a spot of pure ecstasy and she moaned, over and over.

A low rumble of desire growled in his throat. "Eva!" He groaned and stilled, his orgasm engulfing his strong, virile body. In seconds, she came with force around him, acute aftershocks rippling through to every single cell. He kept on moving, extending the exquisite sensation so it lasted and lasted and lasted.

Richard remained inside her as they returned to earth. He kissed her forehead, temples, nose and mouth as their breathing recovered from the exhilarating exertion.

His passion-filled eyes studied hers. "How was that?"

A huge, sated smile spread across her lips. "Amazing!"

"More than amazing." Richard carefully slid out of her and lay on his back.

She closed her eyes, relishing the flood of post-sex satisfaction.

"Aren't you going to give your husband a hug?"

Eva glanced at him, his smile as massive as hers, lifted the doona over them and snuggled into his side.

Richard kissed the top of her head. "Are you warm enough?"

"Yes, you?"

"Yeah, I'm nice and toasty." He caressed her hair and back, his fingers gentle and calming. "Are you sore? Be honest with me."

"A little, but it's hardly noticeable. Definitely not enough to deter me from doing it again."

"Now?" he asked, his voice incredulous.

She laughed. "No, right now I think we need some sleep. Though some wake-up sex would be nice."

"Mmm…more than nice."

* * * *

Eva roused, her eyes fluttering open. The sun shone through the large, floor-to-ceiling window, casting soft, rose-gold rays across the sprawling, winter wonderland. *Not my bedroom.*

Her brain startled, the cogs of the present clicking into place and switching out of sleep. *On my honeymoon with my incredible husband.* And they'd had some sensational sex the previous night.

A sordid array of images from their erotic encounter swarmed her consciousness. The way he'd tongued her down below with a look of love and adoration in his eyes, the way he'd abandoned all control and given himself to her in his release, the way their bodies had fit together like they'd been created for each other.

They had a license to touch anywhere and everywhere, now that they were officially husband and wife. That familiar ache throbbed between her legs. She stared at the clear blue sky and snowcapped mountains reflected in the still lake, in an attempt to cool her hot thoughts.

Richard pressed his chest against her back and cuddled her tighter. "Are you awake?"

"I am now," she said, in a cheeky, just-woke-up voice.

He chuckled, his warm breath caressing her ear.

"Isn't the view breathtaking?" she said.

He scooped her hair aside and kissed the base of her neck. "*You're* breathtaking."

She sighed.

He rolled her nipple between his forefinger and thumb, and slid his other hand over her belly and down to stroke her sex.

"Mmmm…" she moaned, pressing into his skillful hands. He sought out her clitoris, rubbed quicker and harder, and she climaxed, throwing her head back against his chest and crying out his name.

She'd hardly had a moment to recover when he nipped the nape of her neck, sending tingles skittering down her spine, and carved out a sensual path along her back, bottom, legs, soles of her feet, then slowly made his way up to her ear.

"I want you," he whispered.

His voice sounded so damn sexy that she almost came again at the sound of it. Eva turned to face him, kissed him hard on the mouth and pushed him onto his back.

She straddled his narrow hips, ran her hands and lips down his taut chest and six-pack stomach and took the full length of his already-erect cock into her mouth.

Garbled words merged with groans and he gripped her head, his body trembling as she stroked and licked his shaft. Pleasuring him to the point of incoherence turned her on, going by the growing wetness between her legs.

She bathed his cock in saliva and concentrated her sucking on the underside of the head, making him buck beneath her. Then she pulled back, trailed her tongue down to his balls and gave them a slow, deliberate lick.

"Fuck." He squeezed his eyes shut, his face contorted with his last traces of control.

Eva returned to his cock, teasing him until he pleaded for her to make him come. And she did, a guttural groan tearing from his throat as he spurted into her mouth. He tasted hot and silky with a splash of salt. She swallowed and licked her lips. Her husband was all-round post-orgasm delectable.

Richard lifted her up his body and kissed her, sharing the remnants of his release.

"How did I do?" she asked, his body already having given her the answer. But she wanted to hear him say it.

He held her face in his hands, his eyes filled with eagerness. "Fucking incredible."

A victorious smile sprang onto her lips.

"This is way too much fun," he said, with a wolfish grin. "I don't want to leave here."

"Not even to have a shower?"

"Only if you join me."

Mmm...more sex. Was it possible to ever hit saturation point? So far, she couldn't see herself getting sick of it any time soon, not with Richard. Though they were in such a beautiful spot that they should explore what it had to offer, as well as each other. "I'd love to. But after we're done, we should try to see some of Cradle Mountain while we have the chance."

"We have an amazing view from the window."

She peered into his eyes. "Richard."

"Well, we do."

She shook her head and burrowed her face into his chest.

He tilted her chin up and kissed her. "I'm kidding...sort of."

She laughed.

"I promise we'll go for some drives and some scenic walks..."

And have some sex in the bush. The words were unspoken...but implied. "Just not today," she said, finishing the sentence for him.

"Yeah. I want us to relax and thoroughly enjoy each other."

Eva squeezed her thighs together. No argument there. Richard's compelling words were like a caress to her core. And she didn't want the pleasure to stop.

Chapter Eighteen

Homeward Bound

After a mind-blowing weekend of sex, hikes and breathtaking scenery, Richard and Eva embarked on the long drive back home. And even though they slotted in several kiss-and-cuddle stops, she ached for more.

When they were still an hour and a half away, she reached across and rubbed Richard's thigh. He glanced at her with an I-want-to-do-you-right-now look, turned off onto a boat ramp, away from the cabins dotting the main road, and parked overlooking Great Lake.

Snow dusted the tussocks, brush and eucalypts, and fog hovered over the great expanse of inky water, lit only by silvery moonlight. Spectacular, magical, reflecting their relationship.

Richard turned the headlights off but kept the car running and cranked up the heater. He unfastened his seatbelt, threw off his top, and reached across to the passenger side. Her heart slammed against her ribcage and a gush of I'm-ready juices soaked her panties. His smooth, wandering hands warmed her skin and he kissed her as though starved of her touch.

The glass steamed up and he pulled away, opened his window a smidgen and wound his seat back. *Good idea.* They didn't want to get caught by the police, doing it in the car. Eva slipped off her panties, left on her mini dress and long black boots and lifted her leg to straddle him.

Richard's green eyes glowed with lust. "Let me have a quick taste."

He held her hips, as she leaned back, and pulled her wet sex to his mouth. Her breath hitched. With slow, expert tongue strokes, he tantalized her clitoris and continued along the length of her seam, sewing the seed of an orgasm.

Richard glided her down his body and delved one hand between her legs, sending a rush of pre-climactic tingles to her pelvis. Then he cupped her bottom and she slid onto his hard cock and started grinding into his pubic bone. He moved his finger to massage the outer rim of her anal opening and she climaxed.

"Richard!"

"Oh, Eva!" he groaned and stilled, then together they rode out the wave of pleasure.

Panting, she fell against his naked chest, his heart belting out a post-run rhythm. "Wow. Just wow."

"That last little move didn't bother you?"

"I think it spurred me on."

He lifted her head up and looked into her eyes. "I thought I'd just try something. I'm really glad it worked."

"Oh, it worked all right," she said, her voice a soft, satisfied purr.

"Your openness and trust in me are so attractive. The more I get to know you, the more I love you."

"Same here." She dropped her head to his shoulder and rubbed the dusting of hair on his chest. "I can't believe we just had sex in your uncle's car!"

"I'll give it a thorough going over tomorrow, inside and out." He kissed the top of her head. "We should get home...so I can give you a thorough going over, inside and out, tonight."

They arrived home, *home*, and while Richard unloaded the car, Eva stepped inside the cool, quiet house. *Their* house. She shivered with cold and delight and went straight to turn on the heater.

During the week, she'd have to start packing up her place and move in with her husband. *Husband.* She sighed. She still couldn't quite believe it. Even signing to cancel her rental contract was surreal.

Smokey poked his head around the corner of the staircase, prowled over and rubbed against her legs. "Did you miss us, little guy?" Eva bent down, fluffed up the fur on his neck and gave him a pat.

"Looks like it." Richard walked past, loaded up with their belongings.

Eva stood and hurried toward him. "Let me help you."

He continued up the stairs. "Not a chance."

She appreciated his chivalry but asking for help didn't make him less of a man. She'd have to reinforce it to him, reinforce that they were partners and she was more than capable of assisting. If they worked together, they could relax a lot sooner. Okay, maybe not relax exactly. Her face grew hot just thinking about what Richard's 'thorough going over' entailed.

Eva followed Richard up to their bedroom—*their* bedroom—a soft, amber glow warming the hallway. She reached the threshold and halted in the doorway, struck by radiance.

Large white candles, with flames flickering, were strategically placed around the room, and a banner hung from the four-poster bed frame. Individual black squares with white writing spelled out, *Welcome home, Mrs. Hall*, with a red love heart at the beginning and end. She clutched her chest and sighed. *So romantic.*

Now it made sense why he'd insisted she stay away, so he could decorate the space. She ran over to Richard and flung her arms around him. "Thank you."

"Thank *you*. I've never been so happy."

Her gaze met his and she strained to hold back happy tears. "Me either." Richard was her family now. Her life. A part of her heart still wished she had a relationship with her dad—or that she'd at least gotten to meet him, know him. Though maybe he didn't want to be discovered.

He had helped create her, but it didn't mean he wanted the parental responsibility. The empty sliver of her heart would always pine for him, though. Having Richard made her realize that whether she found her father now or not, she'd be fulfilled—at least ninety percent.

Richard smiled and took her hand. "Now, before we christen the bed, come and have a look at this."

He led her into his study-cum-private library, where a gorgeous Gothic desk dominated the room. She didn't remember it from the last time she'd visited. "Where did you get that?"

"It's part of Salvator's wedding gift."

"You're kidding."

"Nope." He picked up something shimmery out of a small, black box. "And this is the other part." A gold chain with a rose-topped, gold-key pendant hung from his hand.

She fingered the intricate charm. "What's this?"

"Outside of being a lovely piece of jewelry, it also has another purpose." He placed his hand over a glossy panel on the front of the desk with a red-painted rose and pressed. It popped open and he slid the panel into a narrow cavity above the space, exposing a drawer with a gold lock.

Her mouth dropped open.

"The key opens it."

She leaned in and studied the pendant, glimmering in the candlelight. "Really?"

"Yep. I've already tried it."

"What a great idea. So ingenious." Eva let go of the key and straightened up. "We can't accept it, though. He must have spent a fortune. It's way too extravagant."

"I agree, but he insisted we have it. Take a look at this."

He gave her the note from Salvator, explaining his decision to pass the present onto them. A pang of sadness stabbed her heart. *Poor guy.* It was as though he'd trialed the Soulmate Serum himself and it had backfired.

Richard skimmed his hand over the shiny desk surface. "You have to admit it does look perfect in here, like it was made for this room."

"Yes, I can see why he thought of us." It seemed like she and Richard were destined not only to be with each other but also to befriend Salvator.

Richard unclasped the necklace and secured it around her neck. "It really looks lovely — delicate and beautiful, just like you."

Eva could feel the flush spreading across her skin like a fireball. "Thanks." She touched the cool, clever charm. "I suppose we should keep everything then. But we'll have to think of a way to repay him."

Chapter Nineteen

Exploring the Norway Experiment

Richard rushed to his office, key in hand, late on the first day back to work. Not ideal but it was well worth it, having awakened to muscle-melting sex with his wife, her whimpers and moans of pleasure still fresh in his ears.

When he arrived at his office door, Salvator stood in front of it.

Richard smiled and shook his hand. "What are you doing here?"

"Thought I'd come and say hello, welcome you back. How was Cradle Mountain?" he asked with a sly smile. *In other words, how was the sex?*

Eva, naked, straddling him, his cock buried deep within her cozy flesh and her head thrown back in ecstasy… "Amazing! Both the place and the company."

"I bet. I've heard it's a reasonably uncharted, breathtaking wilderness."

Richard grinned at his innuendo-infused reply. "Yeah, it certainly is. Oh, and thank you for your very generous gift."

"You're most welcome. I couldn't think of a better home for it," Salvator said with a bittersweet smile.

Richard unlocked the door and put his document bag on the desk.

Salvator hovered in the doorway. "There actually is something else I wanted to run by you, if you can spare a few minutes."

"Sure. Come in and shut the door." Richard gestured for him to take a seat and sat opposite.

"Have you heard about the Norway Experiment?"

"In passing. Some high-security project with handpicked, select staff working on it."

"That's right." Salvator's unblinking hazel eyes stared into his. "I've seen some of your work and I think you'd be a great addition to the team. I hope you don't mind, but I've put your name forward to management. If you're interested and accepted onto the project, it would mean a bit of a pay increase as well."

It looked like knowing Salvator had created a lot of positives — first, the success of the Soulmate Serum, and now a possible promotion. "What can I say? I'm flattered, though I'd like to know more about it first."

An excited glow radiated from Salvator's olive-skinned face. "I can give you an overview now, if you'd like. Then I've arranged a meeting with Harry Kennedy, the senior project manager, at eleven a.m."

"This isn't quite what I expected my first day back. I'd hoped to ease into things…"

Concern washed away his friend's enthusiasm. "The Norway Experiment is a great career advancement opportunity that isn't offered to everyone, but if you're not interested…"

A reassuring smile slid onto Richard's lips. "I am. But you might just need to be a little patient while I reengage my research brain. I'm suffering with a severe case of honeymoon fever."

Salvator chuckled. "I bet you are. I envy you. Eva is a very beautiful woman. I imagine it's difficult to concentrate on much else at the moment."

"You imagine right. A new, interesting project might be just what I need to rein in my thoughts — for a bit, anyway."

Salvator laughed. "Let's test out that theory then, shall we?" He shuffled his chair forward and clamped his gaze on Richard's. "Before I go into the project overview, I need to tell you that part of being accepted onto the program requires you to sign a non-disclosure agreement. You'll be working with some highly sensitive information and it's imperative it doesn't get out.'

"No problem. It makes sense to ensure project security."

"Great."

Richard pulled out a pad from the top drawer of his desk, picked up a pen and re-established eye contact.

"So," Salvator began, his voice low, "the Norway Experiment originated to eradicate faulty genes in the human race. But in order to proceed, Sub Rosa needed a test group. In the 1930s, ethics standards were lax in comparison to now, so it was easy to convince the board to carry out tests on a small group of people who had what was considered to be a 'defective' gene, for the good of all."

Richard scribbled away, jotting down key notes in point form.

"Things really got into full swing around the time of the Second World War. Sub Rosa board members and some of the executive management group had ties with the German Army and found out about experiments they were doing that fit with their aims — to eradicate faulty genes and strengthen the human race.

"However, instead of focusing on existing human populations, as the Germans were doing, Sub Rosa had another, more dangerous target group in mind." He paused, drawing Richard's gaze up to meet his.

Salvator swallowed, his Adam's apple bobbing hesitantly in his throat. "Vampires."

Richard's face screwed up in disbelief. "Vampires? Come on. There's no such thing."

Salvator's earnest stare speared him to his seat. "Believe me, there is. The governments around the world know but they don't want it made public. They don't want the masses to panic."

Richard poked his pen on the pad. "Wouldn't people have seen them? They couldn't pass as human."

Salvator sprang up, walked over and stood at the window of the compact office. "Most people would have seen half- and quarter-castes and not noticed anything out of the ordinary. They're able to mix in more easily and work within regular human conditions and environments.

"Three-quarter to full-blood vampires, on the other hand, are easier to spot due to their extremely pale skin and vibrant eyes. It all depends on whether you know what to look for. If you don't, you'll assume they're a minority group with a small, distinct gene pool. If you do, they'll struggle to disguise themselves

"In addition to their uncommon physical features, the demands of their diet and limited tolerance to sun exposure will be a dead giveaway, excuse the pun."

Richard's hand stilled and he stared at his notes — too shocked to laugh, too shocked to respond at all. His head swam, trying to swallow the concept of vampires and that they lived among human society. They weren't just folklore. They were real. His gaze returned to Salvator. "There must have been some interbreeding."

"Yes. But those humans tend to be sympathizers who wouldn't expose the vampires, or have died through childbirth or because a vampire got hungry."

"I see..." *Kind of.* Richard's mind crammed with thoughts and unanswered questions.

Salvator stepped away from the window and pressed his palms on the desk. "Vampires were seen to be the biggest threat to the survival of the human race, and so, with effective use of fear propaganda — another thing they learned from the Germans — it was easy to get the study ratified.

"Sub Rosa developed a purpose-built facility in Norway where the two vampire clans originated, the cold, harsh, isolated conditions perfectly suiting their lifestyle. And it keeps them as separate as possible from the bulk of humans."

"How are the two clans differentiated and how were they captured?" *Aren't vampires invincible? Can't they break out of barred cells? Crush any human standing in their way?*

Salvator sat back down and crossed his legs. "There's a Jade clan, identified by their jade eyes and fair hair, and a Violet clan, with violet eyes and dark hair. And they hate each other. It stems from some civil war in the Middle Ages.

"In terms of capture, there've been a few effective traps devised. Blood lures are the main one, drawing half- to full-caste vampires from up to a mile away, using a vial with a small amount of animal blood. It's often used in conjunction with a specialized Taser gun. The gun uses beams of concentrated sunlight to incapacitate vampires for up to an hour at a time.

"The ongoing issue is keeping the vampires imprisoned once caught. Overnight, the darkness recharges them and they break out. So, at the moment, it's an endless cycle of lure, capture, escape."

Richard couldn't speak, trying to fit the puzzle pieces together into something comprehensible. He had to keep taking notes, then he could review them later and attempt to make more sense of the overall picture, the ramifications, and put the situation into some sort of perspective.

Salvator uncrossed his legs and leaned forward on his elbows. "The main research aims at the moment are to develop a way to keep the vampires incapacitated for longer, once captured, to enable transportation from farther away, to find a way to stop them escaping from the compound and work on genome cleansing to eradicate the vampire gene."

No matter how overwhelming the concept, specific tasks gave Richard something to focus on. "Sounds like there's still quite a bit to be done. I do like a challenge." He scanned over his last few dot points and tapped his pen on the page. "How is food managed?"

Salvator steepled his hands, his fingers and thumb drumming an erratic rhythm. "It became too hard to try to kill enough animals to feed them all, so the research team developed a supplement, based on the same principles as astronaut meals, providing the vampires with the nutrients they require instead of blood. And it seems to be working pretty well, although, apparently, it tastes revolting."

His colleague sat up straight and wiped his palms on his creased trousers. "Things have come a long way since the inception of the project and its barbaric beginnings. In an attempt to control and genetically alter the captives, staff withheld food, vampires were exposed to twenty-four-hour sunlight in the top end of Norway during summer months, harsh experimental drugs were trialed, and mixed-caste fetuses were aborted and experimented on."

Richard's pen-poking resumed, digging a hole right through the center of his notepad. "I realize vampires pose a potential threat, but using extreme experimentation is appalling, unacceptable."

Is that relief washing across Salvator's face? Has the guy been testing me? Checking to see whether we're on the same moral page?

"I agree," Salvator said. "You'll be happy to hear that the harsh testing has all ceased now. Since I've been on the project, I've pushed for ethical practices and, thankfully, Sub Rosa has embedded them into policy and procedure."

Good. No way could he work in an organization that supported brutal backward thinking. "With all the fear around working with this target group, how did you convince management to tighten up their act?"

A smile pushed at the corners of Salvator's lips. "I focused on the possible legal implications. As soon as I mentioned fines and possible forced closure of the project, they were suddenly more willing to cooperate. I also reinforced that they'd achieve superior and faster results if the vampires were in better condition."

What a great guy. Intelligent, knowledgeable and, most of all, fair. The more he got to know Salvator, the more he was proud to have him as a friend. "Well done. Raising your concerns and pushing for significant changes in practice can't have been easy."

"No. But it should be easier in future, knowing I have another like-minded person onboard."

He and Salvator really did seem to be kindred spirits. Though it still paid to be wary. They hadn't known each other long, and, unlike with Eva, he couldn't confirm the accuracy of his gut feeling. "One other question… Why base the head of operations here, in Tassie, especially when the compound is on the other side of the world?"

"From what I understand, Tasmania offered cheap real estate and operations could remain more easily hidden, covert. The long-term plan is to set up some satellite sites, primarily in colder climates, for easier finding, catching and transporting of Violets and Jades.

"Though, as I said earlier, the main focus at the moment is to work out a way to tranquilize the vampires for longer, to enable hassle-free transportation to the Norway compound and prevent their escape."

Salvator shifted forward in his chair, his gaze glued to Richard's. "So, what are your thoughts? Still keen to sign up?"

* * * *

The nerve-racking elevator ride to Harry Kennedy's top floor office had Richard on edge. His pulse pelted hard in his ears until he could hardly hear what Salvator said. Had he made the right decision?

The challenge of the project fit right up his research alley. It would flex his mind muscles until they were trim, drum-skin taut and terrific. And the increased pay would be handy, too. Both he and Eva wanted children and he needed to be in a position to support a family on one wage in the near future.

The lift doors opened onto a wide corridor, awash with sunlight. Richard squinted. "It's like another world up here."

"It sure is. It's the kind of environment that sparks ambition."

Was that a hint of sarcasm he'd heard in Salvator's voice?

He steered Richard to an office on the right. Inside the open door, a massive meatball of a man rolled around at a large wooden desk.

Harry covered his hand over the telephone receiver. "Come in. Come in."

Richard and Salvator took seats opposite him. Paper piles of various heights were stacked across his desk, interspersed with research and business books. Behind him, the sun had retreated into a clog of white cloud, and the unnervingly-calm sea reflected the light like mirrored sunglasses.

"Right, yes. I understand. But you need to understand this. The deadline is Friday." Harry almost gouged the desk with his gavel-like index finger. "No buts." He hung up and forced a smile, emphasizing his chubby, chipmunk cheeks. "Good morning, Salvator."

Salvator stood and reached across the desk to shake the man's stubby hand.

Harry's narrow gaze moved to scrutinize Richard. He jumped up at the senior manager's silent request to stand.

"And you must be Richard." Harry extended his pudgy hand to him. "Salvator has shown me some of your research reports. They're very good. We could use someone with your skills and thoroughness on the Norway Experiment."

"Thank you, sir."

Harry gestured for them to sit back down. "Harry, please."

Richard fixed his stare on the stout senior manager. "When should I start? Salvator's already been kind enough to give me an overview."

A stay-in-line smile broke onto Harry's lips and he glanced at Salvator. "Thank you." His gaze moved back to meet Richard's. "You can start right away, unless you have any other questions?"

"Can't think of anything else at the moment. I'm still trying to absorb all the information."

"That's understandable. Please come and see me or give me a call if anything comes to mind. Otherwise, I'm sure Salvator can answer most Norway Experiment queries."

Salvator smiled and glanced between him and Harry. "We've got the next update meeting on Thursday. It would be an excellent opportunity for Richard to meet everyone and give him enough time to complete or write up handover notes for any unfinished work."

So much for easing back into things. Looked like the honeymoon period had officially come to an end.

Chapter Twenty

The Dilemma

While Eva luxuriated in the afterglow of their lovemaking, Richard prepared dinner as promised. With the announcement of his new promotion onto a hush-hush project, she assumed he'd be strapped for time, not spoiling her with an afternoon of sex, followed by cooking her a meal and arranging for them to eat it together.

In under thirty minutes Richard returned, still gloriously naked, a tray covering his best bits.

"Dinner in bed? You could have called me. I would have come down."

"Uh-uh. As I said, my treat. I wanted you to just relax and enjoy." Richard had made a special effort, showing the depth of his appreciation for her, like attempting to rack up brownie points, or, in their case, rare-meat points, while he could.

He placed the tray next to her on the bed. "Hang on. I forgot something. I'll be back in a minute. Please start."

Richard walked toward the door and she devoured his remarkable body, all ridges and hard planes of muscle tapered into a balanced, delectable man. Richard took her to places on a daily basis that she had considered outside the realm of possibility.

The sex between them sizzled, intense and addictive. But they also had a much broader, deeper connection that drilled right down to her soul.

When he'd shifted out of sight, her gaze returned to the tray and fell on her white napkin. Writing peeked out from under a lifted fold. She unfurled the diagonal serviette and, in the middle, words in blue cursive, backward-slanted writing formed the shape of a heart.

Mrs. Eva Hall, my wife, has
A fabulous face, Beautiful breasts
Sweet, succulent pussy
Marvelous mind,
The perfect
package.

"Richard." She sighed and pressed the napkin to her chest. He really was too good to be true. Eva couldn't even fault his workaholic ways because, beneath the behavior, it showed dedication and focus that he applied to everything he loved, most especially her, particularly since their marriage.

She opened the top drawer of her bedside table and laid the napkin out flat. She would have to get it framed to protect his words.

After his poetic starter, her hunger intensified...for more than food. Her husband reappeared in the doorway holding a bottle of champagne and two glasses, further stimulating her sexual appetite.

Eva shifted the tray onto her bedside table and crawled to his side of the bed. "Put them down and come here."

He did as she asked, his blazing green gaze locked on hers, and strode over. She knelt on the edge of the bed and licked the entire length of his erect shaft, focusing her tongue on the smooth head.

Richard threaded his fingers through her free-flowing hair. "And did I mention a fucking incredible mouth?" His breathy voice heaved with passion.

Dinner would go cold. Again. But the physical appetizer and first course were hot, hot, hot.

* * * *

It didn't take long for Richard to get back into the work rhythm at Sub Rosa. He finished his preexisting research reports and had a fresh, ready and receptive mind for the Norway Experiment update meeting.

Richard stepped through the frosted-glass door of the top-floor conference room into eye-scorching sunshine that created a glowing golden aura around his colleagues, who were seated at a long, timber table. The bombarding rays of light stabbed Richard's retinas like searing butter knives and he squinted and blinked.

One of the men stood and waved him over. He wore a brown crumpled suit and a brown, gray and white checkered bow tie. *Salvator.* Richard turned his back to the window, walked toward his friend and shook his hand.

A warm, welcoming smile extended to Salvator's eyes. "Have a seat," he said, and introduced him to the six other members of the team.

Right at ten a.m., Harry Kennedy rolled into the room, accompanied by a stiff-suited, gnarled-nosed, middle-aged man—a seasoned red wine drinker, going by the signs. Harry introduced him as the project team leader.

"And this is Richard, our newest, very promising recruit."

The red-nosed team leader glanced at Richard with a forced smile that scarcely reached the corners of his thin lips, and popped open the shiny gold catches on his black briefcase. He pulled out a manila envelope and tilted it until overhead sheets slipped out into his hand.

The man cleared his throat, an unspoken command, sending one of the researchers to close the blinds. The team leader flicked on the overhead projector, beaming a blast of electric light against a white screen.

He slapped on the first transparency, giving a dot point overview of the project, in line with what Salvator had already explained to Richard earlier in the week.

The mundane man spent ages flipping through overhead after overhead, droning on and on in laborious detail about how much management cared about staff and the benefits of the project to the human race. But, ultimately, everything came down to the budget and cost-cutting.

Several times Richard had to rein his mind back into concentration mode. Being the new guy, he needed to look interested and make the most of the information if he wanted to do a good job and make a good impression but it proved difficult. Spending hours in meetings talking felt like wasted time. He wanted to plunge his teeth into the project and start getting some results.

Couldn't they just send around update memos and minimize the management-driven, budget-focused meetings? It would be so much more productive. He pulled a pen and notepad out of his pocket and pretended to take notes. Doodling helped him focus. Usually. But not today.

Eva dominated his thoughts and drove his hand to design her name in gothic letters. He soon intertwined them with his own, developing the doodle into an intricate heart design. Then above it he wrote, 'I miss you' and underneath, 'I love you'.

"Unlike the Aboriginal population, there have been no deaths in captivity and we plan to keep it that way…"

Richard jerked his head up. The smirk on the speaker's face made him want to deck the bigoted prick. The guy thought the Aboriginal people's plight and their struggles were a joke? They were native Australians, categorized not as people but as flora and fauna. Disgusting. So forget foreigners. They had no chance of fair treatment.

Given Sub Rosa's early, barbaric practices, it surprised Richard that all the vampires had survived. And it wasn't like staff would care if they'd died. They were petrified of the prisoners.

The team leader cleared his throat again and had a large gulp of water. "We need to keep the Commonwealth government happy, seeing they're our main funding source."

"And it's a stipulation in the funding contract," Salvator whispered.

"Captive deaths equal death of the funding," one of the other project guys said, his voice even softer.

Salvator's gaze flicked to each researcher in turn and ended on Richard. "And of the project."

Now *that* made sense.

* * * *

While Eva cooked dinner, Richard left his doodled note on her bedside table for her to discover. Now that they were back at work, things were going to get busy and he never wanted her to question his love.

Richard sat at his black, gothic desk and stared at the mountain of paperwork he'd brought home. It had started already and it looked like it would be an ongoing theme, an ongoing expectation. Sub Rosa didn't increase the Norway Experiment staff wages without expecting something in return.

At least he'd been paired up with Salvator to work on a genome-cleansing mini group project with a focus on eradicating the vampire gene. Genetics was not only Richard's area of expertise but also his passion, and with Salvator's support, they'd come up with the most humane outcome, with minimal-to-no side effects.

His first task consisted of wading through what had already been trialed, to get perspective on where the research team's focus now lay, and from there, devise a strategy for how to progress. He needed to get a full understanding of the vampire genetics and the similarities and differences between the clans and humans. Then he had to come up with a working hypothesis to test.

A huge task, but he aimed to rise above the challenge, without compromising his time with Eva. Somehow, he needed to ensure work-life balance and not let things get out of hand like they had early on in their relationship.

A highly task-driven person like him found it far from easy. His default behavior entailed setting his mind on something and remaining fixated until he'd seen it through, until he'd achieved the required result.

Eva rushed into his study and hugged him. "Thank you, thank you, thank you, you wonderful man!"

What did I do this time?

Her joyous, blue-violet eyes registered his unspoken question. "For your note. On my bedside table. I love you so much!"

Oh, that's right. He'd absorbed himself so deeply in Sub Rosa stuff that he'd forgotten all about it. He smiled. "And I love *you*, with all my heart. So, if I'm getting too caught up in this new project, please, *please* come and tell me. Although work's important, I don't want to compromise us."

"Good. I don't want you to either. I love that you're passionate and focused on your job, but it's just a job."

Technically, he couldn't fault her reasoning. However, she didn't know the bigger picture, the importance of what he'd committed to, the fact that his input could be key to preserving the human race. And he couldn't tell her either. He'd already signed away that right. Unease wriggled like worms in his stomach.

Richard kissed her lips. "You, my darling, are my top priority. How does the saying go? Happy wife, happy life?"

* * * *

A month into the genome project and Richard had brought work home every night. He'd have to wade through thirty years' worth of reading before he could even start on a plan.

Working through the pile, he came across a document on the vampire food requirements and an alarming statistic jumped out from the page.

Death by starvation — Jade 11, Violet 13.

Creases of alarm scrunched his forehead. Management had assured them that no deaths had occurred in captivity. It went against the recurrent funding agreement with the Commonwealth government. The document must have been misfiled. Research team members definitely hadn't been meant to see it.

"You look engrossed."

He startled and turned toward the doorway, shoving the rogue report back on the unread pile, face down. Eva wore nothing but a red apron, her delectable nipples pointing against the thin cotton fabric. His pulse went from sixty-five to a pounding one hundred and thirty beats per minute.

She sashayed toward him. "I wondered how long it would take for you to notice me."

"I'm so sorry. I didn't realize it was so la—"

She put a finger to his lips, her beautiful body the perfect distraction. He looked into her come-hither eyes and his cock turned granite hard. Fuck, he wanted her so bad. The craving hadn't stopped, hadn't even come close to easing off.

The more time they spent together, the more they made love, the more he wanted her. Richard reached up to touch his irresistible wife and she grabbed his hands and placed them on his thighs.

Eva shook her head, a mischievous grin on her face. "Close your eyes." He did as she asked but desperately wanted to peek.

She pressed her palm against his chest and slowly dragged it over his stomach, stopping at the waistband of his jeans. She took her time undoing each button of his fly, the occasional brush of her fingers on his cock jolting his hips.

His breath became ragged and impatient with the slow glide of her hands along the inside of his thighs and avoidance of his trigger-happy crotch. If he got any more turned on, one scrape of her knuckles and he'd be gone. And she knew, keeping her strokes on the edge of his climax zone and pressing her lips against his bare pelvis, further drawing out the titillating torture.

His cock strained against his restrictive pants. It felt like forever that he'd been her pleasure prisoner and he couldn't take it much longer. "Eva, please," he begged, his voice rough and raw with desire.

And she granted his wish, freeing his cock from his boxers, holding the base and giving the head a sensual, saliva-filled lick. He gripped her head and groaned.

Her appreciative "Mmmm...", combined with the increasing speed of her hand and tongue strokes, pushed him right to the precipice.

"I'm gonna..."

She didn't ease up. She didn't back off. She picked up the pace.

"Fuck, Eva!" His orgasm soared through him, her hot mouth collecting his cum.

When he'd almost recovered, she said, "Open your eyes."

He did. And what a view. Naked, with her apron tossed aside, Eva stared up at him, a sexy grin on her face, a sheen of cum still on her lips.

Richard bent down and kissed her, twining his hands in her wild hair. Tasting himself on her shot his lust meter up higher than the Empire State Building, making him bar up again. She moaned against his mouth, and he pushed the pile of papers aside and lifted her onto the desk. Coffee stains he could explain away, but semen…

He spread her legs, dropped to his knees and nuzzled into her wet pussy. She was always so ready for him and he fucking loved it. He cupped her ass and pulled her close to the edge of the desk, delving his tongue deep into her folds. He licked her swollen nub, reveling in her inviting, sweet scent, and inserted two fingers inside her.

Heaven.

Richard thrust his fingers in and out, in rhythm with his tongue on her clit, diving deeper and deeper until he reached her G-spot.

Eva threw her head back and shoved her hips into him, a long, primal moan announcing the arrival of her orgasm. He kept his tongue pressed on her sensitive spot and his fingers inside her, as the force of the climax shook through her body.

God, he wanted her, needed his cock plunging to the hilt, her core contracting around him, massaging out a unified release.

As she descended from her high, Richard slipped his fingers out, sucked off her juices then laid her flat against the desk. He bent her knees up, and she watched with lust-filled, half-closed eyes as he coated his cock with her natural lubricant.

"Kiss me," she said, her voice hoarse with want.

Richard planted his palms on either side of her head and kissed her passion-swollen lips. She grabbed his face and stuck her tongue in his mouth. Uninhibited, sexually confident Eva made him horny as all fuck.

Unable to hold off any longer, he entered her, slowly, deliberately, enjoying her snug warmth. He pumped quicker, harder, his tongue mirroring his cock. They breathed into each other's mouths as though one was the other's main oxygen source, an interdependent life support.

Her caressing his balls sent him straight into paradise and he came hard.

She followed right behind, calling out his name, arching her body and writhing against him.

Spent, he fell on top of her, panting into the curve of her neck, their bodies slick with sweat. "I think I might work late every night, as long as that's your method of distraction."

Her laughter reminded him of the melodic tinkling of a wind chime. "Mmm...such a nice diversion."

He propped himself up on one elbow and looked into her eyes. "More than nice. Fucking incredible. You're fucking incredible."

She smiled. "You're not so bad yourself."

He chuckled as he stood, and pulled her into sitting.

She glanced at the piles of papers spread across the desk. "What were you reading?"

"If I tell you, I'll have to kill you," he joked.

She laughed.

"I came across some interesting, unexpected information."

"To do with the project you can't talk about."

"Yeah. Sorry. I'm really turning into a boring husband these days, huh?"

She ran her fingers along the length of his lapel. "I can think of a few ways you can make it up to me."

Richard grinned. He'd hit the libido jackpot, finding a wife as insatiable as him. "My poems and notes not cutting it anymore?"

Eva pressed her lips to his ear and caressed his still-exposed cock. "I'd much rather you be creative in a more hands-on way. And not just hands…"

Fuck. He stood up, cradled her in his arms and charged into their bedroom. No more work tonight…

Normally after a marathon sex session, Richard slept like a well-fed baby—but not this time. His mind was crammed with discomfort and his stomach had tied itself in stubborn knots. He lay on his back with Eva's head on his chest and half her beautiful body resting on his, her breathing slow and steady and her muscles relaxed in sleep. He stroked her long, silky hair.

"What am I going to do?" he murmured. Should he alert Salvator or management to what he had found? Maybe they already knew about it. And if he shouldn't know, it could land him in a lot of trouble.

His gut told him he and Salvator were on the same page, that his friend was a stand-up guy. However, he still didn't know him well enough. And he refused to put all his faith in a feeling.

Even if he did say something, if Salvator didn't already know, telling him could put him in danger too. Maybe he should just let it go. One document didn't provide enough evidence. The deaths were probably accidental. If he raised it, it could mean loss of funding, shutting the project down, losing his job. Risking the survival of the human race.

Chapter Twenty-One

Spreading the Seed of Fear

Hobart, 1944

William sat in his bedroom, his toy car, military tank and soldiers scattered across the floor. He hid in his trench—a quilt hanging over two chairs.

"What is this? No. No. Nooooo!" William's mum screamed.

His dad flew past his room and he snuck out behind him on tiptoes. William followed him to his sister's bedroom but stayed outside. After he overheard his parents refer to his sister as *cursed*, he wouldn't go anywhere near the evil place. Maybe the curse was contagious. He shivered.

"What's wrong, love?" His dad's voice sounded calm, careful.

"Read this," William's mum said in between sobs.

Silence.

More silence.

William stepped up to the edge of the door frame and stole a look inside. His dad held a small black book. His sister's diary. He'd tried to sneak a read so many times but she'd always kept it locked. They must have broken it open. His mum sat back on her legs, dabbing a handkerchief at the tears dripping from her eyes.

Piles of clothes and books surrounded them. They were boxing up his sister's short life. Some people kept a shrine. His best friend's parents had left their soldier son's room untouched, ready for him to return. But he never would — and neither would William's sister.

His dad put the diary down and looked into William's mum's red, watery eyes. "She'd gotten more unwell than I thought."

His mum stopped sobbing and glared at his dad. "Unwell? No. She was the sanest person I know. Ethan and his vampire charm took advantage of her."

Vampire? What? They weren't real. His parents had assured him, several times, after he'd gotten scared stiffer than stiff after watching *Dracula*.

"Come on. That's ridiculous! There's no such thing." His father's voice boomed.

His mum shoved her hands on her hips. "So, you'd rather believe our daughter was insane."

His dad held his hands up in a hang-on gesture. "No…though we need to face facts."

She picked up the diary and pointed to a page. "And they're right here."

His dad stared at his daughter's neat handwriting.

"Whether you want to believe it or not, she got sucked in by the very best." His mum spat out the words like they were poison.

His dad shook his head, like he couldn't believe what the diary said.

His mum grabbed his dad's face between her hands and made him look into her eyes. "Ethan always seemed odd. He just didn't look...normal."

"Foreigners don't look normal." His dad said it as though it was fact.

She looked around then refocused on his dad's red face. "There's foreign, then there's *foreign*."

William leaned back against the wall. *Ethan, a vampire? It can't be true, can it?* He seemed so normal. He ate what they ate. He walked around in the sun. How could he be? But his sister wouldn't lie in her own diary.

"The baby. It isn't a normal baby," his dad said.

Was the baby a vampire, too? William's shaky hands gripped the outer rim of the doorframe and he peeked back into the room.

His mum sniffled. "It killed her. It killed her because of him and his...his..."

His dad put his arms around her and she shoved her wet face into his shoulder. "There, there. We can't do anything now."

"Yes, we can!" Her words were muffled against his woolly jumper. She lifted her head and stared into his dad's eyes. "We can have nothing to do with him or the baby. They both killed her. Who knows what they'll do to us. We have to stay away. We have to keep our distance.'"

His dad grabbed the top of her arms. "But—"

She shrugged out of his grasp. "No buts. It's final. We have to agree on this—for our own safety...and William's."

A few days later, his dad shooed Ethan away when he came by with the baby. Then Ethan put her in care and disappeared. William and his parents were relieved, though still concerned. What if the little girl turned out like Ethan?

So, William took it upon himself to follow his niece's progress through St. Joseph's orphanage to boarding school, to securing a job at Sub Rosa, twenty-one years later. He had to ensure that Ethan had gone for good and his niece couldn't cause his family any more pain.

* * * *

September 1965

The day after Sub Rosa hired William, he came back from lunch and saw his niece, now an attractive young woman, waiting for the lift only a foot away from him. Her long, dark brown hair looked just a few shades lighter than the hideous blackness he associated with her beast of a father. William couldn't believe he'd seen her so soon, like fate had drawn them together.

The distinct violet tinge to her eyes signified her as Ethan's diseased progeny. His heart nosedived into his stomach. She had her father's vampire genetics — and the ability to inflict just as much anguish. He tried not to stare but couldn't stop.

Her chatty friend's incessant conversation and eye contact meant his niece didn't have a chance to notice anything or anyone else on the ride up in the lift, not that she'd recognize him anyway. The last time they'd met she had been a newborn baby and he had just turned eight.

She exited the elevator and he continued up to the business services floor. Working at the same organization would make it much easier to keep an eye on her without his frequent presence seeming inappropriate.

Over the next few weeks, they often shared a lift and engaged in a little small talk and in less than a month into his new job, he'd made some inroads. Then one afternoon, after spying on her during his lunch break, an unusual financial report crossed his desk for the Norway Experiment—some big budget research project.

While working through the financial particulars, ensuring expenses were all accounted for, a word jabbed him right in the jugular. A vile, dreadful word...*vampire.*

"Ouch!" He crushed the flame-eaten cigarette butt into his ashtray. Sub Rosa was experimenting with vampires? He fumbled with the near-empty packet of beloved smokes on his desk, pulled out another one and lit up. William drew in a deep, contemplative breath.

The project was based at the Norway site. *Ethan came from Norway.* No fucking way! He almost laughed. Smoke wafted up and hit the ceiling. It was so ironic and prophetic that Ethan's spawn had been attracted to working at a facility whose core project focused on the critters.

Chapter Twenty-Two

Pregnant Pause

In two months, Eva had settled into the Hall family home…and felt awful. She curled up in the fetal position on the couch, sipping chamomile tea with a hot water bottle or Smokey on her unsettled tummy, trying to give her comfort.

It had been amazing her and Richard having the house to themselves, behaving like a real married couple. But in the last week she couldn't seem to shake a stomach bug. It surprised her Richard hadn't caught it, given their frequent level of intimacy.

Keys jingled in the front door and Richard's footsteps echoed in the foyer.

"How are you, sweetheart?" Richard put his black work bag on the coffee table and leaned in to kiss her.

She lifted her hand to stop him. "You better not."

His concerned eyes scrutinzed hers. "You're not feeling any better?"

She shook her head.

He placed his palm on her forehead. "You don't seem to have a fever, which is good, but I'm calling the doctor."

"No. Please don't. I'll be fine."

"Eva, you need to get over your doctor and needle phobia and get yourself better. If you leave it much longer, it could get worse. Then you might need to be hospitalized. I'm pretty sure you don't want that."

No, she didn't, not after being a sickly child growing up. Eva had been prodded and poked with too many needles to count because of a slightly elevated white blood cell reading that wouldn't resolve.

At one point the doctors had even thought it might be leukemia, but they'd ruled it out when she'd had no other symptoms. In the end, they couldn't explain it and put it down to a natural, genetic anomaly.

After force-feeding herself a dinner of dry biscuits with a thin spread of liverwurst pate and flat lemonade, she had a shower in preparation for the on-call doctor to arrive. The hot water washed away the tightness in her muscles and settled the nausea, at least for the moment.

Eva closed her eyes and rinsed herself off, the high-water pressure massaging her skin and making her moan.

She shut off the taps, opened the shower curtain, reached for a towel and froze. 'I love you' was written on the mirror in large letters. Her heart fluttered, sending ripples of joy along each and every nerve ending. Richard must have snuck in... He should have joined her. Though, if he had, the message would have steamed up by the time they'd gotten out.

Eva returned downstairs just as the doctor arrived. She showed him into the lounge room and sat next to

Richard on the couch. She rattled off her range of symptoms, and the doctor retained a kind, encouraging smile.

"Well, Mrs. Hall, I think I know what the matter is." He started rummaging through his dark brown medical bag. "I just need to test…"

Fear clogged Eva's head and her ears switched off to sound. She squeezed her eyes shut. *No needle, no needle, no needle,* she pleaded, hoping her thoughts could sway reality.

"Mrs. Hall?"

Wild beats pummeled her heart and she pried her eyes open.

The doctor held out a small bottle with a screw-on lid. "I just need a urine sample."

Yes! She accepted the container, her pulse already slowing. "Oh, okay. I'll just be a moment."

When she returned, she gave the sample to the doctor and sat beside her husband again. The doctor stored the bottle in a small plastic pouch and tucked it away in his medical bag. "I'll just need to run some tests and I'll let you know as soon as I have the results."

Richard slipped a reassuring arm around her.

The doctor must have seen the fear on her face and added, "Don't worry, Mrs. Hall. You should be fine."

"When can I expect to hear from you?" Tension refused to loosen its grip on her stomach.

"In a couple of days. Oh, and I'll just write you out a medical certificate for work. Your husband mentioned you needed one."

"Yes. Thank you."

The next day, in between bathroom visits, the phone rang. She rinsed her rancid mouth, washed her hands and rushed to pick up the receiver. "Hello?" Her voice sounded as tired and fragile as she felt.

"Eva. It's Greer. You sound terrible."

"You would too if you could hardly hold anything down."

"Oh, Eva. Stomach bugs are the worst."

"Tell me about it."

"Richard mentioned you saw the doctor yesterday. What did he say?"

"Not much. He's doing some tests."

"It's so strange. Usually stomach viruses don't drag on this long." Greer paused. "Are you sure you're not pregnant?"

Pregnant? Eva gulped. "I doubt it." The idea hadn't even entered her mind. She and Richard had had a lot of sex in a short time, but they'd been careful. It had to be a bug. It would pass. They couldn't be parents. Not yet. She wasn't ready.

* * * *

Richard got home from work and strode over to Eva. "What's wrong? Did the doctor call?"

A rush of words stuffed her mouth and she didn't know where to start or what to say.

His concerned eyes searched hers. "Eva?"

"I think you better sit down."

Richard joined her on the couch, his leg shaking.

She stared into his unsuspecting eyes and swallowed. "I'm pregnant."

"What?"

"I'm having a baby. Our baby."

He shoved his hand through his hair, jumped up and paced, right in front of her. "How did this happen?"

She almost laughed. "I believe it might have something to do with all the sex we've been having."

He stopped and looked at her. "But we were careful."

"From when we got back, yes."

"Before we went on our honeymoon, you said we were safe."

"I thought we were. Even the doctor said we should have been, though sometimes it's not that simple. There may even have been a hole in one of the condoms."

He sat down next to her again and raked a hand through his messy, golden-brown hair. "Shit. I hadn't expected this, not yet."

"Me either." She angled herself toward him, her knee brushing his. "What do you think we should do?"

Resignation replaced the stress in his green eyes. "Have the baby. What other option is there?"

"I could arrange for—"

He shook his head. "No." He held her face between his hands. "I'm surprised, but not unhappy about it."

Her eyes stung with relieved tears. "Really?"

"Yes." A brilliant smile burst onto his lips and he kissed her. "We're going to be a little family."

He'd taken it much better than she'd thought. Much better than she had. And she'd had more time to psychologically prepare for the situation. "Are you sure you're okay with it?"

He smoothed her hair and placed a tender hand on her belly. "Absolutely. It's meant to be. I mean, we tried to prevent it but it happened anyway. Obviously, this baby needs to be born—and sooner rather than later."

"I suppose…"

"Eva, we'll be fine. You're going to make a great mother."

She hugged him. He seemed to know exactly what she'd needed to hear. And she went to sleep that night, cuddled up to her husband with a sense of peace and hope.

When Eva woke the next morning, Richard had already left for work. Disappointment trickled through her. She'd expected a kiss and to bask in the remnants of warmth radiating from Richard's loving embrace. But he'd gone, leaving her without either, well, not that she could remember, anyway. The stress of the past few days had caught up with her and stripped her of a deep, restorative sleep, leaving exhaustion in its wake.

Eva wandered down to the kitchen, the back of her eyes still aching with fatigue, and stared at the pantry. Should she attempt some breakfast? Her traitorous stomach growled. For the past few weeks, as soon as a morsel of food entered her mouth, her gut had roiled and often purged. If it were just morning sickness, it wouldn't be too bad. What she had was a severe case of 'anytime' sickness.

Craving food then throwing it back up was the weirdest sensation. Maybe she should start with a sip of orange juice and see how that went. Eva walked toward the fridge and stopped. A fluffy black cat magnet pinned a message to the freezer door, featuring Richard's distinctive, backward-slanted handwriting. She slipped the note free and began reading.

My dear, sweet Eva,

How do you like your black cat magnet, Thornton? I thought he was the perfect choice for a magnetic romance like ours. What could be more romantic than receiving a love note from someone so dashing – and yes, I may be referring to yours truly here. Ha ha!

How are you feeling, my darling? Is there a word for ecstatically ecstatic? I have the most beautiful wife, in every sense of the word, a great house and now, a baby on the way, our baby. A baby created out of our love and passion for each other.

Anyway, I need to get to work. I just wanted to leave you a little message to let you know I love and miss you and can't wait to see you when I get home.

Make sure you take it easy. That's a demand, not a request. And I'll arrange dinner.

Love you,

Richard x

PS. We're going to be parents. Can you believe it?

Her heart swelled with love until it just about launched into the sky like a helium balloon. Eva read and re-read his note, her eyes so moist the words were a blur. But it didn't matter. She could recite them by memory. She officially had the most wonderful husband on earth.

* * * *

Richard arrived home early, his face beaming, and presented her with a bunch of scarlet, long-stemmed roses. Their perfume smelled so exquisite she struggled to pull the bouquet away from her nose. It was the first strong scent that didn't send her head diving down the toilet bowl.

"Thank you, for these and your beautiful note," she said, tearing up. All the overwhelming emotion had to be related to hormonal changes.

He put his bag on the conservatory table, leaned over and kissed her. "I'm glad you like them. It's always a pleasure pleasing you."

And he sure knew how to please. A surge of arousal blazed between her legs.

His concerned, attentive gaze roamed over her. "How are you feeling?"

Horny. Surprisingly. "I've been able to eat a whole meal without it making a sudden reappearance, so not bad."

Richard chuckled. He shrugged out of his jacket and sat beside her. "I have some good news. I rang the doctor today with a few questions and he confirmed that if you're up to it, we can still have sex."

Her cheeks flared with embarrassment. "You actually asked him about having sex?" She didn't have the guts. It was good to know, though, given the return of her libido.

Richard swept a strand of hair off her heated cheek. "Well, we weren't sure, especially with how you've been feeling, and why stop if we don't need to? In fact, he said it can be comforting for you and the baby."

"Comforting? Really?"

He kissed her forehead. "Yep. We just can't be too...strenuous." He grabbed the flowers from her and stood. "I'll put these in a vase and get dinner started. Feel like anything in particular?"

"Something that won't make me spew, if possible."

Suppressed laughter danced in his eyes. "I'll do my best."

She grabbed his arm. "You haven't told anyone about the baby, have you?" A bundle of nerves wound tight around her stomach.

"No, but I'm dying to!"

A relieved breath whooshed from her body, taking the tension with it. "Please don't. Not yet. I want to make sure everything's okay first. A lot of new, expectant mothers miscarry within the first three months."

"Looks like I'm not the only one who's been doing some research." He kissed her on the top of her head. "I promise I won't say anything, until it's safe."

* * * *

A few nights later, while slaving away in his study, Richard found a Norway Experiment budget report. He held it in a death grip, his knuckles white with tension. It went way over its funding allocation and money had been siphoned from other projects to keep it afloat. Worst of all, the funding bodies had no knowledge of it, so they hadn't given consent.

A toxic mix of anger, fear and frustration fired through him. His blood pressure shot up to high alert. *What the hell?* How many more of these discrepancies would he find? And even if he didn't, these two documents alone were enough to speak up. Richard couldn't continue to participate in something unethical, deceitful and likely illegal.

He dropped the document on his desk and buried his face in his hands. From what he'd read so far, the Violets and Jades weren't as much of a threat as humans first thought. However, fear propaganda and ignorance were a dangerous duo.

The research consistently referred to the vampires' main food source as animals, not humans, except for a very small percentage. Not even their genetics were that different from the human population. Suddenly, eradicating the vampire gene didn't seem so noble. Who was Sub Rosa to decide what and who were worth preserving?

Anger, frustration and fear pumped inside him like an unstable chemical combination. He needed a release valve. If he bottled up the stress and uncertainty for much longer, he'd explode like an atomic bomb, creating widespread carnage. He needed to share his findings and worries with someone, but other than Salvator, who else could he talk to?

"Richard, dinner's ready," Eva called from downstairs.

Eva. Could he confide in her? Not technically. Disclosure about the project to anyone outside of Norway Experiment staff was forbidden. But who would she tell? Her perspective might help him problem-solve how best to proceed.

Richard sat down at the dining table, thoughts ping-ponging around his head. How could he raise the subject? And what if it freaked her out and distressed the baby?

Eva slid her hand over his. "You seem really preoccupied. Is everything okay?"

The perfect opening.

If he didn't say something now, the cracks in his *normal* façade would widen and she'd see right through it.

His dry, unblinking eyes stared into hers. "Not really."

Concern dug deep ditches into the pale skin of her face. "What's wrong?"

Richard looked down at his plate full of food. "I'm not sure whether I should tell you."

"You brought it up, so now you have to."

"It's just...I don't want to upset you."

She sat next to Richard and regained eye contact. "If you don't tell me, I'll definitely be upset."

He put his knife and fork down and stretched out his steel-tight shoulders. "All right. I just have to warn you — it's pretty confronting. It's about the project."

"I didn't think you were allowed to talk to me about your work."

He reached for her hand and held it between his. "I'm not. But I need to."

"Okay…" A big bulge protruded in her throat like she'd swallowed a boulder of worries. "Go on."

Where should he start? "Um…the test subjects aren't voluntary —"

"That's appalling!" Fiery blue-violet embers flickered in her eyes.

"There's more. Some are only part human and the rest are no longer human at all."

Eva puckered her forehead and it crinkled up like an ill-fitting blouse. "What? How can Sub Rosa possibly get away with that? It's not the turn of the century. What they're doing breaches human rights."

He sighed. "Not technically. You see, the test subjects are already changed when captured."

"Changed to *what*?"

Richard hesitated. "Vampires."

"Vampires? As in the mythical, blood-sucking creatures of the night?" She leaned in and sniffed his breath. "Have you been drinking?"

"No." *Alcohol oblivion. Damn tempting.* But then he'd wake up with a hangover on top of the work shit. "I know it's hard to believe. I struggled with it too, initially, but I've seen some lab results and filmed evidence all confirming it's true."

She frowned, as though faith at his words warred with facts. "How long have you known about this?"

"Since I got recruited onto the Norway Experiment after we got back from our honeymoon." Richard rammed frustrated fingers through his hair. "At the start, the project aims sounded totally reasonable. I thought they were for everyone's best interests...but not now. I found some documents showing misuse of research funds, maltreatment of the vampires and some covered-up deaths. I haven't told anyone else."

Conflict flashed in her eyes like a subliminal message, and she shook her head as though trying to shake the revelation from her mind. It stuck now, though, like a piece of gum ground into the carpet.

The wall clock ticked, each stroke loud and ominous in the silence between them.

Eva stared at him, her gaze shifting from disbelief to shooting bullets of disappointment. "I wish you'd told me earlier."

"And how would that have helped?"

"It could have relieved some of the stress."

Richard glanced at his plate, bloody juice seeping out of his steak. "Maybe...but the question remains. What am I going to do about it?"

She reclaimed her hand from his grasp and clasped his face, bringing his focus back to her. "Leave. We'll be able to cope, and with your age and skills, you'll get another job—"

"Possibly, though given the classified nature of the Norway Experiment, not to mention the unethical practices going on behind the scenes, Sub Rosa won't want to risk any information getting out. They might make it hard for me to go."

Richard covered her hand with his. "And even if they don't, morally I can't just move on knowing what they're up to, knowing the things they've done and will continue to do. I need to try to expose them."

Worry and anger ignited blue-violet balls of fire in her eyes, and she tore her hand from his face. "No. It's too dangerous."

"Not if I'm careful."

Her hands trembled in her lap. "See? Now that scares me more. Isn't there someone else you can talk to about this, someone who could help?"

She stopped shaking and her eyes went distant, a slow burn of a smile spreading on her lips. "How about Salvator? Have you spoken to him?"

"No. Although he seems like a good guy, I don't know for sure. Fear can make people do strange things and there's a lot of fear around vampires. Most staff would justify what Sub Rosa is doing and turn a blind eye to unethical practices. They think it's safer to have the vampires locked up but most of their fear is unfounded.

"Contrary to what people think, humans aren't a vampire's main food source. Only a very small percentage feed on humans. So it's unfair to penalize a whole group when only a select few are a real threat. The scientist in me refuses to condemn a species to extinction without knowing and weighing up all the facts."

Eva sighed, her gaze transforming from concern to tenderness and admiration. "It's not just because you're a scientist. You're the fairest, most honest and non-judgmental person I know."

Having her trust and belief in him lifted some of the stressful load. "Thanks. I probably shouldn't have said anything yet, but I couldn't contain it anymore. In your current state, I'm sure it's the last thing you needed to hear."

"Richard, it's fine. I'm glad you told me. I don't want you to hold anything back. I dump my issues on you all the time, so I expect the same in return. We need to support each other. You shouldn't have to bear the whole burden. I know you're the man of the house and you probably feel like it's your duty, your role, but I'd like to think of our marriage as an equal partnership."

He held her warm hand between his and stroked her soft skin. God, she felt good. Good and loving and healing. "You're right. I should have been more open with you. I promise I will be from now on."

She smiled. "Good. So, what will you do from here?"

"Try to get copies of as much evidence against Sub Rosa as I can, then we'll go to the police. I need to make things right, for everyone's sake."

"Just promise me you'll be careful. We have a baby on the way now and —"

He cupped her cheek and brushed the pad of his thumb across her lips. "I won't let anything happen to you or our baby."

"Or you. I couldn't bear it if anything happened to you either."

The sun dropped below the horizon and the room grew gray and dark and shadowy.

"Everything will be fine. You'll see."

Chapter Twenty-Three

The Whistleblower

Richard sat at his work desk, leaning his head on his hand. He stared at his gene-eradication mini project notes and stabbed the page with his pen. Since finding out what Sub Rosa was up to, all his drive and motivation had shriveled up and been replaced with rage. How could he help destroy a community based on false accusations and fear? No one had that entitlement or the right to play God.

From the evidence he'd gathered, the Violets and Jades had and would continue to live alongside humans with no real cause for concern. Just like in the human population, there was good and bad. Working out an effective way to deal with the troublemakers mattered most.

If all went to plan, soon he wouldn't have to worry about vampire gene eradication and instead could focus on fostering a good working relationship between people, whether they be human, Violet or Jade.

"How's the report going?"

Richard jolted his head up and his gaze met Salvator's inquiring eyes. "Um…"

"There's no need to be nervous. I'll be right there with you, backing you the whole way. You've had some really good ideas — gene manipulation, using principles of evolution such as environmental changes to reduce the vampires' ability to thrive, and development of medication to target and eradicate the vampire gene. It's great work. Great innovation."

Now he wished he hadn't rushed to Salvator in an impulsive blaze of excitement early on, spouting off about his destructive concepts. Richard had to think of a way to stall, to discuss his ideas but include compelling reasons as to why Sub Rosa shouldn't invest in any of them. He needed to put enough doubt in their minds to buy him time to shut down the project.

Salvator put his hand on his shoulder. "Are you all right? You don't seem yourself."

Richard plastered the most natural-looking smile he could onto his face. "I'm fine, just a bit stressed about the presentation…" *Among other things.* "I haven't done anything like this before." Preparing to rat on a huge, well-respected organization was definitely a first.

Salvator took his jacket off and rolled up his shirt sleeves. "I'm happy to stay back and help finish it. With two of us, we'll be done in no time."

Richard's temples throbbed with nervous tension. If he didn't convince Salvator to leave, he'd have to abort his 'copy evidence' operation. With the project report due the next day, it gave him a legitimate reason to work late and the perfect opportunity to execute his plan. "No, no, go home. I've got it under control. I just need a bit more quiet, thinking time. I promise I'll call you if I need a hand."

Salvator sighed. "I feel like you've done all the work. It's not fair. Please let me do something to help."

Richard racked his brain for a worthy task. He hated lying to Salvator, but he had no choice. "Actually, there is something you could do. Would you mind dropping Eva home?"

Cheerful surprise lit up Salvator's face. "No, of course not."

Perfect.

Eva entered Richard's office, still buttoning up her blood-red coat. The vomiting had stopped soon after her diagnosis and she'd been back at work for two weeks. People spoke about a woman glowing when pregnant, but Eva didn't just glow. She shone.

"Hi, Salvator." Her gaze traveled from Salvator to him. "Are you ready?"

Telekinetic communication. That's what he needed right now so she'd register the meaning behind his words and not put up a fight. "Sorry, sweetheart, I need to work tonight. I've got a big presentation to finish and all the reference information I need is here." He gestured to the filing cabinet beside him and the piles of files stacked up on his desk.

Disappointment dragged down the corners of her lips.

Richard walked over, kissed the sensitive spot behind her ear and whispered, "Follow my lead." He gestured to Salvator. "Salvator has kindly agreed to take you home."

She turned back to Richard with a resigned smile. "Thanks."

"I promise I won't be too late."

"It's okay. I understand." Eva pressed her palms against his chest, heat seeping through his shirt and into his skin. "Really I do. I'm just going to miss you."

Code for 'be careful'. "Me too." He kissed her lips and lingered.

Eva got it. She got him, even though they'd only been together a few months. Since taking the Soulmate Serum they seemed extra tuned in. It was probably just a coincidence, a placebo response. Chances were they'd be just as connected without the drug. "I'll see you soon."

By six-thirty, Richard had abandoned his desk and done a quick check of the dark, deserted floor. No other lights or staff were in sight…unless they were sitting in their offices, sleeping.

A few other research guys also worked late, though, thankfully, their tasks took them into the lab on the level below. As far as he knew, everyone else had gone. Now he just had to take the fire exit stairs to the administration department a few floors above, photocopy the incriminating evidence and head home.

* * * *

William walked back from the bathroom, and heard the photocopier whirring in reception. He stopped and glanced over. No lights were on, except the strobe-like flash of brightness as the machine made copies. Someone wanted something kept hidden.

He snuck up to get a closer look at the culprit. The next flash temporarily spotlighted a man's face. William had seen him before a few times with *her*, his hybrid niece. *What is the guy up to?*

The man changed documents, placing a new page flat on the glass plate, his eyes darting around before he pressed the copy button. William ducked out of the exposed doorway, his heart pounding and air pouring in and out of his lungs, tickling his throat. He couldn't let the guy see or hear him.

He stifled a cough and slunk across to his office, yanking a cigarette out of the packet in his shirt pocket and lighting it up the second the door shut. Inhaling the smoke and watching it expire from his lungs into a misty cloud felt almost meditative.

He flicked some ash into his scrunched-up, butt-filled ashtray and took a long, deep drag. Cigarettes always helped him think, helped him gain a clear point of view.

The photocopying could be innocent. It could be something personal that had nothing to do with work. Though sneaking up to copy documents out of hours didn't look good. It had to be something sensitive the man didn't want the agency to know about.

As a researcher, the guy had access to a lot of classified data. William wasn't a betting man, but he'd bet his life savings the researcher had copied some classified information for his own, far-from-innocent purposes.

Cigarette hanging from his mouth, William searched through the photos in the personnel files in the adjoining office and stopped on the researcher in question. Then he flipped to Harry's file, jotted down his home number and returned to his desk to make a call.

William stubbed out his finished smoke and lit up another. Propping the phone receiver between his left shoulder and ear, he dialed and sucked on his cigarette, his head dizzy from the huge nicotine hit.

"Hi, Harry?"

"Yes. Who's this?" he asked, his voice muffled, like he had his hand over the receiver, trying to block out background noise.

"It's William Darnel from Accounting."

Kids screamed and shouted and Harry tried to shush them. "And why are you ringing me at home?" A jab of annoyance spiked his tone, like he'd been pulled away from dinner, drinks and dessert.

William had seen him thumping through the office, throwing his weight around—literally and figuratively but never during meal breaks. Harry didn't like to be disturbed, especially when it came to food.

"I thought you might want to know that one of your research staff is photocopying documents in the dark."

"I see," the disgruntled senior manager gritted out. "And which researcher is it?" William could almost hear Harry's heart speed into stroke territory.

William blew out a big puff of smoke. "Richard H—"

The disconnect tone rang in William's ears. The bastard had hung up.

Chapter Twenty-Four

Offering

Chatter drifted down the hallway. Salvator should have been gone by now. *The TV?* Richard laid his bulging document bag on the hallway table and followed the sounds. Closer to the conservatory, a man's deep muttering followed Eva's melodic laugh. *Definitely not the TV.* It had to be his friend. *Of all the times for Salvator to stay and visit.*

"Richard, is that you?" Eva's sweet voice caressed his ears.

He stepped into the conservatory and Salvator sat on the couch, with his back to him. "Yes…"

"I invited Salvator to stay for dinner. Hope you don't mind," Eva called from the kitchen.

Salvator turned with a 'sorry, mate' smile.

Guilt squirmed in his gut like a pit of slithering snakes. Salvator seemed to pick up on his wish-you-weren't-here vibe. Richard usually enjoyed his company, but tonight he and Eva had things to talk about, a plan they needed to discuss. Hopefully Salvator wouldn't stay too long. "Of course not."

Eva returned with three glasses of red wine and placed them on the coffee table, wearing *the* red apron. Richard's mind plucked out an image of the last time she'd worn it...with nothing underneath. His pants were suddenly a size too small in the groin area.

Her warm blue-violet eyes looked cheerful and relieved. "You're earlier than I thought. I didn't expect you back before nine."

If only they were alone, he'd bend her over the conservatory table and show her exactly how glad he was to see her too. Then they could discuss business. Had the room temperature soared up to sweltering in the last thirty seconds? He ran his index finger along the inside of his shirt collar. "Yeah, I got on a bit of a roll. It helps when there are no distractions."

"You got it all done then?" Salvator asked and grabbed a wine.

"Just about." Only one task left. He and Eva needed to get the evidence to the police.

They picked up a glass each and sat adjacent to Salvator on the two-seater couch.

Salvator raised his glass. "To life-changing projects."

Richard glanced at his friend then his wife. If only Salvator knew. If only he could tell him.

"Cheers," Richard and Eva said in unison.

Richard put his arm around her small waist and tucked her in against him, tempted to touch what had been her flat stomach. In the past week, it had developed into an irresistible baby bump and she looked sexier than ever.

Eva's gaze remained fixed on their friend. "Enough business talk. I want to know what's happening with your love life."

Salvator sank deeper into his seat and sighed. "Unfortunately, not much at the moment."

"Really? I'm surprised. You're a good-looking guy and easy to talk to. There must be lots of interested women."

Salvator swilled some wine, protective shutters closing over his open eyes. "There are. I'd be lying if I said otherwise. But...it's me, all me."

Eva shifted to the edge of her seat. "What do you think of my friend Greer? She's been hounding me to find out if you're single...and available."

Richard stared at his shameless wife. "Eva, leave the poor man alone. Since when have you become a matchmaker?" He finished his wine and placed his glass back on the table.

"Sometimes people need a little help."

"Out of anyone we know, Salvator's in the best position to help himself," Richard said.

Eva quirked her eyebrow into a quizzical arch.

"He invented a Soulmate Serum, remember?"

"Oh, yes..."

Salvator's olive skin turned weak-coffee white.

The penny didn't just drop — it rolled into place. "You trialed it on yourself first, didn't you? And it didn't work out. That's why you split up with your fiancée," Richard said.

In one gulp, Salvator sank the remainder of his wine. "Yes. I had to know."

Lines of concern streaked across Eva's forehead. "And you haven't found anyone since."

Salvator stared at the empty wine goblet as though it were a looking glass about to show him a glimpse of the future. "Oh, I've found women I'm keen on, but as soon as I touch them…nothing. I can't even just have a meaningless fling."

"You've already touched Greer," Eva said.

"She touched me."

Eva laughed. "Of course she did. So she's ruled out."

"Unfortunately. She seems like a lot of fun."

Richard grabbed the wine bottle and topped up their glasses.

Salvator's sad, hopeless gaze moved between theirs. "What if I never find the right woman? It's a real possibility."

Eva reached out and squeezed his hand. "She's got to be out there. You just haven't crossed paths yet."

He swirled the red wine in his glass. "I don't know. There are no guarantees."

"Promise me you won't give up," Eva said.

"I wish I could. I think my best bet is to work on an antidote."

The light of recognition flicked on in Richard's brain. "That's what you've been doing, isn't it? While I've been pulling together the project report."

"Yes…sorry."

"Don't be sorry. Remember, I volunteered to take the lead on it." Richard propped his forearms on his knees and leaned forward. "Any progress?"

He shook his head, every smooth, black, Brylcreemed hair remaining in place. "None. I feel like I've hit a solid steel wall. I'm the epitome of 'be careful what you wish for'. I wanted to invent a Soulmate Serum and became obsessed with it to the point where I'd put all my energy, all my drive and focus into coming up with a successful potion.

"And now look where it's gotten me. I've got nothing left to give. Instead of interest and excitement, I'm driven by desperation and hope. But I feel like a result is always going to elude me, always be just out of my reach."

Eva retracted her hand and studied the ruby, diamond and haematite soulmate ring on her right ring finger. "If you believe that, it'll be a self-fulfilling prophecy. It's still early on. You've only just started working on the cure. Give yourself some time. You might be working on something unrelated and the answer will come to you — or you might find *her* in the meantime."

Salvator forced a smile. "I hope so. I really do."

Eva wiggled off the soulmate ring and held it out to him. "Take this."

"Um...how is a piece of jewelry going to help?"

She turned his right hand over and dropped the ring onto his palm. "This is a special ring, designed to bond with and retain a soulmate — or so I've been told."

"But it's yours, for you and Richard. I can't accept it," he said, and tried to give it back.

"Yes, you can. I'll be offended if you don't, like you would have been if we'd tried to return the very generous wedding gifts you gave us." She glanced at Richard and smiled. "I've found my soulmate and, thanks to your serum, I never have to question who he is, ever again. It's helped move our relationship along to where we are now. Without it, we probably still wouldn't be married."

Or having sex. "And we'd be quite frustrated," Richard chimed in, reliving their pre-marital, frottage rule.

Salvator chuckled, picking up on his underlying meaning.

"Maybe this ring will be the added assistance you need to help find your perfect match," Eva said, ignoring his innuendo.

"But—"

She held up her hand in a stopping motion. "When Richard's uncle gave it to us, he specified the ring wasn't intended to belong to one person, but to move to whoever needed it most."

Eva. The most considerate, thoughtful woman. Richard fell in love with her more and more each day. He smiled at her then at his friend. "And that person is you, Salvator. You're a great guy and you deserve the best. Hopefully the ring will help you find the right woman for you."

Straight after dinner, Salvator got up to leave and Richard saw him to the door.

"Thanks again for this"—Salvator patted the ring in his pants pocket—"and your support."

"Anything we can do—"

"Don't hesitate to ask. I know the drill. As long as you also take your own advice."

A resurgence of guilt sprang into Richard's stomach. He should tell Salvator about the Norway Experiment discrepancies, about what he intended to do with the incriminating information. The words congregated on the tip of his tongue, ready to spill over.

Going by their discussions, he and Salvator were on the same wavelength, and Richard's gut insisted Salvator wouldn't betray him. But that wasn't the only consideration. Confiding in him potentially put him in danger. Richard couldn't do that to his friend. He already chastised himself over roping his wife into the whole mess.

Richard swallowed back his confession and smiled. "You're a good friend."

Salvator patted his arm. "As are you. See you tomorrow."

Richard waited until Salvator had driven down the driveway then rejoined Eva at the kitchen sink.

"Do you think your uncle will be okay with us giving the ring away?" Eva asked.

"He won't mind. He trusts our judgment."

She rested her soapy hands on the sink's metal rim. "It just seemed like the right thing to do."

"Yes…" He wound his arms around her waist and placed a gentle kiss behind her ear.

She sighed. "I feel a bit of a gap now, though. It's strange…" She turned within his embrace, her hands dripping dirty dishwater on the floor. "I think I'm just worried about… I'm assuming you got everything you need."

"Yes. I made two copies of the documents. We'll hide one away and take the other with us to the police tomorrow morning."

"And you're sure no one saw you." Second thoughts weighed down her every word.

Richard had to ease her mind somehow. "I seemed to be alone. One of the accountant's offices had a light on but the door was shut and I snuck into reception at the other end of the floor and left the light off."

Stress invaded her face, marching into the lines around her eyes and mouth.

Going by her expression, he hadn't been quite as reassuring as he'd hoped. *Take two.* "Not ideal, I know, but I had to make the most of the situation. No one stopped me, so I'm assuming that's a positive sign." He brushed his lips across her furrowed forehead. "We'll be fine."

Richard interlocked his fingers with hers, steered her toward the staircase, picking up his work bag along the way, and continued upstairs to his study. He pulled one copy of the incriminating evidence out of the bag and laid it on the desktop.

Eva handed him her rose-key pendant and he popped open the front panel of the black, gothic desk and slid it up and away, exposing the hidden, lockable drawer. He hesitated. "I'm thinking about including some photos of us, as well as the evidence and my exposé notes—a bit like a time capsule, just in case."

Her pupils dilated and the blood drained from her skin. *So much for settling her nerves.*

He rubbed the outside of her arms. "Nothing's going to happen to us. However, on the very small chance it does, hopefully my uncle or Salvator will think to try the drawer and take the information to the authorities."

"And the photos?"

"So the police know who they're looking for" — he swallowed, twigs of fear sticking in his throat — "in case we go missing." Saying it out loud made it sound so much worse, like it could really happen. A shiver snaked down his spine.

Eva hid her face in his chest, her body trembling. "Oh, Richard, I'm getting really scared now."

She wasn't the only one. His nerves ran as raw as an exposed, weeping wound. But he kept his worry to himself. Telling Eva would only move her from stress to panic. And that's when mistakes were made. Hopefully his jittery, jack-hammering heart wouldn't give him away.

"Just think. In a few hours, it'll all be over and we can get on with our lives...and so can many others." He tipped her chin up, contained tears changing the color of her eyes to muted violet. They both needed a distraction. Desperately. He needed to stop them from feeding off each other's fear. "Now come and have a shower with me."

She didn't have to say a word. Her you've-got-to-be-kidding gaze didn't just speak volumes—it spoke entire libraries. "You do realize sex won't fix this problem."

Richard locked the envelope away in the drawer, closed the panel over it and handed the rose-key pendant back to Eva. "Sex? Who said anything about sex? I asked you to have a shower with me. The hot, pounding water will do us good, like a soothing massage." He fought back the grin, punching at the corners of his mouth.

She stared at him with a who-are-you-trying-to-fool look.

"Just because our showers often end in sex doesn't mean—"

"Often? Try every time so far."

He chuckled and held her close. "You got me. So come and have sex with me then. It may not fix the problem but it'll definitely help with the stress."

She shook her head and smiled. "How do you do that?"

"Do what?"

"You always seem to find a way to lighten a heavy situation, to make me feel more relaxed."

Finally. He forged on with the winning formula and feigned an upset facial expression. "What are you saying? You don't need sex now?"

She laughed. "I always need sex with you, stressed or not."

"Excellent answer," he said, his tone thick with lust.

They threw their clothes on the bedroom floor and kissed their way into the en suite. Richard turned on the taps, lifted Eva into the shower-over-bath and directed them under the steamy water, jetting out from the large-faced shower rose.

Dripping wet, he walked her backward, sat her on the far corner of the bath and knelt between her legs. The small baby bulge drew him in like a beacon speaking to his soul, and he reached out and caressed it, the hum of connection reverberating right to his heart. Richard kissed Eva's belly button with reverence, continuing down until his mouth enclosed her swollen clit.

She dropped her head back, jutting her beautiful breasts forward in erotic invitation and he accepted, palming one breast and rolling the nipple between his thumb and forefinger, while licking and sucking her clit and caressing her core.

She clamped onto the bath, her breathing quick and shallow, and she orgasmed, bucking her body against him. Eva's feminine flavor and passionate whimpers were so fucking hot that he almost came right along with her.

She started to settle and grasped one of his hands, placing it on her lower abdomen. A strong flutter tickled his skin, followed by another and another.

His eyes searched hers. "The baby?"

"Yes," she said, her voice softer than a whisper. "The little one must like it, too."

"Then we must do it more often."

She covered his hands, resting on her navel, and created a conduit, sending amplified love energy between them. "I won't argue with that."

Steam whirled around the room, and they kissed. It tasted of unity, the bitterness of tomorrow's daunting task washed away. It was a temporary reprieve and they both took advantage of it. She started stroking his ready-to-come cock and he lifted her and pressed her back against the wall.

Eva locked her legs around his waist and he slid inside her, his pelvis rubbing her barely-recovered clitoris. Slow and sensual thrusts progressed to heady and fast, and they both climaxed. Together.

They continued to kiss, breathing into each other like an oxygen mask, and the flutter started up again, like delicate, butterfly wings against his stomach. "Can you feel that?"

"Yes," she whispered against his lips. "The baby likes you inside me too. A lot."

No better feeling existed in the world, not in his experience. "That makes three of us."

She nuzzled the tip of his nose. "Mmm…you're right. This is just what I needed."

"It's what we all needed by the looks of it." More fluttering strummed his wet skin.

Eva's adoring smile tucked into her rosy cheeks. "I think the baby is trying to connect with you, with both of us."

Was connecting with them even possible for a baby conceived less than three months before? "The thought of it fills me with so much love I could burst. I still can't believe we've created a life, that we're going to be a little family." He kissed her passion-plumped lips.

"You'll probably think this is a bit premature, but I've been thinking about names."

"Really? Me too. I'd love Scarlett if it's a girl."

"I like that. And if it's a boy?"

"Couldn't even narrow down a shortlist."

"Luckily for you I have," he said with an impish grin. "With 'Blake' at the top."

"Blake," she echoed, rolling the name around her tongue, as though testing the sound. "I love it."

Loving warmth radiated from his heart. Their baby was no longer just a concept, an idea. Their child reaching out to him, to both of them, made it conceivable, made it real. And now he had to stand up and play his part as a responsible, honorable parent.

Chapter Twenty-Five

Capture

Richard snapped open his eyes to darkness. D-day. Dreary, dismal, dangerous.

He flicked on the bedside lamp, the dim glow highlighting the white, washed-out fear, tainting Eva's face. Richard had watched her most of the night, surprised she'd gotten any sleep. "Are you ready?"

A lightning bolt of stress struck her pupils and she yawned and stretched to try to cover it up. "As ready as I'll ever be."

After breakfast, while she did the dishes, he grabbed a paper-clipped copy of the evidence, had a quick last skim over it and filed it away in his document bag. He checked his skeleton watch. Seven-twenty-nine. His arm shook. *Hold it together. You're doing the right thing.*

"Time to go," he called out, a distinct quiver in his voice, not quite the strong, confident tone he'd aimed for. He crossed his fingers that she hadn't noticed. He had to have her on his side, to believe in him and what he proposed to do to give them the best chance to pull it off.

Eva appeared in the corridor, her attempt at a smile not reaching her eyes, and slung her handbag over her shoulder. He held her hand, and they walked to the car. Although worried and skeptical, she supported him. *So far so good.*

The silent car ride dialed up his thoughts to blaring. He had to keep focused on facts and remain unemotional and methodical, explaining each step to the police until they understood the gravity of the situation. Then, when he and Eva were safe, they could talk and relax.

Only a street away from the police station, a black car cut Richard off, and he swerved to the side of the road.

He yanked on the handbrake, took the car out of gear and let the engine idle. "Are you okay?" He scanned Eva's face and with a shaky hand, cupped her cheek.

Her terrified gaze met his, her breathing stilted. "I think so. That was close."

"Very." He exhaled hard, a fresh jolt of adrenaline thrashing through his veins. "Right. Let's try again." But before he could move, a black car parked in front and one behind, blocking him into the tight space.

Clunking footsteps thudded and crunched on the loose gravel. "Going somewhere?" He'd recognize Harry Kennedy's autocratic voice anywhere.

Richard wound down his window. "To work." He tried to remain calm, but his twitchy smile and trembling hand threatened to betray him.

"If you were going to work, you would have turned off a while back."

Richard's leg started shaking and he forced his foot to the floor, bracing himself. "We needed to detour past…"

"The police station?" Harry bent down, his face a thou away from Richard's. He had the intimidating, interrogation routine down pat.

Fuck. "Why would I go there?"

"You tell me."

"No reason," Richard said, swallowing back the bulging lie.

"Really." Harry's beady eyes darted to the back seat. "What's in the big black bag?"

"Work documents." Not a lie. The information related back to his work, yet his stomach felt squeezed into a small rigid cage.

Harry's lips lifted into a sinister sort of, I-got-you smile. "Then you won't mind me having a look."

A security guard pulled a shocked, silent Eva out of the MG, cuffed her and shoved her in the back of the lead black car.

"You better keep quiet, Missy, or I'll have to put this on you as well," he said, in a menacing voice and shoved a gag into her frightened face.

Heart hammering, Richard's body switched into full fight mode. He wanted to jump out and rescue Eva but he'd be overpowered in a second. Trying to be a hero was not the best tactic, no matter how much his macho brain yelled at him to do something, anything. He couldn't risk either of them getting hurt, especially Eva and the baby. He had to play along, until he could think of a feasible way to escape.

Harry instructed Richard to drive his car to work, as per usual, and leave the keys in the ignition.

"Any false moves and Eva will be just a memory," his boss said with his signature smarmy smile.

Anger boiled in Richard's blood, but he did as commanded and joined the cavalcade back to Sub Rosa, his mind churning over how Harry had pieced it together. *Did a staff member see me photocopying the information?* Someone had been working late on the admin floor that night. Maybe they spotted him and dobbed him in, made management suspicious.

The black car in front stopped and he slammed on the brakes. His concentration dipped and wandered all over the place. He had to drag it away from his erratic thoughts and force himself to focus on the environment. He'd be no use to Eva and the baby if he killed himself in a car accident.

For the next couple of blocks, Richard's attention held to the road but then it delved internally again. *What are they planning to do with us?* They wouldn't just let them go with a warning, not with the information he'd discovered. That only meant...

Fuck. An uncontrollable tremor shuddered through him in an endless, jittery wave. The post-shock shakes. Would Sub Rosa really make them disappear to protect the agency and its reputation? Big money and power drove people to do some strange things, dangerous things. Richard teetered on the verge of hyperventilation, his heart running rampant.

The gated, rear car park loomed ahead and he followed behind the lead car and parked next to it. The car at the back parked on the opposite side of him.

Surrounded.

Trapped.

Sub Rosa headquarters towered above them, the ominous black windows shunting out wayward eyes from prying inside. Nothing was visible, not even a shadow. He shivered, a combination of the chilly morning and flat-out fear.

The security guard wrenched Eva from the back seat. Pure terror slashed her blue-violet eyes. *Do I look the same? Scared, vulnerable, drained.* When flooded with fear, body language became almost impossible to disguise. They'd been forced into fight or freeze, though flight would be his method of choice.

Richard twisted his hands into flexing fists. However, he had to suppress his fight impulse. Freeze offered them the best chance of survival. He stretched out his tight hands, trying to loosen the grip of terror fused with fury.

Patient. He had to be patient and wait for the right fight-or-flight opportunity…if it ever came.

Harry lumbered over, opened Richard's door and ordered him out. Then he cuffed his hands in front and nudged him toward the camouflaged rear exit of the building, where Eva and the security guard waited.

The security guard herded them into the back foyer and closed the door. Sensor lights kicked in, illuminating an empty elevator shaft directly in front of them. Richard's skyrocketing heartbeat reignited his hyperventilated breathing, and his head swam with dizziness. Were they going to push him and Eva down into it, never to be seen again?

Harry pressed the down button, calling the lift up to them. *Thank fuck.* It looked like he and Eva would make it alive—to the basement, anyway.

They piled into the shoddy, claustrophobic service lift, and it creaked and shook and staggered to the floor below. He and Eva had taken to the same elevator to the basement the first time they'd met Salvator, though it felt completely different. Stifling.

They stepped out into the sterile, sectioned-off space, where they had trialed the Soulmate Serum only three short months ago. Harry and the security guard led them through the deserted area into the large lab, now fitted with metal tables, black benchtops with sinks and shelves stacked with test tubes, Petri dishes, Bunsen burners and a range of bottled substances.

Pungent bleach polluted the air. In the opposite corner of the room, a massive metal cylinder was piped up to something. Distress shot his mind into overdrive. Were they going to gas them? Like in the concentration camps?

Harry's soulless eyes stared at Richard. "Get on the table."

Richard obeyed, shuddering as his skin made contact with the icy steel.

"Lie down." Harry's voice was as cold as the metal surface. His beady eyes darted over to the security guard. "Tie him down and remove the cuffs."

The security guard reached under Richard's gurney and began securing a sequence of black, inflexible bands around him. Partway through, he uncuffed him, positioning Richard's arms by his sides, then continued tying until he'd strapped him in from his shoulders through to his ankles. Richard tried to move but the bands restricted any wriggle room.

Eva whimpered and he turned his head, his gaze connecting with hers. Red, swollen, waterlogged eyes stared back at him. Heartbreak stung like a poisonous dart embedded in his aching chest. She stayed stiff and bristled with stress. If only he could cradle her in his arms and comfort her, tell her he had a foolproof plan to freedom.

A red drop.

Blood?

Splashed onto the sterile floor.

A slow trickle down her leg.

And another.

And another.

Creating a slippery red path.

What the fuck? "What have you done to her?" Richard yelled and slammed against the binds, desperate to sit up. He had to get to her. The ligatures serrated his skin but he didn't stop. "You fuck'n animals! You'll pay. You'll pay!"

Harry's confused gaze dropped to Eva's leg then up at him. The slimy manager put his hands up into a stop-right-there stance. "I haven't touched her."

The security guard marched forward, his hands up in surrender. "Neither have I."

Eva doubled over in pain. "Aaaah!" Her tortured cry rang out around the room like an activated alarm.

"What's wrong?" Richard asked, his heart thumping in his throat.

She grimaced and clutched her stomach.

The baby.

Something was wrong with the baby. *No!*

Richard glared at Harry. "Don't just stand there, help her! Or let me do it."

Harry looked from Richard to his baffled partner in crime. "Take her into the bathroom and let her clean up."

The guard guided Eva, still hunched over and sobbing, out of the room. Why help her if she'd be silenced? Killed. A positive sign? But then again, what normal person could decipher the workings of a sociopathic mind?

Now alone with Harry, he'd investigate rather than speculate on his manager's intentions. "What are you planning to do with us?"

"Whatever I see fit."

"Such as...?" Richard wanted to know, yet he didn't. Their punishment would be more than a simple slap on the wrist. Sub Rosa had way too much at stake. Wearing his Mr. Practical science hat, there were two choices — torture or death, possibly both. Cold sweat broke out onto his skin and slid like melted icicles down his back.

"It'll depend on the outcome of further consultations."

If only he could wipe the smirk off the guy's flabby face. Harry enjoyed being evasive, seeing Richard squirm. *Fucking prick.* It was like talking to a brick — a dense, moss-covered, slimy brick. Richard dropped his head against the hard metal. Frustration chewed on his insides like flesh-eating bacteria. They'd know their fate soon enough.

Two sets of footsteps. One shuffling, dragging.

He jerked his head up toward the sound.

Eva.

She had bawled-out, bloodshot eyes and her nose was ruddy red and raw. Richard's heart lurched. Not a good sign. The crimson trickles were gone from her fair skin and her clothes were wet where she had cleaned off the offending blood.

Her somber gaze met his. 'Miscarriage' was stamped all over her face. His heart plummeted, smashing into his solar plexus and shattering his composure. A tear rolled down his cheek and he clenched his jaw, trying to dam the flow of pain. If only he could have a moment alone with his wife to talk, hug, grieve — if she didn't hate him.

The security guard lifted Eva's weary, traumatized body onto the metal bed next to Richard's and strapped her in. She started shaking with nerves, fear, shock. He wanted to wrap her in his arms and hold her, tell her everything would be all right. But would it?

Not likely.

In a totally fucked up way, it was a blessing she'd lost the baby. Richard couldn't bear the thought of their child suffering because of his high-risk decision-making gone wrong.

Harry squeezed into the gap between them. "Right. Well, it's time for me to leave you. But just in case you somehow slip out of the restraints, don't even think about trying to escape." He gestured to the security guard. "He'll be standing watch right outside the door."

Harry thundered out of the room, leaving them alone. *Finally*.

Eva turned to Richard. "I lost the baby," she said, her voice a wafer-thin whisper.

A swell of moisture resurfaced in his eyes. "I thought so. I'm so sorry." His words felt impotent, not offering anything near the apology he needed to give. Though, what apology could ever make up for what he'd done?

Tears ran down her pallid cheeks. "It's not your fault."

"Yes, it is. If I hadn't gotten so fixated on seeking justice, we wouldn't be here and you wouldn't have miscarried."

A steady stream of tears rolled down the side of her face, creating a pool of grief on the metal table. "You don't know for sure." Even after what he'd put her through, she didn't want him to suffer. She should be angry. She should be holding him accountable. She should hate him.

Richard thumped his head against the cold, hard table and stared at the ceiling. "The stress couldn't have helped."

"No, it wouldn't have, but, Richard…"

Relentless guilt gushed up inside him.

"Richard, please look at me."

He yanked his gaze from the ceiling and his stinging eyes met hers.

"You need to stop blaming yourself. I had a choice and I chose to stick by you. For better or worse, remember? We're both responsible. All we can do now is focus on making the best of the situation so we can get out of here…alive." Her voice caught, but she gathered her composure and kept going. "Wishing things were different isn't going to help. For future decision-making maybe, but not now."

What she said made sense. But he had bulldozed her into exposing Sub Rosa. If it were up to her, she wouldn't have chosen the same path. No way. And she knew, too. Yet she focused her attention on them, on salvaging their relationship first and foremost, exactly what he should have prioritized. "I don't deserve you."

"We deserve each other. We're confirmed soulmates, husband and wife. We're committed to each other through thick and thin, till death do us part," she said, trying to smile through her tears.

Such a sweet, brave woman. She was so much stronger and more clear-headed than he gave her credit for. Most people would have fallen apart under the same circumstances, though not his wife, not Eva. He smiled back, his heart swelling with regret, adoration and respect.

She tried to angle herself more toward him, the inflexible bands jolting her back into place. "What will they do with us?" Eva's face screwed up and she choked on the last word.

"Are you okay?"

She nodded, though her expression and the way her hands retracted to her stomach said *no*.

"I don't know what they're planning. But we need to stay strong."

Eva in pain tore him apart. He couldn't even give her verbal reassurance that she'd be okay. But that didn't mean he'd give up. Every cell in his body was primed for survival, to restore their life together and seek justice.

Chapter Twenty-Six

Identity Disposal

William Darnel paced his office, leaving a trail of cigarette smoke spiraling into the air, much like the solution to the latest budget issue — elusive, intangible, insubstantial.

An hour ago, he'd stopped at the window and three cars had pulled up. Two black agency cars had parked on either side of a red MG. Normally, the rear carpark was reserved for management cars only.

He pressed his forehead to the glass and replayed the scene in his head. He'd recognized Harry by his hefty, round physique and a security guard by his gun and burly build.

The security guard had retrieved a woman from the backseat of the farthest black car, and Harry had handcuffed a man stepping out of the MG. The female had looked like his niece and the male like Richard. It had to be them. He hadn't seen either of them at work today. William had a couple quick drags of his cigarette, his hand quivering. His tip to Harry must have paid off.

* * * *

At almost six p.m., Salvator still sat at his desk, writing up some research notes. He'd have finished earlier, if he hadn't been distracted by an article in the most current edition of the agency newsletter about the elusive *God Particle*.

In 1964, Professor Higgs from Edinburgh University had published the conceptual groundwork for a yet-to-be-discovered Higgs Boson particle, nicknamed the *God Particle*, that, if found, would explain the creation of the universe. The European Organization for Nuclear Research, CERN, had shown strong interest in supporting research to find it and Sub Rosa wanted to join the party.

After a year of negotiations, Sub Rosa had had confirmation of their acceptance into the elite research circle, which provided the potential for huge monetary and status-related benefits...once researchers discovered the physical particle. Although extremely nerdy, Salvator couldn't help but be excited. A discovery so huge was a researcher's dream.

Harry barged through the door, out of breath. "I need your help."

Salvator finished the last sentence of his research note and closed the file. "It's late. Can't it wait until tomorrow?"

A bead of sweat slithered down Harry's greasy forehead. "No. This has to be sorted out right now."

Salvator's brow constricted with surprise and bewilderment. Harry had a reputation for being a task master, but Salvator had never seen him so abrupt, so unwilling to negotiate.

"There's been a breach of security and we need to address it before the situation gets out of hand. I hoped you could" — he panted — "help me make things go away."

"What 'things' are we talking about?"

"Let me show you," Harry said, more an order than a request. He thumped down the corridor, stopped in front of the service lift and pressed the 'down' button, his sweaty hand leaving a film of slowly evaporating moisture.

They reached the basement and Harry led him past a beefy security guard to one-way glass overlooking the newly-fitted-out cryogenics' lab. A man and woman were strapped down to metal tables. He blinked then blinked again.

No. No, it can't be.

He leaned in closer to the glass and squinted. His friends, Richard and Eva, tied up. The friends he'd met down here only a few months earlier to trial his Soulmate Serum. They were the 'things' Harry had referred to. His heart stopped.

Salvator banged his chest with his fist and coughed, his heart stumbling back to life. He rubbed his eyes and refocused, just to make sure his brain hadn't played a warped practical joke. No such luck.

What the hell had his friends done? It had to be pretty damn serious. Life-threatening.

"I believe you were at their house last night." Harry looked ready to pounce on his response.

Shit! Did they think he was involved? Maybe he'd inadvertently gotten mixed up in whatever they'd done without knowing it? *Shit, shit, shit!* He swallowed back the mounting dread in his throat. "Yes, I dropped Eva home. Richard worked late, finishing the gene-eradication project update report." *How did Harry know?* Had he or his cronies been following him? Richard? Norway Experiment staff?

"Did they say…anything?"

His eyes fixed on Harry's beady, probing slits. "Like what?"

"Concerns about the Norway Experiment."

"No. Richard just mentioned he'd nearly completed the update report."

"Nothing about Sub Rosa's handling of the Norway Experiment or going to the police?"

Salvator could feel the confusion corrugating his forehead. "Going to the police? With what?"

Harry mopped his brow with a yellowed handkerchief and shoved it back in the pocket of his pants. "Classified documents. Richard had gotten photocopies of a few and planned to take them, along with some notes on an exposé, to the police."

"An exposé on what exactly? Sub Rosa is using tax payers' money to experiment on vampires? Most humans would be grateful."

Harry's lips locked into a shut-down smile. "But we don't want most humans to even know they exist. We don't want those freaks of nature to have any greater power or recognition than they already do."

Salvator stared at the closed-minded man. Ignorant people like him were giving the orders, making the decisions. *Scary.* Outside of checking how much Salvator knew, Harry gave nothing else away.

Whatever Richard had found out, it had to be something worth risking his safety, his life — and Eva's. Why hadn't he confided in him? They could have come up with something together, a better, more foolproof plan. Though, given the outcome, maybe him not knowing had turned out to be a blessing or he might be in the same predicament, with no one to help.

Harry studied him, and he wondered how long he'd been staring back in silence. "What I need from you are your thoughts on how we're going to best manage the situation."

"Manage the situation?" Was this a test to assess how connected he really was to his two captured friends? Salvator watched Richard and Eva through the one-way glass, willing them to disappear, willing himself to wake up from this unrelenting night terror. But no matter how hard he wished, the horrible reality remained.

The unspoken communication between Richard and Eva showed evidence of their solidarity, their impenetrable, deep bond. He had to do all he could to save it, to save them.

"Well, we can't let them go. And given the top-secret nature of the research, we can't turn them over to the authorities. So, I hoped you could suggest an effective way to" — Harry cleared his throat — "dispose of them."

"Dispose of them." Salvator's voice shook.

"In the most humane way, of course."

He can't really mean…

Salvator went from shocked distress into a heart-pumping panic attack. He couldn't kill them and he couldn't stand by and let anyone else do it either. He had to come up with an alternative — and fast. One that could save them while not incriminating him. His mind flipped through options, like scanning through a Teledex at the speed of light.

Harry stepped closer to the one-way glass, his heavy breathing fogging up the window. "I thought an injection, like the ones they give sick animals to put them down. We must have access to those sorts of drugs around here."

Is the man a psychopath? How can he talk so calmly, be so removed particularly from people he knows? Salvator always suspected managers of being cutthroat and ruthless, but in terms of budget, not people.

His mind-Teledex spat out two cards—'cryogenics' and 'memory drugs'. "Whereas I thought something more useful, more beneficial to the organization. A way to turn this around and make it work for Sub Rosa, be a positive rather than a hindrance." Salvator tried to keep his voice even, confident.

"Like what?"

Cryogenic storage of live humans. It hadn't been trialed before, not officially. But just as with many of the projects in his portfolio, who would volunteer for it? This one even more so, with the risk of permanent death a huge possibility.

In prison camps during the Second World War, some rudimentary trials had been conducted, but the set-ups and conditions were questionable and results deemed invalid. Salvator now had an unexpected break, though not quite the break he'd been looking for. Volunteering his friends technically put them to death by experimentation, though he preferred to think of it as 'life suspension'.

Conflict raged inside him like flames from an out-of-control bush fire licking at rising flood water. However, if he didn't suggest it, it left only one outcome — definite, irreversible death. This way, they had a chance, especially given Salvator's theory on their suspected, diversified gene pool.

"What if we use them to trial the memory eraser and filler drugs? I could include Richard and Eva as part of the cryogenics project, cryogenically store them and release them in the future to test the effectiveness?

"We could finally do human testing of the memory drugs and assess the usefulness of cryogenic storage at the same time — no ethics approval required." His voice sounded calm, in control, but his insides shook like a hot can of kerosene ready to combust.

The roly-poly manager scratched his chin.

Silence.

Please agree! Or else what would he do? He could try to help Richard and Eva escape, though the environmental layout made it almost impossible, a suicide mission. Given Harry knew of his friendship with Richard and Eva, not to mention Salvator's access to the lab, he'd be the first person Harry would suspect. He'd track down Salvator and his friends and dispose of them without a second thought.

"I'll record a research note to say they volunteered due to persistent, debilitating post-traumatic stress." Salvator held his breath.

More silence. Time seemed to slow down, stretching each second to a minute.

"Let me run it by the CEO," Harry finally said.

Air sucked back into his starving lungs. A 'maybe', at least not a 'no'. "I'll also need a couple of new researchers to work specifically with me on this. We can't use anyone who's already employed. They may recognize them."

An impressed smile poked the corners of Harry's scaly, lizard lips. "Good point. I'll go to see the CEO and let you know tomorrow."

And Harry actually did follow through, summoning Salvator back to the basement early the next day.

"Everything has been approved."

Relief washed over Salvator like a cool rainstorm breaking an oppressive hot spell. *Thank God!*

"But with the following stipulations... After you sort them out, you're to go to their house and dispose of their belongings," Harry said, already sweaty and struggling for breath.

He yanked a yellowed handkerchief out of his trouser pocket and patted his forehead. "If they make it out alive, we can't risk anything prompting their memories. I've already combed through their place, along with a security guard, for any other copies of stolen Sub Rosa documents and incriminating reports. None were found, but I did collect a number of photos of them. They made great fireplace fodder."

His huge boss smirked. "Oh, and you'll need to tidy up the house too. It's a mess."

"You do realize they live with Richard's uncle and he'll be back from a trip soon."

"You'd better get onto it then." Harry hesitated, tapping his chin with his stubby finger. "I suppose you can leave the furniture, some clothes and toiletries. And park Richard's car in his garage. Make it look like they've packed their essentials and taken off somewhere far away."

"What if his uncle asks me why they left, where they went? Or their friends, colleagues?"

A smug smile slid onto Harry's lips. "Tell them Richard and Eva resigned because Richard accepted a research job overseas. Tell them the opportunity was too good to pass up. That should stop too many more questions."

Salvator spent the rest of the day ringing around his contacts to find suitable research candidates, ones who were available to assist him as soon as possible and keep their mouths shut. And the universe must have been on his side, because he quickly sourced two, who were ready to start tomorrow.

* * * *

At seven a.m. Salvator met the two new researchers in the Sub Rosa basement office. He handed them each a black lab suit and closed the door. "Before we see the subjects, there are a couple of non-negotiable rules. First, the female will be referred to by her project code name, X1944, and the male, Y1939. No real names means no emotional connection. Everything is kept professional. Understand?"

Both the men stopped adjusting their outfits and nodded.

Salvator zipped up his disguise, while their three cold, blank masks laid on his desk. "The other important thing to remember is, no matter what, there will be no speaking, coughing, sneezing, sighing when we're in the lab. It's essential we keep as neutral as possible or results can be skewed." And Richard and Eva might recognize his voice. "You break any of these rules and it's instant dismissal."

"No rooting around in the files and no talking. No problem, boss," the taller man said.

"Just follow your orders. Simple," the other man added.

Suited up in in their black radiation outfits and accompanying masks, Salvator and the two inducted researchers entered the lab. Eva and Richard's eyes filled with fear, panic, uncertainty, as though still unsure whether this meant the end.

Salvator and his colleagues' post-apocalyptic, grim reaper costumes sure didn't help. If only he could reassure them but he couldn't. Even his plan remained full of doubt.

Three men in black radiation suits pulled tight on Richard's restraints, his body banging against the cold, hard, metal table. He could just see Eva, still on the steel gurney next to his, her long, dark hair sprawled over the edge. An emotional vise crushed his heart. As long as they didn't hurt her… They could kill him, but not her. *Please, not her.*

Her red-rimmed, blue-violet eyes nearly destroyed him. Helpless. Angry. Snared-wild-animal afraid. He couldn't do anything to save her, save either of them. He thought he'd have more time, a chance to negotiate. However, Sub Rosa had shut that down and sent in the dirty-work brigade. Their looming presence wreaked of torture, persecution, death.

Unless a miracle occurred, some sort of God-like intervention, Richard would never see his wife again, never feel her in his arms, her smooth skin rubbing against his as they made love, never again taste her sweet, full lips, or hear her soft, sexy voice in his ear telling him how much she loved him. They were meant to be together forever, to have children, grandchildren…

Her sobbing broke the eerie silence and he desperately wanted to comfort her. His choices had been unforgivable and yet, she'd forgiven him. Every tear she shed stabbed deep like a dagger to his heart, a reminder of what he'd lost, what would never be.

One of the black-suited men went to insert an IV line into Richard's arm. His heart kicked into high gear and he rammed against the restraints. The man held Richard's arm firm and stuck the cannula into his bulging blood vessel. Only the tiniest sting registered from the invasion into his vein, the procedure surprisingly gentle and at odds with impending fate.

The man grabbed a syringe filled with a clear liquid, angled it up and shunted the fluid until a bead dripped out the end. What the hell was it? Poison? Richard's temples pounded with frenetic, dizzying beats. The mystery man jabbed the solution into his drip and his mind and muscles melted into a drowsy, paralytic slumber.

Wide, frantic eyes drifted closed as Richard and Eva entered drug-induced dreamland. Salvator turned away and strode toward the storeroom. *Did they recognize me?* They couldn't see his face, but could they tell by his build, gait, height, mannerisms?

He went straight to the bar fridge, opened it up and, with a shaky hand, took out two, blue vials. Then he scanned the shelves for a muscle relaxant sedative, mixed it with the blue memory eraser in a large test tube, grabbed a fresh syringe and rejoined his work colleagues.

Salvator flicked on the second light switch and a row of fluorescent bulbs dominoed across the ceiling. At the cryogenic tank, he and his crew prepped the storage cylinders, due to house his friends in between treatments. The cryogenic component would be the real test. Once frozen, could he rouse them?

Next, he and his two researchers checked the gas flow, temperature and monitoring equipment. All appeared in order, yet adrenaline ran wild in his veins, a primitive response to the unknown.

Salvator closed his eyes. One action step at a time, while weighing in the end goal. That's what he had to do. Like with any other research trial, he needed to turn his emotion switch off or else he'd make a mistake.

Before Richard and Eva were due to wake, Salvator and his mini-team wheeled them closer to the cryogenic storage tank in order to prepare them for freezing. As his colleagues set up the required storage solution and associated equipment, Salvator removed and pocketed Eva and Richard's jewelry. Harry could demand all he wanted, but Salvator wouldn't dispose of it. His long-term plan included placing the items in their exit wardrobes.

Richard's eyelids flittered and he groaned, as though recovering from a hangover. The glaring lights beat down on him and he squinted. Then recognition flooded his face, his muscles tensing, twitching.

Eva blinked back brightness, her bleary eyes darting around the room in an attempt to reorient herself. A sob-like breath stammered in her windpipe. Salvator's heart lurched, threatening to expose his inner thoughts, the radiation suit his secure, black box. He wanted to undo the straps holding her in and hug her. However, he had to remain distant, detached, businesslike. A tug-of-war erupted between his rational mind and emotions.

Richard started to regain consciousness with one thought floating to the surface of his mind.

You set
a raging fire inside my heart,
spreading, consuming, transforming
Everything in its path

Until we are wholly connected,
Joined
Forever in love.

"Forever in love," he mumbled as he came to. Eva's absent warmth chilled him. *Where is she?* He'd lost track of time. Richard tried to reach out and pat her side of the bed. He couldn't.

Caustic bleach corroded his nostrils. Before he opened his eyes, he knew exactly where he was. *The lab. In the Sub Rosa basement.* So no one would ever find them. Except Salvator. *Salvator.* Their only hope. Unless Sub Rosa had relocated him.

Richard coaxed his eyelids open, his pupils assaulted by blinding, white lights overhead. He and Eva had been moved and his watch and wedding band were gone. He squinted through stinging, watery eyes and turned his head away from the onslaught.

Eva lay on a table beside him, still breathing, still alive. *Thank fuck.* Richard went to talk but his tongue tripped over itself, bulky, numb and he could only manage a moan. Whatever they'd drugged them with must have had a sedative base.

Eva's eyelids fluttered and a sob of knowing followed. He wished he could speak to her and tell her how much he loved her. He couldn't see her properly, though it didn't stop him from trying.

Richard had turned to her so many times that he should have repetitive strain injury. These black-suited guys had to be some sort of high-level operatives with a specialty in psychological torture. They were so clinical. Detached. He hoped they suffered the same as him one day.

"Wha-are-you-goin- to-do-t'me?" Richard's voice stumbled out in slow motion, his speech running together. He didn't expect to get a response and he didn't. Not one of the faceless men even sighed. Watching them mill around, scrutinizing, silently communicating felt like living out his own private horror movie. If he wasn't so drugged up, he'd be petrified.

The same man walked over to Richard's drip and prepared a syringe with a bright blue liquid.

"No…pleease doon'tdo this…leeavehim aloone!" Eva begged, her voice strung out and wobbly. If only he could hold her one last time and tell her everything would be all right. But he couldn't. And it wouldn't unless Salvator knew and could do something. But what?

The faceless man continued priming the needle, like he hadn't heard a word of Eva's plea.

Somehow, Richard turned his head more than before, either from a surge of adrenalin or imagination. There she lay, straining against her ligatures, her dark hair wild with rebellion and her watery, bloodshot eyes staring in indignation at the black-suited man.

The ominous guy injected the syringe into Richard's IV. He blinked slow and heavy, and Eva's image began to fade. *Nooooo!* Richard tried to force his eyes open, though they were a stuck gate unable to budge. He willed himself to hold onto consciousness, but it started slipping away.

Tears formed in Eva's beautiful, blue-violet eyes, rolled over the rims onto her stark, white cheeks and she blurred into blackness.

A tear trickled down Eva's face and she jolted against the restraints. Her attempt to break free and reach Richard was futile. Salvator's colleagues stood and watched in a quiet huddle as he sank the syringe into the test tube, slowly drew the full amount of memory eraser-muscle relaxant into the syringe and squirted out a drop to remove any air bubbles.

"No. Pleease doon't," Eva stammered in between sobs.

Holding back the threatening flood of emotion, Salvator pushed through and directed the needle to her drip, squeezing the chemical cocktail into her IV port. Just like her husband, her pulse crashed, one last incomprehensible whisper puffing from her lips, and she fell into enforced sleep.

Salvator stumbled back, swallowing the burning disgust rising like hydrochloric-acid reflux in his throat. If his body continued to rebel at this rate, he'd have an ulcer in no time. And deservedly so. Something so small didn't even compare to what he'd be putting his friends through.

My friends.

But he had to think rationally. He had to keep redirecting his mind to the end goal, focus on each step to provide the best chance for positive progress and hope nothing unforeseen happened, nothing went wrong.

A pounding ache at the building reserve of tears threatening to escape made Salvator move onto the next task. Taking a blood sample was standard procedure, though in this case, he needed to personally receive the results so he knew what to document in their notes. He had a hypothesis about Richard and Eva that he needed to prove or disprove.

"Wha-did-you-give'er?"

Salvator jerked his head around, his eyes meeting Richard's furious gaze. A cold sweat broke out over his body and goosebumps prickled across his skin. Richard shouldn't have roused — not yet, not for hours. But adrenaline could behave in weird, unexpected ways, particularly if a person, or someone they cared about, was under threat, pushed to the limit.

Salvator refilled the syringe in silence. Hopefully another dose would do the job.

"Tell. Me. What. You. Gave. Her," Richard said, his drowsy voice laced with seething anger.

Salvator carried the needle over to Richard's drip, swallowing back the lump of guilt and self-loathing still smoldering in his throat.

"I swear, if anything happens to her..." Richard had gone from sleepy to super-human alert in seconds, thrashing so hard against the inflexible bands that two of them snapped.

Heart racing, pulse punching at his temples, Salvator shoved the syringe into Richard's IV.

Richard gritted his teeth and continued to thrust against the restraints. Another popped open, and he lost momentum. His breathing slowed and his steely, determined stare retreated, his eyes glazing over. Finally, he slumped against the metallic table and followed his wife into a drug-induced slumber.

Drips of sweat slid down Salvator's face and he whipped off his mask and wiped them away with his sleeve. *Close. Too close.* His heart couldn't handle any other surprises.

His colleagues moved fast to remove the broken and compromised bands and fasten new ones to Richard's gurney before he woke. If the memory eraser worked as Salvator anticipated, his friends' unconscious state should give it time to start doing its magic.

Richard's and Eva's clothes were removed and burned, then the team replaced the water from their cells with a glycerol-based cryoprotectant mixture — a sort of human antifreeze. Supposedly, it protected their organs and tissues from forming ice crystals at the extremely low storage temperature — or so Salvator had learned from extensive reading.

The deep cooling without freezing vitrification process put Richard and Eva's cells into a state of suspended animation and their bodies into life suspension, not permanent death. Or at least that's how Salvator rationalized following through with the proposed experiment. Semantics, pure semantics. A few, simple word changes could give reason to anything.

Once the recommended cryoprotectant level was reached, Eva and Richard were cooled on a bed of dry ice until their body temperatures fell to negative one hundred and thirty degrees Celsius.

Next, Salvator and his colleagues inserted his friends head down into individual coffin-like containers and placed them into the large metal tank filled with liquid nitrogen at a temperature of negative one hundred and ninety-six degrees Celsius.

That way, if ever a leak occurred in the tank, their brains stayed immersed and preserved in the freezing liquid, giving Salvator a chance to revive them, assuming the whole process hadn't killed them first.

Chapter Twenty-Seven

The Discovery

Physically, mentally and emotionally exhausted, Salvator stepped into the thick black shroud of night and slogged across the deserted car park to his car. He couldn't drive straight home—not yet, not before he took care of one thing that could stop or at least slow the insidious guilt from spreading like a malicious infection through his blood stream.

In less than twenty minutes, he arrived at his sister's house and she answered the door in her fluffy, pink dressing gown and matching slippers.

"Sorry to come by so late but I just finished work and thought I'd visit on my way home."

A surprised smile stretched her small mouth and sent sharp striations through the center of her forehead. "You're welcome here any time, you know that. Come in," she whispered.

"Are the kids asleep?"

"Yeah..."

"Sorry."

"Don't worry." He stepped inside the compact, front foyer and she hugged him. "It's been ages."

"Yes, I know. I've been so busy at work I've barely had time to sleep."

"You don't have to explain. I understand. Come sit down in the lounge and I'll make you a coffee."

He hesitated. "Where's hubby?"

"Nightshift. He put the kids to bed and had to leave straight away."

Good. The less he saw of the guy, the better. "Oh. Are you sure it's okay for me to be here? I don't want to disturb the kids."

"Of course! Stop fretting and just come sit down!"

Always the bossy big sister. Nowadays it was just the two of them and her family. Salvator didn't get along too well with his brother-in-law, though. The guy drank too heavily and put too much pressure on his sister to hold the family together and keep them afloat financially.

Salvator had tried to speak to her about it but she loved her husband, blindly it seemed. As long as his sister stayed safe and loved... He hoped his brother-in-law felt about his sister as Richard did for Eva. Another stab of guilt pierced his solar plexus.

The flickering light from the TV guided him through the obstacle course of toys strewn across the carpet, and he sat on the closest couch. "Hey, sis, are you still doing the markets?"

"Yeah, why?"

He fingered the cold, hematite ring in his trouser pocket. "I wanted to ask you about something."

She rushed out from the dimly-lit kitchen. "Really? You never ask me about anything. You're the smart one, remember?" she said with a cheeky smile.

Yeah, real smart. He'd created a Soulmate Serum that had ruined his engagement and orchestrated a potentially fatal experiment on his friends. *Genius.* The ring turned icy, as though reading his thoughts, and Salvator squirmed in his seat.

"Not when it comes to jewelry. That's your area of expertise." He pulled the ring out of his pocket, a chilling ache penetrating his palm. "I hoped you could tell me something about this." Deep sadness, regret and helplessness tore through his flesh and infested every cell. He couldn't keep hold of the moody thing.

She snatched it out of his hand and inspected it with her keen jeweler's eye. "Where did you find it?"

"A friend gave it to me."

"This is a very special ring. I never realized it actually existed."

He flexed his frosty hand. "Is it worth a bit of money?"

"I'm not sure. Possibly, though that's not what interests me about it. If the legend is true, it has special properties, ensuring only the right person comes into possession of it. Only a woman who has truly found her soulmate will be attracted to this ring."

Stinging cold sweat formed like sleet on his skin and he shivered. "Really…"

She turned the ring over and over in her hand. "But more than likely it's an 1800s reproduction. It was quite fashionable to make jewelry based on the classics back then." Her gaze returned to him. "Anyway, your usual black coffee?"

Did the room temperature just plummet way below zero or did he imagine the icy drop? "Don't worry about it. I'd better go." Salvator stood from the worn, mission brown lounge chair.

"You just got here."

He edged toward the door. "I know, but it's getting late. Would you mind putting the ring on display — ?"

"No problem."

"And let me know if anyone shows interest in it?

"Sure, but — "

"I'd really appreciate it if you could just do this for me" — Salvator stopped in front of the door and turned to her — "without asking any more questions."

She pinned him with her overly intuitive, sisterly stare. "Is everything okay?"

"Yes, everything's fine," he said, trying to convince her as well as himself.

"If you say so."

He could tell she didn't buy it, but she wouldn't push him any further.

"You know, it's a real shame about you breaking off your engagement. I really liked her. And she adored you. You never told me what happened." His sister had a way of weaseling out people's secrets — from the minute she'd left the womb, according to their mother. He almost admired her special skill...when he wasn't her target.

Salvator shoved his hands into his pockets and fumbled around for his keys. Locked in his heart were now two major secrets. He'd have to padlock his internal safe, secure it against slips and leaks and exposure of the sensitive information. He cleared his throat. "Maybe another time."

The break-up seemed like an eternity ago now. Everything had changed. In such a short time his life had taken on a whole new direction. But forget the road less traveled. Instead, circumstances had steamrolled everything in sight to carve out their own, rough path.

And now he could only appeal to fate to stop his journey from turning into a lifelong detour.

* * * *

First thing the next morning, Salvator strode into the desolate lab and checked the blood analysis machine. A results print-out sat in the tray.

Leukocytosis.

Not surprising. Consistent with his theory, both Richard and Eva had a slightly higher white blood cell count. He put the print-out aside and prepared a slide of Richard's then Eva's blood. Under the high-powered microscope, on the sterile work bench, he studied the proteins in both blood samples.

Just as he suspected, the result was consistent with the elevated white blood cell finding. He shook his head and smiled, proud of his deduction but scared of what it all meant.

Eva and Richard each carried *the gene*, though different familial variations. He collected the slides, washed them in the sink and stacked them in the sterilizer. Then he fired up a Bunsen burner and, holding the results in heat-proof lab tongs, set the dangerous information alight. He'd take the knowledge of his friends' genetic makeup to his grave. Letting on to Sub Rosa equaled the end.

For all of them.

For sure.

The blue-yellow flame devoured the paper until only black cinders floated in the air. He grabbed their files and noted a false reading in each. Had Richard and Eva been aware of their heritage?

From his conversations with them, they'd appeared to have no idea. Though, maybe they chose to play it safe. Or had found out about themselves and it had driven them to go to the police to stop the Norway Experiment.

Salvator had never gotten a straight answer from Harry about what information Richard and Eva had stolen. He leaned on the bench and thought for a moment. Maybe he could subtly investigate and find out on his own.

He approached the lift and pressed the call button. The security guard had seemingly disappeared. *Odd.* The doors opened and he stepped inside, the swift ride up to Richard's office fitting right in with his urgency plan. He needed to be in and out before anyone saw him.

Salvator checked the corridor. No one was in sight, and the place sounded as silent as a cemetery. *No.* Silent as a library. *Much better.*

He slunk inside Richard's empty office and shut the door. On the desk were several piles of paper, but none referred to the Norway Experiment. *Strange.* Richard had definitely been working through those files to familiarize himself with the project. And whatever he had discovered had to be in among them.

Salvator thumped his fist on the desktop. *Crap!* Management must have pilfered the pile and extracted the evidence before anyone else got to it, even him. It showed an agency culture steeped in pure paranoia and lack of trust. Yet the head honchos always went to him to deal with and defuse 'situations'. In all the seemingly contradictory behavior, one theme recurred—Sub Rosa decisions came down to budget and risk management.

How would he ever find out what Richard discovered now? Then again, maybe Salvator would be better off, safer, not knowing. He angled his watch under a strip of straw-colored morning light, jutting through a gap in the blind. It was nearly seven-thirty. Staff were about to arrive. Before anyone saw him, he had to dash back to the dungeon.

He had so many tasks to complete that the day flew. Then that evening, he drove Richard's MG to the Hall home, still debating whether he should have parted with the soulmate ring. Giving it away should have rid him of some of his regret, but it wasn't so simple.

The ring, such a heartfelt gift, left behind residual guilt in the pit of his stomach. He couldn't win either way. However, if the tale about the power of the ring held some truth, Eva should find her way back to it one day.

The gloomy gray sky dulled the usually bright green garden and cast an eerie ambience over the Hall house, like something out of a gothic, vampire novel. Suddenly it seemed perfect that Bram was the sole remaining occupant.

Salvator hid Richard's car in the garage, returned to the front of the house and went inside. Cold, dark and desolate, the emptiness chilled him beyond the bone to the marrow. All the warmth from the wonderful pre-wedding dinner had vanished along with the hosts. Prowling around their property made him feel like a burglar, a traitor. But it had to be done by him and no one else. Anything of importance, he'd hang onto, making sure it avoided the destroy stack.

Where should I start? He wandered into the living room and straight over to the snuffed-out fireplace. Harry had allocated him the whole day to wade through his friends' possessions and he'd need it. He scanned the mantelpiece and something bumped against his leg. He jumped, his eyes darting down, his heart nearly shooting out his mouth.

"Meow."

A *cat*. Harry hadn't mentioned anything about a cat and Salvator hadn't seen one during the dinner party. What should he do with it? He couldn't leave it to starve. He rubbed his temples. Maybe he should try to contact Bram and let him know Richard and Eva had disappeared and he found the cat wandering around on its own. That's what a concerned friend would do.

Salvator crouched and patted the charcoal-gray feline. It purred and butted his hand and legs, the soft, silky fur like a snug velour blanket. He couldn't abandon the cute, friendly little thing and force it to fend for itself. Maybe he could drop by daily or even stay at the house until Bram got back. It could be a sort of house-sitting arrangement, allowing more time to be thorough, to make sure he didn't miss anything.

Decision made.

Salvator stood and surveyed the room. It contained mostly furniture with little space to hide stuff, and nothing specific to Richard and Eva. He returned to the main corridor and passed an antique hall table with a telephone and notepad sitting alongside it. The notepad had Bram's name written across the top and a telephone number to reach him while he traveled.

Going by the sequence length, the number appeared international, with what looked to be a Norwegian country code—Bram, Gothic mansion, vampires, Norway. Could it be a coincidence or something more? One thing he knew for sure. Bram didn't have the vampire gene. His coloring confirmed pure human genetics.

Although Salvator couldn't rule out Richard's dad carrying the Jade gene. He could have inherited a different gene pool from his parents than his brother, Bram, or *changed* later. The more likely scenario suggested that Richard's vampire heritage came from his mother's side. Even so, Bram was probably aware of Richard and Eva's genetics.

After feeding the cat and changing its stinky litter tray, Salvator took a taxi back to Sub Rosa to pick up his car and drove home with Bram's contact number burning a hole in his pocket. He parked in his driveway and hurried to the front door.

"Salvator?"

Shit. He turned as Greer caught up to him.

"What's going on with Richard and Eva? And where have you been? I've been trying to speak to you!" Her probing, chocolate-brown eyes searched his.

She really did radiate raw, natural sex appeal. Maybe they could… "Sorry. I've been seconded to a new position."

"Have you spoken to them? Are they coming back? Is there a number I can call them on?" She clamped her hand on his arm and he flinched.

Hurt flashed in her eyes.

Nope. No chance of any adult physical fun. Bloody Soulmate Serum! "No." He averted his gaze and tried to relax his restless hands. "I wish I had more to tell you but, like everyone else, all I've heard is they've relocated overseas. I'm sure they'll contact us when they're settled. It sounds like everything happened very quickly."

God, he hated lying, but he had no other choice, not if he planned to protect them, not if he planned to protect himself and not if he planned to keep them all alive.

"They could have at least told one of us!" Her words hissed with venomous anger. Too much anger. The signs suggested she'd bundled up her hurt and confusion over his blatant rejection of her with her disappointment and frustration over her friend's silent departure.

"Yes, well, if I hear from them, I'll let you know. Sorry, I need to go." He turned his back on Greer and locked himself inside his safe haven, watching her from the window as she retreated to her car.

So far, she didn't seem to suspect anything, the notion of foul play not even on her radar. *Thank God.* At least one thing had gone in his favor. Sort of. In her case, it should be as simple as out of sight, out of mind. Bram, on the other hand, wouldn't be so easy, but he had to tell him.

Salvator dialed the international number and waited for the click of connection.

"Hello, Bram? It's Salvator. Richard's...ah...friend." His voice quivered out of key, like an untuned cello.

"Hi, Salvator, how are the newlyweds?" Cheer danced in his every word.

"Um...have you spoken to them recently?"

"No. Why?"

"They haven't been at work. Management said they'd resigned so Richard could take up a research job opportunity overseas."

"That's the first I've heard about it," Bram said.

"Me too. So I went by the house today and it was deserted, bar the cat wandering around outside." He had to divert suspicion away from himself and lead Bram up the overgrown garden path, even though it made him sick.

Every poor decision wore away more of his integrity, what little he had left. Though, if Bram became too nosey, too good an investigator, they'd all pay the hefty price.

"They wouldn't have left Smokey behind without telling someone." The wet blanket revelation smothered the joy in Bram's voice.

"That's why I rang, in case they'd already spoken to you and you were on your way back."

"I know nothing about it," he said, his words jittering down the phoneline.

"Um...given the situation, I'm happy to stay at the house and look after Smokey until you get here, if that's okay with you."

"Of course. The spare key's in an envelope in the mail box addressed to me."

"Thanks." Though, Salvator already had a key. But he couldn't admit that to Bram.

"I'll arrange a return flight as soon as I can. I should be back in a few days. If you hear from them in the meantime, let me know." Bram's voice sounded short and sharp and he clicked off, the hang-up tone left shrilling in Salvator's ear.

Over the next few days, Salvator undertook a thorough re-search of the Hall house, tidying the overturned drawers and returning the dumped-out clothes, shoes and linen back into the cupboards. He found nothing of significance...to report to Sub Rosa.

A crumpled black and white polka-dot dress poked through the pile of clothes he picked through on their bedroom floor and he gathered it up. Eva had worn it the night she and Richard had come in to trial his Soulmate Serum, the night he'd first met her, the night he'd solidified them as a couple, the night that had changed their lives forever.

Salvator stared at the limp fabric, blinking back tears. He definitely had to include it as another piece in the exit wardrobe, along with her gold marcasite watch and the rose-key pendant he'd sent her that unlocked the secret drawer in the black, gothic desk.

Giving them the extravagant pendant and desk as a wedding gift had helped mitigate the sad and regretful reminders of the break up with his fiancée, as well as his guilt at his misplaced feelings for Eva.

The desk.

He rushed over to it, lifted the front panel and studied the rose-key lock. Thank God he couldn't see any scratches, dents, any evidence of jimmying. Outside of a few shuffled papers, it didn't look disturbed. Harry and his cohorts hadn't found the hidden compartment. *The secret compartment.* Had Richard stored anything inside?

He drove home, retrieved the rose-key pendant, sped back to the Hall house and returned to Richard's study. With the delicate key slotted into the keyhole, he popped open the secret safe and found an A4 envelope. His pulse pounded, throwing a round of punches beneath the skin of his wrist.

Careful not to damage the seal, he eased the flap open and poured out the contents onto the desk. The information included wedding photos, their marriage certificate, a Norway Experiment exposé and some other typed pages pulled from a larger document, going by the non-sequential page numbers. He picked them up and scanned the contents. "Jade death... Violet death toll..."

Salvator slumped onto the office chair, his mind reeling. He flicked through the pages, reading from sickening start to sordid finish. Sub Rosa had siphoned money from other projects across to the Norway Experiment. And further records showed additional Jade and Violet deaths. The agency had built its reputation on a pile of lies and suppression.

Project staff hadn't been told about any deaths in captivity. And no deaths was one of the stipulations to continue receiving government funding. Richard had collected undisputable evidence of unethical practice. Salvator reread the last page outlining ongoing horrific treatment toward the vampire captives, when supposedly it had all ceased.

Nausea rose in his esophagus and he gulped it back. Sub Rosa's practices were so much worse than he'd thought. Repugnant. Wrong. It didn't matter how scary the target group was supposed to be — no one deserved to be treated that way, not to mention the impact it had on the effectiveness of any studies carried out and the quality of samples taken.

No wonder Richard was disgusted. It disgusted Salvator, too. And nothing could be done about it, especially now. He had to stick by his friends until he could get them out safely. He couldn't compromise their lives, which is what he'd be doing if he went to the police.

Salvator sighed. His conscience screamed for him to act, to finish what Richard had started, to avenge his friend — but not yet. The horrendous situation taught him the importance of patience, persistence and timing to enable the most desirable outcome.

Right now he had to juggle making things as ethical and humane as possible with keeping his friends alive.

Salvator slipped the contents back into the envelope, resealed it and dropped it back in the drawer. He locked the secret compartment and pulled the front panel closed, leaving the information safely in place for Richard and Eva to stumble across again...someday.

Salvator returned to Richard and Eva's bedroom and sifted through clothes in their walk-in wardrobe. He halted on a cream garment bag. Eva's wedding dress. An image of her wearing it with an overjoyed smile infiltrated his mind. Tears burned in his eyes and overflowed onto his cheeks. *How could I do this to them?*

Salvator shook his head and shuffled forward then back, forward, then back. He'd had no choice. The only options his friends had available were to die or maybe die. And maybe die trumped definitely die.

He packed the garment bag in his suitcase, along with the black and white polka-dot dress. When he returned home, he'd hide the items away with the jewelry.

And wait.

* * * *

Day thirty-one – the day of reckoning

Unable to get back to sleep, Salvator left for work at six-thirty a.m. with his heart still smashing against his ribs. His brain had churned all night, terrorized with nightmares about Richard and Eva melting into a cryogenic slime. It was just his subconscious playing tricks. Right? But then again... He shook his head. *No. Not going there.*

With the needle of his car's fuel gauge hovering on empty, Salvator stopped at a petrol station near Sub Rosa to fill up. He paid, shoved the keys in the ignition and dropped the loose shillings and pence into the ashtray. They clinked onto the scratched, metal surface, glimmering in the low, pre-dawn light.

As soon as Salvator arrived at work and entered the basement, he went straight to the cryogenic tank. Richard and Eva had been in storage for a month. The time had come to assess the effectiveness of not only the storage method, but also the memory eraser drug.

Would their heritage affect the results? Normally, that sort of thing worried him. It botched whole experiments, ruined them. In this case, he longed for it, if it meant keeping his friends alive and functional.

He'd decided to go in early, alone, to prepare himself for any hiccups, any horrid surprises. First, he checked the monitoring equipment. All the readings were within expected limits. Then he climbed up the side railing and unscrewed Eva's container lid, his heart hammering like he'd overdosed on adrenaline. He sucked in a deep, bracing breath and peered inside.

A waft of icy cold wind stung his face and he snapped his eyes shut. He inhaled the deep-freeze air and forced his eyes open.

Eva. Still there, in perfect, full-body form.

Holding his breath, he looked in on Richard. Nothing out of place there either. Warm, expired air gushed from his lungs and combined with the frosty vapor seeping out of the tank, creating a chemical smoke signal. *On track, so far.* However, the real test would occur in a couple of hours, when his small research team fished them out to see if they revived.

To see if they'd survived.

"Let's start with Y1939," Salvator said only half an hour later, during the morning handover meeting. "We'll need to get him onto the body-temperature heated bed as delicately as possible, extract the cryoprotectant, rehydrate his cells and hook him up to a nutrition-hydration drip. And have the defibrillator ready, just in case. Got that?"

His taller teammate continued to prepare the revival space. "Loud and clear."

Shallow breaths squeezed past Salvator's strangled airway. "Good." He couldn't relax until he knew exactly what he'd be dealing with. "Then once he's stabilized, we'll wait to see if he rouses on his own."

His stocky research colleague tested the extraction device, the sucking sound conjuring up a dental-disaster flashback. "What if he doesn't?"

Salvator clenched his teeth and swallowed the ball of nerves clogging his throat. "We'll use chemical intervention."

He turned off the apparatus and stared at Salvator. "Such as?"

"Smelling salts, initially. If they don't work, we'll try an acetylcholine imitator such as nicotine. If that fails, we'll try another stimulant like caffeine and work up to the harder substances. If none are successful, we'll hook him up to the defibrillator."

The towering researcher shifted in front of the light, casting a giant shadow over Salvator, like an eclipse. "I'll have the substances labeled, lined up and ready on the side table, alongside the defibrillator."

A nervous smile faltered on Salvator's lips. "Great. Then once Y1939's back with us, I'll start asking him some questions and see how he responds. His answers will determine how best to proceed with treatment."

"What are the indications for administering the memory filler?" the stout guy asked, the awe in his eyes giving away his eagerness for further experimentation.

"We can't use it until the memory eraser has fully wiped Y1939's mind."

The guy's shoulders sagged and the corners of his mouth turned down.

"We need his brain to be a blank canvas, allowing more pliability and receptivity to new information. Then —"

"We'll repeat the same process with X1944. Assuming everything goes to plan," the mountainous researcher said, finishing Salvator's sentence for him.

"Exactly. Any other questions?"

"Yeah. What if one or both don't respond?" the small researcher asked, disappointment dragging down his tone.

Salvator didn't want to think about that. It could realistically happen, but their vampire genetics gave him added hope they'd make it. Their less fragile bodies made it harder for them to expire. *Right?*

He struggled to swallow the bowling ball of stress in his throat. "Then we'll restore them and work on options to revive them. Anything else?" His faint, wispy voice wouldn't convince anyone, including himself.

Within the hour, Richard lay against the heated table, his cells successfully rehydrated and hooked up to the nutrition–hydration drip. His eyeballs rolled behind the lids — a positive sign — the thin sheaths flickering as he woke.

Salvator stood over him, black radiation suit, mask and relieved heart rate in place. "What's your name?"

Richard's forehead creased and he focused internally, searching for the answer. He shook his head. "I don't know. Who are you?" The remnants of sedated sleep slowed his speech.

He didn't even seem scared by the talking, menacing, radiation suit looming over him. Yet. "Let's see if you know me," Salvator said, and removed his mask. The move was a huge risk, but he had a double dose of bright blue memory eraser on hand, just in case.

Richard stared and stared, his forehead crinkling into rutted rows as he scoured his vacant brain. "Should I know you? You seem so familiar but I just can't place you."

Damn! Not quite there. "That's okay. Time for you to rest again."

Richard closed his eyes and Salvator reached over to the trolley beside him, mixed the memory eraser with the sedative and injected it into his drip. Hopefully the double dosage would have the desired result.

Once they'd stored Richard away, Salvator and his team retrieved Eva. After ninety minutes of lying naked on the heated bed, hooked up to the nutrition-hydration drip, she came to. She stared at the still-maskless Salvator.

"Do you know your name?"

Her eyes shifted up and to her left and she frowned. "No. Did something happen to me?"

"Yes. Do you know where you are?"

She shivered and wrapped her arms around herself. "No. It looks familiar, though. Have I been here before?"

Salvator didn't speak. He replied by filling a syringe with the memory eraser and sedative concoction, administering it into her IV and sending her back into life-suspending sleep.

Chapter Twenty-Eight

The Meeting of X1944 and Y1939

Bram paid his taxi fare then lugged his suitcase inside his Fern Tree home. Finally. He'd been held up, his departure delayed after a lead that ended up taking him on a wild dead-end goose chase across Norway.

He dropped his bag in the front foyer and began searching the house. He didn't exactly know what to look for — something, anything out of place, anything to give him a hint as to where Richard and Eva had gone.

One thing stood out. Photos of them were missing. Those on display had been taken out of the living room and conservatory. He lit a candle, opened the hidden door under the staircase and descended the rocky steps, scurrying along the dank, dusty path to the bomb shelter.

When he reached the large metal door, he unlocked it and stepped into the cold, compact living area with kitchenette. Everything looked the same as how he'd left it. Neat. Untouched. He walked into a small bedroom and stopped in front of a carved wooden trunk at the end of the double bed.

Bram bent down, inserted an antique brass key in the central lock and flipped open the matching brass latches. Pictures of him and the love of his life stared up from among her letters and a lock of her golden hair. Mixed in were mementos of Richard, including images from his and Eva's wedding.

He sank back onto the floor and sighed. If anyone had been in the house, they hadn't found his secret stash. *Thank God.* He shut the lid, re-locked the trunk and left the shelter, taking the steps two at a time back upstairs.

Bram checked Richard and Eva's bedroom last. At first glance, nothing but photos seemed to be missing. Their toiletries were in the en suite and the study appeared intact. Next, he opened the doors to their walk-in wardrobe and it bulged with their clothes and shoes, except her wedding dress and maybe a couple of other things. If they'd *chosen* to leave, they would have packed much more to take with them.

Everything pointed to one explanation. Richard and Eva hadn't left of their own accord. Someone had been in the house, confiscated their photos and identifying items like her wedding dress and most likely keepsakes, as though to remove any record of their existence.

Had they been taken too? 'Foul play' flashed in his mind like a faulty neon sign and he shivered. Déjà vu but twenty-five years later.

Bram returned to the conservatory, poured himself a double Scotch and sculled it. The acidic, amber liquid burned his throat and he coughed. *What should I do? If I go to the police, what would I say?*

So déjà vu, almost the same as last time. They couldn't classify it a kidnapping without a ransom request and nothing indicated a struggle. No evidence suggested they'd been taken against their will—from home, anyway.

The Sub Rosa management story about them taking an irresistible overseas job offer? Bullshit. Total and utter bullshit. Richard and Eva would have called to let him know the good news, especially once they'd settled in the new place.

Bram slumped onto the couch, and dropped his head into his hands. His gut filled in the missing pieces of the puzzle. Richard and Eva had met a similar fate to his love.

All the bad luck in his life had a recurring theme.

Sub Rosa.

* * * *

After Richard and Eva's third dose of memory eraser, Salvator and his team extracted them, but at the same time. Meeting each other again would be the true test of the drug's effectiveness.

They lay next to one another on the body-temperature tables, hooked up to their drips. Richard groaned and half opened his still-sleepy eyes.

Salvator stood between his friends and forced a smile. "Have a nice rest?"

"I'm not sure." Richard rubbed his eyes. "It must have been if I can't remember."

"That's good. Are you able to sit up?"

Richard pushed himself into a sitting position, hanging his legs off the side, facing Eva. His pupils dilated as he took in her breathtaking, supine body. Redness flushed his skin and his cock twitched. "What's her name?"

Does she look familiar to him? Is Richard's body's response driven by lust or kinesthetic memory?

Determined, light-jade eyes stared into Salvator's. "Tell me her name."

"Why?"

Richard's expression said, 'do I really need to explain?' "She's stunning."

"And?"

"I have to meet her," he said with conviction, as though driven by an instinctual, survival drive, like the need for food and water.

As if on cue, Eva regained consciousness.

"There's someone here who wants to meet you," Salvator said.

She followed Salvator's gaze, her blue-violet eyes scanning over Richard. Every inch of her blushed.

Richard's smile shifted from relieved, to triumphant, to overjoyed. "What's your name?"

She frowned and pushed on shaky arms until she sat up, facing her forgotten husband. "I don't know. That sounds ridiculous, doesn't it," she said, chastising herself.

"Not as ridiculous as us sitting here naked."

Eva laughed. And they were in their special little soulmate bubble again—alive to each other, like no one else stood in the room, like no one else could interfere.

She glanced at her swinging legs. "What's your name?"

Richard looked around as though searching for clues to help him remember. "I'm not sure."

Her leg brushed his. "I feel like I know you."

"Me too."

Eva peered into her husband's eyes. "But we haven't met."

He wrinkled his forehead, his eyes rolling up to the side, a sign he'd dived deep into his mind, foraging in his erased memory bank for an accurate answer. "No. We haven't. I'd remember."

Salvator jumped in. "I think you're both nearly ready." *After one more course of memory eraser.*

His voice tore their gazes away from each other and they focused on him. "For what?" they said in stereo.

"The next stage."

* * * *

Immersion, January 1966

The bone-chilling suction of Y1939's cells freezer-burned his brain. He should be sleeping. He should be out cold. He should forget...but he remembered. Bits. The memories were fuzzy, blurred around the edges, like they'd smeared Vaseline into the crevices of his mind. *But who are they? And who am I?*

Drowsy, though conscious, he felt time passing and relentless teeth-chattering, body-numbing cold but with no discernible heartbeat. Was he alive or had he died and dropped down into a freezing, rather than boiling, hell? His veins burned with frozen blood trying to flow, like a glacier abrading rock. If heaven existed, it wouldn't be like this, frigid and barren.

Muddy memories clouded his brain, as though stirred up, partially dissolved and eroded. They'd drugged him, for sure. The bitter cold and desolate darkness didn't help. POW camps used drugs and other horrendous strategies to break people. They wouldn't break him, not while he had something to live for.

He missed her. Who, he couldn't be sure, but a cavernous void, a black hole in his heart dwelled where she used to be. Flashes flickered in his mind like an old, broken movie. Dark long hair and flawless fair legs that stretched on forever.

Violet.

Violet.

Violet?

She felt near. He had a clear sixth sense, even in the black, confined space.

They had better not take this away from him, *her* away from him. He latched onto his faint memory, the umbilical cord still connected to her, keeping him alive. If only he could find out who they were and why he floated in limbo. If he could just make sense of things so he could track down this bewitching woman — the mysterious, dark, violet-eyed beauty haunting his soul.

* * * *

The following month, Salvator retrieved Richard and he flunked the memory test. Finally.

"I'm just going to give you a little something to help with your recovery." Salvator picked up a fresh syringe with fluorescent pink memory filler and injected it into his drip.

Richard blinked and closed his eyes and Salvator deposited him in the red, receptive room.

"Here's some information for you to read. Then once you're familiar with it, you can start looking at some pictures, watching some movies, listening to sounds and music — "

"What for?" Richard asked.

"To help you remember..." *Your new self.*

The red room had to work. It supposedly fostered fresh learning by blocking out other stimuli, keeping Richard focused on content—or so Salvator's in-depth research had said. With all his breakable eggs in one flimsy basket, he relied on it. There was no Plan B, only Plan D…certain death.

Within forty-five minutes, he had Richard attached to a nutrition-hydration drip and neuromuscular electric stimulation machine to maintain functional muscle mass. Couched in a state of medically induced hypnosis, a primed Richard sat ripe and ready to absorb information about his new identity.

Richard's muscles pulsed in a steady rhythm and his pupils dilated, soaking up the words to create false memories in his vacant brain—or so Salvator hoped. After two hours of brain infiltrating and repeated reading, Salvator administered a sedative, detached Richard from the drip and muscle stimulator and stored him away.

Next, he brought out Eva and followed the same procedure. He injected the memory filler but instead of priming her into a relaxed, receptive state, she convulsed and fell to the floor, shaking and writhing.

Salvator's heart went into overdrive and he froze, his brain vacillating between cause and effect. If she had an allergy to the drug, a consistent adverse side effect, what would he do?

One step at a time.

His two research colleagues rushed to her side, jolting him into action. He jabbed a sedative into her arm and Eva went limp.

Shit!

Salvator dropped down and cradled her head, his breath buffeting against her blank face. He moved his cheek close to her nose and mouth. Air puffed out at five-second intervals.

Breathing. Good.

Lifting her floppy wrist, he checked her pulse.

Strong. Steady.

He sat back, relief snuffing out the flames of fear, and gently lowered her arm beside her. She'd be fine.

They returned Eva to cryogenic storage and commenced an impromptu debrief session.

"What happened?" the shorter researcher asked.

Salvator shrugged. Could something in her heritage have sparked the unexpected response? A definite possibility. "I don't know. She could be allergic to the drug or had some reaction to the combination of drugs in her system. I'll just have to systematically trial a few things, starting with lowering the dosage, until I get to the crux of it."

Thankfully the lower dosage seemed to work and Salvator commenced regular retention sessions for Eva and Richard in the red room. He injected them separately, combining the adjusted memory filler amount with a sedative to keep them semi-conscious and enhance uptake of subliminal messages between movies to further imbed information.

They were on a force-fed diet of constructed pictures, fabricated interests and formulated scenarios without dates. To further reduce possible problems, Salvator had decided to retain parts of their true history.

They had no family and were put into care as babies — and the material made mention of fictitious friends who had lost contact with them when they'd moved from boarding school, to study, to work. He'd come up with a thorough, self-re-invention program — or at least he hoped it was thorough.

Salvator put down his pen and stretched out his cramped hand. In between monitoring his friends, he continued consultation on the Norway Experiment, resulting in neglect of his Soulmate Serum antidote. He'd been working twelve-to-fourteen-hour days, but even exhaustion didn't stop guilt from eating up his insides like a slow-acting corrosive.

He glanced through his partially open office door, straight at the towering metal cryogenic cylinder holding his friends suspended. He rubbed his throbbing temples. If only he could atone for what he'd done, for what he'd put his friends through. But how? The one thing he could do, had to do, was concentrate on getting them out of there...eventually.

Salvator stood and walked to the window. Dusk had descended across the deserted, rear car park. It would be a long time coming before he could reintroduce Richard and Eva to society. Staff who might recognize them had to leave before he could even consider it. Though, no more security guard meant one less thing to worry about.

Not long after Richard and Eva had been secured in cryogenic storage, Harry had informed Salvator that he'd moved the guard on with a very attractive severance package and a verbal warning to keep his mouth shut or there'd be unpleasant consequences.

Salvator wished he could think of a legitimate way to get rid of Harry and the CEO then fast-track the letting go of Sub Rosa staff who might know Richard and Eva There had to be no complications when his friends returned to the world as their new selves. The smallest slip could be the difference between life and death.

The last sliver of light disappeared beyond the horizon. Instead of 'if onlys', he had to focus on what he could actually do, like prepare for their release by planting some of Richard and Eva's treasured possessions in their exit wardrobes, along with belongings he'd collected along the way to support their new identities. The rest relied on hope.

Hope, one day, that the drugs would break down. Hope that their memories returned. Hope that they would be reunited.

Chapter Twenty-Nine

Executive Decision

Salvator filed away his latest Norway Experiment progress note, shrugged on his jacket and stopped. Voices drifted down the corridor. At seven p.m., he thought he'd be the last to leave.

He snuck behind his office door and peered through the gap. Harry and the CEO skulked past and entered the basement lab. So much secrecy. Working at Sub Rosa often felt like working for the research version of the Australian Security Intelligence Organization.

By the time Harry and the CEO entered the rear car park, twilight had dimmed the sky, bordering on night.

Oh shit! They'd see Salvator's car and realize he hadn't left work and that he'd probably seen them prowling around. If they asked him about staying late, he'd confess to hauling up in his office to further refine the Richard and Eva project. That should satisfy them.

Salvator moved to the window and shoved his shaky hands into the front pockets of his pants. But if they didn't buy his explanation, they might decide to add him into the memory drug-cryogenics experiment as a participant, along with his friends, leaving no one to save them, no chance of survival.

Harry leaned against the driver's side door of his black BMW, so deep in conversation with the CEO that he didn't seem to notice, or care about, Salvator's car.

A tornado spun out of the nearby bushes at high speed. Between blinks, Harry and the CEO went from two business men chatting to a couple of stiff, white, exsanguinated humans, lying on the asphalt.

Dead.

A spear of shock lodged in Salvator's lungs. Vampires were on the loose and not too happy about Sub Rosa's genocidal scheme. And he was one of the despised scientists employed by the company, still hiding inside.

He rubbed his constricted chest and shivered. With only one more vehicle unaccounted for, would the vampires wait around? How would he know? How could he get to his car without getting killed?

The bodies. *Shit!* What should he do with those? If he moved them and someone saw… And what if someone recognized his car leaving afterward? Things were going from bad to horrendous. Salvator took a few forced breaths to stave off a major meltdown.

Call the police. That's what a decent person would do. Plus, it might make any lingering vampires move on. With no weapon or trace of his fingerprints near the murder scene, he should be fine. He lifted the receiver of his phone and dialed.

"I need to report an attack…"

* * * *

CEOs came and went over the next fourteen years, with none taking much interest in the Sub Rosa program specifics...until Andy Falon.

"What's this basement lab used for?" the newly appointed, over-zealous CEO had asked, his voice competing with the hum of the cryogenics vat in the vast, open space.

Salvator had patted the large cylinder. "I've been assigned a cryogenics and memory drugs trial. Two humans with post-traumatic stress volunteered." *Forcibly.* He'd drip-fed information to Andy on a need-to-know basis. And the new CEO had needed to know as little as possible.

"Sounds interesting..." the CEO had said.

No. No it doesn't.

Andy had looked around the sterile space. "How long has the project been running?"

"Since October 1965."

The new CEO had stared at him, his arctic blue eyes disbelieving. "Fifteen years? And the volunteers were happy to give up so much of their lives?"

Salvator had swiped his sweaty hands across his trouser legs and swallowed the skewers of truth stabbing his vocal cords. "At the time, they were so distressed that they were willing to do whatever it took to give them peace. I explained it could take a while—"

"'A while' is right. How much longer do you think it'll be before you have some significant results?"

"I'm not sure, but they're not ready to re-enter society yet." Some staff who knew them had lingered at Sub Rosa, including Greer, and he'd needed to pad out Richard's and Eva's new identities to foolproof level— or as close as possible.

"I see. Well, make sure you keep me informed of their progress."

"Of course." *The bare-boned basics, anyway.*

Salvator had led him back into the main corridor and shown him the basement office area. Once Andy had become entrenched in the CEO role, he'd been so involved in the Norway Experiment he hadn't had time to think about a small, cryogenics-memory drugs trial. The Norway Experiment had taken precedence. It always had. For once, management's obsession with it had had its benefits.

According to Salvator's sixth sense, Andy had seemed about as trustworthy as a con artist. However, over time, the guy had proven he knew how to motivate people. By 1981, he had encouraged and supported brainstorming, as well as lateral and creative thinking, resulting in studies into a vampire tranquilizer.

By 1986, six years into his role as CEO, researchers had developed and implemented a sunlight barricade system across the Norway compound, stopping vampire escapes.

Salvator placed his palm flat against the ice-cold vat until his hand ached. Freezer burn finally made sense. When he pulled his pallid, almost-blue hand away, it throbbed, the heat sucked right out of it after only thirty seconds. And that was on the outside. His friends were on the inside, their bodies fully immersed consumed by a brutal ice sea.

Salvator switched off the lab lights, grabbed his brown weathered satchel and walked to his car. His tight-knit little team of scientists had been great. They'd both stayed on, eager to see the results of their work, which he'd always hoped for. The less staff turnover and the more consistency the better.

He locked his car door, fed the key into the ignition and turned. Nothing. Stranded at Sub Rosa. *Great.* Then again, he almost slept there most of the time anyway. Outside of the threat of a vampire attack, it almost made sense camping out in the car park.

A sad, resigned, chuckle stumbled from his lips. This is what his life had become. He tried the key again and the engine chugged but didn't turn over.

Salvator slammed his hands against the steering wheel. The stubborn keychain swung in the ignition. *Third time lucky?* He tried the key again and pumped his foot on the accelerator and the car sputtered to life.

Yes! Home gave him some respite, though maybe he required a longer break. Before he could consider going anywhere, though, he needed to increase his colleagues' responsibilities and ensure they could cover his role during his absence.

When convinced of their competence, he might even apply for a secondment to the Norway site. With any luck, it would provide him with a fresh perspective and allow him to see some of the good he'd done. It would give him the chance to check out the facilities in person, including Andy's revered, infallible sunlight barricade system and refurbishment of the Jade and Violet compounds.

Salvator could use his position to make things even better for the captives — atone in a third party way. But would that be enough to halt the regret from rotting his heart?

Chapter Thirty

Y1939 — Living in the Eighties

The red-tinged room. Y1939 squeezed his eyes shut and shook his head, trying to dislodge the lingering slumber from his hazy brain. A big screen. Familiar? His misty mind hovered part way between dream and reality. The red padded seat cradled his body, his muscles pulsating. A movie played about an extra-terrestrial, followed by *Tootsie*...

Music played. "Tonight, I celebrate my love for you... Precious to me-e-e-e... We close our eyes..."

A photo album sat on a small side table and he picked it up, long lines draping from his arms, leading to... He looked around. Something made his muscles twitch all over. So weird, but not unpleasant.

Did I have an accident? Go into rehab? Maybe the album held the answers. He began flipping through it — him with a group of others at boarding school, him with his friends at the football, him with friends at a bright, glowing bar, him with his new-look goatee and moustache... Nothing there. He slapped it shut.

Diary. He'd seen a diary...somewhere. He put the photo album down and patted the floor. The back of his hand knocked a pointed edge under the side table. Lifting it to his lap, he started scanning through the pages.

Romantic, loving, smart and loyal formed the essence of the undated entries. *Did I write them?* It read more like a biography than his personal account of events and record of random reflections.

Poetry. He wrote poetry for his girlfriends but hadn't met 'the one' yet, apparently. His stomach twinged in disagreement. A ghost of a woman haunted his thoughts, but she disappeared before he caught her in a memory.

He flipped a few pages and read halfway down. He had a science degree but had a passion for construction and renovating. An odd combination, which matched the incongruent writing style.

Something didn't sit right. There was a strange disconnect, an absence, a vacancy. He stood, his legs wobbly, and a sea of sticky patches ripped the hair from his skin like a kinky waxing session.

"Ouch!"

The rhythmic muscle twitching ceased. He fell forward and gripped the armrest of the couch to steady himself, weak and dizzy. Furniture walking, he staggered into the bathroom and studied his reflection in the huge mirror. His golden-brown hair glinted under the fluorescent lights and his light green eyes flickered, as if trying to communicate in Morse code.

No dark, dehydration rings. No headache. No hangover. No pain. No dream. However, his naked body had been hooked up to muscle stimulation machinery, so he had to be in some sort of hospital, which meant something was wrong with him. Very wrong.

Chapter Thirty-One

Captive Audience

Sub Rosa Norway compound, 1996

A couple of grim-faced researchers in white coats came to Rhoda's cell. It was that time of the month — DNA and body fluid extraction. She had stopped trying to struggle. Each time had ended in tears, convulsions and paralysis.

So, she went along with them, every fiber of her being in silent protest. Better to go with the flow than against it until she could find a way to freedom.

No longer did they escort her into the lab to join a line of tasered Jades, waiting their turn, subdued with just enough sunlight to control them and keep them moving, like drugged dogs on a lead.

Since the sunlight bars had been installed, the scientists visited each captive individually, inflicting pain without the vampires leaving the comfort of their cells and reducing their risk of escape.

One researcher shoved a cotton bud in her mouth, while another syringed a blood sample out of whatever shadow of a vein he could see.

"Owwww!" She lurched forward, the pain from the syringe shooting like a stab wound to her neck. She passed out on her bed and woke up to the blaring hum of sunlight bars.

"Hello?"

The voice sounded friendly, foreign. *Someone new.* She blinked, rubbed her dry, aching eyes and entered the living room. A middle-aged man, around the age her son would be, stood on the other side of the bars.

He wore a crumpled brown suit, crooked bow tie and white shirt. Years of worry lined his face, and the dark smudges under his hazel eyes were a beacon of unrest. Jetlag could have played a part but the blackness stamped into place signified insomnia.

A tentative smile hesitated on her lips. "Can I help you?"

"I'm not sure. I'm new here…"

Not a native Norwegian, not with such bronzed, olive skin. He had to be visiting from abroad. From the Australian site, perhaps.

"I can tell," she said.

Two pink spots of embarrassment spread across his bony cheeks. "Is it that obvious?"

A nerdy, shy scientist but likeable. "Yes. Sorry."

"And I'd tried so hard to fit in," he said with no trace of humor.

She sidled up to him and whispered, "Just a word of advice. If you want any of us to work with you, fitting in is the last thing you will want to do."

He smiled, deep wrinkles creasing the corners of his eyes. "Good to know. Anyway, I'm Salvator. I'm a researcher from the Tasmanian head office."

"Please sit, Salvator."

He stepped inside, stripes of golden sunlight scanning over him like a barcode.

She moved toward the kitchenette. "Would you like something to drink?"

"Just a coffee if you've got one."

When Rhoda returned, Salvator flipped through a notepad full of messy cursive handwriting, a pen behind his ear. She placed his mug down on the coffee table in front of him and cradled hers, seeking solace from the warmth permeating her cold skin.

"Thank you." He blew on the steaming coffee and took a sip. "You know, there's something really familiar about you."

"I bet you say that to all the Jade girls."

He laughed, a real, rich belly laugh, but his body remained stiff, rusty like he had not laughed in a very long time. "I'm serious. There's something about you... Do you have other relatives in here?"

Her chest constricted. Hopefully he could not decipher body language. "I do not know for sure."

"How about on the outside?"

She hesitated. *Should I tell him?* He might track down her son and husband. He might help her see them again. But what if his motives were not so innocent? What if his kind manner was an act, a ploy to find and capture them? Hurt them?

He leaned forward. "You do, don't you?"

Her heart thrumped in her throat. "Yes. But—"

"You're worried about putting them in danger."

She stared at him. Maybe persistent silence would shift him onto another subject.

Salvator shuffled forward. "I promise what we talk about is confidential. Believe it or not, I want to help you."

A sardonic snort shot out her nose. "Really."

"Honestly," he said, his tone imbued with the word. "Though I can see I'll need to gain your trust. I understand." Salvator drank some more of his coffee. "How about you start by telling me what life is like in the compound?"

Lonely, miserable, stressful. But should she admit her honest feelings to a Sub Rosa researcher? The agency should know the truth, but what if they used the information she shared to make her life more miserable, not less?

Salvator had said he wanted to help, so maybe she could use her disclosure as a test to see how he responded. "Hard. When I am not being poked and jabbed and manhandled for testing, I am stuck in my cell, alone, recovering from the physical and emotional pain and trauma.

"Before the sunlight bars, I could see a broad range of other Jades when we were huddled together in the lab, awaiting experimentation. But even then, we were too — what is the English word? Deadened, numb? — to interact."

She waved her hand like a game show hostess. "Now, in this maze of cells, I can only just see my Jade neighbors opposite, overhear them, yell out to talk above the constant hum, but there is no privacy, no private discussion, no quality conversation. There is very little quality of life. If it were not for my family..." She trailed off. She could not offer him too much. Not yet. "I feel on display, like a dangerous animal in a decadent zoo."

Salvator's eyes shone with unshed tears of pain, sincerity, and...admiration? Like he truly understood. "It sounds very difficult indeed." He swallowed the rest of his coffee and put his cup on the table. "You've dealt with all this for a long time without going crazy. It's an impressive feat and speaks to your strength of character."

He stood up suddenly, nearly tipping the chair over and kept his eyes downcast, hidden. Something in his own words, in the situation, had struck a nerve. "Thanks for the drink, Rhoda. With your permission, I'd like to visit again tomorrow and speak some more." The crack in his voice said, *when I have collected myself.* The sentiment acted as a good reminder for her to do the same.

* * * *

"A-hem." Salvator adjusted his checkered bow tie, haloed by the glowing bars.

"Come in." Coils of anxiety wound around Rhoda's stomach and squeezed. Could she confide in him about Abe and her son?

"Thanks." He sat, pulled a pen from behind his ear, thumbed through a few pages of a dog-eared notepad then back a few and glanced up. "I forgot to ask you yesterday — How do you find the vial meals?"

"From what I have heard, they are quite literally vile. Thankfully, I have avoided having one. They are saved for the full vampires because they have no other food option, other than blood. Whereas three-quarter and half-castes like myself can manage with eating a human-type diet with a bit of blood in between. It is not ideal. We cannot function quite as well, though we will not starve."

"I've heard the taste is more like medicine than food." He frowned, as though soured by the thought. "It's not the most appetizing, but practical under the circumstances, I suppose." In other words, survival always took precedence over flavor, leaving no strong argument for the scientists to spend time and money on improving it.

Salvator checked the corridor and moved forward as though to reveal a secret. "I'm trying to push management to review them, particularly to improve the taste."

He came across as a kind, mild-mannered man, in an adoring, son-like way. She held back the urge to ruffle his salt-and-pepper-streaked hair. "Let me guess. They could not care less."

"I won't let their lack of interest stop me. I'll take the broken record approach if I have to and annoy them into it."

Maybe he did care about the vampires' plight or else why go to all the trouble?

He reviewed a few more pages of his notepad and regained eye contact. "Have you thought about our conversation yesterday?"

Her heart went from steady to racing in a split second. "I have. A lot."

"And?"

"I have decided…" Rhoda's voice shook, wavering between instinct and rationality. She hesitated. Sub Rosa would not have interest in or use for her human husband, except maybe to get to her son. But not even Abe knew where he resided anymore.

"I bore a son in 1939, just before my husband, Abe, and I migrated to Australia. Abe thought it would reduce my chance of capture. We had only just bought a property and confirmed plans for the house when Sub Rosa snatched me and brought me back here. Richard was still a baby…"

Salvator stopped writing. He discarded his notepad and pen on the coffee table and fell against the backrest, his face unreadable. *Shock, surprise, fear, guilt?*

Rhoda edged forward. "Salvator? Is something wrong?"

His eyes traveled back and forth inside his head, as though trying to decipher one of Abe's codes.

"Salvator?"

He focused on her, his eyes full of surprise and stress. "It's Rhoda Hall, right?" he said, with a heavy emphasis on 'Hall'.

"Yes."

Salvator rubbed his hands along the length of his thin thighs, as though to stretch out the creases in his rumpled slacks. "I'm not quite sure how to tell you this."

"Tell me what." Was Richard dead? She squeezed her eyes shut. *Please, he cannot be dead.*

"I know your son."

"What?" she choked out, trying to dam the tears building behind her eyes. "Where is he?"

"I can't go into detail or it could compromise his safety. But I can tell you he's okay." His voice was so soft, barely audible, even with her hypersensitive hearing.

No more question time. She did not want to endanger her son. But the rational decision did not stop the gnawing curiosity. Maybe Richard was in hiding and

Salvator could not risk being overheard. As long as he stayed alive, safe, that was her top priority, what she deemed most important. Now she just had to find a way to see him again — and her husband.

A broad, grateful smile lifted the corners of her lips and she jumped up. "Wait here…"

In her bedroom, she pulled out a red velvet pouch from her top bedside drawer then returned to the living area and handed it to Salvator.

He turned it over in his hand, his confused hazel eyes lifting to meet her stare. "What's this?"

"There is a gold and black cross pendant and ring inside. My husband gave them to me as a gift, as protection, and I want you to pass them on to Richard. Hopefully, they will help him stay safe, stay free. Promise me you will get the pouch to him."

Salvator held it tightly in his hand, his gaze steadfast. "I promise."

* * * *

Salvator left his suitcase at the foot of his bed and flopped onto the springy mattress. *Home.* He folded his hands behind his head and stared at the ceiling. He'd returned to Tasmania with some information on Richard's father and had also given Rhoda some peace of mind. She knew her son was alive, though not exactly in what condition.

Visiting the Norway compound had been the start of his path to redemption. He'd come back, more determined than ever, to resume preparation of Richard and Eva's successful re-entry into society, with the secret hope their *new selves* were only temporary.

If things turned out as he'd planned, they'd eventually remember who they were and be together again. And the possible addition of Richard's parents' love and support filled the missing family gap his friends had both craved.

Now that Greer had married and moved on, along with nearly all the 1965 Sub Rosa staff, Salvator could finally start working toward a date for Richard and Eva's release…in the next five to ten years. It was still a while away, but better than indefinite.

After the best night's sleep he'd had in over thirty years, Salvator got into work early and reviewed Richard and Eva's progress notes. *No problems.* Next, he surveyed the cryogenics machinery output readings. *No issues with their vital signs.* He smiled. It felt like things were starting to come together.

With safety goggles in place and his stained, white lab coat buttoned up to the top, Salvator sat at the high bench and resumed construction of his memory solidifier concoction. He held a red-fluid-filled test tube in one hand and a blue-fluid-filled one in the other.

If the memory solidifier drug worked, it would consolidate Richard's and Eva's implanted memories upon their release. It provided a safeguard to ensure the new memories stuck and held, at least for a while, at least long enough to report back on the success of his friends' integration. And deter Sub Rosa from further follow up.

He poured the blue substance into the red and it bubbled and spat. Lavender-scented smoke invaded his nostrils, like sweet tear gas, and he coughed and spluttered, trying not to spill the new bright purple solution.

"Salvator. Salvator!"

He glanced up and stared through his moisture-coated lenses. One of the researchers ran toward him.

Salvator slotted the test tube into the wooden holder. "Yes."

The rotund researcher stopped in front of him, short of breath. "It's the cryogenic samples, they…"

Salvator threw off his goggles and jumped up. "What about them?" His heart pounded so loud in his ears he could hardly hear the guy.

"They're not reviving."

"Not reviving?" His chest tightened, squeezing air out of his suffocated lungs and refusing to admit more. His friends. They'd revived every other time. "Let me see."

The researcher led him to two chilled chimpanzees, lying on heated gurneys. "I've tried everything."

No sign of Richard or Eva. "What about X1944 and Y1939?"

The guy's brow crinkled. "What about them?" His eyes searched Salvator's and his forehead unraveled. "Oh. No, they're fine. It's these new samples."

Oxygen rushed into Salvator's lungs and a wave of relief undulated through him. *Thank God!*

"Only one percent of the monkeys have responded to the experiment. The rest never wake up. And I haven't been able to restore life to any that have died and been stored. I know we've only done limited human testing, but going by the broader results, it's unlikely we'll get ethics approval to expand the study. And I can't see anyone else volunteering. Cryogenic storage looks like it'll only work on a very small population." The short, fidgety researcher couldn't hide the fear and frustration cutting into his voice.

Salvator stared at the cold, lifeless monkeys. "Cryogenics is still in its infancy. Part of this research is about coming up with ways to make it work."

He'd spoken out of pure hope, his cognitive bias. But hope didn't mean it wasn't possible. At the moment, success seemed remote, though it often did before a major scientific breakthrough. And one could come at any time.

"I agree, but there's only so long they'll continue to fund something showing limited results."

Tension gripped Salvator's gut like an unforgiving fist. They'd been working with the technology for thirty years now, and although that didn't constitute a long time in research terms, budget-wise it equated to a long time pouring money into a project with no foreseeable benefits. As his colleague suggested, they needed to come up with something promising, and soon, or the funders would pull the last little grip on the loose pin.

Chapter Thirty-Two

X1944 — Living in the Nineties

Sleepy blue-violet eyes. *Her* eyes. And her body, naked again, except for clear round patches with wires pasted across her pale skin. When had she last seen the sun?

She combed through her long, dark cocoa-brown hair with clumsy fingers then slung it over her shoulders. A half-smile pushed at the corners of her dry, cracked lips. She needed balm — and to get out of the air conditioning.

She put the silver, handheld mirror down on a small side table and searched the red-tinted room. No personal belongings were in sight — no handbag, no clothes and no identity, just a comfy, red leather couch and a large screen, a cinema room for one. But why would she sit in her birthday suit to watch a movie unless...

No. *No.* She wouldn't, would she? No matter how desperate she was for cash she couldn't. She couldn't work in a...a...brothel, no matter how exclusive, no matter how high-end and...and...sell her body.

A titanic wave of nausea rocked her stomach and she swallowed the rising swell. What else had she swallowed? *Errr!* Bile clogged the back of her throat and she gagged. She'd rather starve, wouldn't she? Her brain scrambled to find a feasible alternative. Maybe she'd stayed at a boyfriend's house. *Yes, that has to be it.*

She closed her eyes, relaxed back into the couch and did a quick body scan. No hangover. No soreness. No post-sex elation or revulsion. But then, why the loss of memory? A strong sedative? Had she been drugged? She shook her head. No. *No, no, no, no, no!*

Her muscles twitched like falling dominoes, one, then another, then another, distracting her from her disgust. She straightened in her seat. Maybe this formed part of those once-a-month beauty treatment regimes. *Oh yes, definitely.* At the salon. *Yes, the salon.* Relief doused the spot fires of anxiety raging inside her and she settled into the cozy, cloud-like couch.

Pictures of her drinking in laser light clubs with her girlfriends, a dot in a sea of people at a music festival, hiking in the mountains, dressed in her uni graduation gown, clutching her degree and sitting around a colossal campfire with friends flipped through her mind, like a *This Is Your Life* slideshow.

Some of her friends stood out across a series of photos and were mentioned in undated memorabilia — birthday cards, letters, gifts — but it seemed disjointed, like a jigsaw puzzle where the pieces didn't quite fit. She'd lost contact with all of them over the years, for one reason or another, and she'd apparently described every instance in detail in her secret diary, so it had to be true.

The large screen flicked to life. *Pulp Fiction*, moved onto *Matrix*, onto *Total Recall...*

The bloodied scent of fresh, raw meat aroused her brain and she snapped her eyes open. A plate of steak steamed on the side table in place of her diary and photo albums. *How did it get there?* She must have drifted off.

The sirloin sat in a puddle of pinky-red juice that had trickled into the side of carrots and green beans and stained the fluffy white mashed potatoes. Saliva pooled in her mouth and she licked her cracked lips. She sat forward, cut a thin sliver of steak and chewed on it, a mouth-watering, metallic tang teasing her taste buds.

"Oh... Ohhh!" she moaned. And suddenly she understood the O in 'orgasm', not that she could remember the last time she'd had one. Her pictures showed a serious lack of men, so maybe she'd only ever used her hand, had never shared the intimate experience. *How depressing.*

Hunger commandeered her train of thought and she devoured the rest of her meal but refrained from licking the plate clean. Just. It was tempting, very tempting, like she hadn't eaten for decades.

Behind the empty plate were two more. Her stomach gurgled. One saucer contained a white whipped sugary coating atop a lemon filling with a dollop of cream and the other a selection of shaved cold meats, pickled vegetables and cheeses.

Saliva spurted into her mouth like tapped spring water. How had she not seen the tempting morsels earlier? They had been right there in front of her. Her meat love affair had put a spell on her, creating tunnel vision every time. A chuckle bubbled up from her throat. Love really was blind.

Gobbling down what should have been the first course, she saved the sweet for last. The lemony flavor zinged her palate and she slowed down to savor the dessert. Sated, she lay back in her seat. Soft music played through hidden speakers. *Baby One More Time*, *Smells Like Teen Spirit*, *Bittersweet Symphony*, *Truly Madly Deeply*.

Post meal contentment seemed to have stimulated another type of hunger — a whole-body, erotic-feast type of craving. A familiar, longing ache throbbed between her legs, a physical memory suggesting there had been someone special. So why didn't he stick in her head?

A weird inkling niggled at her brain and she searched internally. A memory of a man grasped onto the precipice of her mind but lost its grip, slipping down, down into the deepest ravine. Maybe he'd just been an incredible fling but nothing serious. Or he'd hurt her and she'd blocked him out.

Tensing muscles and an involuntary head shake refuted that thought. Maybe he'd been the love of her life and she'd lost him, burying him with other difficult experiences, like boarding school.

She shuddered. Thank God she'd gotten out of there and had started studying business administration at uni. And she loved animals. Cats. She couldn't wait to go home and play with her special, charcoal-gray purr-baby. A recap of memories slid through her thoughts like a PowerPoint presentation, searching, searching...

There was no cat in any of the photos or mention of one in her diary. *Strange.* And something else nagged at her, like a story with missing pages or a vault inside her head that she'd lost the combination to, a vault storing sensitive, important information she guarded for some reason...like her heart. But what...and why? Maybe someday, some way, she'd find the key.

Chapter Thirty-Three

Reintegration for One

Hobart, August 2005

"What do you mean the funding's been cut?" Salvator leaned across Andy's desk and glared at him, anger and fear playing tug-of-war with his emotions.

Andy remained reclined in his big, black leather chair. "The cryogenics project just isn't working out. You and the team have had long enough to get some results and—"

Salvator slammed his palm on the desk. "What will happen with the samples?"

Andy eased himself into an upright position. "For the moment, we'll continue to store them, but all experimentation needs to cease. There'll be no more cryogenic subjects or funding."

Beads of sweat slid down the center of Salvator's back, his mouth as arid as the Great Sandy Desert. He pushed himself off the desk and breathed—in and out, in and out, in and out. Storage hadn't been affected, so that meant his friends were still safe for the moment. Maybe he could use the news to his advantage.

"Given the situation, it sounds like the perfect opportunity to release my memory drug subjects—"

Andy held up his hand in a stop motion. "How many have you been working with again?"

"Just the two—a male and a female."

Andy rubbed his chin. "And we don't really know how the memory drugs stand up yet, do we?"

"No...but—"

"Then I can only give you permission to release one. I'd like to see how successful their reintegration is first before I consider releasing the other. There may need to be more tweaking." Andy propped his elbows on his desk and leaned forward. "I'd like you to report back to me on the reintegrated subject's progress over a five-year period. Then I'll make a decision about a release date for the stored subject...if it's appropriate."

"And if not?" Salvator shook, stress and anger vibrating through every frayed nerve and clenched muscle.

"We'll have to dispose of the sample, just like any other failed experiment."

Salvator's heart jumped into his mouth. The guy contemplated killing off humans like swatting a fly! *What kind of heartless pig do I work for?* Andy had never hidden his budget-focused, taskmaster side but Salvator hadn't realized his boss could be quite so ruthless. It looked like Harry and the parade of CEOs over the years, particularly Andy, had been cut from the same soiled cloth.

Although not an aggressive type, it didn't stop Salvator from wanting to grab the guy's pristine

Versace shirt and knock him to the floor. "But I could release both and do a comparison study."

"You could but I won't approve it. It's too risky and way too difficult for you to follow up both effectively." His steely stare nailed Salvator to the spot. "You can choose which one goes free, though choose wisely," Andy said with a smirk.

The whole thing — people's lives — was just a game to him. *Bastard.* Salvator forced a smile through clenched teeth. "Thanks for your consideration, Andy. I'll get right on it."

If he could only release one of his friends, he knew who he had to choose. Even though Richard had parents he could possibly reunite with, Salvator couldn't leave a woman, especially Eva, suffering any longer.

He didn't want Richard to suffer either but... Richard and Eva should be freed together. However, he didn't have permission, so he just had to stop wishing things were different and get moving on the first reintegration — and make sure of its success.

He raced back to his basement office and punched the number of the cryogenics government funder into his office phone. The guy had been in the role for a number of years and they'd developed a you-scratch-my-back, I'll-scratch-yours arrangement. Otherwise, Salvator would have no chance of pulling off Eva's reintegration, not after 9-11. That incident brought a whole new meaning to 'security'.

He drummed his fingers on the desk as the phone rang...and rang...and rang. "Come on!" he muttered.

It rang a couple more times, then the line connected. "Hello, Salvator. I'm assuming you heard the unfortunate news."

"Yes. Andy just informed me." His voice sounded breathy, tremulous, his pressured speech giving away his desperation

"What can I do for you, outside of providing more funding?"

"Well, I hoped you could help me get some official replacement documents for my cryogenic memory drug recipient. You see, I've been given permission to release her with a new identity and assess the impact of the memory drugs and cryogenic storage, but with the tightened security and amount of red tape hoops I need to jump through…"

"You're worried you won't be able to get her an official license, passport…"

"Exactly. So—"

"No problem. Consider it a thank you for all your work on the project, as well as the extracurricular bits and pieces…even though the results weren't what we were hoping for. Anyway, send me through the subject's details and what documents you require and I'll get them to you by the end of the week."

As promised, Salvator received the required documents by Friday, noting Eva's new identity—Eden Freberg. Hopefully his contact in the department stayed in the same role and remained as forthcoming when Richard's turn arrived for release.

Salvator checked the documents, put them in a plastic sleeve and stored them in his satchel. Then he extracted Eva from her cryogenics container for the last time.

She lay bare before him, her skin as smooth and fair as it had been the day he'd met her, her dark brown hair just as glossy, not an ounce of beauty stripped. Just her mind but hopefully not forever.

His loyal research team of two approached. "Is there anything you'd like us to do?"

"No, thanks. I just need to set her up for a final red room session on the laptop and mobile phone to consolidate the skills she's learned through the YouTube tutorials, then drive her home." His gaze remained fixed on her, still amazed he'd succeeded in pulling it all together. It had taken a long time, but she was almost free.

While Eva completed the red room session, Salvator entered her DNA into the mini CODIS DNA-like index system on his computer and checked it against those contained in the Norway compound.

The search identified a familial match to a Violet, though no other details were available—no name, no sex, no age. Could it be her mother? Father? Sister? Brother? Salvator might have even met her relative during his mid-1990s secondment.

One day they both might find out the identity of the person, assuming their luck had changed for the better. For the time being, he'd lock away that little tidbit in his mind-safe and get Eva ready to go.

He pulled into the driveway in front of the refurbished house in the hilly seaside neighborhood she used to call home in 1965, before she'd moved in with Richard. Had he risked too much taking her back there?

Possibly. However, the area and outside appearance of the house had changed a lot so he figured it shouldn't ring too many bells. Not too soon, anyway.

With the new Eva still sedated in the front seat, Salvator grabbed his brown bag, containing proof of her new identity and opened up the compact house. He'd fitted it out in French provincial style, carrying the theme of white and warm honey-toned wood furnishings throughout. Having never seen inside her place, he took inspiration from Richard's descriptions at the time. And looking at it now, the style really did suit Eva.

Salvator placed his bag on her bed and took quick stock of her bedroom wardrobe. Grandmother's wedding dress, *check*. Black and white polka-dot dress, *check*. Doctored photo albums, *check*.

On her bedside table, he planted an iPod with a range of music from the 1960s all the way to current pop and opera next to her gold marcasite watch. In the cabinet under the TV were a range of DVDs from *The Sound of Music* right through to the spy series, *Spooks*, *Pride and Prejudice* and the latest-release romantic comedies.

He retrieved the plastic sleeve of ID documents from his brown satchel, removed her license and put it in a small pink purse along with a credit card and some cash. Then he filed away her replacement birth certificate and passport in her bottom, bedside drawer.

Back in the living room, he'd filled a small bookshelf with a range of books spanning from classics such as *North and South* right up to thrillers, murder mysteries and romances. He had one last glance around the new, Eva-inspired home. Spending some of his own savings to get it just right had been worth it, the least he could do after everything. A sharp sting burned the back of his eyes.

Before he broke down, he coerced his lips into a smile and returned to the car. Eva's head lolled to the side, leaving a trail of dark glossy brown locks gleaming in the midday sun, but other than that, she'd stayed how he left her. He opened the front passenger side door, scooped her into his arms and carried her inside.

At sixty-eight, his strength had waned. But after years of bare minimum nutrition and muscle stimulation, Eva fell into the featherweight category, as easy to carry as a babe. And now marked the beginning of her rebirth.

He lowered her onto her double bed and pulled out a purple, fluid-filled vial and syringe from his satchel. Salvator filled the syringe with the slow-acting revival tonic and purple memory-solidifier chemical cocktail, and injected it into the only visible vein on the inside of her exposed elbow.

If all went to plan, she should rouse in fifteen minutes and feel the full effects of the caffeine-based, reviver-solidifier solution by the end of the hour. It gave him plenty of time to get out of there without being seen or remembered.

The implanted memories should be fully embedded into her brain, which meant she should think and behave like she'd been living in the house since finishing university. If it all worked as he anticipated, she would continue to lay down memories normally and no Eva ones should pop through. Yet — and hopefully not for a while, for her sake and Richard's.

Sleeping Beauty. Eva embodied the full essence of the sentiment, laid out in a peaceful slumber. Now she just had to make the transition from subconscious to conscious. She began to stir. A grateful breath gushed from his lungs but his heart ached, wanting to be there for her when she woke.

Enough. Hurry up and move before everything is ruined.

He packed away his emotions, along with the empty vial and syringe, and kissed her on the cheek. Her neck. Bare. *Shit!* He patted his pockets searching for the key while his mind retraced its steps.

He detected a lump inside his jacket pocket and stopped. Of course...so he wouldn't forget. He pulled out the gold chain with the red-rose-topped key pendant and secured it around her neck.

Salvator stood back and smiled. "The key to a wonderful new life ahead," he said, as though stating a fact rather than a desperate wish.

Chapter Thirty-Four

The Birth of Eden Freberg

Eden woke up from a long, intricate dream. One of those cheese-before-bed ones with colors, snippets of memories, conversations, people's faces. A nondescript feeling nibbled away at her mind, a wary unease mixed with excitement like emerging from the womb, fresh with a subconscious history working behind the scenes, guiding thoughts, behavior, actions.

She yawned and stretched out her stiff body. Exhaustion tugged at her like an attention-seeking child. Amazing how searching for a job ate up more energy than being at uni all day.

She needed to start making some new friends and earning some money. Her savings buffer would run out soon. And she had no family support to fall back on. If her calculations were correct, her meager Austudy earnings should last a couple more months, assuming she reduced her diet to a staple of mincemeat and rice.

For three weeks, she'd searched the classifieds both in print and online with no bites. "Please let me find something soon," she prayed. It had become her mantra, and she repeated it hour after hour after hour.

Newspaper in hand, Eden sat on the couch, with a mug of decaf coffee, and flicked to the classifieds section. She scanned the job vacancies, starting at administration and stopping only partway down the page. An ad for a Personal Assistant at a large research organization, the Sub Rosa Corporation, caught her eye. And the place was located nearby, another big bonus.

A surge of adrenaline shot through her veins. "Sub Rosa…" she murmured. The name sounded so familiar. She must have read about the highly esteemed facility or heard about it on the news.

She picked up a pen from off the coffee table, marked the ad to come back to later and had a sip of coffee. After a few more sips, her eyes hadn't budged. The Sub Rosa role drew her attention for some reason. Was it a gut instinct, letting her know this was the one?

Rather than getting her heart set on a job that might fall through, she should also consider other options. Her dwindling bank account concurred. But she couldn't move past Sub Rosa. It felt like a massive, double-brick wall built up around her brain, preventing her from scanning farther down the page.

Ignoring the seed of resistance embedded in her stomach, she emailed the contact person, Ms. I. Zoffany. She'd wait for her reply before trawling through the rest of the employment pages. If she got a good feeling from the woman, she might not have to look any further. She might have found what she'd been searching for at Sub Rosa.

Chapter Thirty-Five

A Change of Plans

Hobart, January 2007

Salvator stepped out of the lift into the corridor leading to the basement lab. *The light. It shouldn't be on.* He'd turned it off the previous day when he'd left and he was always the first one in. He hurried past the glass and froze.

A blur.

Two blurs.

Men, tinkering with the cryogenics vat. His heart plummeted from his chest and slammed into his stomach.

With a pulse rate just short of a heart attack, he threw the door open. "Hey! What the hell are you doing?" he asked, but he already knew. Fear flared inside him like he'd been exposed to nuclear radiation.

The two men stopped and stared, black and yellow biohazard bags laid out on the floor between them. One came forward and said, "Dismantling the cryogenics unit. What's it to you?"

Hyperventilated air ratcheted along Salvator's windpipe. "You have to stop," he said as he approached them. "I have samples…"

Golden-brown hair poked out from the top of one of the biohazard bags. Salvator's heart stuttered and his lungs clamped down, locking air into his constricted chest. Richard wouldn't be the only person dying today.

"Are you okay?" the other guy asked and guided him to a seat.

Salvator's skin turned cold, clammy, cadaver-like and his vision went blotchy, like focusing on a camera flash for too long. "Turn it back on." The air leaked out of his lungs, his voice below a whisper.

The men fussed around him, one taking his pulse, one grabbing a glass of water.

His heart kicked back into gear, arrhythmic beats reviving his weary body. "Turn. The. Machine. Back. On."

The men stopped fussing, their eyes as wide as a stunned doe.

"Now!" Mustering up every last bit of energy, he staggered over to Richard and touched his skin. Still frostbite cold, still within saving limits.

"And put my samples back," Salvator shouted.

Both men jumped. "But Andy…" one of them protested.

"Just do it! I'll deal with Andy."

Salvator stabbed the 'up' button for the lift, went straight to the top floor and stormed into the CEO's office.

"Happy New Year!" Andy said, with a super-sized smirk.

Salvator stood in Andy's face and jabbed his finger into his chest. "You said I'd be able to release Y1939 if X1944's reintegration proved successful."

Andy's steely stare usually bullied him into backing the hell off, but this time he refused to stand down.

A flicker of fear flashed in his boss's eyes, dilating his pupils. Had Salvator found a weak spot in Andy's armor? "I did, but we had a five-year deal. It hasn't even been two." Andy held his position, adjusted his Armani shirt and tie then retreated to his black leather throne.

It looked like arrogance overrode whatever threat Andy felt. Anger and desperation rose, like acidic reflux, scalding Salvator's insides. Like an over-inflated tire ready to pop, he loomed over Andy's desk and shoved his finger into the stack of quarterly reports he'd lodged on Eva since she'd been freed.

"I assure you, she's well and truly reintegrated. There hasn't even been a hint of a lapse." Except her returning to work at Sub Rosa as a personal assistant less than a month after she'd been released. That, he'd conveniently omitted.

Sitting in his safe haven, Andy scrutinized him with beady, slitted eyes.

Salvator poked the pile of reports. "If you'd read these, you'd see." Outside of selecting Sub Rosa, Eden—the new Eva—showed no other hint of remembering. In fact, she fit right into the workplace and her new identity.

Other than Salvator, William Darnel, the current senior manager of business services, remained the only other longstanding staff member, and Salvator doubted he'd remember her. The guy hadn't been at the agency long when she had disappeared, and given his accountancy role at the time, Salvator didn't think their paths would have crossed.

"Two years doesn't seem long enough to provide an accurate result. Releasing Y1939 at this point is risky. I don't know…"

Salvator scowled. What options did he have if Andy refused? Salvator's uncharacteristic anger may have unsettled him, but Andy still had the upper hand. And no matter how much he wanted to punch the smug CEO to a bloody pulp, it definitely wouldn't get him on Salvator's side. He had to try another tactic.

"If you won't let me reintegrate him now, I won't have another opportunity. Two contracted men literally pulled the plug on the cryogenics tank today, compromising Y1939. I resurrected him and the tank but I don't know for how long."

Andy rubbed his bristly chin.

Maybe Salvator could appeal to Andy's research sensibilities and the possibility of making more money in future. "Just think, with him reintegrated, I'll be able to conduct a comparison study —"

"Sub Rosa has spent enough time and money on these two subjects. There really needs to be a bigger memory drug study commissioned to get any real results."

Salvator's heart pounded in his ears, a repetitive sonic boom, threatening to blast his head right off his shoulders. "What are you saying?" His mind mulled over how to steal Richard in the middle of the night, without being seen, and set it up as though he'd been sent along with the other lingering specimens to get destroyed.

Andy hesitated, drawing out the suspense, reminding him who had the power, the control, the final say about everything Sub Rosa, including whether someone lived or died.

After ten long, excruciating seconds he said, "You can release him, but forget about the ongoing surveillance and reporting back. I can't warrant spending any more of our limited research dollars on you chasing them up. We've got more pressing projects taking precedence. I'll wait until we have a larger sample size, if we get it sanctioned."

Thankfully, Andy had no idea how important it was for Richard and Eva not to remember. Remembering could cause catastrophic fallout for the Norway Experiment and for Sub Rosa as a whole. If Salvator retired, it wouldn't be his problem anymore. He could leave in conjunction with Richard. They'd finally all be free after forty-two years.

Salvator straightened his creased, tan jacket. "Then, with your permission, once Y1939 is released and set up, I'll tender my resignation."

Chapter Thirty-Six

The Nerve-Racking Release

The sandstone house stood on top of the hill, as palatial and proud as Salvator remembered. He hadn't ventured past the Hall home since Bram had returned from his vacation all those years ago. He couldn't. It meant facing Bram, and what he'd done to the guy's nephew, not to mention putting them all in increased danger if he slipped up, even in the slightest way.

To his relief, Bram hadn't caused any trouble. He'd half expected him to call the police and have them show up at Sub Rosa. Part of him wished Bram had stirred things up, giving his friends an earlier chance at freedom. But, equally, things could have gone bad, and instead, he, Richard and Eva would have been telling the tale from the grave.

A spider-web-addled intercom sat to the side of the gate. He didn't remember the system installed there last time he visited. Had Bram arranged for it? Or someone else? Nausea rushed up his esophagus, the sickening sensation sitting at the back of his throat.

What if someone else lived there? He hadn't even thought of that. He'd just assumed... However, he should have learned by now that assuming meant trouble. It would cause the death of him one day.

Salvator lowered his window and pressed the intercom — and waited, and waited, and waited. Five agonizingly slow minutes passed on his scientific watch. Maybe no one was home or the house remained deserted. It didn't look like the intercom had been used in a while.

Salvator went to close his window and the gates creaked open. Someone lived there. But who? And why had it taken them so long to respond? He threw the car into gear and drove up to the house. Instead of green and luscious, the previously manicured garden had turned into an overgrown, tangled brown mess.

He parked in front of the large bay window and walked over to the Psyche and Eros fountain. Rust-tinged water now spouted out, and the statue had become grimy, streaked with soot and weathered from acid rain. Weeds had sprung up around the base, extending like a trail to the foot of the front steps, and creeper had grown like cataracts over a quarter of the house, choking out light.

The large oak door at the top of the steps stood ajar. "Hello?" he called through the gap and peered into the darkness.

"Come in." The soft, shaky voice sounded like a frail, elderly man. Could it be Bram? He would be around ninety, if still alive.

Salvator stepped inside and closed the door behind him. He tried to adjust his eyes to the dim lighting in the cold dusty corridor. Once he could see clearer, he continued down the passageway and turned into the living room. A wrinkly, white-haired yet distinguished-looking man lay across a worn, aged couch, a thin, blue blanket pulled up over him.

He smiled, the wrinkles spreading across his face like a run in a sheer stocking. "Hello."

"Bram?" The twinkle in his eye hinted at the man he'd met all those years ago, a kernel of him beneath the fragile façade.

"Yes, and you are?"

He moved closer but remained standing. "Salvator."

Bram appeared to search his memory. "Richard's friend?"

Questionable, but... "Yes."

Bram's smile grew. "It's good to see you. What brings you here?"

Scoping out the place to return the new Richard. That's what he wanted to say. The truth. He ached to, but he couldn't. It would raise too many questions, opening up not just a can but a slab of worms. "I was passing through and—"

Bram struggled up into sitting. "I never found them, if that's what you were hoping. I would have told you if I had."

Salvator gulped back the rising shame. "I thought so, but—"

"It's always worth checking. I understand. So how have you been?"

Outside of tired, scared, racked with guilt? "If being a lifetime workaholic is considered not too bad, then not too bad."

"I've been there. Believe me. It's far from ideal, though it can be a good distraction."

"Yes... I never got married so...I needed something to keep me...occupied. I'm in my late sixties now, though, and I've done what I needed to do, so I'm retiring."

"It'll be a big adjustment. I remember how it felt when I stopped work at the university. What do you plan to do with yourself?"

"I'm not sure yet. Travel, maybe tinker with some personal research projects I never got to finish. And I have a sister and a niece and nephew and their kids I'd like to see more often. How about you? How did you keep busy?"

Bram hesitated, as though weighing up whether to confide in him. "If I tell you, you have to promise it won't go any further."

What could he possibly say? Had the man involved himself in something illegal? It didn't matter. Salvator couldn't judge after spending most of his working life involved in prison-worthy activity. "Okay."

Bram swung his feet off the couch and patted a spot next to him. "I should probably start at the beginning. You see, I'm not really Richard's uncle."

Salvator dropped down onto the seat and stared into the old man's spirited eyes.

"I'm his father. I'm Abe. 'Abraham' on my birth certificate." A sparkle broke through his cataract-clouded eyes, accompanying his roguish grin, Richard's grin.

Not just Richard's dad, but also Rhoda's husband. Sweet, beautiful Rhoda. Apart from freeing Eva and being on the brink of releasing Richard, Salvator hadn't felt true joy since his secondment to the Norway site, where he'd met Rhoda in the mid-1990s.

Abe went on to explain how he and Rhoda had met, fallen in love and fled Norway to prevent her being captured, how she'd been kidnapped from their

Tasmanian home, sent back to Norway and held in the Sub Rosa compound. How for years he didn't know if she was dead or alive and how he'd given Richard away to a boys' home and passed himself off as his uncle to protect him.

He stopped speaking and studied Salvator. "You don't seem shocked to hear of Richard's part-vampire heritage."

"No. The more time I spent with him, the more signs he showed. They were subtle but enough for me to question his humanness." *Not to mention the blood test confirmation.*

"And it didn't bother you?"

"No. I always felt comfortable and accepted around Richard."

"Yes, he grew up to be a wonderful young man."

"He did. I consider it a privilege to know him." Pity Salvator had lost his chance for the sentiment to ever be reciprocated.

Abe smiled, then it withered away. Salvator couldn't imagine the level of grief Abe had endured, losing a wife, a son and a daughter-in-law. "I tried for years to find a way to free Rhoda but the Fort Knox, high-security set-up made it extremely difficult. I couldn't get anywhere near the compound, but I didn't give up on finding a successful option to get her out of there permanently. But once the sunlight bars were in place, they shut down every avenue of escape, which made it impossible.

"I worried Richard had also been kidnapped by Sub Rosa given his part-Jade genetics, but if they'd taken him to the compound, my wife would have found out and probably even seen him. If someone else had kidnapped him, there would have been a ransom note."

Abe repositioned the blanket over his knobby knees. "It doesn't matter now what agency or faction was behind it. The outcome ended the same. My son and daughter-in-law disappeared somewhere..."

Into Sub Rosa storage in a vat of liquid nitrogen, to be exact. Salvator couldn't tell him, or anyone else, ever — only if Richard or Eva ever asked. Then he promised himself he'd be upfront. They deserved to hear the truth about what had happened, at the very least, even if they hated him for it.

"Seeing as I couldn't help my wife or son, I focused on doing what I could, on helping others. Though, I never gave up on trying to find Richard and Eva or rescuing Rhoda." Abe's jaw tightened. "I know you work for that despicable place — "

"Not for much longer."

"True. So, my confession shouldn't bother you then."

Confession. I should be the one confessing. No amount of Our Fathers or Hail Marys could ever absolve him of what he'd done. Even though he didn't have much of a choice, it still didn't make it acceptable. It would never make it acceptable.

"I've been helping to hide Violets and Jades coming through town." Abe paused, his eyes searching Salvator's for any hint of shock or revulsion. But he felt neither shocked nor revolted — more curious, impressed. And it obviously showed, because Abe kept talking. "I suppose you could say I set up a sort of refuge. And in a way, it's helped me feel purposeful, like I'm doing something to assist."

That displaced sort of assistance when unable to help those who are the real target. Salvator knew all about it. His Norway secondment was a prime example. "That's...incredible. Dangerous, but incredible."

"So, you aren't against helping the vampires?" He scrutinized Salvator through wrinkled, yet vibrant eyes.

"No. Even though I'm afraid of some of them, it doesn't mean the whole vampire population deserves to be imprisoned and experimented on. In fact, I stayed at Sub Rosa to try to make things as ethical and humane as possible, sort of trying to do what you've done, but from the inside." *Among other less-honorable things.*

"Overall, I'd like to think I helped. I made some difference. The greatest positive gains were when I did a stint in the Norway site in the mid-1990s. I met some amazing people who changed my life, including your wife.

A tear trickled down Abe's undulated cheek. "You met Rhoda?"

"Yes, and she's amazing, inspiring. We developed a strong platonic bond. So much so, she entrusted me with some cross jewelry you had gifted to her and asked me to give it to Richard. So, I'm hoping I can leave it here for when he returns one day."

Abe wiped the wetness away from his face with the back of his hand. "Of course."

Salvator put the red velvet pouch housing the cross jewelry on the dusty lamp table. "I'm curious. What did you think of Richard and Eva working at Sub Rosa?"

"I didn't like it. I worried about them, their safety, as well as them being fed false information and developing skewed, flawed biases." He wrung his gnarled hands in his lap. "They're both smart, so I thought they'd do the right thing and hopefully stay out of trouble."

"Yes…" Salvator shot up. "Anyway, I'd better go. It's been good to see you."

Abe stretched out his hand and Salvator shook it. The guy had a surprisingly strong grip, despite his eggshell-like frailty. "All the best."

On the drive back home, Salvator reflected on their conversation. What a great man, a man who deserved to see his son. And a son who deserved to know his father. Salvator knew what he had to do, even though it went against everything he'd planned for. It meant coming clean and hoping they didn't hate him. No matter how difficult, Richard and Abe required a reunion.

That night, Salvator took out a small, white, drawstring pouch from his bedside drawer and tipped the contents into his hand. Richard and Eva's wedding bands and the ruby heart engagement ring Richard had given Eva tumbled out and glinted under the lamp light. They'd be reunited with Richard, along with his father tomorrow.

Finally.

After a sleepless night, watching shadows duck and weave and slither across the ceiling, he rose before dawn and drove to work. He needed some alone time...to prepare. If he planned to introduce Richard to his dad, should he prep him to remember?

Salvator switched on the lab light and stared at the large, metal cryogenic cylinder. Instead of things getting easier, winding down, they'd become more complicated. If he stayed much longer in fence-sitter state, he'd lose sensation in his legs.

In his basement office, a hot coffee in hand, he made a pros and cons list. Partway through, an idea struck him. Ring Abe first, arrange a suitable time to drop by and allow their conversation to aid his decision.

He glanced at the time in the bottom, right corner of his computer monitor. Only seven-forty-five. Way too early to call. So, he dove back into his backlog of paperwork until it hit mid-morning. The old guy should be up and about by then.

Salvator scrolled through his archaic, mobile phone to Abe's home number and pressed the call button. With each ring, his stomach coiled into a tighter and tighter spring. No answer. He called straight back. Maybe it took a while for him to reach the phone. But it rang out again. And again. And again. Abe could have gone out. However, it didn't look like he went out much at all these days.

Salvator's gut clenched. Something didn't sit right. Maybe one of the vampire refugees he'd tried to help had helped himself. He shook his head. *Bloody over-active imagination.* But it was possible.

Right before he left for the day, he tried again.

"Hello, Hall residence," a woman said, her voice shaking.

"Hello. Who's this?"

"I'm Mr. Hall's housekeeper."

"My name's Salvator and I wondered if you could please put Abe on the phone?"

A sob broke the static-filled silence. "I'm sorry." She sniffled. "But he...he..."

"What happened?"

She blew her nose. "He" — more sobbing — "got rushed to hospital" — more nose-blowing — "this morning. They think heart attack or stroke." She broke down in a deluge of tears.

"What hospital? Is he going to be okay?" He'd have to rethink everything. He'd have to get Richard over to see his dad as soon as possible.

The crying intensified, sorrow pouring down the phone line. "No. He didn't make it."

Salvator stood frozen, holding the phone well after the housekeeper had hung up. Emerging from his catatonic state, he stumbled into the lab and pressed his palm on the cold, metal vat. "I'm sorry." He leaned his forehead against the icy exterior. "I'm so, so sorry — about your dad, about this, about everything."

He'd planned to do something right, to help in some small way. Then… He patted the striated steel. Blinking back tears, he levered himself into standing straight. "You're just going to have to wait here a bit longer, my friend." His heart froze. *My friend.* Two words that used to bring him so much joy, now delivered only heartache.

With the heartbreaking turn of events, he couldn't release Richard back to his old home. Not yet. Not with people coming and going, sorting out Abe's funeral.

But he could do something else, something factoring in the change of circumstances.

After everyone had left, Salvator extracted Richard, set him up in the red room and, after a computer-and-mobile-phone-usage consolidation session, handed him a document. It stated that on his twenty-sixth birthday, he'd received a solicitor's letter notifying him of his Uncle Bram's passing and inheritance of the house in Fern Tree.

The new Richard had finished his Master of Science degree at Melbourne University and so returned to Tasmania to follow it up. Ownership wouldn't take effect for the next couple of months so he'd based himself in a unit close by, one Salvator had just found through a Google search on his desktop computer.

While Richard absorbed the information, Salvator went to his office, printed off the rest of the doctored documents, including a mock Melbourne University degree and birth certificate and photos of Richard growing up — with friends at the beach, on fishing trips, at bars and on his own — and arranged them in files and albums.

And just as he had with Eva, he obtained an updated driver's license and passport from his acquaintance in the government funding department.

Salvator slid Richard's new 'Rick Hartman' ID documents into a plastic sleeve and put them in a box with the remainder of his exit wardrobe paraphernalia. Nearly an hour had past. It was time to re-sedate and re-store Richard to his cryogenic cylinder in preparation for his reintroduction into the world. Tomorrow.

Once he'd stored Richard away, Salvator stocked up his satchel with the memory solidifier and sedative concoction, collected the box holding Richard's new life and drove to the temporary, furnished house in Fern Tree he'd arranged for Richard to rent.

Inside the small red-brick home, Salvator filed Richard's ID documents away in his bedroom drawer, slotted his license in the new-Richard's small black wallet and packed away the photo albums in the spare room. Then he returned to the car, picked up a box filled with clothes and shoes and put them away in the new-Richard's wardrobe.

The last box contained a music-filled iPod, books and DVDs, similar to those put together for Eva's new identity, though with a few additions to cover him right up to 2007. Salvator also included research and scientific books, as well as cookbooks and poetry and some rock and alternative music to fit and strengthen Richard's new persona.

Two hours later, everything was in place. Salvator surveyed the new-Richard's pad. It looked neat but still bachelor-ish — minimalist, simple, angular, black and silver. Salvator's mobile phone buzzed, and he unclipped it from his belt. A reminder flashed onto the screen to pay the new-Richard's bond and two months of rent. He deleted it, called the real estate agent and got it organized.

On the way back to his unit, Salvator did a detour past Richard's old — and what would soon be his newly inherited — sandstone house. It looked deserted, so he snuck inside and put the small white pouch containing the wedding bands and ruby heart engagement ring in the attic, along with a range of other stored items.

The next morning, he got in to Sub Rosa extra early and extracted Richard from his steel cylinder for the last time. He drained the cryoprotectant from Richard's body, placed him on the body-heated bed and rehydrated his cells.

As always, Richard was an amazing male specimen. He'd lost some muscle mass, as Salvator had expected, even with the monthly muscle stimulation sessions, but other than that, he appeared perfect. And just like Eva, he hadn't aged a day. It was one of the positives of their mixed heritage combined with the years of cryogenic storage.

After grooming Richard's facial hair into a Johnny Depp-style mustache and goatee, Salvator dressed his friend and fastened the gold and black skeleton watch to his right wrist. Then he transferred him into a wheelchair, loaded him into the car and drove him to his temporary home.

Once inside, he wheeled Richard into the bedroom, deposited him onto the double bed and injected him with the purple memory solidifier, slow-acting revival tonic.

If he responded like Eva, he should begin to revive in fifteen minutes, though not be fully conscious until the end of the hour, giving Salvator plenty of time to leave without the risk of being seen or recognized.

He had everything crossed that Richard's implanted memories were successfully embedded and it would be like he'd just returned from Melbourne University after receiving notification of his uncle's passing and inheritance of his home. Hopefully he'd mimic Eva's success and continue to lay down memories normally and have no past life ones slip through.

Yet.

Richard began to stir. "I hope it all comes together," Salvator whispered.

After lunch, Salvator returned to work and packed up his desk. With his satchel slung over his shoulder, he said goodbye to Andy, and he and his loyal basement research team left together.

Salvator swung open his car door and stared up at the black, shiny skyscraper, his second home, housing his dysfunctional scientific family over the majority of his life. A sense of finality and freedom filled his bone-tired body. Shackle-free for the first time in over forty years, he finally turned his back on Sub Rosa.

Chapter Thirty-Seven

Déjà vu

Several years later

Sweat poured from Rick Hartman's skin, his singlet wringing wet. He'd been scrubbing the sandstone façade of his house with PH-neutral soapy water for twenty minutes, though it felt like hours. He swiped his beaded forehead with his forearm, spreading rather than soaking up the sweat.

He climbed down the ladder and dropped the sponge into the now-tepid bucket of water, his eyes stinging and limbs burning. He needed a shade break on the front porch. Now.

Removing his sunglasses, he squinted into the sun's glaring rays, beaming down like lasers through the breaking cloud. He really should have waited for a cooler, more overcast day to finish up the outside facelift.

It had taken almost three years, but the renovations were nearly complete. The major stuff, anyway. When he'd taken ownership of the Fern Tree house, it had needed some serious maintenance work. And he figured he could do it up in his free time. It sounded easy…in theory.

Now he understood how projects ran way over schedule and way over budget. Poking around inside had exposed a whole heap of stumping and other issues that needed fixing before he could even start on the aesthetic changes.

Since moving to Hobart, after completing his science degree, specializing in genetics at Melbourne Uni, Rick had worked in casual construction jobs that paid well but had been insecure. What he really wanted, what his heart desired was to follow his passion and find a permanent research position. But so far, he'd had no luck.

He emptied the dirty water down the drain at the back of the house, cleaned the bucket and sponge and left them out to dry. Then he grabbed a beer from the kitchen fridge, collapsed onto a dining chair and drained the bottle in less than a minute. Normally, he preferred red wine, but nothing beat a beer on a stinking hot day.

After a much-needed shower, he retrieved his laptop from his black, gothic desk, returned to the conservatory and got comfortable on the couch. He flipped open the laptop lid and began his weekly scour-the-Internet-for-Hobart-research-jobs routine.

Ba-ling.

An email. A job offer? He clicked on Outlook in the menu bar at the bottom of the screen and opened the bolded, unread message. *Nope. Damn.* A jeweler he'd recently contacted had replied, regarding some pieces Rick had found when cleaning out the attic.

He skimmed through the body of the message. The jeweler had found no information on the cross jewelry or wedding bands but included a short note about the ruby heart ring.

Its origins traced back to the Middle Ages, which made it impossible to price. It had to be a family heirloom. How else would it have wound up in his uncle's possession?

From his understanding, the old guy had never married, so it couldn't be from his partner's side. And going by the state of the house, he doubted his uncle had had a lot of money so he couldn't have purchased it — unless he'd turned jewel thief and stolen it from somewhere. A romantic idea, though not likely.

If Rick's life panned out the way he planned, he'd be offering it to his intended wife…once he met her. He closed his eyes and shook his head, reliving his most recent disastrous date.

The woman rolled out her beach towel on the golden sand, her lustrous, dark brown hair glistening in the sun. While Rick anchored a large, multicolored, beach umbrella, she stripped off her summer dress, revealing a white, almost see-through bikini. The barely-there outfit contrasted with her smooth, milk-chocolate skin, and her natural C-cup breasts strained against the thin, stretchy fabric.

His cock stood to attention, saluting her impeccable beauty. Thank fuck he'd gone with loose board shorts.

"I'm just going for a swim," he said. A dip in the ocean was the closest thing to a cold shower he could get.

"I'll wait here and soak up some more sun."

Not that she needed to with her perfectly sun-kissed body. But each to their own.

The water worked its magic and gave him the extra benefit of perving on her from afar. He still needed to suss out her personality, but so far, physically, she hit the spot. He'd never wanted to fuck a woman so badly in his life. Although he didn't do the whole one-night-stand thing, he needed to know he could do her…when they reached that point.

To date, he hadn't been able to tolerate, let alone enjoy, touching any woman of interest…romantically. The idea of getting naked with them repulsed him. Hopefully things were different with this hot beach babe.

He dove into the cool, blue water, dousing his desire enough to swim back to shore. The hot sand coated his wet feet like golden-crumbed schnitzels by the time he reached her.

She sat up, covering her breasts with her untied bikini top. "Hey, go drip on someone else!" A huge smile hijacked her lips and she patted a space in the sun next to her. "Going to join me?"

"Sure am." He laid his towel right next to her but in the shade.

Her smooth brow furrowed like a Flake chocolate bar. "Don't you want to work on your tan?"

"Not really. My skin burns in the sun." If only it just affected his skin. The sun's rays were like daggers, stabbing searing heat into his muscles, nerves and bones. Too much direct exposure felt excruciating, like being thrown into a furnace filled with scalding hot switchblades.

He'd had tests to check it out and the doctor had cited a slightly elevated white blood cell count as the only anomaly. Outside of avoiding the sun, there was no cure.

"Maybe you just haven't used the right sunscreen." She pulled an SPF 50+ tube from her beach bag and squirted some cream into her hand. "Here, let me…"

Before he could utter a word, her lips were on his and she started massaging the UV protection into his back.

All the lust drained from him, like he'd kissed his sister rather than a love interest, and he pulled back, ready to run — or vomit. She stared at him, her eyes filled with seduction, *longing. She wanted more, just like the others. Another emotional vampire, sucking him dry of any sexual feelings.*

"I'm so sorry, but I really have to go."

She edged closer to him. "We only just got he — Oh, I get it." By the ecstatic smile on her face, she presumed they were going back to his place or hers, to take things further. Her assumption couldn't be more wrong. He started to believe women really were from another planet, possibly another universe.

"No. No, it's not like that. I'm not like that."

"What a shame." She ran her palm down his chest and he used every ounce of control to stop from recoiling. "I think we could be good together. Very good."

Hadn't she heard what he'd said? Didn't women have a knack, a gift, a genetic predisposition to pick up on the vibe of a situation? Apparently not, going by his experience. So, just like the others, he'd have to leave no room for gray areas. "Look, um, I'm not sure how to say this, but we're not suited."

She retracted her hand as though he were an iron set on blistering-high heat. "What?"

Rick retreated. "It's just not going to work. Sorry."

The drive back to her house felt beyond icy and more like an Antarctic blizzard. The outcome was a one-hundred-and-eighty-degree flip from the start of their date. He'd rather be direct, blunt, honest, earlier than later, even though she probably saw it as prick-like behavior. It didn't make sense to lead her on when the relationship had no future.

Yet he couldn't help but feel disappointed. She'd had such great potential. If only sex didn't require a physical connection, like in the virtual world. If his poor success rate continued, he might have to cross over into the land of make believe to get some action.

Rick opened his eyes and refocused on his computer. It had gone into black-screen sleep mode. Miss Right was long overdue for an appearance. A niggle, an unscratchable itch teased the deepest corner of his mind. A woman... A dark-haired woman, with an hourglass figure, unusual eyes...and...and...

He strained for more details but they wouldn't come, as though he'd hidden her precious memory somewhere special, for protection, so he wouldn't lose it. But that's exactly what he'd done...forgotten. Irony could be cruel.

Maybe she was a figment of his imagination or a fragment from a dream, possibly a premonition. One concrete thing — all the women he'd been attracted to fit the mystery mold, yet none had been 'the one'. He'd just have to keep trying until he found *her*.

The laptop grew hot on his legs, a prompt to stop day dreaming and recommence his job search. Midway down the page he stopped scrolling. A research position was available at a Hobart agency called Sub Rosa. *The* Sub Rosa. They were renowned for their good work, particularly in the genetics field, his field of interest. Now he just had to apply and get selected.

Smokey, his new, charcoal-gray fluff-ball of a kitten, bounded into the room and rubbed against Rick's legs, purring in agreement. A clear idea of his dream woman, a dream house and now possibly a dream job. *Could I be so lucky?*

Chapter Thirty-Eight

Full Circle Renaissance

Sub Rosa Corporation, May 2010

Andy Falon, the Sub Rosa CEO, walked around to the other side of his enormous, Italian designer-style desk and extended his hand. "Welcome aboard, Rick. With your knowledge of genetics, I think you'll be a real asset to the team."

"Thanks, Andy." Rick shook his steel-grip hand. "This is such a great opportunity. I won't let you down."

Andy escorted him to the door and smiled, his thin lips like brittle elastic bands about to break. "Good to hear. Report to reception on Monday and they'll send down Simon Fidelis, also on the research team, to give you your department orientation."

Rick couldn't wait to get started. Sub Rosa's vision, mission and culture seemed to align with his own values and beliefs. The agency was renowned for taking risks, lateral thinking, going where other research organizations were afraid to go and coming up with groundbreaking results. They had to be flush with money and resources.

He rode the lunch-rush-packed elevator down to the ground floor and checked his black and gold skeleton watch. Already twelve-fifty-five, which meant he should hurry home and finish off some of the house renovations. He'd only have weekends to play *Bob the Builder* once he started full time work next week.

The lift doors opened and two stunning women stood, waiting — the taller one with the hourglass figure and long, dark brown hair fully fit his fantasy woman mold. She listened while the shorter, curvy, vivacious woman filled her in on her recent hot date. Did the statuesque beauty have a man to report on, too? Was she still single? *Please be single.*

Rick walked past them and the taller woman swayed his way but stayed tuned in to her friend so didn't see him. He turned and stared as the lift doors closed on his introduction opportunity.

There was something about her eyes, her striking, unforgettable, blue-violet eyes. No, it was so much more than that. She had a familiar, magical aura about her, like she'd been his long-lost love from a past life, calling him to rekindle their flame. The overwhelming draw to her felt like fate. The indescribable, all-consuming attraction created a whole mind, body and spirit craving and it floored him.

Transfixed, he focused on the lift and relived the encounter over and over, trying to understand why her presence had hit him like a sensual sledgehammer to the heart. He'd seen and met some fuckable women, but this seemed different. Deeper.

Since when did he fall so hard for a girl by sight alone? There was always a first time, though the lurch in his heart didn't feel like a first time. His brain searched for a connection but came up vacant, like pockets of his memory had been recorded over. Erased.

He chuckled. He'd been spending too much time on the house and not enough on his poetry. That would explain it. He needed a creative outlet. Maybe she was a muse, sent to reconnect him with his creativity, to remind him not to get too overloaded with work.

Rick walked to his car, still lost in thought and inspired to write a poem about her and him and being together. He'd gotten way ahead of himself, but his gut told him otherwise. He sat in the driver's seat of his red MG, started the engine and glanced back at the shiny, black skyscraper.

"I need to know her."

Want to see more from this author?
Here's a taster for you to enjoy!

The Cure: Discover
Sandra Carmel

Excerpt

Sub Rosa basement lab, Hobart, October 1965

"Help! Help us!" Eva screamed, but no sound came out. Her breath caught in her throat. She had to be dreaming.

Wake up. Wake up! She closed her eyes, opened them again. *No!* She was still in the Sub Rosa basement. In hell…but not the biblical fiery type. It was stark and sterile, lab-like, the pungent odor of bleach stinging her nostrils.

We'll find a way to get out of here, she wanted to tell her husband, but she couldn't. They had an audience, a black-radiation-suited audience, their shielded inhuman-looking eyes peering at them—studying, analyzing, deciding whether to keep them alive.

Do I know them?

Does my husband?

None of the frightening figures had said a word.

The one in charge held up a fluid-filled syringe that glinted in the grim light. Her gaze darted between the man and the needle. The man and the needle. The man and the… He squeezed out a drop and she gulped down frenzied gushes of air. In one swift move, he stabbed the syringe into her IV. *No no n...*

She roused. Still a prisoner, strapped down to a stone-cold gurney. She should be petrified. It had to be the injected drugs that dulled her fear.

Adrenaline lay dormant in her system, her heart droning on and on and on. *Thrump. Thrump. Thrump.* Her circulation slowed, shunting her lava-like blood through her veins and clouding her brain.

Hazy, scattered thoughts swirled about, mostly out of conscious reach. She tried to open her eyes, the lids hanging heavy, almost immobile, as though each lash were weighted with a ten-pound dumbbell.

Artificial calmness enshrouded her, further dulling her sense of reality—not bad, but not good. Floaty, relaxed...but she was trapped, with no way to escape.

She tried to turn to see the love of her life and her body slammed against the steel table. "Ugh," she groaned. Thick black rubber bands encircled her chest, hips, knees, ankles and wrists, holding her in place, keeping her prisoner.

Craning her neck only got her a glimpse of her husband's golden-brown hair. The agency had made sure of that. They'd made sure to sever the connection to her soulmate.

Her husband, Richard, had discovered stuff—things, sensitive information and now...

He wasn't at fault. He'd tried to do the right thing and had convinced her to join him, but they'd gotten intercepted.

They hadn't been married long. The twenty-third of July 1965. Three, short amazing months. They were still in the honeymoon phase.

Mesmerized by Richard's light green eyes, his tender passionate lips, his sexy whispered words, she'd made love with him day after day, night after night. And each morning, she would wake up snuggled into him, safe and secure in his strong arms.

But he wasn't just a wonderful lover, he was a romantic, considerate man, frequently leaving her a sweet sentiment or poem in different spots — on the notepad by the phone, on her bedside table, on a coaster, on her dinner napkin, pinned to the fridge by a fluffy cat magnet and even on the steamed-up mirror for her to see when she got out of the shower.

Just when she thought he'd run out of places to hide them, he'd find a new one. Richard — always so thoughtful, loving and full of surprises…

His slurred words jolted her out of her drowsy state and she snapped her eyes open to brightness. Interrogative-spotlight intensity. She squinted, furiously batting her eyelids in an attempt to adjust to the glare.

She'd been moved, and her precious heart engagement ring, wedding band and gold marcasite watch were gone. Would she and her husband be disposed of next?

She sucked in a sob-like breath, choking on noxious air, and her womb cramped. Still sore, stripped, raw, she tried to focus her blurry, tear-filled eyes on Richard's handsome face. He lay only a few feet from her, but she could hardly make him out. If this formed part of Sub Rosa's torture plan, it worked a thousand times better than any physical suffering.

If only she could reach out and touch her husband, tell him she loved him, reinforce that she didn't blame him for any of this and they'd make it through. They'd be together again, stronger than ever. However, she struggled to form words in her head, let alone speak them, her tongue numb, heavy, defective.

The same black-suited man walked over and prepared a syringe with a blue liquid. "Nooo! Pleease don't dooo this... Leave him alooone!" she pleaded, her words slack and slurred.

The faceless man jabbed the syringe into her husband's drip. Tears sprang from her eyes and a burst of adrenaline kicked her heart into overdrive, frantic beats thrashing against her ribcage.

Within seconds, Richard's eyes fluttered and he went as limp as a puppet with slashed strings. She strained at the obstinate ligatures, desperate to break free to reach her lifeless husband, but the man approached and stuck the same needle into her IV.

Black.

Bright.

Black, bright, black, bright, black, bright. The flickering fluorescent lights blacked out and her pulse plummeted, her scream barely a whisper.

Home of Erotic Romance

Sign up for our newsletter and find out about all our romance book releases, eBook sales and promotions, sneak peeks and FREE romance books!

About the Author

Sandra Carmel is an Australian-based author of engaging, thought-provoking romance novels, novellas, short stories and poetry, who writes for the pleasure of stimulating herself and others with words. An obsession with classic romance novels, particularly *Jane Eyre*, combined with marrying her own Mr Rochester were key motivators in commencing her romance writing journey. So far, she has taken the scenic route from contemporary to paranormal to erotic, creating provocative stories that delve beneath the surface of desire. She reads and writes a lot, frequently disrupted by her ever-attentive, cheeky cats, and sinfully amorous husband.

Sandra loves to hear from readers. You can find her contact information, website details and author profile page at https://www.totallybound.com